THE HOTT TOUCH

BOOK FOUR OF THE TOUCH SERIES

STONI ALEXANDER

SILVERSTONE PUBLISHING

Copyright © 2019 by Stoni Alexander
First Edits by Johnny at Better Together
Copy Edits by Nicole at Proof Before You Publish
Cover Design by Johnny & Stoni
Cover Photo by iStock
All rights reserved.

Published in the U.S. by SilverStone Publishing, 2019
ISBN 978-1-946534-08-8 (Print Paperback)
ISBN 978-1-946534-09-5 (Kindle eBook)

To my most beloved son

ABOUT THE HOTT TOUCH

Everyone adores ex-SEAL Maverick Hott, especially the ladies. That's the way it's always been. But he keeps things casual, so no one captures his heart. And no one gets hurt.

Most of all, him.

Then, there's beautiful Carly Stone. His bestie since they were kids. The girl who breathed life back into him when tragedy struck. The same one who runs him ragged on the racquetball court and sees into his soul with those piercing hazel eyes.

Yeah, *that* best friend.

Returning home after a near fatal hostage rescue mission, the fearless and cocky CEO of ThunderStrike has a brand new set of priorities...starting with her. But he stumbles upon her secret, which has him questioning how well he really knows her.

When a powerful senator calls in a favor and Maverick refuses, the ruthless politico exacts his revenge. So Maverick turns to the person he trusts most.

Carly's investigative skills are an asset. Her assets, a major distraction. And while posing as husband and wife, their chemistry is downright lethal.

Together, they're unstoppable...until Carly gets caught in the crosshairs, and the most important mission of Maverick's life is saving hers.

THUNDERSTRIKE'S HOSTAGE RESCUE MISSION

Ashton "Maverick" Hott lived for the challenge of turning the impossible into *possible*. As CEO of ThunderStrike, he understood that every mission came with risk, but this one had him on full tilt and high alert.

Leading his team into enemy territory, locating the American hostages, *and* getting everyone out alive was an arduous undertaking. But Maverick ran *toward* danger. He lived to rescue and protect.

His strong sense of responsibility extended to the employees working alongside him at his paramilitary security firm. Their lives were just as important as the prisoners they rescued. Every mission demanded the same outcome. They all went in together and they all got out together.

There was never any other option.

Zero three hundred meant black skies and quiet streets. Maverick and his elite team had studied the maps and completed the drills. They were prepared, and they were ready.

He led them due north. They hugged the buildings, avoided lights. Every crew member was committed, smarter than hell, and driven to succeed. They also entered each mission knowing it might be their last.

The deserted warehouse was located on the outskirts of some shithole town in the middle of fucking nowhere, Middle East.

Twelve American physicians had been working there, offering free medical care to the residents, when a terror cell raided the camp, killing most of the locals. The doctors were taken hostage. That's when Maverick got the call.

He located the door in the building's southwest corner. Though Maverick had no expectation the heavy metal fire door would be unlocked, he tried it.

Locked.

He acknowledged his four-man team before aiming his Glock. "Breach," he said into his comm.

He fired his weapon, the silencer helping to mute the sound. The deadbolt snapped free. He shoved open the door and entered, weapon drawn, his teammates close on his heels.

They'd be flying blind without their night-vision goggles. The five men entered a dark, windowless room, trash strewn throughout, several metal chairs tossed in the far corner. No hostages, no guards.

Two hand signals, and they filed toward the far door. Despite their gear and weapons, they made no sound, like big cats on the prowl for their next meal. If his sources were accurate, that door would be unlocked. Maverick waited until everyone had moved into position, submachine guns at the ready.

Through the door, they hoofed it down two flights of stairs and through a second door at the end of the dark corridor. As they charged forward, Maverick maintained control of his breathing. Slow inhale, hold two beats, and exhale.

Powered by adrenaline, he was keenly aware of his surroundings. The smallest sound magnified in his ears. Every odor, no matter how faint, penetrated his nostrils. His eyes were trained on his next target, yet his peripheral vision guarded against a surprise attack.

A creak in the rickety floorboards. He raised his right hand and they halted.

Footsteps.

Dreaded, fucking footsteps.

A man appeared dressed in military fatigues and pointing an Uzi. ThunderStrike's second-in-command, Marshall "Gunner" Young, fired a single shot and the man dropped.

"Move." Despite the surprise, Maverick kept his voice low and even-keeled. Gunner stayed as lookout while Maverick led the remaining three forward. According to the intel they'd received, the twelve American hostages were on the other side of this door.

He turned the handle, eased it open.

Seven men. Five women. All sitting or lying on a filthy cement floor. A small lamp in the corner cast eerie shadows on the wall. Despite knowing the truth, he searched their faces for her. Always seeking. Never finding.

"Target achieved."

He approached and flipped up his night goggles. "We've come to bring you home."

Another muted gunshot from the corridor. "We gotta go," Gunner said through the comm.

Maverick and his team hurried the group onto their feet. The hostages were in bad shape, but he had to move them out. One of the men couldn't stand, so Maverick hoisted him over his shoulder. The injured doctor groaned.

Per protocol, he led them in, but he was last man out. His team ushered the group down the hall toward a stairway.

Gunner fired another shot.

"Penelope, talk to me," Maverick said. "We're sixty seconds to rooftop."

Maverick waited, but his lead helicopter pilot didn't respond. They hustled up three flights of stairs and exited through a doorway onto the rooftop. Breathing hard, Maverick propped the American against the cement wall.

Between the weight of the man and the flak jacket, sweat soaked Maverick's back. He searched the dark sky. *The helos should be here.*

"Penelope, I need your location."

"Twenty seconds," she replied. The edginess in her voice didn't bode well.

The fire door burst open and four terrorists started spraying the rooftop with bullets. Maverick's team released a torrent of gunfire and the enemy dropped.

"We have to land on the north side of the building," Penelope said into Maverick's earpiece.

Maverick shouldered his submachine gun and retrieved the injured hostage. "Follow me. Gunner, take the rear."

As they charged across the roof, the Black Hawks touched down. Maverick placed the injured man inside, then helped two women. Three ThunderStrike crew guided six of the hostages to the second craft, then jumped in behind them.

After assisting the remaining three Americans, Maverick did a quick head count. They were one shy. The other chopper lifted off and he surveyed the area. Gunner lay writhing on the ground. Maverick sprinted back, hoisted the two hundred and fifty pound man into his arms, and bolted back toward the helicopter. "Talk to me."

"Fuck."

"Where are you hit?"

"Chest."

He laid Gunner into the belly of the craft.

As he was about to hop in, a barrage of gunfire exploded behind him. Searing pain shot through him. He tried climbing in, but collapsed on the ground.

"I'm hit," Maverick said. "Penelope, go."

"Gunner." Penelope's smooth voice rolled through the comm. "Make it happen."

Gunner grunted. "I can't move—"

"Two seconds, Gunner." Penelope sounded far, far away, like she'd already left him to die in enemy territory.

An arm reached out...as everything faded to black.

2

CARLY'S BAD NEWS

Carlyle Stone glared at the Excel spreadsheet. Not even her death stare could change the bottom line. "Not good."

Her assistant's shriek sent her hurrying into reception. "What's wrong?"

Desiree Hott stood barefoot on her desk, her eyes wide with fear. "Another mouse."

Carly sighed. "Those traps aren't working. Did you see where it went?"

"Wherever it went isn't far enough." Desiree shuddered. "You know how you hate spiders? That's how I feel about mice."

"I was hoping we could get rid of them ourselves, but I'll call an exterminator."

"Why don't you tell your dad?"

"I did, but he hasn't done anything. Maybe this is the universe telling me to step away."

"Not true. The universe wants you to stay because if you don't, the bad guys will win."

"Well, then, the universe is going to have to throw us some meatier cases, and by meatier, I don't mean in the form of a rodent."

"It's that bad?"

Carly nodded. "Another few months and Stone Investigations won't exist."

Frowning in that oh-so-familiar way, Desiree twirled a chunk of pink-streaked blonde hair. "Don't say that."

"I'm behind on rent. If I don't pay the electric bill, we'll be working by candlelight."

"Can't you work something out with your dad?" Desiree climbed down, slipped into her stilettos, but kept her gaze glued on the floor.

When Carly's grandpa passed in February, her father took over as building landlord and her free ride came to a screeching halt. Though her dad charged her less than the going rate to rent the Pennsylvania Avenue office in southeast D.C., it was still a big chunk of change that she didn't have.

Carly's sigh was laced with frustration. "He hasn't been so great about returning my calls."

"Okay, so what happened to the new clients Sinclair sent our way?"

"Two still haven't paid. One wants to barter. She doesn't believe money is the best way to do business." Carly groaned. "My grandpa would hang his head in shame at what I've done to his beloved business."

"You haven't done *anything* wrong. People don't seem to need private eyes like they used to. They hunt for people on the Internet. DNA testing is done by spitting into a test tube. I'll make it a point to ask everyone who comes in for a referral. No worries."

"Thanks," Carly said before returning to her office. But she *was* worried. She needed a lot more than referrals to turn her business around. She needed a solid case, something that would put her investigative agency back on the map.

And make Grandpa Pierce proud of her.

Because God knows, her parents weren't.

The doorbell chimed. *Must be my three o'clock.* She rolled the silky lip gel across her lips, then tugged her suit jacket down. *I need this, so git her done.*

Desiree tapped on her office door. "Craig Pluckett is here."

With a smile, Carly rose as her prospective client walked in. "Mr. Pluckett, I'm Carly Stone." She shook his hand. "Have a seat."

"Call me Craig." He settled into the chair across from her large antique desk.

"Craig, your assistant explained that you're shopping PI firms. Who are you working with now?"

"I'm not at liberty to say. What I can tell you is that they've jacked their prices way up."

"Are you looking for routine background checks for your hotels in the D.C. region?"

"No, the entire country. My department oversees as many as a hundred and fifty background checks a week."

Carly did the math in her head and perked up. If she landed this gig, she could pay her overdue bills *and* have money left to advertise, something she desperately needed to do.

After discussing particulars, Carly determined she could save the hotel giant tens of thousands. "I'll email you my proposal. When are you making your decision?"

"In three months, when my current contract expires." Craig glanced at his watch. "Where's Carlyle? I'd like to meet him before I leave."

"You already have. *I'm* Carlyle."

Craig paused. "I thought Carlyle was a man."

Ah, crap. She let the silence speak for itself.

While shifting in his chair, he cleared his throat. "I...um. Every private investigator I've *ever* worked with has been a man. How long have you been in business?"

Her stomach dropped. His tone had changed. "My grandfather, Pierce Stone, founded and ran Stone Investigations for almost forty years. I have a college degree in criminal justice and have worked here for a decade. I'll include references with my proposal."

"Is Mr. Stone here?"

"Unfortunately, he passed away in February."

"I'm sorry for your loss." Craig rose. "Sure, send over those references along with your proposal."

As she pushed out of her seat, her cheeks heated. This wasn't the first time she'd been overlooked because she was a woman-owned business or because she was running her own investigative firm. Sometimes she hated how the world worked.

After showing him the door and watching her opportunity vanish down the hallway, she shook her head at Desiree. Back at her desk, she reviewed the agency's financials one more time while fiddling with her stackable rings. *If things don't turn around, I'll have to let Desiree go. That's gonna suck.*

The door chime rang. *Maybe Craig changed his mind.*

"Hey!" Desiree called out from reception. "I thought your kind only ventured out after sundown."

Sinclair's deep chuckle filled the office. "Hey, sis. Carly here?"

In addition to being one of her closest friends, Sinclair Develin was Desiree's brother. Not by blood, but by the strong bonds of family he had with the Hott clan.

Grateful for the distraction, Carly rolled into reception.

Sinclair's embrace was tighter than usual and, when he released her, the lines around his eyes were etched deep. He was every woman's dream, except Carly's. Carly's heart had been captured decades ago. While she could appreciate Sinclair's intense blue eyes, luscious dark hair, and that devilish smile, he'd always been the brother she never had.

In all the years she'd known him, Sinclair had never dropped by unannounced and he never went anywhere without an agenda. Laser-focused, he was a Washington power player, known as The Fixer. His business prowess and connections had opened doors for her professionally, but her history with him dated back to middle school, when he was Ashton Hott's biggest rival turned adopted brother.

"Ash has been shot."

The air got sucked out of Carly's lungs and she clutched her chest. Desiree's guttural scream made her jump.

"Ohmygod, ohmygod, what happened? Is he okay? Where is he?" Desiree's sentences blurred together as she flew around the reception counter.

Sinclair stopped her with his body, wrapping her in his massive arms while she clung to him. "He's in a Frankfurt, Germany hospital. He's going to be fine. No worries."

Towering over her, Sinclair locked gazes with Carly. His usual calculated, controlled confidence had yielded to alarm. Ashton was worse than Sinclair was letting on. For Desiree's sake.

Desiree broke away. "When are we leaving?"

"I'm flying out today," Sinclair said. "Dad's meeting me at Dulles."

Desiree grabbed her handbag. "Let's go."

Sinclair stopped her, his large hands cemented on her shoulders. "Dad wants Carly to fly out first."

No way am I getting in the middle of this. Carly threw her hands up. "Family first."

"Dad's—Warren's—instructions were explicit. You, Colton, and I accompany him."

As Desiree's cheeks pinked, she flicked her gaze between them. "So, what? I'm the B team?"

Sinclair raised his thick eyebrows. "Desiree, Dad wants to ensure the first visit is chill." Intensity shone in his eyes. "You can get...well, sometimes you get...er...emotional."

"Oh, that is such a load of—" Then, Desiree eyed Carly. "I'm sorry. I'm being selfish."

"Can you clear your schedule?" Sinclair asked Carly.

Before she could answer, Desiree blurted, "I'll handle everything. You go. Ash would want you there."

"When I bring Carly and Colton back, I'll fly you and Hudson out," Sinclair said. "Crockett, too."

"Desiree, thank you." Carly fetched her handbag.

"My driver is outside."

Sinclair's feet ate up the pavement and she double-stepped to keep up. After they slid into the backseat of his Lincoln Continental, Sinclair instructed his chauffeur and they pulled into D.C. traffic.

The silence helped Carly collect her jumbled thoughts, but she couldn't slow her frantic heartbeat. Ashton had been her closest friend since second grade. Once, in middle school, things had almost ventured outside the friend zone, but his life had spun out of control and he needed a friend—not a girlfriend—to help him manage through the loss.

Over the years, she'd watched a revolving door of women come and go. But she'd remained steadfast in the friend zone, ignoring the innermost desires of her heart.

For as long as she could remember, he offered his support every single time her parents expressed their disappointment in her. Several months ago, her beloved grandfather had died and Ash had been her rock. And, over the years, he made her guts burn from all the belly laughing they'd done together.

So, she'd cling to that beloved friendship, knowing that one day someone would come along and claim his heart. A sharp pain stung her chest and she glanced over at Sinclair. He stared out the window, muscles in his jaw ticking again and again, as if keeping time to some tune running rampant through his mind.

"You're overly protective of Desiree, so what didn't you want her to know?" she asked.

Sadness tinged his eyes. "He might not make it."

Adrenaline raced through her. "Oh, God, no."

"Warren is out of his mind with worry. He didn't say anything about who should visit or who shouldn't. I made that decision."

"Of course you did."

"You hold it together when it counts. He needs that. He needs *you*."

"I'll be strong."

"Desiree and Hudson can't see their big brother fighting for his life. Some would say I have no right to keep his family away." His lips quirked at the corners. She'd seen that sinister smile hundreds of times. "But you know I don't give a damn what anyone says or thinks."

The six men who'd graduated Harvard together had an unbreakable bond. When one was down, the others would rally around and lift him up. Throughout the years, she'd witnessed that over and over again. Tears clouded her eyes and she turned away.

The driver pulled up in front of her modest brick-front home in Arlington. Sinclair waited in the car while she threw clothing into an overnight bag. An hour later, they boarded his private jet at Dulles International Airport. Colton Mitus and Maverick's father, Warren Hott, were seated.

Colton, CEO of Mitus Conglomerate, had a brilliant mind. Normally reserved and stoic, there was no denying the concern in his eyes. Ashton's cocky, bold, larger-than-life personality seemed to be the glue that held these men together.

Worry lined Warren's face, his eyes red from crying. Her heart broke. He looked so damn scared.

Both men rose to hug her.

"Thanks for the call," Colton said to Sinclair. "What do you know?"

Sinclair placed a hand on his shoulder. "Give me five with the pilots, unless *you* want to fly this bird."

"I'm in no condition to pilot anything."

Silence hung heavy, the atmosphere thick with tension, as they taxied to the runway.

Once airborne, the flight attendant took their drink orders. Sinclair perked up, the familiar twinkle in his eyes returning when he glimpsed her long legs. Carly bit back a smile. This would have made Ashton laugh out loud while he encouraged his friend to take care of his personal business with her *after* the plane touched down. But Carly was confident that if she *hadn't* been there, and Ashton had, both men would be vying for that flight attendant's *personal* attention.

A moment later, the attendant returned with their drinks. Carly needed something strong to numb the shock, so she tossed back a whiskey, welcoming the burn. Only after the alcohol had calmed her palpitating heart did she ask for the rest of the story.

"Warren, how are you holding up?"

Ashton's dad didn't fake it where she was concerned. "I can't lose him, Carly."

Her heart stuttered, the pain reverberating through her. "He'll pull through." For his sake, she tried smiling. "Can you talk about what happened?"

He patted her hand. "Of course." He regarded the two men sitting across from him. "Thanks for dropping everything. I know you both have a lot going on. In fact, I got your save-the-date wedding announcement, Colton. I look forward to the big event."

"Thank you, Warren," Colton said. "Tell us what you know."

"Penelope called me. Both he and Gunner were hit. Gunner's in stable condition with a gunshot wound to the chest that punctured his lung. It would have been fatal if he hadn't been wearing his vest." Warren cleared his throat. "From what she explained—though I kinda blanked out—they'd gotten the hostages out. Gunner was down. When Ashton returned to get him, he got sprayed with gunfire."

"Oh, no," Carly whispered.

Colton shook his head. "Jesus, no."

Pausing, Warren's lip quivered and he stared out the window.

Carly shifted her attention to Sinclair. With raised eyebrows, she pleaded with him to step in and say something—*anything*—but he shook his head and remained silent.

After a moment, Warren continued. "Penelope flew the copter out of enemy space and landed. Both men were triaged on site, then flown to a hospital in Frankfurt. Emergency surgery for both. Like I said, Gunner is in stable condition. She said Ash is in and out of consciousness. Shrapnel was removed from his leg, but the Flak jacket couldn't stop a bullet from entering his back. If he makes it, the doctors aren't sure if he'll be able to walk."

And that's when Carly lost it. On a gasp, she pushed out of the seat and rushed toward the restroom tucked in the back of the plane. Ducking inside, she sobbed. *He can't die. He just can't.*

When she'd been in second grade, her family had moved to Northern Virginia. That first week she felt lost and alone, but when Ashton plunked down beside her at lunch, he made her laugh. At recess, she challenged him to a race. Back then, she'd been fast enough to beat him. The day he stepped forward to be her friend was one of the best days of her life.

Determined to stay strong for his sake, Carly wiped her eyes and returned to her seat.

"You okay?" Sinclair asked.

She nodded.

"This is tough." Warren offered a sad smile before addressing Sinclair. "When we bring Desiree and Hudson, I'll need you with me, son."

"I'll be with you every step of the way, Dad."

The eight-hour flight featured two movies, neither of which Carly watched. She sat in numbed silence, rearranging her stackable rings. At one point, she dropped one, but couldn't find it. Colton plucked it from under his seat and handed it to her.

"He's a fighter," he said, though his eyes were tight with worry. "He'll pull through."

"He has to," she whispered.

Colton and Sinclair spoke quietly for over an hour. And then, Colton and Warren slept. In the darkened cabin, Sinclair retreated to the back. Thirty minutes later, he returned, a smile hovering on the corners of his mouth.

Her smirk elicited a wink from him. Though never attracted to him, she could see how women would be. He was handsome, wicked smart, and powerful. In addition to their bad-boy reputations, he and Ashton were emotionally unavailable, so women flocked to them.

Sinclair had helped her navigate through a time in her life when her sexual fetish had reached a crossroads. Not only had he pointed her in the right direction, he had given his heartfelt guidance when she'd needed it most.

Though she never told him how she really felt about Ashton, she had every confidence he knew that, too. Nothing got past Sinclair Develin.

Nothing.

Lucky for her, Sinclair kept all her secrets.

"Is he going to die?" she whispered.

"He fucking better not," Sinclair replied.

3

MAVERICK'S VISITORS

Maverick could manage through the pain. But the meds they pumped into him kept him bathed in a murky fog. When the morphine wore off, he'd open his eyes and have a brief moment of confusion, then clarity. Then, pain. He'd no idea if he could move his legs because he couldn't fucking feel them.

He wanted to speak, shout. But he couldn't make his mouth move. His vision was blurry and his thoughts jumbled.

He remembered going into ground zero. He remembered carrying out one of the hostages. All of them had been deposited into the copters. After that, things got wonky. Gunner was down. Maverick bolted to him and high-tailed it back to the bird. That's where his memory cut off.

His next recollection was waking in a white room. Initially, he thought he was in heaven, a destination he didn't think he'd ever see. Then, Nurse Ratched came in and the shit got ugly real fast.

Hospital. The eye-stinging stench of antiseptic mixed with the smell of blood. The thick outline of his legs beneath the thin bed linens sent relief coursing through him. *Can't beat Carly in racquetball if I can't outmaneuver her. Can't train for the Ironman.*

But he had no idea if they worked.

Nurse Ratched entered his room and checked his vitals. When she lifted his head and adjusted his pillows, he groaned.

"Mr. Hott, you have visitors." Her thick German accent punched through the silence. "I add painkiller to your IV. You like, yes?"

He closed his eyes as the cool blast of medication entered his vein. He wanted to object, but he couldn't. He wanted to ask about Gunner. Where were the hostages? Were they safe? Did his team make it out okay? So many questions but he couldn't utter the damn words.

The familiar scent of his father washed over him and he breathed a little easier.

"Son, it's Dad." His father's warm hand blanketed his. "You look good. Can you open your eyes?"

Maverick fought against the constant dull ache and sharp pains shooting through him. He struggled against the drugs, but he couldn't. *I'm trying, Dad, but I can't.*

His father spoke quietly about his work, and about how the mower broke and Hudson tried to fix it, but now it's a heap of scrap metal in the garage. His father's laugh made Maverick smile, but he doubted his lips were moving. He lay there floating in and out of consciousness, his dad's soothing voice a godsend.

"Ashton, you are my life and I need you to pull through. You hold our family together, son. I'm praying hard for you. You've been strong your entire life. Dig deep and do it one more time. I *cannot* lose you." His dad cleared his throat. "All right, my boy, I brought a few surprises with me."

His father kissed his forehead and squeezed his shoulder, then spoke to someone else. Maverick strained to hear, but couldn't.

"Hey, Maverick. You look good."

Colton.

"You're in Germany, of all places. Oktoberfest is *never* going to be the same."

Maverick could hear the anxiety in his friend's voice. *I'm okay. Just a little dinged up.*

"You were quite the hero, per usual. Gunner is okay. We're going to visit him next. I need you better, Ash, because I can't get married if you're not standing up there with me. Plus, you and I are in business together. There's no way I'm letting you off the hook that easily. You owe me money."

Jackass. Maverick wanted to laugh, then punch his golden man in the arm.

"We're staying for a few days, but the nurse standing over us has an iron fist. I'm going to let someone else say hello. I'm pulling for you, my friend. Get better."

Thanks for the visit, brother.

More quiet chatting. Then, someone sat beside him. He knew it was Sinclair before his brother uttered a single word.

"Jesus, Ash, you smell like a fucking pharmacy."

Maverick was closer to Sin than his biological brother.

Sinclair wrapped his large hand around Maverick's arm. "I could beat the living hell out of you and there's not a damn thing you could do about it." Sinclair's chuckle made Maverick laugh, though no sound escaped his lips.

You hit me, you'll regret it, Jackoff. He wanted to laugh at their familiar childhood warning, but his body wouldn't cooperate.

"I gotta thank you for getting banged up like this. Because of you, I got a blowjob on the flight," Sinclair whispered into his ear. "I need you back home, brother. The Ironman is coming up and I won't train if you aren't dragging my sorry ass. I'm staying in Germany until you're so sick of me whispering sweet shit into your ear that you deck me. Get your ass home and I'll make sure you have a *true* hero's welcome. I brought you a surprise. She's been keeping it together real good. You gotta get better, you hear me? I love you, brother."

The warmth from Sinclair's breath on his cheek vanished, as

did the firm grip around his arm. The medication kicked in and Maverick stopped trying to fight through the fog.

Warm breath and the softest lips touched his forehead, his cheek, and a delicate peck on his mouth. "Hey, Ashton. Somehow you look good in a hospital gown."

My Carly girl. I must be a mess if she flew all the way out here.

She held his hand, stroked his skin, combed delicate fingers through his hair. Her touch felt like the best medicine and he relaxed even more. "We haven't seen your doctor yet, but when I learn something, I'll tell you. Ash, I'm sorry this happened." Her voice cracked. "You'll be okay. I know you. You'll get better. You have to. You know it and I know it. My life would be empty without you."

Despite trying to fight it, he was slipping into another drug-induced sleep.

Her breath warmed his ear. "I love you, Ash. I always have and I always will. Don't you *dare* die on me."

THREE WEEKS LATER, Maverick pushed out of bed, wincing at the knife-like pain shooting down his leg. The pain was a godsend because it confirmed he could feel.

While he was no stranger to beat up muscles, constant bruises, and achy joints, he struggled to absorb so much discomfort in so many places. Pushing himself to his physical limit was something he loved doing, but the challenges he faced were unlike anything he'd ever experienced before.

And like everything else in his life, he bore the weight without complaint. He gripped the walker for support and ambled out of the hospital room and down the hallway. He forced himself to do this five times daily, though he struggled come nightfall. But he could feel slight improvements, which spurred him to push harder.

Gunner walked around the corner and grinned. "Looking good, my man."

When at home, Gunner kept his Afro short and his facial hair closely cropped. He hadn't shaved since they'd arrived and looked almost as wild as Maverick.

Normally, Maverick would slap his friend and fellow ex-SEAL on the back, but he wasn't confident enough to let go of the walker, so he clung to the aluminum and smiled. "One step at a time. You ready to get out of here?"

Gunner broke eye contact.

"Don't go there," Maverick said. "It's time for you to go. Your family misses you. Plus, Penelope said she needs help running ThunderStrike."

"I hate to leave you. I wouldn't be here if it weren't for you."

"Right back atcha." Maverick wanted to throw an arm around him, but the stabbing pain down his leg reminded him to clutch the support device. "Nurse Ratched informed me that I'm getting promoted to the rehab facility. Probably getting your empty bed. Now, you get your ass home and don't look back."

"I can grab you a cell phone before my flight leaves."

Per ThunderStrike protocol, overseas missions were completed without them. If a mission went wrong, teams couldn't risk top-secret emails or contact information being made available to their captors.

"Hell, no." Maverick resumed his walking and Gunner fell in line beside him. "My phone never stopped ringing all the damn time. Quiet is good." Truth was, he hated that he wasn't needed. Despised that someone wasn't calling him for something. Being at the top of everyone's list was something Maverick craved. He wanted to be the one everyone thought of when they needed someone to help them out.

But what could he do from his hospital bed? In truth, he was grateful the visits had stopped. No one needed to see him like this. "Mayhem can wait another week or two."

Gunner threw an arm around him. "'Thanks for saving my life' sounds pathetic. I owe you one."

"We're even, my friend. You saved mine, too." Maverick stopped at the elevator bank. "Your lung is healed. You're well. Now get outta here. I'll call you when they free me from the castle."

Laughing, Gunner stepped into a waiting elevator. "Get better." The doors closed.

"Damn, I wish that was me." Fighting through the pain, Maverick ambled onward, determined to get healthy.

4

A HERO'S WELCOME

I *need a shave, a shower, and a fuck.*
Released after forty-five days in the Frankfurt hospital, getting laid was at the top of Maverick's list.

The first two weeks, Maverick couldn't shake the haze from the pain meds. The past thirty days, he'd pushed through his limitations, determined to get stronger. The physical therapy had been grueling. He fought for every step, gritted through the obstacles, refusing to go easy on himself.

The payoff?

Returning home three days ahead of schedule. He couldn't fucking wait.

The hospital doc had told him to go easy, continue with his physical therapy, and pay attention to the various types of pain.

"Some are good, others not," said his doctor.

As far as Maverick could tell, all pain sucked.

The only things that didn't hurt were his self-induced orgasms. Try as he might, nobody at that facility would give him a hand. Literally.

Sinclair had offered to send his private jet, but Maverick flew commercial. He didn't want special treatment. He wanted to blend in and fly home under the radar. No fanfare, no press. Just a normal guy returning to his normal life.

He wouldn't be leading another overseas mission for months. Even he knew that. Running ThunderStrike from base camp would have to suffice. Small steps, like the first ones he'd taken in the hospital.

His dad had visited him on two different occasions. When he'd first landed there, and again, weeks later. Maverick had no memory of that initial visit, nor could he recall any of his other visitors. But his father had assured him that all three of his siblings had visited—Sinclair, Desiree, and Hudson—along with his closest friends, Colton, Crockett, and Carly. Jagger had flown in from California, too. He wished he could remember, but the first few weeks had been a hazy blur.

The jumbo jet touched down at Dulles. Passengers grabbed their phones, but Maverick didn't have his. After weeks of being unplugged, he was ready to jump headfirst into the fray.

When he exited the craft, he followed the crowd. His plan? Head outside and grab a ride home. After passing through customs, his attention fell on a large handmade sign.

WELCOME HOME ASHTON!

As his family waved him over, he shoved down the well of emotion. *Showtime.* He threw out his arms and grinned. "I'm back, baby!"

Desiree flung her arms around his neck. "I'm sooooooo happy to see you!"

Damn, it felt great to be home. Better than great. Fucking sensational. "Thanks for coming out. I wasn't expecting to see you guys."

Hudson didn't do his usual handclasp, one-armed hug, either. Like his sister, he bear-hugged him. "Heya, Ash. Love the beard, man."

His father didn't even try to fight the tears. "Welcome home, son," he said, pulling him close.

"How'd you guys know I got released ahead of schedule?"

"Seriously, you did not just ask us that," Hudson said.

"Sinclair?" Maverick asked.

"Of course," Desiree replied.

Maverick slung his arms over his siblings. "I never told him. Hell, I never told anyone."

"Sinclair knows all," Hudson said with a chuckle.

Maverick regarded three of a small handful of people he loved most in the world. His closest friends were missing, as was his favorite gal pal.

"Where's Carly?" Maverick asked.

For the last several weeks, he couldn't stop thinking about her. And some of his erotic dreams—all starring the beautiful blonde —had woken him with a stiff one that could *not* be ignored.

Before his family could answer, a torrent of reporters gathered around. Seconds later, a leggy brunette emerged from the swarm and sauntered close. Alexandra Reed, local news anchor and fiancée of his close friend, Crockett Wilde.

Maverick grinned, full on. "Hey, baby girl. What's going on here?"

"The press caught on to your homecoming. If you can spare a minute, I've got some questions."

Maverick puffed out his chest. "Ask away."

"You accomplished something the government couldn't. Tell us about the rescue."

"We kicked some serious ass."

The group laughed.

Maverick lost the bravado and rubbed his aching thigh. "Seriously, our goal at ThunderStrike is to ensure a safe return in a hostage situation. Lives lost are unacceptable. I'm damn proud of my team. We did what the client hired us to do. Got in, grabbed the Americans, and got the hell out. I was the one who got a little detained."

He surveyed the mob of reporters, their phones shoved close. When he locked eyes with a cute one, she smiled, her cheeks flushing. Normally, he'd check her out, grab her name and number. Depending on circumstances, he'd hook up with her. Might even take her to dinner. But that's as far as things would go.

Instead, his thoughts jumped to Carly. Again.

Despite his dad's detailed report of every visitor he had, Maverick had no memory of her being there. But now, with his feet firmly back on U.S. soil, he could finally address the pressing need to see her.

"You fought your way back to us, so how are you doing now?" Alexandra asked.

"Good as new and ready to roll." Maverick shot the group a big smile, ignoring the constant ache that had latched on like a leech.

"What's next for ThunderStrike?"

"Business as usual." He nodded, more to convince himself than anything. Maverick was hurting. If there was anything he detested, it was weakness. He'd throw on a smile and muscle through it. He'd keep his chin up and his pain to himself. Maverick measured most things against seventh grade. Seventh grade was the gold standard, the benchmark for things sucking. He had managed through worse. He would do it again. His family and friends expected it. His employees demanded it. He had an image to uphold and he'd do it if it fucking killed him.

Maverick answered a few more questions before the throng of media trickled away. Only Alexandra stayed.

"My phone is off. My cameraman long gone." She stepped close. "It's just us. Everyone's been so worried about you. How are you doing?"

But it wasn't just the two of them. Maverick's family hovered, eager for the real story. *Not happening.*

"Thanks for coming out, Alexandra. I'm good. Really. Tell me about you. What's happening with my boy?"

Alexandra beamed and Maverick chuffed out a laugh. A twinge pinched the back of his thigh and he rubbed the spot.

Her gaze followed his movement. Per usual, Alexandra missed nothing. "I thought so. Well, your secret is safe with me," she whispered. "You've got to take it easy."

"I'm on the top of the world, baby girl. Got too much going on to slow down. You didn't answer my question. How's Crockett?"

She beamed. "We tied the knot."

"Holy hell. I missed the wedding?"

"Crockett thought my mom would want to be there. It was small. Nothing like Colton and Brigit's this December." Her smile fell away. "We wanted you there—"

"It's okay. When was the big day?"

"Last month."

He kissed her cheek. "Congratulations. How is Mama Mitus doing?"

Alexandra's smile fell away. "She passed, but she was so happy to see us marry."

Sadness cut through him. "I'm sorry, honey."

"It's been tough. Crockett has been amazing and so supportive. How did you get through it when your mom died?"

The short answer: Carly.

Maverick's family hung on his every word. He didn't want to talk about his mom. Not here, not now. Not ever, really. Like everything else, Maverick clamped down on his feelings. "We leaned on each other. Got through it the best we could." He threw his family a brave smile. "Our boy Crockett is strong. You're smart to lean on him. Tell him I'll call him once I get settled."

"I will." She hugged him. "You're our hometown hero. The press has been talking about your return for days. They're probably camped out at your home waiting for you."

Christ, I hope not.

"Wait, you live on a boat, don't you?"

"Let's keep that our little secret."

Before leaving, Alexandra addressed his family. "Good to see you guys. Can I get a couple of quotes from the fam?"

"We're very relieved Ashton is home," Warren said.

"And so proud of his heroic efforts," Desiree added.

"Thanks," Alexandra said. "Enjoy your homecoming."

Maverick shot her a wink. "See ya, Goth Girl."

With a smirk, she headed out. Maverick shifted his gaze to his family. Their expressions were a mix of curiosity, concern, and glee. He chuckled. "We're a motley crew, aren't we? Where's Sin?"

"He said he'd catch up with you later," Maverick's dad said. "Let's get you out of here. You're hurting, aren't you, son?"

"Nah, I'm fine."

Maverick was back on American soil, surrounded by his family, and eager to jump into the mayhem. He couldn't wait to shove the past aside and turn toward the future. Pain hadn't stopped him before and it wouldn't stop him now.

On the way out, Hudson pulled up alongside him. "Sorry you missed my grand opening."

Maverick fastened an arm around his younger brother. "How'd it go?"

"Awesome. You would have been proud."

Maverick smiled. "I'm always proud of you."

Strange, even now, Hudson considered Maverick more like a second dad than an older brother. Despite just five years separating the men, Hudson had been struggling to find his way. Two years ago, he approached Maverick with a restaurant idea and Maverick had done everything possible to make that happen for him.

"Are you free tomorrow night?" Hudson asked.

"Absolutely. You want me to stop by?"

"I'm throwing you a welcome home party."

"You didn't have to do that."

"Oh, hey, I almost forgot." Hudson handed Maverick his cell phone.

Maverick hesitated. "How the hell did you get that?"

"Sinclair gave it to me."

"It was locked in my safe at work."

Hudson laughed. "You don't think a gated office complex and a safe are going to stop him, do you?"

"Yeah, I kinda thought it would."

"Whatever. Just take it. It was already turned on, too."

Maverick rolled his eyes. "I left my wallet in the safe. Did he give you that, too?"

"Sorry, no."

They left the airport and, for the first time, Maverick appreciated the thick September humidity. Dusk blanketed the sky, vibrant hues of violet and fuchsia lingering on the horizon. He soaked in that sunset like it was his first, gratitude filling his heart. *Damn, it's great to be back.*

Over the next forty minutes, his family chatted away, updating him on everything they'd already told him via their phone calls. But hearing the stories in person, being able to reach out and touch them or punch his brother in the arm, was the best damn homecoming. When Desiree mentioned Carly, Maverick took control of the conversation.

"How is she?"

"She's okay," Desiree said, twirling a chunk of hair.

"Why didn't she come to the airport?"

"She doesn't know you're back because she's been testifying in Baltimore all afternoon. Sinclair called Dad an hour ago and we scrambled to get here. Do you want me to text her?"

"No. I'll surprise her later. Hudson, did you invite her tomorrow?"

"Duh," Hudson replied.

"Is she coming?"

"Duh, again." Hudson snort-laughed. "Of course she is."

As they crossed the bridge into the district, Maverick's phone rang. *That didn't take long.* "Senator Internado, how are you?"

"That's my question for you, Maverick. I saw the local news. Glad you made it home safely."

George Internado wasn't the type of man who made small talk. "What can I do for you, George?"

"I'm enjoying a burger at Rudy's. Join me."

"Now?"

"Yes, *now.*" The senator let the silence linger an extra beat. "I wouldn't have gone to the trouble of calling if it wasn't important. Enter through the alley behind the restaurant. I'm at a table in the kitchen reserved for Rudy's special guests."

"Roger that." He hung up. "Dad, can you drop me at Rudy's? It's a few blocks from the Capitol."

"Can't the senator wait? You haven't even been home yet."

"Internado doesn't know the word 'wait.'"

Five minutes later, Maverick stood on the sidewalk outside the popular dive restaurant and peered into the car. "Thanks for coming to the airport."

"The party starts at six tomorrow," Hudson said. "I'm closing the restaurant for the big event."

"Thanks, bro." Maverick smacked the top of the car. "Love you guys."

His dad drove away. Maverick headed into the alley and pounded on the back door. Rudy flung it open and grinned. "Hey, Maverick, long time no see. I caught the end of your interview on the news. Congrats. You're our hometown hero."

"Nah, not me. Just damn happy to be home." The smell of grease and burgers filled Maverick's nostrils and his stomach growled.

Rudy stepped aside. "I'm making your favorite burger. It'll be out in a minute. Come on in. The senator's waiting."

The sixty-eight year old politician was a pillar of power in Washington. He'd held his senate seat longer than the thirty-three years Maverick had been on planet earth. In the year since Colton had introduced them, the senator had become a staunch supporter of ThunderStrike. He made calls, set up meetings, but Maverick never expected his generosity would be one-sided. He knew going into this relationship that the seasoned politician would want something in return.

His gut told him that day had come.

George Internado wiped the ketchup from his chin and extended his arm. Maverick grasped his greasy hand and shook it. After dragging the rickety chair over the concrete floor, he sat.

"Thanks for coming, Maverick."

No choice. "Absolutely."

"I heard you were in bad shape. Feeling better?"

"Doing great." He rubbed his aching thigh. "I appreciate the concern, but I doubt you summoned me to discuss my health."

Rudy set a cold bottle of beer in front of Maverick and left.

"This situation might have been brushed under the rug, had your homecoming not been plastered all over the local news." Internado shoved a French fry into his mouth, chasing it with a swig of beer. "I fully anticipate the media will play this up. Hometown boy saves the world. A fucking syrupy-sweet story."

"What *situation?*"

"While you were in the hospital, someone leaked word that your privately-funded mission wasn't so private, after all. Those cock-sucking vultures have been scrambling to see which government agencies were involved. If this gets out, we're in deep shit." Internado threw down his napkin. "Why couldn't you slip back into town without all that fucking fanfare? Does your dick need to be stroked that badly?"

"Actually, it could use a good stroking."

"Dammit, Maverick, get serious." The senator leaned forward and Maverick whiffed the booze on his breath. "The State Department couldn't get the job done through diplomatic channels and a military op was ruled out due to the political climate. So, the families of these poor prisoners pooled their pennies and off you went. Only, you and I know it wasn't that simple. Someone had to point you in the right goddamn direction. How are we going to sweep this shit under the rug when there's no more room under the rug for any more shit?"

"They aren't going to find anything because this mission was completed like every other ThunderStrike rescue. Pointing us in the right direction isn't a crime."

"Who the hell loaned you that second Black Hawk? We pulled a few strings to make that happen."

"So, you're the Wizard of Oz." Maverick tossed back a mouthful of beer. "Good to know. I'm scared to death of the Wicked Witch, so thank the good Lord you're not her."

"Cut the crap. It's just you and me. No cameras. No pussies. We've got a serious problem that's got to be dealt with."

"Senator, I think—"

Rudy delivered Maverick's burger, along with a giant side of fries. "Thanks, Rudy. Looks great."

"Enjoy, my friend," Rudy said. "Senator, can I get you anything?"

Drilling Maverick with a death stare, the senator shook his head. "Not a goddamn thing."

"If that's all you wanted to tell me, I'm rolling out of here." Eager to leave, Maverick shoved out of his chair.

"We're not finished. Sit your ass down, boy."

Taking orders worked when Maverick went through Officer Candidate School. It also worked when he became a Navy SEAL. But he left the military to call his own shots and bark his own damn commands. Gritting his teeth, he eased back down.

"I read the intelligence briefing. You were told to abort the mission because the terrorists had intel when you were going to strike. Instead, you went rogue. You risked the mission and the lives of everyone affiliated with it."

"The only thing that went wrong is one of my men took a bullet."

"What about the bullets you took?"

"My welfare doesn't count."

"That's very noble, Maverick, but it doesn't erase the facts. The Senate Select Committee wants answers. Being that I'm the head of that committee, I was forced to open an investigation."

"Then you know we did nothing wrong."

"This is bureaucratic bullshit. But..." he shrugged a heavy-set shoulder, "I *might* be able to delay the hearing for the indefinite future."

Here we go. Maverick stayed silent.

The senator leaded forward. "I'm announcing my run for Governor of Virginia. Not only could I use your public support and the support of your influential and very wealthy friends—like Colton Mitus and Sinclair Develin—I could use your assistance with my opponent."

"What does that mean?" Maverick popped a fry into his mouth.

"Keep in mind, I'm not suggesting you do this. I'm simply answering your question."

Maverick hated playing games. His stomach grumbled and he shoved the bacon burger into his mouth. At least the greasy food tasted good.

"You have those surveillance devices," George said. "Would those work for keeping an eye and ear out for what's happening on the other side of the fence? Hypothetically speaking."

Refusing to answer, Maverick tossed back another mouthful of beer, the frosty brew doing nothing to cool his anger. *What a cluster fuck.* Now he knew why Sinclair had gone out of his way to get him his cell phone. *I'm supposed to be recording this conversation. Wake up, dummy. You're back in D.C.*

"And in exchange, your little problem goes away," the senator continued.

"What you're asking me to do is illegal. Ever heard of Watergate?"

Internado threw back his head and forced out a laugh. "Pshaw, Maverick. I'm not asking anything of the sort." He glanced around, though they were alone. "You have a problem, son. I'm merely throwing out a lifeline. Take it and you're saved. Don't and you drown."

Maverick grunted. *What a crock of shit.* "I see."

George drained the beer and wiped his mouth. "Give it some thought. I'll be in touch." Groaning, he pushed his rotund body off the old, wooden chair. "Thanks for dinner." The senator bustled out through the employee-only entrance.

Seething, Maverick wolfed down his burger. After guzzling the beer, he reached for his wallet, forgetting he didn't have it. Rudy hurried over and cleared the table. "Everything good?"

"Great meal, Rudy. I don't have any money—"

Rudy held up his hand. "You're an American hero. This one's on me."

"Thanks." Maverick shook Rudy's hand and strode out through the back door.

At the end of the alley, a black sedan waited at the curb. As Maverick approached, the occupant in the back seat rolled down the window.

"Get in."

5

SHOCKED

Maverick slid inside and the sedan rolled out of the alley. "How'd you know I got summoned here? Dad call you?"

"He didn't have to," Sinclair said. "I know everything that goes on in this cock-sucking town, including the crap Internado just pulled."

"I'm going to ignore his request for Watergate, the sequel. I'd rather take my chances at the hearing."

"If you don't help him, he'll rip out your jugular."

"I won't become his bitch and I'm sure as hell not going to do something illegal."

"I know that." Sinclair stiffened. "I've got dirt on him and I'm here if you need anything."

"The hearing will amount to a hand slapping."

"And if he sticks it to you?"

"Then we'll bury him under all that dirt you've dug up."

Sinclair flashed a smile. "I'll love every second of it." Pausing, he eyed Maverick. "You look like hell. Need pain meds?"

He studied his brother's face. The intensity radiating from his eyes was stronger than usual. He'd pursed his lips. Never a good sign when Sin kept things bottled up. "I got off those as soon as I could drag my sorry ass out of bed. Don't tell me *you're* taking them again."

The car stopped at a light. "Not at the moment." Sinclair stared out the window. "Sorry I missed the media frenzy at the airport."

"I didn't expect you'd be there. Don't your kind only come out after dark?"

Sinclair chuckled. "You're the glue in this family. Everyone will sleep easier now that you're back home."

"Thanks for my cell phone. How'd you get it?"

"Penelope buzzed me in. I cracked open your safe." He handed Maverick his wallet. "I threw in some cash for you."

"Thanks, brother. How are you doing?"

"The club runs itself. My firm is going through a growth spurt. Everyone who's anyone in D.C. is in crisis mode."

"What do you expect? You're The Fixer."

Sin flashed a smile. "Colton and I have been talking about a new business venture. You in?"

"Sure. Maybe. No clue. I don't even know what time zone I'm in. Check with me in a few." Maverick glanced out the window at the familiar surroundings.

"I've got something planned for you at the club later. A *real* hero's welcome. Swing by around eleven."

"When the vampires come out to play."

Sinclair waggled his thick brown brows. "These lovely women will suck a lot more than your neck."

Both men laughed as the driver pulled into the marina. Sinclair held down a button on the side panel. "Drive to the end."

"Yes, sir."

"I love you, brother," Maverick said. "Thanks for everything these past several weeks. You were really there for me."

"I'm still paying you back."

"You don't owe me anything."

"Just a better life," said Sinclair. "By the way, you'll get a lot more pussy with that wild-man look." Sinclair chuckled. "Looks good on you."

Laughing, Maverick got out. "See ya later." He shut the car door and headed toward his yacht, berthed in the last slip on the left.

He entered the ship's main cabin and bit back the raw emotion tightening his throat. There were days he doubted he'd get back. After downing four ibuprofens, he poured himself a finger of whiskey and made his way toward the ship's bow. He parked his butt on the upholstered bench and silently cursed all the evil he couldn't eradicate.

Like every rescue mission, he risked his life to save others. While he should have felt a tremendous sense of accomplishment, the emptiness in his soul wouldn't leave him.

It hovered over him like one of his prized drones. For the past twenty-one years, he couldn't shake the loss, no matter how much success he achieved or how many lives he saved.

And now, after overcoming every damn obstacle to get back home, he had to deal with a senator who decided *now* was the best time to call in a favor.

Thirty minutes later, Maverick felt little pain. He took a relaxing shower, ignoring his raging boner. Any surprise Sinclair had planned would be better than his fucking hand.

Wiping the steam from his bathroom mirror, he couldn't recall the last time he'd let his hair get this unruly. After scraping his fingers through the mangy mess, he examined his beard. Not shaving for two months had turned him into a wildebeest.

In his stateroom, he pulled on his old, reliable button down jeans, no underwear. He slid into a pressed white shirt and eyed his reflection in the mirror. As he tucked in the shirt and rolled up the sleeves, he didn't recognize himself. He peered through the facial hair and wavy, dark blond mane to the root of the problem. Pain stared back. He painted on a smile, but the anguish in his eyes didn't vanish. He'd grown used to the mental toll of each mission, but the physical agony was something he'd never encountered. Like everything else he shouldered, he would manage through this, as well.

Let's roll.

Rather than text Carly, he'd swing by her place and surprise her. When Carly's grandfather had died earlier in the year, he'd left her his Arlington home. That had caused a Stone family uproar. Despite her sister's temper tantrum and her mom's snide remarks, Carly had moved in.

His Porsche purred to life and he peeled into traffic. He couldn't wait to see her, but as he rolled onto I-395, he realized she could be on a late-night stakeout. It was after ten thirty when he pulled down her quiet residential street. *If she's asleep, I'll wake her ass up.*

Just the opposite appeared to be true. The front exterior light shone brightly and several cars lined the street in front of her house. No sooner had he knocked on the door than his heart started pumping faster. *I've missed her...a lot.*

The front door opened to a woman wearing a gold masquerade mask. "Hiya, handsome."

Temporarily baffled, he paused. "Wrong house. I'm looking for Carly St—"

"Shhh." She pressed her index finger on his lips. "Good to see you. No real names, tonight. Come on in."

What the hell?

Several masked guests mingled in the cozy living room. Definitely the right place, but since when did Carly have masked parties? She was more of a chill-with-a-six-pack kinda gal.

As the woman handed him a black, leather mask, he realized it was Carly's roommate. Rather than put up a stink, he tied the mask on. "Anything else I need to know?"

"If you like someone you see up here, you can invite them to join you in the basement. Upstairs is off limits. You'll find drinks and munchies in the kitchen. Help yourself."

Silenced by confusion, Maverick headed toward the kitchen. Normally, stacks of dirty dishes filled the sink. Tonight, however, there were two platters of fancy finger foods on the tablecloth-covered kitchen table, glasses of bubbly on a silver platter, and beer bottles plunged into a mountain of ice cubes in the sink.

Maverick confirmed he was standing in Carly's kitchen when he spied the picture of them from her second grade birthday party. He was the only boy she'd invited and the only one she'd gotten into a mud fight with. They were grinning like idiots, both missing front baby teeth and bathed in clumps of wet dirt. Decades ago, her mom had placed that photo in a magnet frame and slapped it on the refrigerator as a reminder of why Carly got grounded for a week.

After grabbing a beer, he swiped off the water, and downed half the bottle. He felt like an idiot in the mask, but once he found Carly, he'd remove it.

Over the past six weeks, the constant need to see her wouldn't go away. Sure, the phone calls had been great, but that hadn't been enough. Something had changed while he'd been gone, but he wasn't sure what it was, how to define it, or what to make of it. As soon as the plane touched down, he had to see her.

No Carly on the first floor, so he ventured into the basement. His heart kicked up speed. *She's probably playing pool or darts.*

Instead of the usual glare from the harsh overhead spotlights, floor and table lamps bathed the room in a soothing incandescent glow. A masked woman bending over the edge of the pool table wasn't playing pool. A man, also masked, stood behind her, his pants around his ankles. Her bare ass was in full view and she was getting screwed. Royally.

His brain shorted. *What the hell?*

Behind him, groaning grabbed his attention. A masked threesome was getting it on in a chair. A dude was kissing one lucky lady while a second chick was on her knees blowing him. A blonde slunk into his field of vision, snapping him out of his sex-induced trance.

"Hey, there, big boy. Wanna play?"

Maverick's straining cock twitched. Not having sex in over two months had turned him into a raging horndog, but he couldn't do it. Not here. Not now. And where in the hell was Carly?

"Thanks, darlin'. I'm here to see someone."

"No problem. Have fun." She moved on, leaving Maverick firmly rooted in place.

Maybe she's on a stakeout or working late at the office. Her roommate could have thrown this together without her knowledge.

After tossing back more brew, Maverick strolled around the corner. He spied three masked people tucked against the wall behind the sofa. The brunette—wearing a bustier that exposed her breasts, plaid panties, and thigh-high patent leather boots—was getting it on with two dudes. She stood with her back against the wall, her arms raised overhead and gripped at the wrists by one of the men who sucked her nipple, while the second guy had yanked aside those schoolgirl panties to feast on her.

She writhed and groaned, her gritty, sexy sounds sending heat rocketing through him. The man sucked her other tit while fondling the first one. Her breasts were just shy of oversized. Pliable, yet firm, with engorged pink nipples made red from being bitten and sucked. *Those tits are fucking perfect.*

She wiggled one of her hands out and pressed the second guy's face into her crotch. Another blast of energy pummeled Maverick. This chick was on fire, her raw, unfiltered moans turning him rock hard. He wanted to throw the two men off and take her with everything he had. Ravage her until they both collapsed on the carpeted floor, too boneless to move. But not too drained to do it again.

As if she could hear his filthy thoughts, she opened her eyes and locked on his. The charge jolted him to his core. With the intensity of a tigress hunting prey, she stared into his eyes.

And then, her body jerked. Her guttural groan made his balls ache, and she convulsed so hard her head rolled back and her eyes fluttered closed.

Fucking hell. It's Carly...my Carly. His tomboy, smart-ass friend of twenty-five years stood fifteen feet away getting her rocks off by two masked guys.

A kaleidoscope of emotions flooded him. A dangerous elixir of anger and envy. But those were nothing compared to the surging need to take her against that wall until they both surrendered to the mind-blowing euphoria.

Desire pounded him hard enough to steal his breath and he turned away to compose himself. The image, now tattooed on his brain, rocked him. She'd marked him for life and she hadn't even laid a hand on him.

No way in hell would he stick around to catch up. What would he say? You really know how to rock an orgasm. Wow, those are some fantastic tits you've got there. Two men because...what... one wasn't enough?

He tore off the mask, threw it on the floor, and hoofed up the stairs. Then, he powered toward the front door.

"Hey, did you find her?" asked Carly's roommate.

He set the bottle on the table. "I sure as hell did." Maverick didn't stick around long enough to hear her reply.

Oh, my God. Carly couldn't catch her breath, but her inability to suck down air wasn't from her orgasm. It was from the man who'd been the reason she'd had one.

Ashton.

Her *friend* Ashton.

THE HOTT TOUCH | 41

Even the mask, the wooly beard, and wild hair couldn't hide his identity, though she doubted he was trying.

A pang of panic clouded her thoughts. "Wow, that was intense," she said, pushing off the wall.

"Natasha, you're not leaving us, are you?" asked one of the men.

She brushed her fingers over his smooth chin. "I am. Please clean up the area. An old friend just got here."

"Yes, ma'am," said the second.

After pulling on her silk robe, she retrieved the black leather mask Ashton had dropped and hurried upstairs to catch him. The sex high had been replaced with a sinking feeling in the pit of her stomach. Had she known he was coming home ahead of schedule, she would have canceled the party or asked her roommate to host it without her.

When she'd seen him lying in the hospital bed, she'd confided the innermost secret of her heart. She loved him with her entire being. But that secret paled in comparison to this kinky one.

Ashton wasn't in the kitchen and she didn't spot him in the living room, either.

"Hey," said her roommate. "One of your friends stopped by. Did I do the wrong thing by letting him in?"

Tabitha was an acquaintance "in the scene" who needed a place to stay short-term after relocating to the area for grad school. Carly had offered her the spare bedroom.

"Of course not," Carly said, forcing a smile. It wasn't her roommate's fault. "I checked the kitchen, but he's not there. Where is he?"

"He blew out of here five minutes after he went downstairs to find you." Tabitha's eyes widened. "Oh, crap. Did he see something he wasn't supposed to?"

Carly nodded. "Something like that."

"That would explain his surprise at putting on the mask and why he looked pissed when he left. I take it he's not a player."

Oh, God. Carly's stomach roiled. "I don't know. We don't talk about sex. We're rooted in the friend zone. Have been for decades."

"Too bad. He's so handsome. Sexy, too. Maybe you should uproot him."

"Maybe I should," Carly said.

But she had no intention of doing any such thing. In fact, the only thing she wanted to do was damage control.

6

UNINHIBITED

M averick bypassed the long line of scantily-clad women and men dressed in their best duds. Everyone waited to gain access into the warehouse-looking structure located at the end of a dark street in Georgetown. He slipped a hand into his pocket while the bulky bouncer examined the ID cards of three women. Normally, Maverick would engage the women in small talk, but his mind was still reeling from what he'd seen moments earlier.

While the Uninhibited employee checked their names against his electronic list, the three women eyed Maverick.

"Hi," said one of them. "Wanna join us?" She slicked her lower lip with her tongue.

"Thank you, doll." He glanced at her chest, but only because her breasts were on full display. His raging hard-on had calmed on the way to Sinclair's kink club, but if he so much as thought of what those two men were doing to Carly, his dick would shoot straight to the moon.

The second woman tilted her head upward until her gaze locked on his face. "Ooooieee. My God, I could climb you, that's for sure."

The third woman wrapped her fingers around his biceps. "He's got enough for all three of us. Like a share toy."

He grinned. *Damn, it's good to be back.* For the first time in a long time, pain wasn't hogging the spotlight. "Ladies, where can I find you?"

"At the bar, waiting impatiently for you," said the first.

Maverick winked. "Be good until then."

Big D opened the fire door. After waves and more giggles, the women scooted inside.

"Welcome back, Maverick." The chocolate-skinned man grinned. "Great to see you. How you feelin'?"

Maverick extended his hand and the bouncer clasped it. "Good to see you, Big D. What have I missed?"

"Hey, buddy," said a guy standing in line. "The line *starts* here. You need to wait in it like the rest of us."

Big D strolled over to the man, dwarfing him in stature. "Sir, this is Mr. Sin's brother. Mr. Sinclair Develin, the *owner* of Uninhibited. I'm a pussycat when compared to him. He'll rip out your heart and *then* tell you to get the hell out of his club. Take it down a few."

The customer offered a sheepish smile. "Sorry."

Maverick tossed him a nod. "It's all good."

"Hey, listen up, everyone," Big D boomed. "This is Mr. Maverick Hott, the man who rescued all those American hostages. Let's show him some love."

The group broke into hoots and applause. Maverick grinned at the crowd. "Thanks for the warm welcome."

After opening the metal door, Big D slapped Maverick on the back. "Enjoy."

Maverick handed the bouncer a folded fifty. "Where can I find the devil himself?"

Big D laughed. "In his office. Knock first. He's rarely alone."

Maverick strode down the dimly lit hallway made darker by black walls, and entered the bar. The place was packed, so he threaded his way toward the back of the large room, past the linen-covered tables and smartly dressed wait staff.

He heaved open the door and entered a different world. One filled with kinky delights and dark fetishes. Here, BDSM wasn't just encouraged, it was nurtured, taught, and explored. While Maverick liked sex as much as the next guy, he stayed on the side of vanilla. Not because he didn't want to explore what Sinclair offered, but because he'd never found anyone who intrigued him enough to take that first step.

Plus, Maverick never had to try when it came to women. Rather than chasing after one woman in particular, the ladies flocked to him. Always had. Only thing, none of them ever stuck. Not a single one.

As he walked down the hallway, he paused in front of one of the performance rooms. *This is new.* The sign on the wall said, "The Farmer's Daughter."

Maverick stood in the back. At his height, he had no problem seeing over everyone's heads. A woman wearing a checkered dress was bent over a bale of hay while a man with overalls around his ankles took her from behind.

The couple ground and thrust, cried and groaned. Though he grew hard, he couldn't connect with them. All he could see was Carly pinned against her basement wall. The same wall he'd leaned against when they'd played pool, time and time again. Heat streaked through him. How long had she been doing this? Who, of their close-knit group of friends, knew about her secret? *And which one of them had screwed her?*

Seeing red, he strode down the hall. Rather than wait for the elevator, he yanked open the fire door. Taking the steps two at a time, he continued climbing until he reached the third floor. As he barreled toward the office marked "Private", at the hallway's end, he grabbed his burning thigh.

He needed some damn answers and he had every confidence

his brother had them. Instead of taking Big D's advice and knocking, he barged in.

Sinclair was leaning back in his executive chair, eyeing a topless woman, her hands resting on her hips. As he flicked his gaze to his brother, his eyes burned brightly. "Perfect timing."

Maverick shut the door.

"Tiffany was showing me her new breasts."

Maverick eyed her tits. "Nice."

"She's all yours," Sinclair said.

"What? Oh, yeah, is this my surprise?"

"It can be." Sinclair furrowed his brow. "What's wrong?"

"Tiffany, your breasts are lovely," Maverick said. "Can you excuse us for a minute?"

"Why don't you go play?" Sinclair suggested as she slipped into her shirt.

Tiffany caressed Maverick's crotch. "I'll take extra special care of your brother, Sin."

It would be so easy to take this woman into a private room and have some late night fun. He could screw her until the sun burst over the horizon, but he didn't want her. He wanted someone else.

After Tiffany left, Maverick eyed his brother. If anyone knew Carly's secrets, it was him. Sinclair kept everyone's secrets, including his. Why should Carly be any different?

Sinclair opened his credenza and pulled out a bottle of Macallan Scotch Whisky and two glasses. "It's great to have you back." He filled them, then handed a glass to Maverick. The two men downed their drinks.

Maverick closed his eyes as the alcohol burned a path to his stomach. He placed the empty glass on the desk. "Hit me."

Sinclair hesitated before pouring more. Maverick tossed that back, then set the glass down. "I have a question. And I expect an honest answer."

"Always. You wanna sit?" Sinclair relaxed back down into his chair.

Maverick glared down at his brother. "Did you fuck her?"

"Sure. A couple of times. She's a good time. Gives great head."

Maverick grabbed Sinclair by the lapels of his suit jacket, lifted him out of his chair, and thrust him against the back wall. "You mother fucking asshole."

"Jesus, man, what the hell? You don't have to have sex with her. She wasn't even the surprise I had planned for you. Hell, Ash, what crawled up your ass and died?"

Maverick blinked. "Who are you talking about?"

"Tiffany, the woman showing me her boob job."

Maverick shoved Sinclair against the wall, then wrapped a hand around his brother's throat. "Did you have sex with Carly?"

"*Your* Carly?"

"You have three seconds before I beat the living crap out of you."

Darkness flashed in Sinclair's eyes. "You hit me, you'll regret it, Jackoff."

That made Maverick chuckle. Before they became brothers, they were archenemies and called each other that on a regular basis. On a deep breath, he released his hold. Sinclair raked his hands through his hair, smoothed out the wrinkles on his white dress shirt, and tossed back the remains of his drink.

"We used to beat the living crap out of each other." Maverick poured more Macallan for them both before easing onto the leather sofa. "We were insane back then."

Sinclair sat in the brown leather chair. "I'm not convinced we're any *less* insane now. What the hell's going on with you?"

"Answer my question."

"I've never had sex with Carly. Nothing more than a brotherly hug. I did, however, cheat off her during the final exam senior year in U.S. Government."

Maverick laughed. "You've come a long way, bro. Did she know?"

"Of course not."

"But you know, don't you?"

"Know what?"

"About her kink?"

Sinclair arched a brow. Seconds passed before he answered. "I do."

"Why didn't you tell me?"

Sinclair crossed his legs, sipped his drink. "I wouldn't betray her or anyone else who confides in me."

"You two ever play together?"

"Never."

"Why not? She's beautiful, sexy. She likes to play on the dark side."

"She's not interested in me."

"How do you know?"

Sinclair's eyebrows flew up. "I've seen the way she looks at you."

"We're friends."

"You want to tell me what provoked you to put me in that choke hold?"

"On my way here, I stopped by to surprise her and got one hell of my own. She's having a masked sex party." Maverick shoved off the sofa, but he couldn't shake that image. "I saw her with two men."

"That's rough."

"It was the sexiest thing I've ever seen and I can't get her doing *that* out of my mind. How long has she been having these parties?"

"Ask her. She's *your* friend." Sinclair grew silent for several seconds. "Ready for your surprise? I've got a few lovely ladies lined up who are very interested in taking care of your wildest needs."

"*You* have fun with them."

"I'm not the hometown hero, you are." Rubbing his whiskered chin, Sin studied his brother. "You chase skirts like the apocalypse is around the corner. What is up with you?"

THE HOTT TOUCH | 49

"I'm too pissed off to enjoy myself." Maverick opened the door. "I'm sorry I almost beat the crap out of you."

Sinclair's lips curved. "You didn't stand a chance."

"No way you'd win."

"Fortunately, we'll never know, will we?"

"I hope not, for your sake. That's a pretty face. I'd hate to mess it up." As Maverick closed the door, Sinclair's laughter followed him into the hallway.

THE FOLLOWING MORNING, Maverick was the first to arrive at ThunderStrike's headquarters, nestled behind a chain-link fence in Anacostia. He flipped on the lights and stared at the company's motto painted on the wall behind reception.

ABOVE & BEYOND

There were days when he doubted he'd make it back to run the private security firm he founded, and manage a business he loved. Feeling a sense of pride, he strode down the hallway to his office.

He sat in his chair and powered on his computer. Despite the worn furniture and the windowless room, he felt like a king returning to his castle.

The next hour was a flurry of staff welcoming him back. At zero eight hundred, he led his regular morning staff meeting with his executive team. Gunner was more than eager to pass the torch and Maverick gladly took it. His staff went around the table, updating him on projects, missions, and new opportunities.

"One final note," Maverick said to the group sitting around the conference table. "Senator Internado advised me that I'm going to be called to testify before the Senate Select Committee about our last mission. He claims we went rogue and didn't follow orders. I'm not concerned anything will come from their investigation, so let's move forward with any government-related missions." He paused. "Any questions? Any issues I need to know about? Any problems you want to dump on me?" His focus shifted from one employee to the next.

Everyone stayed quiet.

"Last chance."

"Welcome back, boss," Penelope said.

As his top-ranking female, Penelope Stein piloted most every mission where Maverick had feet on the ground. She had a mind like a steel trap and took zero shit from anyone. Him included.

"Thanks for handling things while I was gone."

"Don't ever leave again." She shot him a cool smile. "Running this company is way more difficult than I'd anticipated. The logistics of who was in what country when drove me nuts. Plus, that brother of yours is a total nightmare. My God, Sinclair is like your evil twin, only he barely utters a word."

"Well, he must have said something because he wormed his way into my office *and* into my safe."

Rising, Penelope threw her hands up. "Unbelievable. He told me you asked for your phone and wallet." She shrugged. "Normally, I can detect a liar. He's good."

"Yeah, he's smooth. Don't sweat it. I trust him."

"I'm glad you're okay."

He tossed Penelope a nod before eyeing his crew. "Good job everyone."

"How are you feeling?" Gunner asked after the team filed out.

Discussing meant reliving, and Maverick would just as soon put the mission behind him, focus forward, and let his body heal. "How's your lung?" he asked.

"Good as new. When do you start physical therapy?"

"I quit PT when I walked out of that facility."

"Mav—"

Maverick held up his hand. "I appreciate the concern, but no lectures. I was training for an Ironman before that asswipe's bullets found my body. The sooner I can get back to that, the happier I'll be."

Gunner rose. Instead of leaving, he closed the door. Maverick resisted the urge to roll his eyes. Remaining silent, he braced for the healthcare lecture.

After dropping back into the chair, Gunner cleared his throat. "I know it's short notice, but I've got to take Friday off. Brianna and I haven't had a moment alone since I got back. We're running the kids to Pennsylvania for a weekend with the grandparents."

"Take more time if you need it."

"You've got me on the schedule for Monday's assignment. It's a local protection gig for Ella Kayson and her exec team at Qualitation. I'm still a 'go', unless you're rotating me out."

Maverick checked the schedule. "Not rotating you out. We need to get our asses into gear and back out there ASAP." Maverick rolled the chair back. "Is that it? Are we good?"

Gunner's jaw ticked. "I've got something else to tell you."

Crap, he's resigning. "Okay."

"Dom died."

Maverick's chest squeezed and he clutched the arms of the chair. Dom could only mean Dominic Delriccio, their ex-SEAL teammate. "What happened?"

"He was shot during a convenience store robbery. Wrong place, wrong time."

Pushing out of the chair, Maverick tried reeling in his sadness, but emotion made his throat constrict. "When?"

"Three weeks ago."

"Did you make it to the funeral?"

"Yeah. Brianna came with me. I didn't think I'd need her, but burying Dom was rough. Brought back memories of how close we'd all been, you know?"

Maverick swallowed down the grief. "How's his family doing?"

"Hanging in. The guys started a fund to help them out."

"I'll contribute," Maverick said.

"I'm sorry to tell you this on your first day back, but I waited long enough. You needed to know."

"Dammit, he was a good guy. This kills me."

Rising, Gunner patted him on the back. "I know it does."

After Gunner closed the door, Maverick shut his eyes, refusing to give in to the mounting sorrow. Losing anyone gutted him. Reminded him of his own loss. He slammed his fist on the table. Not even the throbbing in his hand could distract him from the sadness in his heart.

7

HUDSON'S HAPPY HOUR

A s a matter of course, Carly faced work issues head on. She didn't shy away from having the tough conversations and, most times, she welcomed problems. For Carly, a victory was a problem she'd overcome.

But as she shut down her computer to leave for her best friend's welcome home party, butterflies zoomed around her stomach at light speed. Rarely rattled, she couldn't remember the last time she'd been this nervous.

Over the past two months, Carly had missed Ashton…a lot. She'd lost her running partner and she hadn't played a competitive game of racquetball since he left. She loved playing pool with him or joining him on boat rides down the Potomac. She missed his boisterous laugh, his too-loud voice, his generosity and loyalty, and how he'd make her laugh so hard her insides hurt. She also missed staring into those bright eyes or imagining what his lips would feel like pressed against her. How intoxicating it would be to run her fingers down his rock-hard chest. Or how good he'd feel inside her.

She'd debated whether or not to bring up his surprise visit. In her typical assertive approach to life, she mulled saying, "I'm sorry you didn't stick around until after I'd finished coming." Ultimately, she ruled out that conversation-starter. She'd also eliminated, "You looked like you got quite an eyeful."

In the end, she decided that saying nothing was the smartest way to handle his pop-in. Maybe he'd forgotten.

Yeah, right.

Desiree bounded into her office. "You ready?" She narrowed her eyes. "No, you're definitely not."

"What's wrong?" Carly slung her handbag over her shoulder.

"It's Ashton's homecoming. Let's glam you up a little."

When finished, Carly's amateur makeup artist smiled. "Beautiful. He won't be able to take his eyes off you." Then, Desiree stepped back and crossed her arms. "Why don't you show some boobage, woman? If you've got 'em, flaunt 'em."

Wearing a black suit and long-sleeved white shirt, Carly had dressed to blend in. Hours earlier, she'd camped out in a five-star hotel lobby waiting for a client's spouse to arrive with his alleged mistress. Once she'd snapped photos before *and* after his tryst, she returned to work. Doing right by a client sometimes meant proving they'd been deceived by the one they loved. With each betrayal, her conviction to guard her heart magnified.

Desiree scurried out, returning with a burgundy shawl. "Why don't you undo a button or two on your shirt and take off that jacket? This pretty shawl adds some sexy-sexy."

"I didn't realize I was going for sexy-sexy." But Desiree had a point, so she shrugged out of her jacket and draped the shawl around her.

"Don't forget the button."

She hesitated, then unbuttoned. *Compared with what he saw, this is nothing.*

Desiree scrunched up her face. "This is a *party*. You still look kinda…I don't know…um…uptight."

Boy, can she read me. Carly unclipped the second button. "I think we're good. Let's go."

Time to face Ashton.

Fifteen minutes later, she parked on a side street, and she and Desiree walked toward the D.C. eatery, conveniently called "Hudson's". The restaurant was so busy, the crowd spilled onto the front patio. Clearly, everyone loved Ashton.

Not as much as I do.

"I'm helping Hudson behind the bar," Desiree said.

"Maybe I should join you," Carly said.

Desiree laughed. "That's crazy! How will you talk to Ash if you're busy pouring drinks?"

Exactly.

As soon as they squeezed inside, Desiree bolted, leaving Carly alone.

Though Ashton towered over most, she heard him before she spotted him. His booming voice thundered through the space. The familiar huskiness of his timbre paired with that contagious laugh sent tingles streaking through her. Freshly shaven, but still sporting that wild head of hair, Ashton stood in the center of a group doing what he did best.

Entertaining the masses.

Laughter reverberated from the group hovering around him. Pausing, she soaked up his beauty. She hadn't seen his dirty blond hair that long since middle school. He had the most beautiful blue-green eyes that lit up whenever he smiled. But it was that smile that melted her heart.

I've missed him so much.

Rather than approach the man of the hour, Carly headed toward the bar. She needed a moment to calm her frenzied heartbeat and shake out the pins and needles in her fingers.

Desiree had slipped behind the counter, while Carly squeezed into a tight spot at the bar. Desiree dropped two napkins on the shiny wooden counter, then set down two bottles of beer. "For you."

"Why two?" Carly asked.

"One's for Ash." Desiree beamed at someone behind her, so Carly turned.

And her heart jumped into her throat.

Ashton's massive chest blocked her view. She tipped her chin up, their eyes locked. His familiar earthy scent surrounded her and she breathed deep. He was home and inches away, drilling her with that smoldering gaze. She wanted to throw her arms around him and confirm he was standing right in front of her. But the fiery look in his eyes was anything but friendly.

He cocked an eyebrow. "Avoiding me?"

"Of course not."

The second he wrapped his arms around her, she melted into him. He tightened his grip and held her there, locked in place. The best damn spot in the entire world.

"Welcome home, Ash."

He broke the bear hug and stared into her eyes. Inches away, she tried ignoring the pull. But she couldn't. Electricity flowed between them, the charge energizing her. She'd missed him so, so much. Ticked off the days before she could see him again.

So what if he'd seen her getting off? It's not like he didn't have his own stable of women, ready to drop everything...especially their panties.

"It must be two hundred degrees in here. Let's go outside." He swiped the trickle of sweat from his temple. "You probably have a story or two you can entertain me with," he said with a wink.

There it is. He'd taken the offense and flung the first ball. She could catch or she could duck.

"What about your guests?" She handed him a beer.

"They can chill without me for ten."

She loved how he placed his hand on the small of her back as they inched their way toward the entrance. He shoved open the door to the patio. "After you."

"Hey, can I get your attention, please?" Hudson hollered over the din of the crowd.

Someone whistled.

"Hey, be quiet," shouted another guest. "Hudson wants to make a toast."

Standing behind the bar, Hudson raised his bottle of beer. "I have something to say."

Conversations continued.

Ashton stepped back into the restaurant, threw his finger and thumb into his mouth, and belted out a whistle. "Quiet!"

The room fell silent, all eyes on him. He grinned. "Much better. Hudson, you've got the floor, bro."

"Thanks. First, thank you all for coming. Ashton—*Maverick to most of you*—has always been my hero. Now, he's everyone's, but I don't mind sharing. Second, if you've got a drink in your hand, thank him, because he's footing the liquor bill." Hudson raised his bottle. "To my brother. I missed the hell out of you. We all did. How 'bout a speech?"

"Speech, speech, speech," friends chanted.

Always the showman, Ashton jumped on a chair. His boyish grin fooled everyone, except Carly. She caught the wince, the shock of pain in his eyes. Definitely physical. Maybe emotional, too. She wanted to help him, but he'd created this impenetrable wall around himself and wouldn't let anyone in. Not even her.

The room quieted. All eyes fell on him again.

He peered around. When his gaze locked with his brother's, he smiled. "Thank you for this party, Hudson." Pausing, he eyed the guests standing shoulder to shoulder. "To my family and friends who flew to Germany. I got my butt kicked…and hard, so while I don't remember seeing you, thank you for dropping everything to visit me. To my coworkers, especially Gunner and Penelope, you are never going to be allowed to run ThunderStrike again. *Ever.*" He winked.

Lighthearted laughter filled the restaurant.

"Seriously, you two saved my ass more times than I can count."

"We love you, Mav," Penelope called out and raised her wine glass.

"Thank you all for being here." He shifted his full attention to Carly, his untamed energy drilling into her. "I've missed you." She held his gaze, the air crackling with wild energy. Then, he raised his bottle. "I'm no hero. I'm just a guy doing his job. Thanks for being here to welcome me home."

After glasses were raised and drinks were downed, he stepped off the chair. As his foot hit the floor, he winced and grabbed the back of his thigh. "I need some air."

He's one Hott mess. Instead of following, Carly took the lead. She curled her fingers around his hard biceps and nudged her way through the tight crowd.

In that moment, she didn't care that he'd seen her half-naked with two men. Maybe it was time they discussed sex. Over the years, they'd talked about everything else. She wasn't ashamed, nor should she be. On occasion, she liked to get a little wild. Throw off her inhibitions and live out her fantasies. So what? It was no big deal to her. Why should it be for him?

They'd talk about it, have a few laughs, and move on. Though she remained hopeful, she wasn't convinced he'd be joshing about her two-manned orgasm anytime soon.

Once outside, the cacophony of voices faded away. The late summer breeze blew through her hair and cooled her clammy skin. She eased away from the door and spied a just-vacated table, dirty plates and glasses not yet cleared away.

"Come on."

Ashton was in turmoil, something she was familiar with. Only, years ago, the distress had been from loss, not injury. Because he viewed pain as a sign of weakness, he'd hide it. She'd helped him then. She'd do the same for him now.

She piled the dishes up and moved them out of the way. "Sit."

"What can I get you? Are you hungry?"

"Nothing, Ash." She sat. "Someone will be by."

As he eased onto the wrought iron chair, the tightness around his eyes faded.

An attractive woman waved from a nearby table. "Hey, Maverick. Welcome home."

"Thank you, darlin'."

"We should catch up sometime."

"Absolutely." He flicked his gaze back to Carly. "What's shakin'?"

"I'm relieved you're back. How's your leg holding up?"

"All good."

She wanted to hear the truth. Would it kill him to show some damn vulnerability? "What's been going on?" *Way to go, dummy.*

He chuckled, leaned back. "You tell me. You've been *much* busier than I have."

Ignoring that, she said, "You're in pain."

"So?"

"C'mon, Ashton. Talk to me."

"We talked every week. I don't have anything new to add to the conversation." He hitched a brow. "You might, though."

A server moseyed over. "Hey, guys. What can I get you?"

They ordered more beer and the waiter cleared the dirty dishes. Tapping her fingernails on the table, Carly waited. His bravado bullshit worked on everyone, but not her. He refused to make eye contact. So, she drilled into him with a piercing stare, determined to get him to open up.

Knowing him, it would be a long night.

Maverick shifted on the hard seat and fixed his gaze on the most intense hazel eyes on the planet. If Carly could ignite fire with that stare, he was confident she'd burn down the whole damn city. He knew that look. Seen it a zillion times. She was determined to get to the truth, no matter what.

That's what made her such a damn good private eye. But he didn't need her questioning the hell out of him. Asking probing questions about his health, his injuries, his next steps. He wanted to kick back in the midst of this party and chill with his friend.

Only the more he regarded her, the less the evening breeze cooled his skin. Damn, the woman had brought her A-game. From the flowing mane of blonde hair and dark eye makeup, to the swell of her breasts, he drank in her beauty.

A gust of wind blew her hair across her face. He leaned over and tucked it behind her ear. Then, he grasped her chin and gave her a gentle squeeze. "You look beautiful, Carlyle."

Calling her by her real name always elicited a smile. He loved how her eyes crinkled at the corners.

"Your homecoming deserved more than sweats." She smiled. "I'm a Desiree original."

Her sweet expression reminded him of happier times. Playing together on the jungle gym. Racing each other around the playground or down the street in their neighborhood. The mud fights and all the times his mom would invite her to stay for dinner or for family sleepovers.

Carly never liked being at home. She considered his home hers. His family was hers, too.

Tonight, however, he was grateful they weren't related because he wanted to do some dirty, filthy things with her. *Easy, brother.*

He needed to keep her in the friend zone. Wanted to ensure that they always stayed connected to each other. Losing her would kill him. But things had shifted between them. And because Maverick had one direction—*forward*—he couldn't turn back time and he couldn't erase the jarring, erotic image of her.

He wished he could exorcise it so he could focus on the woman—or women—he'd be hooking up with when the party was over. If there was anything that grounded him, it was a hard run, an adrenaline-pumping, balls-to-the-wall mission, and a good romp with an eager partner.

His gaze floated over Carly's face. She raised her eyebrows, took a swig of beer. Those full, glossy lips surrounded the rim of the bottle and a groan Maverick couldn't stop escaped his lips.

I want her. And only her.

The waiter delivered their beers, along with a giant plate of nachos smothered in ground beef and melted cheese. "My apologies, Maverick, sir. Your brother pointed out that you're in my section. I'll be right back with your plates." The server darted off.

"At least I'm not the only one having a rough night," Maverick said.

"Ash, I'm sorry you saw me last night. We need to get past it. It was no big deal."

"How was *that* no big deal?"

"It just wasn't." She shrugged, then nibbled on a tortilla chip. "I don't ask you about your sex life. Don't want to know. And I sure as hell am not going to chat about mine."

"Why not?" he boomed. Most everyone outside glanced in his direction, so he lowered his voice. "It's way more interesting than mine."

She pursed her lips. Carly speak for "conversation over".

The waiter jetted over with place settings. Maverick tossed back a mouthful of beer, then shoved a chip loaded with meat and cheese into his mouth. She said nothing while he chewed, but those piercing eyes were doing a number on him. That woman could see into his soul.

"I had no idea you were into kink," he said, breaking the silence. "It was sexy as hell. Seeing you like that turned me on *and* pissed me off." The truth spilled out without censor. Not one to hold back, he hadn't planned on putting it all out there quite so soon.

The air grew thick with tension, the need burning a trail to his hardening cock. He wanted something he shouldn't want, with someone he could never have. Because Carly was not a one-and-done kinda gal. If they crossed that line, there would be no going back. But the biggest reason was Maverick's refusal to give his heart away.

His broken heart had finally mended, but it wasn't whole and never would be. He would stick with what he knew and what he did best. Casual screwing with women who couldn't snare his love.

Only one woman held his heart and she was six feet under.

"Why are you angry?" She folded her hands in her lap. "You have sex and I've never said a word about it."

Rather than answer her question, he tossed back more booze. It was one thing to assume her intimacy with faceless men, but a completely different thing to witness it. Truth was, he needed to be that man.

"I want things to go back to the way they were," Carly continued. "I've missed you, Ash. I miss you more now and you're sitting right in front of me."

Acid churned in his stomach. He didn't want to hurt her. "I'm sorry. You're right. I saw you getting off with two men. So what, right?"

Reaching across the table, she squeezed his hand. "Exactly."

Her soft touch sent streams of energy surging through him. His phone rang. Close friend and SEAL teammate, Enrique Rijado. Had Enrique driven up from Virginia Beach?

"Hey, bro!" He glanced around. "Are you here?"

"Maverick, it's Julia, Enrique's sister." Her somber tone snagged his attention. "Can you talk?"

Enrique Rijado had enlisted in the Navy, earning a coveted spot as a SEAL. Maverick had been fresh out of OCS and the junior of two officers leading an eight-man squad. He and Enrique had hit it off right away. Stayed tight while they served.

Three years ago, Maverick left the Navy. Enrique retired last year after twenty years of service. Regardless of where they were,

THE HOTT TOUCH | 63

the men remained close. Enrique and his wife, Elena, had asked Maverick to be Godfather to their second child.

Maverick's guts twisted. "What's going on, Julia?"

"Enrique's gone."

The muscles running along his shoulders turned to lead. "What do you mean, *gone?*"

"He died." Her voice trembled. "I'm sorry I didn't call sooner. He left us Monday. Elena was so grief stricken, she had to be hospitalized. We're in shock."

Maverick struggled to comprehend what she was saying. "Was he in a car accident? Was he sick?"

"He took his own life." Her voice broke and she choked back a sob.

Maverick's heart jolted to a stop and he shoved out of his seat. "*What?*"

"Elena found him."

"Oh, God. I'm so sorry."

"They did an autopsy. Now we're awaiting the drug test results. It's so upsetting. Enrique didn't do drugs."

"I know he didn't." Maverick forced down the billowing emotion. Had to get a grip. "Can I do anything? Help with arrangements? I can't believe this."

"Somehow, we got it all done. The funeral is Saturday. I'm sorry for the short notice. It's just that everything has been so crazy. I hope you can make it."

"I'll be there."

"Elena wanted me to ask if you'd be a pallbearer."

His heart broke. "I'd be honored."

"She and the kids are staying with me in Virginia Beach. She hasn't been able to go home. We're receiving visitors at my home tomorrow night. I'll text you my address."

"Thank you."

"Enrique talked about you all the time."

"Yeah, we're close. I'm sorry, we *were* close." He cleared his throat. "Do you have Gunner—Marshall Young—on your list?"

"Um…yes, I do."

"He's with me. I can let him know, if you'd like."

"Thank you. See you tomorrow."

Maverick hung up and a mountain of grief barreled toward him. *Enrique killed himself?* He texted Gunner. "Come outside NOW."

When he shifted his attention to Carly, she stood and hugged him. He wanted to crumple in her arms. Instead, he gritted his teeth, refusing to let grief overtake him.

"I'm so sorry," she whispered.

Gunner bolted over to the table. "What's wrong?"

"I should get out—" Carly blurted.

"Don't leave," Maverick said.

"You're making me nervous," Gunner said.

"Enrique's dead."

Gunner stared in disbelief. Then, he gripped the back of the wrought iron chair. "Jesus, no. Was he in a car accident?"

"Suicide."

"*What?* Where did this come from? I just saw him at Dom's funeral."

"I don't know." Struggling to process the news, Maverick threw an arm around his ex-SEAL teammate.

Gunner bowed his head. "I wish he'd said something to me."

Maverick felt sick to his stomach. "Funeral is Saturday. Visitation is at his sister's tomorrow night in Virginia Beach."

A tear streaked down Gunner's cheek. "He never let on. Never said a word that he was going through anything. We could have helped him."

Maverick's throat tightened. Several seconds passed while he waged war against himself. He would not allow grief to win. Not here in the middle of his party.

When he'd gotten control of himself, he cleared his throat.

Only then did he realize Carly had been stroking his back. While her gentle touch soothed him, it didn't change a damn thing. His friend was dead.

Gunner wiped his wet cheeks. "Man, this is devastating."

"Yeah," Maverick replied. "Seems surreal."

"I can't make the funeral," Gunner said. "We'll be in Pennsylvania."

"Don't sweat it."

"I've gotta get out of here," Gunner said. "Good luck at the hearing tomorrow. A slap on the wrist and we'll be back to full-throttle."

Maverick pulled Gunner in for a hug. "Thanks for coming tonight. Go home and be with your family."

Gunner's gaze met Carly's. "He needs you, Carly." After patting Maverick on the back, he left.

For the first time in his life, Maverick envied what Gunner had. A wife who adored him and three young children who couldn't get enough of their daddy. Feeling raw and vulnerable, Maverick no longer wanted to party. He needed to be alone with the tsunami of sorrow barreling toward him.

8

BENEATH THE STARS

Carly's concern was warranted. Ashton didn't process death in a healthy manner. He absorbed it. Obsessed over it. Somehow felt responsible for it. Even believed he could have prevented it.

Enrique's suicide could send him spiraling down a dark hole. Years ago, she'd seen how losing his mom had wrecked him. And while she did everything possible to help him, he was like a tornado hurtling across an open prairie. Back then, women weren't his crutch. Explosive violence was. Until he met his match in Sinclair. Two wild rams who would have battled to their bloody deaths if his dad hadn't intervened.

Rather than question him or express her concern, she waited. He'd been thinking. Overthinking, more like it. He'd been staring at her, but he wasn't actually seeing her.

"I've gotta go," he said.

"Let's tell Hudson you're heading out."

"Right." She felt his sadness and her heart broke for his loss.

They entered the bar and a swarm of people surrounded him. In a flash, he turned the switch. Maverick the showman joked and grinned. He waved people over and included them in the conversation. He bear-hugged the guys and kissed the gals on their cheeks. He let everyone know how much he appreciated them. He was a pro at shining the spotlight on others. Asking questions meant he didn't focus on himself. Though genuine, she'd seen his performance hundreds of times. His humility was one of her favorite qualities. He had a lot he could brag about, but he chose to remain silent.

"Can I steal you for a minute?" asked a woman Carly didn't recognize.

"Darlin', I'd love to, but I've gotta fly."

Then, he turned his full attention on Carly. The intensity in his stare had her biting back a moan. That man had a way of stripping her bare and exposing her soul without uttering a single word. When he placed his hand on the small of her back, an undeniable connection passed between them.

"After you," he said.

They inched their way through the busy eatery. Everyone wanted their moment with the hometown hero. Though he denied no one, he kept Carly in his sights and took every opportunity to place his hand on her back and usher her forward.

Twenty-five minutes later, they arrived at their destination. The bar. Hudson mixed drinks and chatted up the partygoers. Ashton gestured to a spot between two guests, so she squeezed in. And then, he joined her.

In that tight little space.

Being wedged against him in a public place triggered her fetish. She envisioned them making small talk while she dropped her hand beneath the bar and caressed him. On occasion, her fantasies included public places, and Ashton had a starring role in fulfilling her wildest ones.

Her breath hitched while her thoughts wandered to what could happen if she kissed him. Really kissed him. *How would his tongue feel in my mouth?*

"Hey, Babe."

How would his hands feel caressing my skin?

"Carly."

Would we slink away and...

"Carlyle."

She flicked her gaze toward him, her cheeks warm with desire.

"Whoa, mama, where'd you go?"

She couldn't stop the sly smile. "I'm right here."

"Could've fooled me. The stool beside you is open if you want to sit."

Of course, she didn't. She liked being smooshed against his strong, hard body. A man slid onto the seat and congratulated Ashton, leaving Carly pressed against his granite chest.

Hudson bounded over. "Hey, guys! Is this a party or is *this* a party?"

Ashton chuffed out a laugh before clasping his brother's outstretched hand. "This was the best. You knocked it out of the park, boss."

"Wait? You're leaving?"

"I'm getting grilled by the senate tomorrow morning. Can't be late for my own execution."

"Nah, you'll be okay." Hudson's eyes darted to Carly. "He will be, won't he?"

"Totally fine," Carly assured him. Though, in truth, she had no idea.

Desiree bounded over. "I wish it was this packed every night. Your friends are great tippers, Ash." Her gaze darted from one to the other. "What's wrong?"

He painted on a smile. "All good."

"Are you two taking off?"

"I've got an early meeting, so I'm headed home," Maverick replied.

"Are you working 'til closing?" Carly asked Desiree.

"Uh-huh."

"Come in late tomorrow," Carly replied. "I'll handle the office by myself in the morning."

Desiree grinned. "You're the best."

"Do you have a ride home?" Carly asked her.

"I'll drop her off," Hudson replied.

"I'm gonna bolt." Ash's voice boomed over the noisy crowd. "I love you guys." When he stepped away from the bar, Carly's heart dipped. Then, he turned and extended his hand. "I'll walk you to your car."

When she slipped her hand in his, her heart skipped a beat. She'd held his hand before. In elementary school, when they were field trip buddies. During his mom's funeral, he clutched her hand for support. Was he in need of her support again? She would give it willingly.

This time, they managed to break out of there in fifteen minutes. Once outside, he heaved in a deep breath. "Where are you parked?"

"Couple of blocks away."

"I'll walk you to your car."

"You don't—"

"Right, like I'm going to let you walk alone."

"I'm this way." They headed north on 16th Street, hand in hand.

"I'm going to target practice this weekend," she said. "Maybe you'll join me." Licensed for concealed carry, Carly had only used her weapon a handful of times in her career, but she found time for target practice every week, regardless of her schedule.

"I will if I'm around." His phone buzzed and he read the incoming text. Instead of replying, he shoved his phone back into his pocket.

Assuming it was someone interested in a booty call, her chest tightened. *Maybe that's the distraction he needs. No...I'm what he needs.*

She fished out her keys. "Get in. I'll drive you to your car."

"I'm fine."

"Please. I'll worry."

He laughed. "What? You think someone's going to jump me?"

"I'm concerned if someone did, you'd kill *them*."

"I've got this. No worries."

Bullshit.

"Gimme a hug goodbye." Before she could respond, he hauled her close and held her tightly.

He always smelled so good…and so familiar. When she patted his back and broke away, she glimpsed the sadness he was working so hard to conceal.

"Welcome home, Ash."

His eyes darkened as he peered into hers. "Be good, Carly girl." He headed back down the street, favoring his right side. She wished she could take away his anguish, but she knew the deaths of his friends hurt more than his injuries.

As soon as he rounded the corner, she slipped into her car. Knowing him, he'd go home and obsess over his friend's death, convinced he could have prevented it. Or, maybe, phone someone for a late-night hookup. She doubted he'd bring a woman back to his boat, so, as she pulled onto the deserted street, she formulated a plan.

After stopping for a six-pack, she headed toward the live-aboard marina in southwest D.C. If he wasn't home, she'd leave the beer. No harm, no foul.

Always on the go, Ashton had sold his condo and purchased a fifty-foot Azimut yacht after leaving the Navy. He felt as comfortable on or in the water as he did on land. The vessel slept eight comfortably and was equipped with a state of the art navigation system and top-of-the-line everything else.

She pulled into the marina. To her surprise, his car was in his assigned spot, so she parked beside him and walked down the pier toward the darkened yacht, her stilettos tapping on the wooden slats.

He's here, but he might not be alone. Her chest squeezed.

Until yesterday, Carly and Ashton didn't do pop-ins. But being that he'd broken protocol, she'd reciprocate. She spotted him alone on the ship's bow. A solitary man bathed in the soft glow of the moon. She hated that he was hurting. But more than that, she hated that he bore his heartache alone.

She slipped off her heels and stepped onboard. The closer she got, the faster her heart pounded in her chest. When he hurt, so did she.

A friendship stands strong in the best of times, but a true test is how that relationship weathers the worst of times. Theirs had survived both.

"Hey."

He turned. "Hey."

"You didn't finish your beer, so I brought you a few more."

"Couldn't stay away, could you?" His playfulness was an attempt to deflect.

"I'm not staying. I'm leaving this for you."

"Sit your ass down. You didn't drive over here to deliver a six-pack."

She shrugged. "Busted."

His tight smile eased some of the tension running down her back. She sat beside him, pulled out a bottle, and handed it to him.

He unscrewed the cap, took a swig, and offered it to her. "I'll share."

"Generous to a fault," she said, and tossed back a sip.

They drank in silence, their attention fixed on the moonlit water while the rhythmic lapping of waves against the hull attempted to soothe their tormented souls. But the gentle rocking had a different effect on Carly. Her thoughts drifted to how he'd feel on top of her, their bodies undulating in time with the rolling water.

Once, she'd felt her body on his. The memory still stirred her, all these years later. During their middle school years, the snow gods had dumped two feet on the D.C. region. Sledding down the hill together, they toppled over at the bottom. They were covered in snow and laughing hysterically, until they realized she had landed on top of him. Raging teenage hormones kicked in and she kissed him. Maverick needed little prodding. He kissed her back with tongue.

"Will you be my girlfriend?"

Though she wanted to be, she liked the way things were, especially since her home life was in constant turmoil. Ashton's mom and dad made her feel welcome and included her a lot of the time. If they broke up, she wouldn't just lose her boyfriend, she'd lose her best friend *and* his family.

"I'll think about it." She snagged one more kiss from the cutest, boldest, and loudest boy she'd ever known.

A week later, before she'd given him her answer, tragedy struck the Hott family and Ashton's mother was dead. He sunk into the depths of depression and Carly maintained her role as best friend. Even though he tried to push her away, she refused to abandon him. He'd been there for her plenty of times, so she stood by him through that horrific ordeal.

And she would stand by him now, too.

Maverick wasn't balls deep in some chick because the only woman he wanted sat inches away from him. He gazed in her direction. Her beauty had become so familiar he took it for granted. Long, mussed hair, those hypnotic bedroom eyes, and deliciously sexy lips. She had a rockin' hot body he tried not to check out. But sometimes he couldn't help himself. The other night, he'd seen the full monty. Spectacle aside, she was packing the goods in all the right places. And her unexpected wild side was crazy hot.

Tonight, she tried hiding her concern, but she was terrible at it. Always had been. But he loved that she cared about him.

He was struggling to process the deaths of his friends. He needed to talk with someone who knew him well and would listen without trying to make everything okay. Carly was one of a handful of people who met those requirements.

"Thanks for sticking around," Maverick said, breaking the long silence.

"You want to talk about it?"

"Let's go inside." He pushed off the porcelain surface and extended his hand.

When she grasped it, energy surged up his arm. He pulled her to her feet with more force than he'd intended and she crashed against him. Her moan ripped through him. He strapped his arm around her and kissed her. Like fireworks on the Fourth of July, desire exploded through him. She dragged her fingers through his hair and plunged her tongue into his welcoming mouth. Their clash of teeth and lips added to the mounting frenzy. When he tugged her closer still, she ground against him. His desire to sink inside her sent lust surging through him.

She broke away, gasping for breath. Even the darkness couldn't hide the arousal in her eyes. That kiss had awakened him from the dead. But he needed more—a hell of a lot more—to bring him back to life.

"Oh, no," she whispered. "That was…" Never at a loss for words, she couldn't finish her sentence.

"Good? Bad? On a scale of one to ten?"

She shuddered in a shaky breath. "Intense."

He smiled. Not because he was happy, but because she liked it. Probably not as much as he did, but *this* wasn't a competition. This time, they were both on the same side. But tonight wasn't going to be *the night*. If he had sex with her, it could mean the end of their friendship. The death of his friends was difficult enough. Losing her would kill him.

She combed shaky fingers through her hair. He wanted her hands on him, raking her fingernails down his chest.

"Okay, so let's get ourselves back on track," she said. "I know you're hurting."

"My balls are killing me."

Her lips curved. "C'mon, Ash. I'm serious."

"So am I, babe." He winked. "Let's talk. Because God knows, I could use more of *that*."

They entered the ship's cabin. He flicked on the recessed lights, then dimmed them. Sleek lines and cool colors, the large room was filled with two sofas and a coffee table, a state-of-the-art galley for cooking, and the captain's bridge. The lower level housed three staterooms. The upper level offered a flybridge where he could captain his vessel outside.

"You want something to drink? If you're hungry, I can order a pizza."

Carly eased onto the light gray sofa while Maverick kicked off his boots so his bare feet could breathe.

"Ashton, talk to me."

He sat beside her. *Go on. Get it out.* "You saw me in the hospital, so you know I got banged up pretty good. I've never had my ass kicked like that before."

"I know."

"I'm not a hundred percent, but I'll get there." He rubbed the underside of his thigh.

"Let me massage your leg."

"No."

"Lay down."

"Carly."

"Do *not* argue with me."

"My God, woman, you like to boss me around." He lay face down on the couch and she moved beside him.

"Where does it hurt?"

"Hamstring is messed up. I've got a knot by my ass that won't stop aching."

"Do I need to stay clear of any scars?"

"No, those healed."

"Can you take off your pants?"

"*What?*"

"It would be easier if I could massage your leg without the clothing."

"Don't tempt fate, babe. Jeans stay on."

She shook her head. "We had an accidental kiss. Relax, would ya?"

That was no accident. He'd feel much better after having that ever-loving orgasm. And he'd relish in the pleasure of taking care of her needs.

Because I'd do it a hell of a lot better than those two cads.

Now that he'd gotten a taste, he was hungry for a bite. A big bite.

Determination shone from her eyes. She wouldn't leave until she'd massaged his damn leg. He had every confidence she'd stick with his leg and not stroke what he really needed.

"Rub away." He rested his head on his folded arms. She ran her hands up and down the back of his thigh before homing in on his knotted muscles.

"Is this the spot?" she asked.

"One of many. Feels great."

As she worked his taut muscles, he heated from her rhythmic caresses. Losing himself in her would be the perfect escape. He'd carry her into his stateroom and peel off her clothing. He'd dote on every inch of her heavenly body until the ecstasy had her screaming his name. Then, he'd slide inside and forget about the shit storms that had wreaked havoc with his life over the past several weeks.

As much as he needed the release, he wanted to pleasure *her.* Watch her unravel around him. Discover all the things about her that he'd only imagined. Marry fantasy with reality.

"Gunner mentioned Enrique's death was the second," she said. "Who else passed away?"

He winced while she worked on the cramped knot. "I think you met—whoa, that hurts—Dominic Delriccio. One of my SEAL buddies."

"I met him a few years ago. Doesn't he live in New Jersey?"

"He did. He was killed a few weeks ago in a convenience store robbery."

She stopped rubbing. "I'm sorry. And now Enrique, too?"

He rolled over and propped up on his elbows. "If he'd told me he was suffering, I could have helped him." Maverick shook his head. "I fucking hate death."

"I know you do."

They grew silent while Carly continued rubbing his thigh. While the massage helped, her stimulating touch distracted him. He started to harden and flipped back onto his stomach.

"When this three-ring circus of a hearing ends tomorrow, I'm heading to Virginia Beach. Pay my respects. Maybe someone can help me understand what went wrong."

"I'll go with you."

"I've got this."

"No, you don't. You *just* said you feel responsible. How could you have prevented it if you didn't even know the circumstances?"

The deaths of his friends had ripped open a wound that had never fully healed. Grief and loss had crippled his family when his mom had been killed. His dad had lost his way and Maverick had stepped up for his younger siblings, but he, too, was spiraling into the depths of depression. Carly had been his rock. Though he'd tried pushing her away, her unwavering friendship had been his one saving grace.

The atmosphere grew thick with unresolved tension. He wanted to pull her onto him, envelop her in his arms, and forget. But he wasn't going to drag her into his mental drama. Better to go it alone this time.

Craning his neck, his eyes met hers. "Carly, thanks for the beer and the massage."

Rather than take the hint and head out, she massaged harder, though, this time she shot him the death stare. He'd seen that look dozens of times. She was like an angry dog, tied up in the sweltering heat without a bowl of water in sight. You get too close, that damn mutt will rip your leg off.

"I've got a late morning appointment," she said. "Text me when the hearing ends. I'm going with you." She gave him an affectionate squeeze. "I'll be your buddy. Remember what Mr. Nesbaum used to say before our field trips?"

Maverick cracked a smile. Nesbaum was their second grade teacher. "Stay alert and hold your buddy's hand." He recited it like it was yesterday.

She smiled at the memory. Every damn chance they got, they'd been each other's buddies. And she'd never once pulled away when he'd taken her hand. Because Mr. Nesbaum said that buddies *must* hold each other's hands. So they did.

Maverick didn't have the energy to argue. In truth, he wanted her by his side. This time, he needed her, though there was no way in hell he'd admit that.

She patted his leg and stood. "I'll send you my bill."

He pushed off the sofa. Though his leg still burned, her massage had helped. Her loving touch always worked. "Thanks for taking such good care of me."

He wanted to kiss her again. Softly, this time. Feel her lips pressing against his. Welcome her tongue into his mouth and carry her to his bed. He never brought women here. This was his private sanctuary. But he wanted to lay her down and smother her with kisses before covering her body with his. Lose himself in her while their eroticism washed away his pain and loneliness. Even if just for a little while.

Then, cradle her in his arms all night long.

They exited the cabin and walked onto the stern. A soft breeze blew past him and he inhaled the crisp night air. *She's right. I can't do this alone.* "I'll grab us a couple of hotel rooms." *Though, one would work better.*

She slipped into her stilettos. He walked her to her car and she pulled him close for a hug. "Thanks for not arguing with me."

He tightened his hold, closed his eyes, and savored her. She always smelled like summer peaches. He loved peaches. "Thanks for coming over."

"Good luck at the hearing," she said. "But you and I don't believe in luck, do we?"

"No," he replied. "No, we don't."

9

THE HEARING

Wearing a dark pinstripe suit, a crisp white dress shirt, and red power tie, Maverick was ushered into the packed hearing room in the Dirksen Senate Office Building across from the U.S. Capitol. His eight o'clock time slot had been pushed back to half past noon, which meant, he had an additional four hours to stew over this dog and pony show. *What a time suck.*

As he took his seat at the rectangular table facing the tiered rows of committee seats, cameras clicked like machine guns. While labeled a hearing, this had all the markings of a trial with the accused presumed guilty.

He'd been advised to lawyer up, but Maverick didn't want someone speaking for him. He refused to be silenced because he'd done nothing wrong. He'd accepted a job the military couldn't. He'd placed his team in mortal danger. His second-in-command had taken a bullet and he'd almost gotten killed.

Even with all that mayhem, ThunderStrike had gotten the job done. All twelve American hostages had been rescued. The terrorists didn't bully the United States into submission and they didn't get the millions they'd demanded, either.

An intern hurried over and poured Maverick a glass of water

before adjusting the mic. "You're live now." The reverb made several in the crowd wince. The young man slid the stand away. "Sorry. Is there anything I can get you?"

Maverick shot the kid a tempered smile. He'd save his winning grin for *after* the hearing. "I'm good."

The senators filed in and seated themselves.

George Internado sat in the center, his pudgy face swollen, his tired eyes glazed over. While the senator had been affable over the past year, he wore no smile today.

Internado struck his gavel. "I call this hearing to order. This Senate Select Committee has been formed to investigate a recent mission undertaken by ThunderStrike, a high-security firm that provides surveillance, protection and rescues, here in the United States and overseas, for both the U.S. government and private corporations. The mission in question, code named 'The Twelve', occurred in defiance of government direction and possibly violated international laws."

As if to punctuate what he'd just said, he paused to sip water from his glass. "Good afternoon, Mr. Hott. We appreciate your speaking with us."

"Good day, Senators."

Internado referred to his notes. "Mr. Hott, you're the CEO of ThunderStrike."

That isn't even a damn question. "Affirmative."

"And you personally led the mission known as 'The Twelve'."

"I did."

"Isn't it true that you executed this mission contrary to direction given by your government contacts?"

"The mission to which you're referring is top-secret. I'm not at liberty to discuss details."

The senator held up what looked like a two hundred-page bound document. "According to this subcommittee report, you were advised to abort the mission because it was believed the terrorists holding the American hostages had learned the date and time of your strike. Instead of standing down, you went rogue, risking the mission and the lives of everyone affiliated with it, including the hostages."

"I was confident we could complete the assignment successfully."

"But it wasn't a complete success, was it? There were serious casualties."

"The twelve American hostages are now home. No one on my team died. So, in my eyes, the mission *was* a success, Senator."

"But you didn't follow explicit orders, now, did you?"

"My goal was to bring our fellow Americans home and ensure the safety of my team."

Internado gestured to the committee. "Perhaps my colleagues have questions of their own."

Other senators began hurling questions at him, many worded to prejudice the public's opinion of him and ThunderStrike. He answered those he could, refused to comment on anything he couldn't. Round and round they went. No resolution. Just talking heads. It seemed like a witch hunt, but he refused to get burned at the stake.

Over the course of the afternoon, he removed his jacket, rolled up his sleeves. He kept his voice low and steady, but he wanted to jump to his feet and scream. When the team's competency was questioned, he couldn't hold back.

"Senators, I am an ex-SEAL who proudly served my country for eight years. After my honorable discharge, I formed ThunderStrike to do the work the military could not. The armed forces are not in the business of rescuing American hostages. My highly skilled team and I risk our lives to protect those in need and bring them home. Many of these hostages are tortured, raped, mutilated. In the particular case for which I've been called to testify, the families of the twelve American hostages hired us. We ran surveillance, studied maps, memorized routes, and ran drills at ThunderStrike's Eastern

Shore location. All while flying well beneath the enemy's radar. And—"

"Mr. Hott," interrupted one of the senators. "What's your point?"

"My point?" Maverick grunted his frustration. "We run *towards* danger and are willing to die to save others. We steadfastly believe in the American constitution. We love our country and its citizens. This mission was a private matter that doesn't involve the United States government. By your own admission, the American government does *not* get involved in hostage rescues of private citizens. Simply put: ThunderStrike does."

"Even if it means violating international laws," Internado quipped like a parrot repeating himself. Then, he looked at the senators to his left and his right, each giving him a nod. "Mr. Hott, it is the committee's decision to suspend award of any new government contracts to ThunderStrike pending the outcome of this investigation. We'll reconvene one week from today with our findings. Thank you for your time. Meeting adjourned." Internado rapped his gavel.

Maverick's blood boiled. As he pushed out of the chair, he forced down the anger and flipped on the charm. Out he went to face the media.

After surveying the reporters, he said, "Good afternoon. ThunderStrike will continue to fight the good fight on behalf of Americans everywhere. Our commitment to defend and protect remains steadfast. While the committee debates next steps, our teams will continue to stay active both here and abroad."

"How can you do that, Maverick, if ThunderStrike's government missions get stripped away from you?" asked a reporter.

"That won't happen. In the meantime, we have plenty of private-sector assignments in play to keep us busy."

But Maverick *was* worried. In this town, bad press traveled fast. He might be grinning like a happy fool, but he was wise enough to know that some of his key clients would disassociate themselves from his company. If the committee found them in violation of *anything,* that could signal the end of ThunderStrike.

As he strutted down the hallway, he clenched his hands into fists. The press surrounded him like a caged bird, shouting questions and snapping pictures.

Feeling suffocated, he loosened his tie, unfastened his top button. Week in and week out he put in sixty to seventy hours. He didn't save lives for the glory or the ego stroking. He did it because he could change the outcome for innocent people who didn't deserve to die like his mother had. He did it because it was his calling. He'd been put on this earth to make a positive difference in the lives of others.

Saving lives pushed him out of bed after four hours of sleep. It forced him to train harder, hone his skills, and risk it all to reunite a mother with her child or a spouse with his mate. He wanted to help families because he couldn't heal his own.

He slipped on his shades and shoved open the exit door. The bright sunlight made him squint, even behind the dark lenses.

He texted Carly. "On my way."

Dots appeared as he walked down the sidewalk toward his car. "How'd it go?"

"Be there in ten."

Stone-faced, Maverick drove away. After turning the corner, he muttered, "Mother fucking assholes." He parked in a garage near Carly's office and walked into the row house building with "Stone Investigations" over the doorway.

"How'd the hearing go?" Desiree asked.

"Slap on the wrist." Maverick raked his fingers down his unshaven cheeks. "They'll find we did nothing wrong and this fiasco will soon be forgotten."

"I hope so. Sinclair says Internado can be a piranha."

"Nothing we can't manage." He eyed Carly's office. "Where's the boss lady?"

"She figured you'd be hungry, so she ran next door to grab something for the road."

He grinned, his first *genuine* smile of the day. His stomach had been in knots all afternoon, but knowing food was on the horizon rekindled his appetite.

The office phone rang.

"Stone Investigations." While she listened, Desiree shook her head. "I'm sorry to hear that, Mr. Pluckett. I'll let Ms. Stone know. Thanks for calling."

Desiree hung up. "Damn, we needed that."

Maverick peered at his sister, who'd gotten busy nibbling her fingernail. "What was that all about?"

"Carly had this great opportunity. Check that. The opportunity wasn't great, but it was steady work. Things have slowed way down." Rising, she leaned forward. "I think I'm going to have to resign."

"Why?"

"She used to have meatier cases, but lately she's been snapping pics of cheating spouses. But, hey, it's something, right? That guy who just called works for a major hotel chain and needs someone to run hundreds of background checks on a regular basis. The work is routine, but we needed that gig."

"What's she doing to bring in new clients?"

"Money's tight, so she hasn't advertised in a while. A lot of the clients she had from her grandpa died, retired, or moved away."

"What can I do to help?"

"Don't say anything," she said twirling a chunk of hair. "I shouldn't have told you."

"I have a top-secret clearance, honey. I won't breathe a word."

She grinned. "Best brother ever."

"You say that to all three of us."

"But I only mean it when I say it to you."

He chuffed out a laugh as she giggled. The door opened and Carly breezed in with a tray of drinks and a large bag. She'd clipped her hair up, soft wisps framing her face. Her navy dress and heels were sophisticated and conservative, yet the knit hugged her curves like a glove. *Damn, she looks hot.*

She slid her gaze from one to the other. "I'm happy to see you two laughing."

"Desiree claims I'm her favorite brother. Do I look that gullible?" Maverick took the tray of drinks and set it on the reception counter. "Thanks for buying all of this." He pulled out a twenty.

"Put your money away." She set the bag on the counter. "Desiree, I got you an iced tea."

"Thanks." Desiree stabbed a straw through the lid. After inhaling half the liquid, she sucked down a breath. "Whew, I was crazy thirsty. Craig Pluckett called. He's going with someone else."

Carly's shoulders slumped. "Damn." Then, her gaze darted to Maverick and she pinned on a smile. "Ready to roll? I checked traffic. There are a couple of accidents on I-95. Give me a second to shut down, then we'll head out." She sashayed into her office, the knit dress clinging to her swaying ass.

Clear out the dirty thoughts and get your shit together. We're going to a funeral, for God's sake.

When she returned, he said, "Let's keep an eye out for anyone trailing us."

Her brows furrowed. "Why?"

"The press followed me to my car."

"Are they *that* desperate for a story?" Her smarmy smile made him chuckle.

"Internado suspended the award of any new government contracts pending the outcome of their witch hunt."

"Ouch."

"Thanks for the compassion."

She shot him a little smile and the gnawing frustration in his gut settled down. He loved that she never pitied him.

"ThunderStrike is going to be fine," she said. "You did nothing wrong."

"Those are the facts, but I'm dealing with Internado and he writes his own set of rules."

"Do you think the media is going to follow us so they can get an exclusive on the *real* Ashton Hott? The one who turns into a hangry savage when he doesn't eat massive amounts of food every few hours? Or maybe the grumpy one when he doesn't get enough sleep."

"Boy, does she know you," Desiree said.

"I'm messing with you," Carly said.

"Like only you can," he replied. "Let's roll."

"I'll close up," Desiree said.

"Come on," Carly said. "It's Friday at four thirty."

Desiree rose, then plopped back down. "So, what do I do with this upgraded surveillance system again? Do I activate it?"

"It's activated by voice and movement, so we do nothing." As they walked to the parking garage, she asked Desiree if she was working at Hudson's over the weekend.

"Yup," Desiree replied. "Hudson needs my help. He's got employees who show up late for their shifts or they don't provide the level of customer service I think his clientele should receive."

Carly stopped at her vehicle. "I'm sure you're great at it."

"Thanks," Desiree said. "I'm sorry about the hearing, Ash." She pecked his cheek, then turned back to Carly. "Thanks for being with him this weekend." With a wave of her hand, she took off toward her car.

"Do you want me to drive?" Maverick set his bags in her car.

"No, you might need to duck and hide from all the press." She slid behind the wheel. "I'll drive the getaway car." With a boisterous chuckle, he got in beside her.

As she wove her way out of the city, Maverick chowed down.

"What happened today?" she asked.

"Let me get Gunner on the phone, so I can tell you both." He dialed, Gunner answered. "You're on speaker. I've got Carly with me."

"Hey, Carly," Gunner said. "Glad you're going to the funeral with Mav. Hold a sec. We just got to my in-laws. I've gotta put the dog out back."

Carly took the entrance ramp to I-95 south. The sounds of Gunner ushering three excited children and a maniacal-sounding dog out of the van made her smile.

"What?" Maverick asked her.

"That mayhem reminds me of your family when we were kids."

"Do you remember when my folks took us to Hershey Park?" he asked.

They shared glances and a smile.

"We had a blast," she replied. "We rode those baby rides with Hudson a dozen times."

Bittersweet memories had Maverick swallowing down the lump in his throat.

"Hey," Gunner said. "How'd it go today?"

Maverick relayed the news.

"Do you think they'll find us guilty?" Gunner asked.

"I hadn't been back in the States an hour and Internado asked me for a favor," Maverick explained. "It stunk like rotting fish, so I stayed clear. This could be his way of telling me he didn't appreciate my lack of allegiance. He did grease the skids for several of those government jobs he just suspended."

"Sounds like a power play to me," Gunner said. "Regardless of the outcome, we did the right thing. You did good today, but I know you're pissed. What's next?"

"Follow-up hearing. One week. 'Til then, it's biz as usual." Maverick wrapped up the call and hung up.

"What did the senator ask you to do?" Carly asked.

"Spy on his opponent." Just thinking about that conversation made his blood pressure skyrocket. "He's running for governor and has no intention of losing."

A growl shot out of her, the sultry sound landing between his legs. "What is wrong with that man?"

"That's what happens when people go unchecked. He thinks he's above the law."

Shifting his attention to her, he drank in her beauty. With her hair up, he had a clear view of her profile. Big, expressive eyes, an adorable button nose, and heart-shaped lips he'd finally kissed. She glanced over and the worry lines between her brows deepened.

"How are you holding up? You know, regarding Enrique." She slowed in heavy traffic.

"I wish he would have told me he'd been struggling. I would have flown back early to help him."

She squeezed his hand. "I know you would have. Tell me about him."

Maverick talked about their friendship and how Enrique's strong faith had filled him with hope, especially during missions. The miles passed while Maverick shared stories of a man dedicated to his children, deeply in love with his wife, and proud to be a sailor. "I talked to him when I was in the hospital. After twenty years in the military, he was adjusting to civilian life, but he downplayed it and I didn't press him. I regret that now."

"Maybe there's more to the story, you know? Could he have been involved in something illegal? Was he carrying a huge debt? Was there a cheating spouse? Could he have been murdered? My job is like putting together a thousand-piece jigsaw puzzle, but the pieces aren't in the same box."

"I appreciate your efforts, but the answer to those questions is 'No'. You're here as my friend, not my PI."

"Right, sorry."

"Thanks for wanting to help." He gave her shoulder a tender

squeeze. "You know, I've never seen you in action." He paused. "Correction. I did see you in action. I've never seen you *working*."

She glared at him. "Never gonna let me forget that, are you?"

"*I'm* never going to forget that."

"Ashton, we have *got* to move past it."

Silence.

The congestion cleared and she sped up. "I don't want my sex life to interfere with our friendship. But, I have to admit, I'm frustrated by your behavior."

"What did *I* do?"

"You have sex. It's none of my business. Same goes for me. My fetish has nothing to do with you."

Maverick sighed. His honesty might trigger a completely different set of problems. "We know so much about each other. I made assumptions. They were wrong."

"Such as?"

"You have sex with men you're seeing. I was surprised you never talked to me about it. And envious that Sinclair knew. I thought I knew all your secrets."

"You two are still so competitive." Their gazes met in the darkening car. "Thank you for being honest."

Tell her more. "Seeing you like that was very erotic. I can't get that image of you out of my head."

Hoping she'd share this intimate part of her life, Maverick waited. In truth, he didn't just want to know. He wanted in. Something changed in him when he saw *other* men taking care of her needs. *Those dudes shouldn't have been touching my Carly.*

Years ago, when Maverick had wanted to make her his, she'd kept him squarely in the friend zone. Then, he'd been too wracked with grief to fight her. He needed someone to lean on and she'd been there for him, despite trying to push her away. She held all the power then and she held it now, too.

The air crackled with mounting tension. She'd gone silent on him. And he wanted her to spill every dirty little detail. "Well, woman, are you going to tell me or what?"

She veered onto the ramp for I-64 toward the beach. "I will, but you have to swear to me this isn't going to affect our friendship. When I visited you in Germany, I was terrified you were going to die. I can't lose you, Ashton, *ever.*"

"I'm not going anywhere. I promise."

Their eyes met and the connection between them intensified.

"Okay. I'll tell you." She held out her pinky.

He wrapped his around her delicate one and squeezed. "Don't make me say it."

With a smile, she shrugged.

"I pinky promise to keep your secret forever."

More silence as a shadow fell over her eyes. Then, she squared her shoulders. "There are times when my sexual needs are a little extreme."

That much he'd figured out on his own, so he stayed quiet.

"In college, my fantasies started changing. I imagined others watching while I had sex. I fantasized about sex with strangers, but I never acted on that one. Picking up a guy wasn't my thing."

He shifted in the seat. "I see."

"I thought something was wrong with me, so I ended up repressing my fantasies further, which only made things worse. Turns out, that while I love vanilla sex, I also have exhibitionist tendencies, something I came to understand after doing my own research. A couple of years ago, I was at my lowest point, sexually. A friend told me about Uninhibited, so I went with her. I had no idea Sinclair owned the club. When I found out, I decided I wouldn't return. That same friend encouraged me to talk to him, so I did. He helped me navigate the club. But that was it. I love him like a brother, but there's no chemistry. Not like how I feel about—"

He waited, silently begging her to finish that sentence, but Carly had clammed up.

"Feel about who?"

"No one." Her attention stayed glued to the highway.

Does she mean me?

"Anyway." She breathed deep. "Sin introduced me to a few people he thought would be helpful and also safe. That group grew to about thirty. We get together every few months. I wear the wig and call myself Natasha. And that's where you enter the story."

"You've had boyfriends. Are they into kink, too?"

"I don't date men in the scene. I'm into guys who like vanilla sex. I've never found the right person where I could blend my fetish into the relationship." She glanced over at him. "It sounds complicated, but it works for me."

"Thank you for confiding in me."

"We've been friends pretty much our entire lives. I would miss you if you weren't in my life. I don't want this to come between us."

"Neither do I."

"So, are you good?" At the same time she glanced over at him, she ran her tongue over her lower lip.

He paused, mesmerized by her seductive action. "Totally. I'll forget about it and we can go back to the way things were." His guts twisted. He hated lying to her. He couldn't get beyond it because he wanted her to unleash her dark fantasies on him.

And *only* him.

THE PAIN AND THE FURY

Carly was pissed. Ash was lying.

He was struggling with her story, but she didn't know what troubled him. Was it that she was sexually active? Was it that she had a fetish? Was it that she'd kept it from him? Whatever his issues, if he wouldn't talk about them, she couldn't fix the problem.

But now wasn't the time to bust his chops. He was going to have to deal with death and a family in mourning. He'd shove down his loss in order to help them with theirs. And she'd push aside her own feelings to be strong for him, because that's what he needed from her...her friendship.

A light rain dotted the windshield as she drove into the Rijados' neighborhood of well-kept brick homes. Cars packed the street, so she parked around the corner. Ashton slipped into his suit jacket and, as they walked toward the house, he draped his arm around her shoulder.

"Thanks for being here with me."

"Always."

He rang the doorbell and a heavyset woman greeted them.

"Hello, Julia."

"Maverick, thank you for coming." She stepped aside and they entered the home.

"This is Carly," Ashton said. "Carly, this is Enrique's sister, Julia."

"I'm so sorry for your loss," Carly said.

"Thank you." She slid her teary gaze to Ashton. "We're really struggling with this."

When he hugged her, Julia sagged in his arms. "Our lives won't be the same without him."

"I know."

"Enrique never let on that he was suffering, not even to Elena. I know she'll be grateful you're here. Let me take you to her."

As they moved through the home, Julia introduced them to a few family members and close friends. Ashton offered a hug or shared an uplifting story about Enrique. Tears pricked his eyes when he spoke with Enrique's mom and dad, but he didn't break.

Julia led them into the kitchen and over to Elena. "Maverick, thank you for coming."

"Elena, I'm so sorry," he said and hugged her.

Looking much older than her forty-something years, Enrique's widow fought to keep it together, but her hand shook as she soaked up her tears with a tissue.

"You must be Carly," Elena said. "We've never met, but I feel like I know you. Maverick talks about you all the time."

He mentioned me to his friends? "I am Carly. I'm so sorry for your loss, Elena."

"Would you like something to eat?" Elena asked. "Everyone brought so much food."

"Have *you* eaten?" Carly picked up a plate. "Can I get you something?"

Elena's rueful smile tore at her. "Thank you, but no. I can't eat, can't sleep. Somehow, I have to be strong for my children." Her eyes filled with tears.

Carly set the plate down and stroked Elena's back. Losing someone like this was gut wrenching.

"I talked to him when I was in the hospital." Ashton slid his hand into his pocket. "He said his new job was working out and that you and the kids were doing great. He mentioned some challenges, but only in passing. I wish—"

"I completely forgot about your injuries," Elena said. "How are you doing?"

"I'm good. I have a lot of unanswered questions about Enrique."

"So do I."

"Did he talk to you about what he was going through?"

"He was struggling, but he got help. He said he was feeling better and I had no reason to doubt him."

"I wish he would have told me."

"None of this seems real." Pausing, Elena shook her head. "I want to go to Enrique, then, I realize, he's not here, and the emptiness and panic and grief starts up all over again."

Tears filled Ashton's eyes and he wrapped a comforting arm around her and kissed the top of her head. "If I could take your pain or fix this, I would."

Elena sniffled. "Enrique and I were very close. We were friends before we fell in love." She glanced from Ashton to Carly. "Like you two."

Ashton peered into Carly's eyes. His undeniable grief sliced through her like a thousand knives.

"What can I do?" Ashton asked Elena.

"I appreciate your being here and being a pallbearer. You're welcome to speak at the service. Enrique would have liked that."

"Whatever you need."

"Tomorrow, we're coming back here after the…" Her voice cracked and she shuddered in a deep breath. "Join us."

"Absolutely," Ashton replied.

Julia entered the room with more visitors.

Elena sighed. "My aunt and uncle drove up from North Carolina." She wrapped trembling fingers around Carly's shoulder. "Thank you both for coming. I'll see you tomorrow."

As Carly stroked Ashton's back, he leaned into her. Desperate to console him, she hugged him. He tightened his grip and choked back a sob. Her heart broke.

"This is too much," he said.

"Come on." She clasped his hand and headed toward the front door.

They found Julia in the living room, greeting the constant stream of guests paying their respects. While waiting, Ashton massaged the back of his thigh.

He's hurting and I've got to help him.

"Thank you both for coming," Julia said. "The service is at Our Lady of Grace, not far from here. Do you need directions?"

"We'll find it," Carly said. "What can we do to help? Do you need us to pick up floral arrangements? Does someone need a ride to the church?"

"Everything's taken care of. The service starts at ten." The front doorbell rang and more guests entered the home. "I should say hello."

When Julia stepped away, Ashton said, "I've gotta get out of here."

A steady rain fell as they walked down the sidewalk. By the time they'd gotten to the car, large droplets pelted them. They both jumped in and she started the engine.

"I failed him." Ashton's voice was so low, Carly wasn't sure she'd heard him correctly. "I need to punch a wall, go for a run." He threw open the door and pushed out, slammed the car door shut and powered down the street.

Carly ran after him. "Ashton, stop."

He continued walking. "I can't do this. Not again."

Rain pelted her face and she two-stepped it. "*Stop.*" She

grabbed his arm. His eyes were wild, unseeing, his breath coming in short bursts. "Look at me."

Panting, he jerked back. "Dom and Enrique didn't deserve to die. I could have stopped it."

"No, you couldn't." The rain came down harder, soaking them. She grabbed his shoulders and squeezed. "Ash, look at me."

He was hyperventilating, like he was about to have a panic attack. His eyes darted around. She wanted to slap him back to reality. Instead, she backed up and gave him space.

"Death sucks, honey, and you can't stop it from happening. All you can do is be strong for their families."

He threaded his hands through his hair and threw his head back, toward the dark sky and pounding rain.

Just when she thought he was going to lose it, he stared at her with a penetrating gaze. Had these deaths, on the heels of his own accident and the senate's investigation, pushed him over the edge?

"Ashton," she murmured. He blinked several times and swiped the water from his eyes. "Come back to me."

He snaked his arms around her waist and hauled her against him. His jagged breath heated her face. As she peered into his eyes, the pull was impossible to resist. She should push him away and order him into the car to escape the drenching rain.

Instead, she did the one thing—the only thing— that made sense.

She pressed her mouth to his. He tightened his hold and kissed her with so much passion, her legs shook. His teeth grazed her lip, the force of his tongue against hers turned her inside out. Overtaken by his intensity and his vulnerability, she moaned into him while clawing at his back. And he devoured her sounds in a panty-melting embrace.

She would do whatever he needed to help him through this. *Whatever it takes.* She slowed the kiss down until their lips were barely touching.

"Holy hell," he murmured, breathing hard.

Barely able to see, and dizzy from their scorching kiss, she wiped the water from her eyes. "Let's get out of the rain." Her words came out in a breathy whoosh. A stupid response, but her mind had been blown. That kiss had been packed with a raw, untamed ferocity.

They hurried back to the car. "Get in." She ran around and jumped behind the wheel. They were dripping wet. "You okay?"

"Of course not. You just had to walk me off the ledge. I'm sorry."

"Don't apologize. You're hurting and you refuse to let anyone help you, *ever*. Let me be that person."

He regarded her for a long moment. "I can't. I can't lean on you again."

She swiveled toward him. "That's what we do. It's what we've always done. I would not have gotten through my unorthodox childhood without you and your family. You were my rock when my grandfather died. Please," she whispered. "Let me help you."

He stared at the constant stream of rain pelting the windshield for a few seconds while she held her breath and waited for his answer.

"I will."

Exhaling her relief, she gripped his hand. "Thank you."

Then, his eyes met hers. "Christ, we're drenched."

"So, we're partners in this, right?"

He trailed a heated gaze over every inch of her, from her dripping face and hair to her soaked dress, down her legs, then back into her eyes. "Yes. Partners."

He plugged the hotel address into his phone's map app and she drove away.

Being with Ashton was exhilarating and arousing as hell. She'd opened Pandora's box, rubbed the genie's lamp. That second kiss had unleashed desires she could no longer control. But, she'd agreed to help him through this difficult time, so she'd tamp down on her needs and focus on his.

The hotel parking lot was chock full, so she pulled up to the covered entrance. "Let's check in and find out where we can park."

They grabbed their bags and hurried inside, trailing water droplets like breadcrumbs.

"Good evening," said the front desk clerk. "Oh, my. It's really raining out there. Checking in?"

"Yes." Ashton tossed his driver's license on the counter. "Why is the hotel so crowded?"

"There are a ton of fun fall activities going on," said the clerk. "We have the Neptune Festival. That's a blast. There's also the International Sand Sculpting Festival. Totally phenomenal. If you like wine, the wine festivals are the place to be. But my absolute favorite is the Blue Angels airshow."

"Thanks for the suggestions. Two rooms. Hott."

"Yes, it is a little warm." The clerk clicked away on the keyboard, then laughed. "Ah, I see. Your name is Hott." He tapped the keyboard. "Hmm." More clicking. "I have you down for two king rooms." He crinkled his nose and adjusted his glasses. "We seem to have had a glitch. There's only one room left."

Carly slid her gaze to Ashton. They'd never slept in the same room before. Ever. Sharing a hotel room seemed like a mistake that would only end in heartache. Ashton waggled his eyebrows. Relieved he was behaving more like himself, she smiled before turning back to the clerk.

If they shared a hotel room, she would *not* be able to control herself. She'd want to comfort him. That would lead to a hug. A hug would lead to a tender peck on the cheek, which would morph into another rocket-fueled kiss. As the fantasy continued, she had them naked on the bed doing the bump-n-grind. A breathy moan escaped her lips.

Ashton glanced over.

"Oh, wait," said the clerk. "Okay, my bad. I'm still getting used to our updated system. It's...well. Never mind. We're all set. Two rooms with king beds. Fifth floor."

Damn.

The employee set the keycards on the counter and Carly picked then up. "Mr. Hott—great name, by the way—would you like me to charge the card on file?"

"That'll work."

"Rooms 518 and 519. Elevator is down that hallway." The clerk pointed. "Have a great stay."

"The lot is full, so I pulled up out front," Carly said. "Where can we park?"

"There are three spots in the first row marked fifteen-minute unloading," said the hotel employee. "Park in one of those."

"Stay inside," Ashton said. "I'll move the car."

She handed him the keys. "Push the seat back or you won't be able to get in."

His lips quirked up. "I've driven your car before. I've got this."

Right.

A moment later, he returned, droplets beading down his forehead. On impulse, she caressed away the wetness. The atmosphere became charged, the impulse to kiss him tugging her closer. She stared at his handsome face, the knot between his brows thick with worry.

All she wanted to do was pull him against her and erase his grief. She hated that he was hurting. He glanced at her mouth, plucking her from her trance.

"We need to dry off," she said.

"I need to go for a run," he said. "Burn off steam."

A run? Now? You've got to be kidding. Carly had to play this one cool. "Great idea."

With bags in hand, they walked to the elevator bank. He punched the button, the doors slid open and they stepped inside the small space. The air turned electric. He raked his hands through his dripping hair and she found herself staring at his profile. His eyes, sharp as razors, cut into her.

The elevator opened and she dragged her attention away.

Forging forward, she stopped in front of room 518. "This is your room." Using the keycard, she entered the room and flipped on the light.

"Let's map out a run-route before we dry off and change." She was stalling until she could come up with a smarter and safer option. No way could they go running at night in a rainstorm in an unfamiliar place.

The door banged shut behind him. Heat warmed her chest as she glanced at the king bed. But she pulled a hand towel from the bathroom rack and patted his face dry while he gazed into her eyes. Energy flowed between them, smoldering desires that teetered on an uncontrollable wildfire.

"I'll go for a run on the beach."

Repressing the urge to roll her eyes, she dried her own face. "What does your physical therapist say about that type of workout?"

"I don't have one." He removed his soaked shirt.

She wanted to strip off his undershirt and drag her fingernails down his hard chest. "Ashton, if you run, you're going to further injure yourself."

"Today's been a bitch. Two friends are dead and I could have prevented one of them, for sure. Hell, maybe even Dom's, too. Several of my missions have been suspended because I won't play by Internado's fucked up rules. I can't sit here and do nothing. No way in hell."

Her thoughts were racing. *I need a plan B.* "I'm sorry."

"I want to put my fist through a fucking wall, but I don't need to add broken bones to my list of problems." He gripped his hips. "Now, are you running with me or not?"

As she gazed into his eyes, an idea popped into her head. *I have no other choice.* "Give me one sec." Pulling up an app on her phone, Carly typed in Virginia Beach. Up popped the name of two clubs. She raised her face and stared at him.

He'd stripped down to his black boxer briefs. Pausing, she admired every beautiful, hard-muscled inch of him.

God, help me.

She sashayed close. He ground his teeth, flexing the muscles in his cheeks. His earthy scent engulfed her. Seeing him with someone else would be gut wrenching, but she was committed to help him. Her proposal was extreme, but a smarter alternative than running on the beach.

"Get dressed, Ash. There's a kink club nearby. We're going to play on the dark side."

No way had he heard her correctly. *"What?"*

"I don't have my wig, but I don't know anyone down here," she said. "Bring your own condoms. Do you have any?"

"Uh-huh." He was dreaming. That was the only logical explanation.

"I'm going to see if I can get us on the list." He could see the striations of blue and green in her exotic eyes. He started to harden but had to redirect his thoughts. He was in his underwear. No need to behave like a perv.

"Carly."

She hitched her hand on her hip. "Ashton, you have a soft tissue injury that's going to take time to heal. If you push too hard, you'll make things worse. Plus, it's raining and it's nighttime. Running is *out* of the question."

So damn bossy. So incredibly hot.

"I'm not familiar with this club, but we'll check it out. Come to my room when you're ready. I'm going to shower." Without waiting for a response, she grabbed her bag and left.

He stripped out of his underwear and stared at his growing boner. How in the hell was he supposed to have sex with another woman when all he wanted to do was play with Carly? Over the years, she'd had some crazy ideas, but this one...this one topped them all.

After a quick shower, he raked his hands through his wet hair. Since he'd brought clothing for the funeral, he had to wear his white button down shirt and black suit pants.

This is insane.

Truth was, she was right. Running would result in a setback. When she'd decided they were going out, the determination in her eyes had aroused the hell out of him. Secretly, he loved when she ordered him around. No one else had the balls to do it, probably because they knew he'd never listen. But Carly had this special hold over him. Always had, from day one.

Two months of yanking his own dick had been enough. *I need a stiff drink and a woman—a curvy, wild one named Carlyle Stone.*

Returning to the bathroom, he fished two condoms from his toiletry case. Then, he brushed his teeth and stared at his unshaven face. "Let's roll."

He crossed the hall and knocked. When she answered, his heart stuttered. "You look pretty." He wanted to keep things chill, not play his hand. In reality, she looked sensational in her black dress and stilettos. He closed the door.

"This is my funeral dress. I'll be two minutes."

"You got us on the list?"

"Sure did."

Following her, he leaned against the bathroom doorframe while she coated her lashes in mascara. *My god, she's gorgeous.* He wanted to tell her to skip the face paint, but he liked watching her get ready.

"You go to Uninhibited," she said. "Do you play there?"

"No. I visit Sin. Sometimes I watch. Does that count?"

As she stared at his reflection, her pupils dilated. "It does for us exhibitionists. We'll give this a try. It'll either work, or it won't." She turned to him. "I want to help, so be honest with me. Okay?"

"Always am."

"My kink friends know me as Natasha. Do you want to use a different name?"

"I'm not going to be doing much talking."

She turned back to the mirror. "You can't just walk in there, dick-a-blazing." She paused, a brief smile flitting over her face. "Well, maybe *you* can. Let's talk rules. You and your partner will choose a safe word."

"For what?"

"If you don't like what's happening and you want your partner to stop, you use the word and vice versa."

"Why not just say 'stop'?"

"If you're role-playing a scene where there's no consent and you say 'stop', your partner might think it's part of the play. But if you say, 'grapefruit', you'll know to stop. And checking in with your partner is good."

"I do that."

She brushed blush over her cheeks. "What about consent?"

"Carly, relax. I *have* had sex before. Granted, it's been a few months, but I think I'll remember how to do it. I talk to them. I make sure they're sober, they're in agreement, and they're having fun."

"Right. Of course. I'll settle down once I get there."

"We don't have to do this."

She steeled her spine. "Yes, yes we do. You need this. Plus, I like trying new places. There is one more thing."

"Hit me."

"We go in together. We leave together."

"I'm not leaving with anyone else. And I would never leave you there with some stranger."

Her sweet smile made his heart pound faster. "Do you know about aftercare?"

"After what?"

"Spend a few minutes snuggling or touching her in a nonsexual way. Check in. See what worked, what didn't. You know, talk to her a little."

He arched a brow. "Do I have to propose to her, too?"

She laughed. "Only if you fall madly in love and can't imagine your life without her."

Staring at her reflection, the strangest feeling came over him. He couldn't imagine his life without *her*.

"I'm sure muscle memory will kick in." She pulled a condom from her toiletry bag, sashayed past him, and dropped it into her black clutch. "All right, my friend, this might be the wildest thing we've ever done together."

She took the words right out of his mouth.

11

UNLEASHING THE BEAST

After a lifetime of being friends, Maverick wasn't convinced they'd be able to maneuver through this and come out unscathed. How could he get it on with some random woman while Carly played nearby with a stranger? Sex changed things, even if the intimacy wasn't theirs to share.

Both sofas in the club's greeting room were filled. Members gathered in small groups or in pairs. Maverick hadn't expected the kink club would be so crowded. He threaded his hand around her waist, heat shooting up his arm. "Thank you for going above and beyond."

Her sweet expression slayed him. She knew *exactly* what those words meant to him. Going above and beyond was his mantra; how he lived his life. He kissed her cheek, savoring her soft skin and inhaling her beautiful scent. Then, he clasped her hand and headed to the bar.

While waiting for a spot at the rail, a woman sidled up beside him. "Hey, handsome."

Maverick shot the gal a smile. "How ya doin'?"

Carly let go of him and his chest tightened. He didn't want to flirt with this woman.

"Wanna chat over a drink?"

"Darlin', I'm taken, but I appreciate you stopping by."

After regarding Carly, the stranger said, "Lucky lady," and sauntered into the crowd.

Maverick slipped his hand around Carly and pulled her so close her hair tickled his lips. "Trying to get rid of me?"

"I don't want to be in the way."

Pain speared his chest. "Don't say that. Don't even think that."

Two patrons left the bar and Carly and Maverick slid onto the stools.

"Be right with ya," called the bartender.

A man sidled up to Carly. "Hiya, beautiful."

Maverick gritted his teeth. *Here we go.* He was not okay with this situation. No way would he hang around while some dude got it on with her. Maybe this wasn't such a good idea.

"Hey, guys," said the bartender. "Sorry for the delay. What can I get you?"

"Top-shelf whiskey," said Maverick. "Make it a double."

"Ma'am?"

"A Manhattan?" Maverick asked Carly.

"Please."

Maverick addressed the bartender. "A Manhattan, but make it a little on the sweet side and two cherries." He knew how she liked her drink because he knew a lot of things about her. The chump beside her knew nothing and Maverick would keep it that way. Dropping a protective hand around Carly's shoulder, he stared the guy down. "How you doing?"

"Hey, man. Good. You?"

"I'm doing all right."

"I was hoping to spend a little time with this lovely lady."

Maverick flicked his gaze to Carly. "Natasha *is* lovely. She's breathtaking, really, but I'm biased."

Her smile was subtle, just a brief upturn at the corners of her mouth. No way would this dude put his grubby paws on her.

The bartender set down their drinks. "Wanna start a tab?" Maverick handed him cash. "No, this'll do us. Extra's yours."

"So, Natasha," the guy said. "Interested in sharing a table with me?"

Not happening. "Can you give us a minute?"

"No problem." The guy's gaze lingered on Carly before he wandered away.

"I don't like the idea of you jetting off with the first guy who wanders over," Maverick said.

"Playing things chill works for me." Her gaze hovered on his while the air between them hummed, the undeniable attraction swirling around them.

He wanted to kiss her. No, strike that shit. He *needed* to kiss her. His aching balls would hurt no more if they both surrendered to their pent-up passion. Maverick raised his glass. "Here's to whatever the night brings us." They toasted and he tossed back a mouthful.

"Good?" she asked.

"It hits the spot. You like whiskey. Try it."

She sipped the amber liquid. "Mmm." She licked her lips and his cock stirred. "Try mine."

Maverick sipped the cocktail. "Exactly how you like it."

Carly pressed the glass to her mouth and drank. Her sultry murmur was a direct hit to his libido. He was about to tell her he didn't want her playing with anyone else when the woman from earlier appeared.

"Hi, again. I'm Jane. This is my husband, Harry. We've never seen you guys before. Are you new?"

"First time," Carly said.

"This is a great club," said Jane. "Everyone is easy to talk to. Are you guys here to play or just check out the place?"

"We haven't decided yet," Carly replied.

"We like to start with dancing. Join us."

"We'll be in," said Carly.

Jane smiled at Maverick. "See ya."

Screwing a married woman was not his thing. And he'd rather leave than watch Carly. He couldn't shake the memory of her with two dudes. No desire to see an encore performance with someone else.

Carly ran soft fingers through his hair and electricity thrummed through him. "What are you thinking?"

"How 'bout we finish our drinks, then dance?" he said.

Playfulness filled her eyes. "Dancing with you is always an adventure."

He chuckled. "Me and my two left feet."

They leaned close to hear each other over the chatter. She told him his dad had started physical therapy for his tennis elbow and that Sinclair had mentioned a real estate opportunity he wanted to discuss with him. Carly was more plugged in to his family than he was. While listening to her sultry voice and staring into her hypnotic eyes, he weighed his options. In the end, one clear answer rose to the top. He wanted to experience her fetish with *her*, and bring her the ecstasy she craved.

When they finished their drinks, they headed toward the back of the club. He held open the door and she sashayed past him. A slow song pulsed through the speakers while clubbers moved in a seductive rhythm to the sensual beat.

On the dance floor, Carly's hips swayed, her body glided. She turned away and danced into him, pressing her backside close. He grew hard. He wrapped his arms around her while they swayed together, moving as one. Inhaling her peachy scent, he held her like she was his. And she fit, plain and simple.

The song ended and the DJ switched tracks. A song by Welshly Arms pulsed a strong rock and blues vibe and Carly broke away. Heat infused him as he cemented his full attention on the sultry blonde with the soulful rhythm dancing inches away. *His* Carly girl...the one and *only* woman he had to have.

Jane and her husband shimmied their way over.

Not again?

Laser-focused on him, Jane spun and gyrated. Harry moved and grooved as he homed in on Carly. The song ended and another slow song brought couples close.

"Wanna dance?" Harry asked Carly.

Feeling overly protective, Maverick pulled Carly flush against him. She slipped her arms around his neck.

"No, thanks," Carly said.

"We'll be hanging at our table if you change your mind." Harry escorted his wife off the dance floor.

"What do you think?" Carly asked as they glided to the music.

For several long seconds, he stared into her eyes while his innermost desires burbled to the surface. *Be honest.* "I've entered your world and I want *you* to teach me. I need *you*. And *only* you."

Her breath hitched. "Do you know what you're saying?"

"I do. Do you want me, babe?" He braced for a shit storm.

Instead, a shadow darkened her eyes and she pulled him closer. "Yes," she murmured, her voice filled with a husky need. "Yes, I do."

Carly's core slickened with need. *Oh, my God. Sex with Ashton.* She could *finally* marry fantasy with reality.

But she was committed to taking care of *his* emotional needs and helping him forget his overwhelming grief, even if just for a little while. She threaded her fingers through his and tingles skittered up her arm. "Do you want another drink?"

"No. I want you and only—"

She stopped him with her mouth. Their scorching kiss only heightened the throbbing between her legs. "So, you're placing yourself in my care."

"Completely."

"Do you trust me?"

"One hundred percent. But, let me be clear: I won't share you. And I'm not playing with anyone else."

Her heart leapt. "Me, too."

Hand in hand, they entered the playroom. Soft lighting set the mood while bowls of condoms and wipes reminded players to be safe and sanitary. Red sheets covered the futons that filled the large space where half naked or sexily-clad couples and threesomes moaned and thrust their way toward nirvana.

The hedonistic scene triggered her fetish. Her nipples pebbled, her breath quickened. She closed her eyes and inhaled the rich aroma of sex. As they picked a path through the space, she promised herself she wouldn't mistake their lusty experience for anything more. *Once, for Ash.* "Does this look like something you'd like to do?"

"Hell, yeah." Ashton nudged her against the wall and pressed close. "I trust you. Show me what you like, what you need. I'm ready to serve you."

She melted. *Oh, God.*

When his mouth found hers, her body tightened with desire. The ache between her legs screamed for a release. He broke the kiss. Backed away, his eyes dark with greed.

She spied an empty futon in the center of the room. Tugging him toward the bed, she tried regulating her breathing. Normally in complete control, she was out of her mind with desire. This wasn't about her fetish, this was about being with a man she'd desired for years and years.

As if staking her claim, she set one foot on the mattress. He snaked his arm around her and pulled her close.

She was trying to play things cool, but she was on fire. "I never allow penetration when I play, but I will because that's what *you* need."

He dropped a tender kiss on her lips. "I'll do it to please *you.*"

His playful tone made her smile. Being with Ashton was so familiar, yet here it was so foreign. Despite her concern that they'd be awkward or the experience would feel forced, she didn't hesitate to touch him. She trailed her hands through his hair and fisted chunks of luscious waves. Her exploration continued as she traced the tips of her fingers over his beautiful, tempting mouth.

The power behind his embrace had her clutching him for support.

"Is there something you don't want or won't allow me to do?" Her voice was low as she fought to control her breathing. So eager to take this man inside her, she had to force herself to ask him everything she would normally ask a kink partner.

"Whatever you give me, I'll take."

Their mouths met in another explosive kiss. This time, his tongue searching, eager to stroke hers, sent heat pummeling through her. His intensity and power thrilled her. He raked his hands down her sides and gripped her ass like he owned every inch of her. Like she was his.

Though Carly kissed men in her private group, she did so to enhance the sexual experience. Kissing Ashton felt personal and intimate. When their riveting embrace ended, she stared into his eyes.

"Is there anything that's off limits?" she asked, nuzzling his neck.

"I'm not a fan of the poo-poo place."

She cracked a smile. "Still can't get away from calling it that, can you? We have to cover the futon and put down one of those pads." Together, they prepped the bed.

"No condom?" he asked.

"Yes, a condom, but we have to keep the play area hygienic. I'm soaking wet."

"Oh, God." He drew her into his arms and pressed his hot mouth against her neck and worked his way up to her ear. A low, needy moan shot out of her while she clawed at his back.

Despite the couples and threesomes playing around them,

Ashton's attention never strayed from hers. She felt like the center of his universe and drunk out of her mind on him.

One button at a time, she unfastened his dress shirt. Trembling with anticipation, she pressed her mouth on his beautiful, bare chest. For years, she'd marveled at his strong, defined pecs, but when her tongue laved his pink nipple, she couldn't stop the moan. He tasted like male perfection.

She left his shirt on and trailed her fingertips over his granite abs while he toed off his shoes and dropped his pants. Ashton hadn't bothered with underwear and his jutting cock snagged her complete attention.

Long, thick, and saluting her like the patriot he was.

"Oh, wow," she murmured.

"Naked," he commanded.

"I don't play naked." In one slow movement, she tugged her dress over her head.

"Jesus."

She wore a black, lace bra and a matching black thong.

"You are fucking perfect."

And then, her endorphins kicked in as they always did whenever she entered her fetish-driven world. But this time, the fetish manifested itself in a whole new way. Instead of wanting others to see her, she needed him to see her. He inhaled, his already massive chest expanding to its full size. Her heart thumped hard and fast. Dizzy, she swayed.

He threaded his hand under her hair and wrapped his fingers around the back of her neck. "You okay?"

"Uh-huh." She couldn't look away, didn't want to. He commanded her full attention. "Lightheaded."

He held her close. "I got you."

By God, he did. She didn't need to instruct him. She didn't need to check in. She needed to let go and lose herself. An action filled with consequences that could ruin everything.

But, as she stroked his chest, his abs, and finally his cock, she would face those hurdles another day. On this day, she'd go freely down a dangerous path, without reservations.

"How can I make this better for you?" he murmured.

His selfless words filled her soul. She'd brought him into her world and yet, he wanted to please her. She couldn't tell him that she needed him to make love to her, to be as intimate with her as he would dare. So, she said the next best thing.

"This is for you. To help you forget. To ease your fury. I can take everything you give me."

"Then, fuck me." His raw words weren't a request. They were a command. He was ordering her around. Always had to be in charge. His eyes burned brightly, his jaw set in a hard line.

But his busy hands hadn't stopped roving over her shoulders, her back, her ass. When he cupped her breast, she gasped.

Desperate to pass the point of no return, she fished the condom from his pocket. "Sit."

He filled the futon, his large body taking up most of the space. She straddled him. Caressed his cheeks, the rough whiskers grazing her fingertips. His cock bobbed between them and she eyed his massive junk. Reaching down, she scooped his balls and gently massaged. His groan begot one from her. With her other hand, she stroked his shaft. Beautiful and thick, she wanted to put him in her mouth. Feast on him in the dirtiest of ways and swallow him down.

Tonight, however, she craved a deeper level of intimacy, one that could only happen if she took him inside her. He framed her face in his hands, the lust pouring from his hooded eyes. Gasping for air, their mouths met in a ravenous kiss. The embrace continued, their tongues tangling, the passion escalating.

Desperate to touch him, she stroked his shaft and streams of pleasure flowed through her. His oozing head made her moan. She had to taste him.

With her gaze anchored on his, she slid her fingers, wet with his juices, into her mouth and sucked. He tasted exactly as she'd always imagined. So damn delicious.

"If you keep doing that I'll come all over your phenomenal tits."

That was a warning.

His penetrating gaze, paired with the huskiness in his voice, ignited a deeper level of passion. She'd seen so many different sides of this man. But this sex-crazed one, the dirty-talking Ashton was brand-spanking new. And she couldn't get enough of him.

She placed his hands on her breasts. Even though she was busty, his large hands owned every feminine inch of her.

"You. Are. So. Fucking. Hot." The grittiness of his deep voice had her panting. "I can't wait to make you come while I'm deep inside you."

His words undid her. As he fondled and pinched, she ground against him, but when he pulled aside the lace covering her hardened nipple and took her tender flesh into his mouth, she cried out.

Several nearby looked over.

And her dirtiest, darkest desires exploded into full view. Groaning, she dug her fingers into his wavy hair. She instructed him to bite her, to fondle harder. She could feel the ecstasy building. He hadn't even entered her and she was about to shatter into a million pieces.

She couldn't wait any longer. She tore open the condom wrapper and covered him. "Ash, do you want this?"

Panting, he stilled. "Jesus, woman. Yes. For years and years."

Her throat constricted, the emotion threatening to escape. Refusing to get snared in anything remotely romantic, she rose to her knees and waited.

He stared into her eyes. "Did you change your mind?"

"No." She paused to breathe. "I want you *in* me."

In one swift move, he tugged aside her thong and positioned himself at her opening. "Sink down on me."

Another toe-curling command.

His warm breath mingled with hers. His hard body was finally hers for the taking. She took him inside her and, together, they moaned through the exhilarating rush. Overwhelming pleasure coursed through her. *Everywhere.*

He filled her intimate space completely.

She opened her eyes. He was watching her. She leaned down, kissed him. Then, she started moving.

She wished this were a simple fuck. Another emotionless journey that nurtured her hedonistic needs. But as she pressed her tongue into his mouth and he met her stroke for stroke, she silently acknowledged how badly she needed him. How badly she'd always needed him.

His sexy, masculine hands roamed over her body like she was truly his. Her sensitive skin tingled, the pleasure so powerful her body careened toward an orgasm. He fondled her breasts, pushed aside the lacy material to pinch her erect nipples. Euphoria washed over her and she glided faster. And then, he planted his hands on her hips and took control.

"You feel incredible, Car—Natasha. I need this. I need you. Oh, hell. Is this good? Talk to me."

"Yes. So good," she said, her voice a breathy whisper.

Gripping her, he forced her to stop. "Can I touch your clit?"

"This is…" *Perfect. You're perfect.* "I'm good."

"Are you about to call out the name of a fruit?"

Even with him nestled deep inside her, she couldn't help but laugh. "No, no fruit."

"Kiss me, then."

She brushed her lips over his, dropping tender kisses on his mouth.

"You are so damn beautiful."

His words melted her. "Thank you, Ash," she whispered. But

she couldn't allow herself to get swept up in their intimacy because that's *not* what this was. "Take me. Hard and fast."

Ashton Hott could have fucked the hell out of her, but he didn't. He stayed in control and dictated her movements, forcing her to glide slowly. All of them slow, deep, and deliciously intense. The man owned the word sensual and her kinky needs took a backseat to being with *him*.

He severed their fiery connection. "You've got an audience, babe."

There must have been a dozen people watching them.

"Oh, hell, I'm going to come." She kissed him hard. The intensity of his tongue against hers, his rough grunts, and those amazing slow, deep thrusts were too much. Crying loudly, she shuddered and convulsed, the climax ripping through her, sending spasms of euphoria undulating over her.

"Fucking hell." With his hands anchored on her hips, he whispered, "I'm coming, baby." His eyes closed, the orgasm flushing his handsome face while he moaned through the ecstasy and poured himself into her.

Seconds passed. Mindless, blinding, deafening seconds of nothing but Ashton nestled deep inside her. Sated, she relaxed against him. He snaked his arms around her and released one final, throaty groan. "Wow. You brought me back from the dead." His soft kiss was filled with gratitude.

"How does that hold up against a run on the beach?"

"No comparison." He tucked stray tendrils behind her ear. "Was that good for you? Did I take care of your needs?"

Better than good. You were as good as it gets. "Yes."

"This kinky world is way more exciting than I'd thought. Maybe I should reconsider my sexual priorities."

Her heart dropped. Normally, she got off on having others watch her, but tonight, *he* drove her wild. *He* brought her pleasure. Being with him had tipped the scales. He was her escape, her ecstasy, her nirvana.

She should have known better. He'd gotten a sampling of a vanilla sex exchange at a kink club and was ready to rumble. Her issue? She did *not* want to share. Not now, not ever. She'd opened Pandora's box and she'd unleashed a beast.

Her own.

This marked the end of Maverick's dry spell. He was reborn a new man, with Carlyle Elizabeth Stone his chosen religion. Worshipping her could easily become his drug of choice. *I'm in trouble. A lot of trouble.*

Carly was the complete package and he was fucked. Royally fucked.

Over the years, he'd described her as smokin' hot, a total sweetheart, a kick-ass private eye, and his best gal pal. He could add sensual goddess to that list. Why would he ever have sex with anyone else, ever again?

I can't. I won't.

She had the most sated expression, yet intensity still poured from her eyes. For all he knew, that was round one and she was ready for more. Now that he'd played with her in her world, he wanted to play with her in his. Sex on top, on the bottom, bent over, backwards, forwards and upside down.

Her erotic needs weren't just sexually stimulating they were emotionally riveting. Clearly, he was getting ahead of himself. They'd just crossed a line and he didn't want to scare her away. Had to play this low key. "Thank you. You're amazing. That was exactly what I needed."

A flicker of sadness dashed across her face. Had he said something wrong? *Ah, shit. Maybe she wanted more.* "I don't want to rush us. If you—"

"Shh, you're fine." Rather than lifting off him, she stayed connected. He loved how their intimacy extended beyond the sex.

"How are you doing?" He caressed her back with tender strokes.

"I'm good. Feel better?"

"Good as new." He leaned in to kiss her.

The peck was painfully short. "Let's meet by the locker rooms," she said before lifting off him.

They removed the bedding and dressed in the gender-specific locker rooms. When he exited, Harry was chatting it up with Carly. *Christ, he's persistent.*

As Maverick got closer, his heart pounded faster. Not only was Carly a natural beauty, her relaxed expression and flushed cheeks were his doing. Or so he'd like to think. But he was along for the ride. She'd grounded him in the absolute best way possible. She regarded him with a cool stare. But when he snaked his arm around her and pulled her close, her lips curved.

He could see past her aloof exterior because he knew her. Her eyes told him everything he needed to know. While her smile was discreet, the happiness in her eyes was not. She might be Natasha here, but when she lifted her face to his, *his* Carly girl stared back. He kissed her temple. "What's happening?"

"Are you staying nearby?" asked Harry. "We could join you in your motel room. Jane really likes you guys. She's a great time and won't disappoint."

Is this guy for real?

"We're gonna pass." Maverick tightened his hold. "Are you ready, baby?"

She hitched a brow. *Was that too much?*

"Sure, *honey*."

"Your wife...er, girlfriend, um, friend is worth pursuing."

"Let's just call her *mine*," Maverick said before ushering Carly out of the club.

On the way to the car, Maverick slung his arm over her shoulder. Never one to hold back, he blurted, "I feel reborn." Then, he dipped his head and kissed her. "I kinda got the impression you wanted more. Are you sure you're okay with leaving?"

"Positive."

He opened the passenger door and she slipped inside. Her well-toned calves stole his attention and he wondered why they'd waited so long to get together. On the short ride back to the hotel, she said nothing.

He clasped her hand and she tensed. "How do we do this?" he asked.

"We don't." Her harsh words sliced through him.

"What the hell does that mean?"

"I wanted to help you."

He tightened his grip on the wheel. "So, what? That was a pity fuck?"

"Come on, Ash. You needed that and you chose me. It was good for me, too. We…we go back to the way things were."

"Is that what you want?"

Pregnant pause. "Yes."

Muscles running down his shoulders tensed. *Tell her how you really feel.* Instead, he let go of her hand. "Whatever you think best."

She stared out the passenger window. "I'm here to help you manage through your loss."

He rubbed the back of his neck. "Now what?"

"We attend the funeral tomorrow."

"Right. Got it."

They drove the rest of the way in a frigid silence. As they walked into the hotel, she hugged herself. He wanted to hold her close, warm her, but she kept her distance. Never at a loss for conversation, they rode the elevator in continued silence.

The chilly atmosphere followed them down the hallway. He pulled her to a stop outside her room. "I know you and something is off."

Her smile didn't touch her eyes. "I just need some sleep, that's all."

He threw out his arms and painted on a grin. "How about a Hott hug goodnight?"

She embraced him. Did she regret what they'd done? Did she want sex with that other man? Had she wanted more sex with him at the club? He had no fucking clue.

"Thank you for tonight." His sincere words sounded crass. He wanted to ask her to come into his room. He wanted to hold her while they slept. He needed her and that scared the living hell out of him. Ashton Hott had never needed anyone.

Ever.

By design and on purpose.

She steeled her spine. "Let's grab breakfast on the way." She opened her hotel room. "G'night, Ash." Her door banged shut.

He stood alone in the hallway. *Dammit, this was a mistake. I've lost her.* He entered his room and undressed. *How the hell can we go back to being just friends? How are we supposed to do that?*

He wanted her in his bed, beneath him. He wanted to explore her and ravage her. He wanted to please her and learn from her.

Because of her, he'd pushed past his fury and loss. The pall of death messed with his head and his heart. But she'd torn down his walls, this time with ecstasy, then smacked him back into the friend zone.

Frustration had him seeing red. Had their sex been a mistake? He had no roadmap because there was no one like Carly. He'd bedded numerous women, but he had no deep, meaningful relationships with them. With Carly, he'd had a rock-solid relationship, but no sexual intimacy. How was he supposed to marry the two with someone who wasn't even interested?

It would be easier to call it what it was—a pity fuck—and move forward. But Maverick never took the easy route.

Carly had breathed life back into him. For those moments

they'd been together, he'd locked out the world and locked in on her. After brushing his teeth, he slid beneath the linens.

Alone. Always alone.

But that was his doing, his choice. No one could see him unravel when the demons came racing back.

He turned off the bedside lamp and closed his eyes, but sleep wouldn't come. So, he locked his fingers behind his head and stared at the ceiling. His thoughts drifted back to Carly and a friendship that had begun decades ago.

In second grade, Carlyle Stone had been the cute new girl with the pretty hair and smiling eyes. That first week, he spotted her eating lunch alone, so he joined her. But his motives were more selfish than selfless. Beyond being able to stare at her without getting caught, he would make his parents proud.

His mom believed the best things in life stemmed from random acts of kindness. During dinner, Sarah Hott would ask her family who did something nice for someone else without expecting anything in return. *Everything* counted. Even when his little sister proudly announced she found a spider in the "bafroom" and put it in Ashy's bed to keep it warm.

Even now, he could see his mom's smile and hear her sweet voice. *"I'm so proud of you, Ashton. You made a positive difference in someone's life today."*

It wasn't until he was older that he realized the power in doing something kind for someone else.

In middle school, his mom left for a two-week stint with an international physicians organization. She was spending time in the Middle East helping citizens through a health crisis. Two days after their group arrived, a terrorist group took the doctors hostage. A week later, they were dead. Tortured and murdered by their captors.

His sweet, dedicated, giving mother must have gone through hell before she died at the hands of pure evil.

Rolling over in bed, Maverick fought against the burn in his throat. Even alone, his reaction embarrassed him. It had been twenty years since her death, but some nights it felt like he was right back there. In the pain and utter heartbreak.

Through that grueling year, Carly had showed him the true meaning of friendship. She'd been his rock and he'd leaned on her, hard. Ever since, death was his trigger. And here she was again, by his side, offering herself up to him. Only, this time, she'd given him much more than her friendship.

Armed with that knowledge, he came to a sobering realization. Everything, including their twenty-five-year relationship, had changed in an instant.

She might be able to put him back into the friend zone, but he could not. He could never reverse course because he had one direction.

Forward.

Always forward.

12

A STONE FAMILY DINNER

The funeral had been beautiful. There wasn't a dry eye in the church after the priest's eulogy. Carly held his hand, said all the right things to let him know she cared, but she'd created some kind of force field around herself. After they buried Enrique, family and friends returned to Julia's and spent the afternoon honoring his friend. Again, Carly was right there, offering her constant support, but she wasn't herself. Maybe she regretted what they'd done, but Maverick sure as hell didn't.

On the ride home, they'd talked about everyone and everything but the elephant in the room. It was like the intimacy never even happened. But Maverick couldn't *stop* thinking about their hot connection. She hadn't just revived him physically, she'd lifted him emotionally, too.

As the sun dipped below the horizon, Carly pulled up in front of Uninhibited.

"I like your idea about starting a foundation," Maverick said. "If I do something, you'll work with me."

Up went her eyebrows. "I will?"

"Damn straight."

She shot him a smarmy smile. "And you think *I'm* bossy. All right, I will, but only because it's for a good cause."

"Text me when you leave your parents' house," he said.

"I won't last there three hours. I'll get to target practice by nine."

"Thanks for coming with me." He kissed her cheek and she tensed. "Having you with me made all the difference."

"I'm glad I could help." He didn't like the strain in her voice much, either.

Maverick opened the car door. "I'll see you in a few. Tell Lisa and Ed hello." He winked and got out. "Have fun."

"Ugh."

After she pulled away, he texted Sinclair. "Let me in."

Maverick cracked his neck as Sinclair opened the front door, then led him to his private dining room on the first floor. The room was cozy and elegant with a table setting for six.

"Are we expecting company?" Maverick asked.

"Did you forget?" Raising his brows, Sin waited. "You forgot. Colton and Brigit, Crockett and Alexandra. You and me."

"We need women."

"You have one, and I'm surrounded by them." His phone buzzed with an incoming text.

"So, pick one."

Sinclair shook his head. "Not from here."

"What about your company?"

Sinclair arched an eyebrow. "I'm a fixer, not a fucker."

Maverick laughed.

"Are you staying for dinner?"

"Yeah. Meeting Carly at nine."

"Sounds promising. Why didn't she stick around?"

"Dinner with Lisa and Ed. I'll see her later at target practice."

"How romantic." On a chuckle, Sinclair shook his head. "How was the funeral?"

"I couldn't have gotten through it without her."

"You always say that."

"We had sex."

A satisfied smile lifted his brother's lips. "About time. Vanilla or kink?"

"Vanilla at a kink club. She got off on being seen. I was drowning and she threw me a lifeline."

"She was topping from the bottom."

Maverick chuffed out a laugh. "Whatever the hell that means. Look, all I know is that she's my new addiction."

Sinclair's phone buzzed with another incoming text. "You two gonna make a go at it?"

"She shoved me back in the friend zone."

A waiter delivered two tumblers. "Your Macallan, Mr. Develin."

Sinclair raised his glass as his phone vibrated again on the table. "Bottoms up." He tossed back a mouthful.

"What's going on with you?" Maverick asked.

"Shit storm's a brewin'."

"Talk to me."

"Dakota needs my help."

"With what?"

"You know I can't talk about that." He flashed a wicked smile. "Let's circle back to Carly. Do you love her? Never mind. I know the answer. The question is: What will you *do* about it?"

"She's clammed up." Maverick sipped his whiskey. "And she's pretending our intimacy never happened."

"Friends with benefits?"

"No, she's too special to me."

"I know that." Sin tossed back the amber liquid.

Leaning back, Maverick crossed his legs. "In high school, she told me she's never getting married. Maybe I won't, either."

Sinclair chuffed out a laugh. "Are you for real? I see you married —to Carly—with five loud children and three stinky mutts."

Maverick smiled. "Controlled chaos sounds damn fun."

"You live for a good challenge."

"I do, don't I?"

Carly sat at the kitchen table in her parents' house massaging the back of her neck. Her muscles always knotted whenever she spent any time with her mom. Though she'd tried begging out of this, her mom had insisted.

"It's business-related," her mom had said. "Be here by seven. I want to make sure dinner is over by eight thirty. I have plans."

So, Carly had no choice but to suck it up and go.

"You're all dressed up," her dad said. "You look nice, dear."

"Thanks, Dad." Over the years, his hair had thinned and his signature moustache had turned mostly gray, but he'd stayed in decent shape.

"She looks morbid," her mom replied. "You look like you're going to a damn funeral."

"I did go to one."

"Did one of Grandpa's clients die?" asked her dad.

"A SEAL teammate of Ashton's."

"Who?" asked her mom.

"*Ashton*. Ashton Hott."

"I'm sorry to hear that," her dad said.

"Doesn't he go by Maverick now?" Her mom popped a pickle chip into her mouth.

"His college friends nicknamed him that," Carly said. "Everyone who knew him before Harvard still call him Ashton."

Her mom scrunched her nose. "What a snob. Harvard is a playground for the elite."

"Lisa, enough," said her dad. "He's been a good friend to Carly."

Glaring at Ed, Lisa set down her burger. "He's a total player and he's been stringing Carly along for years. I read the story in

The Washington Post and I caught that news segment. They're painting him as a friggin' hometown hero. What a crock!"

"Lisa, he almost died saving those hostages," said her dad. "Have a little respect, for God's sake."

"Shut up, Eddy. Who asked you?"

Carly was about to take a second helping of onion rings when her mom cleared her throat. "You already ate three. Don't be piggy."

Her face heated as she held the tongs over the bowl. "Two. I ate two and they were small." She hated that her mother still monitored her food intake.

Lisa Stone patted her stomach. "We gals need to watch our hourglass figures." Carly was the first to admit her fifty-six-year-old mom looked fantastic. She colored out the grays. She had minimal wrinkles because she'd always been adamant about using sunscreen. Regardless of her mother's appearance, her horrid disposition overshadowed any physical beauty that she had.

"Fine, whatever," Carly said setting down the tongs.

Ed Stone rolled his eyes. "Stop badgering her, Lisa." The retired IRS auditor had the patience of a saint, so his brusque tone caught her ear.

"Shut your trap, Eddy. Unlike Cassandra, this one's no lightweight."

Her dad sighed. The only time she'd received her mom's approval was during college when she'd practically starved herself and dropped to what Ashton had called, "A bag of bones with a few layers of skin."

"Mom." Carly steeled her spine. "Not everyone is skinny. I run. I lift. I play racquetball. My body is so different from yours and Cassie's."

Her mother glared at her. "Would it kill you to call her Cassandra? You could stand to lose ten pounds—and let me be frank—that's a conservative number, missy. I'm just trying to help you catch a man."

Carly wanted to throw up. If "catching a man" had been her endgame, she sure as hell did *not* want her mother's help. She pushed away her unfinished burger. "I have to go."

"Like hell you do," said her mom. "Time to talk business." She snapped her fingers. "Ed, clean up."

"No." Her dad never pushed back. "I'm done taking orders from you. If you don't tell Carly why you called her over, I will."

"Save it, Ed." Lisa eyed her daughter. "Your dad and I are getting a divorce."

Carly snapped to attention.

"Things between me and Ross have gotten serious," her mom said. "He's moving in."

"Where are *you* going?" she asked her dad.

Pushing out of the chair, he leaned his backside against the counter. "Florida. Time for me to start over."

Who can blame you? "Okay."

"I've agreed to give up my half of your dad's pension," said her mom. "In exchange, he's turning over management rights for the office space in that shitty rundown building your idiot grandfather worked out of. Going forward, I'm your new landlord."

Her guts twisted. This was a total appetite killer. "Seriously, Dad?"

"Yeah." His sheepish expression might have been his version of an apology. Carly had no freakin' idea.

"How much are you jacking up my rent?" she asked, glaring at her mom.

"Not one little penny!" Her mother's flamboyant smile sent shivers racing down Carly's spine. "I've found someone willing to pay me *triple* what your dad's been charging you. You have two weeks to clear out." She brushed her hands together, as if clearing crumbs off her fingers.

Carly's heart dipped. No way could she afford to pay double, let alone triple. "Dad, why don't you sell the building?"

"I will, at some point," he replied. "I'm ready to put this sham of a marriage behind me and move on." He rose. "I'm going to finish packing." Then, he patted Carly's back. "You can meet clients in a coffee shop or on a park bench."

She grimaced. "I'm a private investigator, not a spy."

"Once I'm settled, I hope you'll come visit me."

"Oh, sure, *her* you invite," quipped her mom.

"Lisa, let's be civil with each other. We had some good times and we've been blessed with two wonderful daughters. For too many years, I put up with your cheating, then I endured our open marriage while you've paraded men through here. I doubt Ross will stick around for long, but good for you if he does. And just so that we're clear, this marriage isn't open or closed. It's *over.*"

And with that, he left the room.

After a nonchalant shrug, Lisa turned to Carly. "Be out of the building by the end of the month. And take a look at your ass in the mirror, young lady." Her mom left the kitchen, taking her haughty expression with her.

Carly wanted to fling her glass against the wall or flip over the kitchen table. Instead, she fiddled with her stackable rings, forcing herself to calm down. *Maybe she's doing me a favor. I won't have to deal with her anymore. She'd be a witch of a landlord.*

She found her dad in the guest bedroom packing. She'd no idea their marriage had deteriorated to the point that they were no longer sharing a bedroom. He looked tired. Not from lack of sleep, but from years of putting up with a loose cannon. He closed his suitcase, then zipped his duffel. "I just texted you my new address. I'm moving to a retirement community in central Florida. Most of the residents get around on golf carts." He hugged her. "I love you, honey."

"I love you, too. Safe travels."

A mix of emotions—anger, frustration, and sadness—swirled in her head. As she headed out the front door, she almost collided with her mom's boyfriend. *Great.* She mumbled hello.

Ross sported a sleazy smile, slicked-down hair, and a suit that screamed Saturday Night Fever. His dark shirt, unbuttoned to his naval, revealed a thick rug of chest hair billowing through the gold chains dangling around his neck. "Carly, hey. Did you hear the big news?"

"Sure did." He reeked of so much cologne she had to turn away.

"I'm the new sheriff." He stepped close and she backed up. "Are you as wild as your spicy lil' mama?"

"Get lost, Ross." She walked to her car.

"I was hoping we could get to know each other," he called out. "You know, I bang the cougar *and* her hot daughter."

Refusing to acknowledge his disgusting comment, she jumped into her car and drove away. Once out of sight, she stopped at the curb and pounded the steering wheel. "They are soooooo fucked up!"

She didn't even try to stop the tears. She was alone. No one was there to criticize her or tell her to eat less or stop eating altogether. Her business was hanging by a thread *and* she was getting evicted. *The universe is definitely sending me a sign.*

Though surprised, she was glad her parents were splitting up and her dad was starting over. Initially, her dad had gone along with her mom's interest in "branching out". After a few years, he stopped seeing other women and had asked Lisa to do the same. She refused. At long last, his patience had run out.

Mom isn't his problem anymore. Lucky guy.

In light of these changes, Carly had no intention of returning to her mom's house, especially now that creepy Ross was moving in. *Total effing weirdo.*

She wiped her cheeks, punched up her playlist, and drove toward the firing range. "I wish you were here, Mrs. Hott. You were always so kind to me and you always had the best advice." Carly sniffled. "Ash isn't the only one who misses you."

Carly parked in the lot, pulled her Glock 19 from the lockbox in her trunk. She removed the cartridge and packed it and her gun in its case, then shouldered her duffel and grabbed her range bag.

After checking in, she changed in the locker room. Emerging in jeans and a long-sleeved shirt, she headed over to the firing area.

Once there, she covered her ears and eyes in protective gear before taking her position in the fifty-yard lane. After loading her weapon, she took a moment to center herself. Still raging mad from the conversation with her folks, she tried settling down. Despite years of practice, she was still wielding a dangerous weapon.

She closed her eyes and envisioned her happy place—a sunrise stroll at the beach, the morning sun warming her face. She breathed deeply and took aim. She homed in on the target, widened her stance, slowed her inhale, and fired on exhale.

She hit the paper dummy in the shoulder. *C'mon, concentrate.*

Ten minutes into it, the tension in her neck still wouldn't release. She hoped the evening with her parents would blur into the background, but with each shot she fired, her frustration mounted.

On the way to the firing range, Sin's driver made a quick stop at Maverick's so he could collect his range bag. Having confirmed Carly's location, Maverick made his way to the far side of the building. The lane beside her was empty, so he donned his protective gear, pulled his Glock from his case, loaded it, and stepped into the space. He loved watching her practice. Her form was terrific and she hit the target way more times than she missed.

Tonight, however, something was off. Tension had hiked up her shoulders and her stance wasn't right. After lowering her weapon, she looked over at him.

Her tight smile didn't touch her eyes. When she turned back, she centered herself, raised her gun, and fired, completely missing the target. *Whoa, woman, what's up with that?*

Over the next hour, they practiced side by side until she lowered her weapon and removed the cartridge. He fired for another five minutes before stopping. Together, they headed toward the range's clubhouse.

"You want a drink?" he asked.

"I'm gonna head out."

"You were off tonight," he said.

Frustration radiated off her. "No shit."

"Should I guess?"

"You won't even need three."

"Lisa and Ed."

"You win."

He stepped close. "What's my prize?"

"Me, full of piss and vinegar," she said with a smirk. "I suggest you find someone fun to hang out with."

"I know just the remedy."

She shook her head. "Don't even go—"

"Let's motor up the Potomac," he said, cutting her off. A late night booty call was not the answer. "You love the river at night."

They left the firing range, got in her car, and she headed back to his place. "My folks are divorcing."

He studied her face. "That's big."

"You know my mom's creepy boyfriend, Ross?"

"Yeah, I've met him."

"Well, he's moving in with her." She locked eyes with him in the dark car. "I don't blame my dad for getting out. Their open marriage was doomed, but that is *not* my problem."

"No, it's not." He was surprised that bothered her since she was so against their arrangement from the get-go. Knowing Lisa Stone, there had to be more. She'd always been Carly's toughest critic. "What else happened?"

THE HOTT TOUCH | 133

Carly sighed. "The usual. She lectured me about food and told me to drop ten. I feel so fat every time I'm around her."

He bit out a grunt. "I hate when she does that to you, which is *every* fucking time you see her. You shouldn't go over. You know you're not fat."

Silence.

"Carly, honey. You aren't."

A growl shot out of her. "Thanks, but I can't talk about it anymore."

She pulled into the marina, but instead of parking, she stopped in front of his car, hopped out and handed him his overnight bags.

"You ready for that nice, relaxed cruise down the river?"

"I can't, Ash."

"Dammit, Carly."

"I'm sorry. I've gotta go. Talk to you next week." She dropped a peck on his cheek and drove away, taking his heart with her.

13

EXPECT THE UNEXPECTED

Monday morning, zero seven hundred. Maverick parked in the lot behind the four-building office complex and exited his black Suburban, one of six company vehicles used for local assignments. He scanned the area. Aside from the tweeting birds and constant hum of D.C. traffic, the area was quiet.

In less than three hours, a crowd of onlookers would be witnessing a high-profile business executive announce the launch of her newest venture. And ThunderStrike would ensure she and her team received the best possible security.

Despite the mayhem of the past few months, standing in the empty parking lot filled him with immense pride. Internado might be interfering with his government-related missions, but the private-sector division of ThunderStrike was forging forward.

Four months ago, Ella Kayson, CEO and President of Qualitation, had hired his company for this one-day gig. While Maverick lived for the intensity of rescue missions, the short-term surveillance and protection assignments kept ThunderStrike sharp and in the game.

Following the brief speech and ribbon-cutting ceremony in

the courtyard, the attendees would move inside so Ella and her exec team could address the audience.

Two aspects about this job concerned Maverick. First, Ella had opened the event to the public and, second, she was an independent thinker and a strong-willed woman who spoke her mind. She used her voice to empower women, especially other black women, to follow their vision and live their dream. Not everyone was an admirer or supporter of Qualitation and its founder. For that reason, Maverick and his team were committed to ensuring the events went off without a hitch and that Ella and her team stayed safe.

Gunner arrived next, also driving a ThunderStrike SUV. Maverick walked over to meet him. "Good weekend?"

"Yeah. How was the funeral?"

"Hard to bury a friend."

"Always is."

Penelope and Trevon Williams rolled in at the same time, each driving a ThunderStrike vehicle.

"Morning." Trevon extended his hand. "Good to have you back in command."

Maverick shook it. "Great to be back." He eyed each of his teammates. "You three doing okay this morning?"

"Yes, sir," Trevon said. "I'm looking forward to this."

"Absolutely." Gunner tipped his shades and peered at Maverick. "I'm glad Ms. Kayson didn't cancel."

"Me, too," Penelope said.

"Before we secure the perimeter, let's check our comms." After completing a sound check, Maverick said, "Let's get started. Penelope, you're with me. We'll clear the perimeter of this building and the one called North. You two take South and West."

"Meet you back here," Gunner said. "Once the building opens, I'll set up on the roof."

Unlike hostage rescue missions, where they're loaded down with protective gear and weapons, today's uniform was a breeze.

Dark suit, dress shirt, dark shoes, dark shades. Ties were required for men, optional for women. Beneath everyone's clothing lay a bulletproof vest. Their Glocks were tucked into their waist holsters. Only Gunner used a sniper rifle.

They retrieved their explosive trace detectors and split up. Maverick and Penelope circled the North building checking for anything out of place. A piece of PVC pipe, a small package, even a trash bag. He spotted a brown paper bag beneath a picnic bench. He knelt, ran the detector strip over the outside of the bag, then inserted the strip into the detector. Someone's lunch remains.

"Clear." He tossed the bag in the trash.

After completing their exterior building sweeps, Maverick glanced over at his partner. Penelope hadn't uttered a word.

He slowed to a stop. "What's going on with you?"

"Nothing."

He furrowed his brow. "That's a load of crap. Talk to me. If you're not up for today's assignment—"

Her expression fell. "Someone leaked the timeline of our mission."

"Which mission?"

"The one that landed you at that senate hearing." She shook her head. "I read an article and it got to me."

"There's been press about us before."

"The writer concluded that if I'd arrived at the extraction site according to plan, you and Gunner wouldn't have gotten shot." She paused. "I can't argue that fact. It's tough to swallow my part in what happened to you two."

Maverick had little time to determine whether she was clear-headed for their assignment. If she weren't, he'd have to replace her, pronto. He slid a hand into his pants pocket and relaxed his stance. "Why didn't you call me?"

"I was with Gunner when you texted him at Hudson's last week. I was worried something had gone wrong with one of our overseas missions, so I called him when he left. He told me a

SEAL teammate had died. I couldn't pile on about a stupid article."
She broke eye contact. "But it got me thinking...maybe I should
step down."

Oh, boy. She's coming unglued. "We've always done our best
when we face issues together as a cohesive team. I would hate for
you to bail on me...or on yourself." Maverick offered an
encouraging smile. "Here's how I see it. You *did* find a way to land
that bird under extreme conditions, and you *did* get us *both* out.
Alive." He tossed her a nod. "Keep in mind that writer didn't have
to make any split-second decisions about whether or not to abort
a rescue mission or find a secondary landing location. That
person got to review everything from the comfort and safety of a
computer. You're the best at your job and you love what you do.
That's what counts."

Her expression lifted, her eyes brightening. "Thank you."

"Now, stop reading that garbage, will ya?"

She cracked a smile. "Yes, sir."

"You okay?"

"Better."

"Ready to rock this?"

She squared her shoulders. "Definitely."

The team reconvened out front.

"All clear?" Maverick asked.

"Affirmative," Trevon replied.

In addition to employees arriving for work, two catering vans
and a party rental truck had parked out front. After clearing the
vehicles, the ThunderStrike team went inside and introduced
themselves to the security guards. Wall-to-wall windows on three
sides of the building made the lobby a fishbowl. Not the best
situation, but Maverick and his team would remain vigilant.

At eight fifteen, Ella Kayson walked through the front doors.
Her vibrant red suit was as bold as her personality. "Good to see
you, Maverick."

"How are you, Ella?"

"Excited the big day is finally here."

After introducing his team, Maverick explained that, going forward, Ella would be escorted by a ThunderStrike employee at all times.

Ella acknowledged all three. "I'm happy to see a female amongst the ranks."

"I'm a big fan," Penelope said. "I've read both your books."

"When my next one comes out, be sure to call my office for a complimentary copy."

"How many are you expecting today?" Maverick asked.

"Around a hundred and fifty, but reservations weren't required. The good weather and free food might bring in foot traffic. We heard back from the mayor's office. She'll be here, along with several other government officials."

Maverick curled his hand into a tight fist. *Internado better not show up.*

Ella reviewed the agenda with the team. Following the outside ribbon-cutting ceremony, they'd move into the lobby. Four Qualitation executives would speak, she'd finish with a short keynote address, open the floor to questions, then leave an hour for networking. "I like to call it power-mingling."

"And we'll be right there alongside you," Maverick said.

"I'm heading upstairs to my office," Ella said. "Who's coming with me?"

"One more thing," Maverick interjected. "Four SUVs are parked in the rear of the building, adjacent to the exits. In the event of an emergency, we'll escort you and your executive team into those vehicles. We're each responsible for five of you and we'll find you. You'll be taken to a secure location until it's safe to return here."

"You've thought of everything. I caught the evening news Friday. Internado is putting you through the paces. He's barking up the wrong tree if he wants *you* to roll over and play dead."

Maverick's stomach roiled. "My thoughts, as well."

"If I could help you, I would." Then, she leaned close and whispered, "He reeks of rotten fish."

He sure as hell does. Despite wanting to voice his opinion, Maverick got back to business. "Penelope, Trevon, please escort Ms. Kayson to her office. Radio us when you're on your way downstairs."

"Understood," Penelope replied.

The three took off toward the elevator bank. While Gunner retrieved his rifle from his vehicle, Maverick called his office.

"Good morning," said Anne, his office manager. "The phone hasn't stopped ringing."

"I'm not surprised," he said. "Clients are overreacting to Friday's hearing."

"They want reassurance from you."

"We're at Qualitation until approximately fourteen hundred. I'll return calls when I get back."

Dammit, this should not be happening.

Over the next thirty minutes, Qualitation employees filed into work while Maverick and Gunner kept a watchful eye. The party rental company readied the lobby with a podium and several rows of folding chairs. The catering company rolled carts of refreshments through the front doors and set up on tablecloth-covered tables.

"Time for me to head to the rooftop," Gunner said.

"Let me know when you're in position."

"Always do." Gunner flagged down a security guard.

Five minutes later, Gunner told Maverick he was at-the-ready.

"How is it up there?" Maverick asked.

"Hot."

"Need a spotter?"

"I've got this."

"Keep me posted." Maverick stood along the wall, a silent sentry designed to blend in as everyone scurried about. While it would be easy to let his thoughts wander, he'd trained himself to stay on task. Years ago, he learned a skill called temporary facial recognition that allowed him to track most everyone at an event. In a sea of strangers, he watched for gestures, nervous tics, or even a sheen of perspiration dotting someone's brow.

A young woman pushing an empty serving cart stopped in front of him. "Are you security?"

"Whatcha need?" Maverick asked.

She shot him a flirty smile. "I was just admiring your...um... your suit, and wanted to say hello."

"Thank you."

"The strong, silent type." Then, she cocked her head. "Maybe I could give you my number, you know, so we could get together for drinks sometime."

Maverick never let himself get distracted while on assignment, especially by a woman. That was the oldest trick in the book. "Thank you, darlin', but I'm taken."

"The good ones always are." She rolled the cart outside.

Am I taken? Focus, dammit.

At zero nine fifty, Ella and her executive team returned to the lobby.

Gunner's low, deep voice rumbled through Maverick's earpiece. "Rough count puts the crowd at two hundred. It's a big group."

"Sixty or so in the lobby. I'm heading out." Maverick slid on his sunglasses as he stepped into the bright morning sunlight.

Ella stood at the podium. She welcomed everyone, thanked the mayor, and acknowledged her special guests and VIPs. While the mayor spoke, Maverick continued his visual sweep. More people congregated in the courtyard, their phones outstretched.

"There's an abandoned army-green backpack east end of the refreshment table," Trevon said through the comm. "I'm going to scan."

"Roger that."

A few more government officials added their comments

before Ella and the mayor cut the ribbon and the audience broke into applause. When finished, Ella led the energetic group inside.

Once the audience was seated, the overflow of guests stood in the rear of the lobby near the elevator banks. Acting as emcee, Ella introduced her executive team.

"Trevon, what's the backpack status?" Maverick asked.

"All clear," Trevon replied.

Maverick scanned the attendees. The constant movement in the back of the room snagged his attention. Catering staff scurried to refill coffee carafes, a few people chatted by the elevators. Things were as he anticipated. The executive addressing the audience touted how this was going to be *the* year for Qualitation. Maverick tuned out the speech to study the faces. He'd been trained to watch for any sudden movements, anyone pulling something from a pocket. With cell phones in use, Maverick's attention was in continual motion.

"I've got a four-door sedan that's circled the parking lot twice." Gunner's steady voice rumbled in his ear.

On instinct, Maverick wrapped his fingers around his weapon while studying the crowd. No one appeared uneasy.

"Disregard," Gunner said. "It parked out back."

Clank! One of the caterers dropped an empty plastic water pitcher and the loud crash made several jump.

The audience broke into applause as one Qualitation exec replaced another at the podium.

"The four-door sedan is on the move again," Gunner said. "Single occupant. Male."

Maverick moved toward the front door. "Position?"

"Northwest side of building," Gunner replied. "All eyes on target. He's circling the parking lot again."

"Is the lot full?" Maverick asked.

"Affirmative in the front, but there are spaces in the rear," Gunner replied.

Silence for another moment.

"He's driving toward the courtyard. Gaining speed. He's barreling toward the building. I've got to stop him."

Maverick bolted toward the front door as Gunner opened fire.

As the vehicle sped toward the building's lobby, people started screaming and running in every direction.

Fueled by adrenaline, Maverick grabbed his Glock and ran outside.

"I hit him," Gunner said. "He must have rigged the gas pedal. I'm on the way down."

The chaotic scene faded into the background. Maverick heard nothing but the sound of his controlled breathing as he aimed at the gas tank and fired repeatedly.

The car exploded in a burst of flames, metal and glass went flying in every direction. The force propelled Maverick backwards. He hit the ground and rolled away, protecting his head from flying debris.

After grabbing his weapon, Maverick tried pushing to his feet, but searing pain had him dropping to his knees. *Fuck me.* "Gunner. I'm down." In addition to a bloodied hand, his shoulder had become dislocated.

"I'm in the staircase," Gunner said into his earpiece. "Where are you?"

"Out front." Gritting his teeth, Maverick forced himself to stand. "Penelope, find the security guard in charge before you grab your five."

"Copy that," she replied.

Gunner ran over. "Talk to me."

"My shoulder."

"Hell, no, not again?"

Maverick winced from the pain shooting down his arm. "Again."

"I've got my five execs and am heading toward the back stairs," Trevon said.

"Roger that," Maverick replied.

"Do it now," Maverick said to Gunner.

"I hate doing this."

"Trust me, I hate it more."

Gunner placed one hand on Maverick's back, the other on his arm while Maverick inhaled. "On three. One...two." Gunner jolted his shoulder back into place.

Excruciating pain exploded through him. "Christ, that's a bitch." He rubbed his arm. "Thank you, brother."

Together, they ran inside. Pandemonium filled the lobby. Three of the large windows in the building's front lobby had cracked, but none had shattered. Had that glass blown out, attendees would have been peppered by flying shards and casualties would have been high.

Gunner bolted to retrieve his execs while Maverick strode toward Ella and her two vice presidents. "Are you injured?"

All three shook their heads, though they appeared to be in shock. He located the other two and ushered all five toward the rear of the building. Once outside, he hurried them to his SUV. Then, he contacted his crew.

Trevon had loaded up his five and was ready to roll. Gunner was fifteen seconds out. But Penelope was nowhere in sight.

"Penelope, talk to me," Maverick said.

"One of mine has fainted," she replied. "I'm sending four outside to you."

"You need help?" Maverick asked.

"I've got her," Penelope replied. "I'm headed down the stairwell."

When the four employees rushed outside, Maverick escorted them to Penelope's SUV and helped them inside. Breathing hard, Penelope set the woman into the vehicle and Maverick checked her pulse.

"Slow and steady," Maverick said. "What's her name?"

"Glenda," replied one of the others.

"Glenda, can you hear me?" Maverick asked.

The woman's eyes fluttered open. Though she looked dazed, she recognized her coworkers.

"How are you feeling?" Penelope asked her.

"I think I'm okay."

"We'll have you checked out by a paramedic once we're at the safe sight," Maverick said. Hurrying back to his vehicle, Maverick spoke into his comm. "Everyone ready?"

After receiving three affirmatives from his team, he jumped into the driver's seat of his SUV. "Let's roll."

On the drive back to ThunderStrike, he phoned his office manager. "Code red. Seven minutes out."

"Ambulance?"

"Affirmative."

As they drove the route back to ThunderStrike, Maverick checked in with his teammates again. Status reports indicated everyone was shaken up, but no one reported any injuries.

He called his office manager again. "Fifteen seconds out."

"Gate is opening."

Each of the vehicles whizzed into the parking lot and the shaky Qualitation execs were escorted into ThunderStrike's safe room.

The spacious room had two sofas, a conference table, phone and computer chargers, a cot tucked against the wall, and a television mounted on the wall, along with two private restrooms. People sat huddled on the sofa, a man rushed into the bathroom, and the woman who'd fainted lay down on the cot.

"An ambulance is on the way," Maverick said to the group.

"We're okay, but you aren't," Ella said. "I would suggest you get that gash on your hand looked at."

Maverick hadn't noticed his blood dripping on the floor. Anne entered with a roll of paper towels. Maverick unrolled several and jammed them against the wound.

"Penelope, can you help our guests get settled?" Gunner asked.

"Of course." She slid her gaze to Maverick. "Go."

"Let's get you to the hospital," Gunner said.

"Can you excuse me for a moment?" Maverick said. "Gunner, join me."

Maverick found the super glue in the break room drawer and washed his hand beneath the faucet. After drying the gash, Gunner examined Maverick's hand. "I'm not sure this'll work. I vote for stitches."

"I'm fine. Close it up."

"So stubborn." Gunner sealed the wound shut with the super glue.

"This year is kicking my ass."

"Just stop dislocating your shoulder." Gunner rubbed his own. "I'm starting to have sympathy pain."

As the two men returned to the safe room, Maverick's phone rang. The lead officer at the scene needed an update on the whereabouts of the Qualitation execs. Maverick gave her their address as Anne escorted the paramedics into the room.

"How's everyone doing?" Maverick asked Ella.

"I've got a tough crew. We appreciate you and your team for jumping into action."

"That's what we do."

Maverick addressed the group. "You've been through a lot today. Take it easy for a few days. Post-traumatic stress is common after an event like this. If that happens, please tell your healthcare professional. We're here if you want to talk."

"Thank you," Ella said and her team echoed her sentiments.

At sixteen hundred, a detective called with an update. Casualties were limited to cuts and bruises. The Qualitation building had been cleared of any explosives, but the building and courtyard were now considered a crime scene.

"I'm relieved no one was seriously hurt," Ella said. "It's all over the news."

Anne popped her head in. "Two reporters are holding. Lines one and two."

"Excuse me while I take those calls," Maverick said.

"Hott here," he said from his office.

"It's Alexandra. How are you doing?"

"All good."

"Let's see if we can reverse some of the bad press you've gotten over the past few days."

"Here's my quote: 'Qualitation hired us to protect them. Mission accomplished'."

"What specifics can you tell me about the alleged terrorist?"

"All I can tell you is ThunderStrike and the local security team worked in tandem to ensure the safety of all civilians present. Check with Metro Police for anything else."

"That's perfect. I'm glad you're okay."

"Thanks for the call." He hung up and spoke briefly with the other journalist.

At the close of the workday, Maverick and his team drove the Qualitation execs back to the building. Yellow police tape cordoned off the area. The remnants of the car lay scattered in the courtyard, on the grass, and in the parking lot. One of the giant windowpanes had fallen out and shattered glass lay strewn on the cement. Numerous law enforcement officers clustered in small groups.

Maverick spoke with the officer in charge. After explaining that these employees needed access inside to retrieve their personal belongings, they were assigned two officers.

"I'm here if you need me," Maverick said to Ella. "I'm sorry today didn't go as planned."

"Months ago, I debated whether we even needed protection. I hate to think of how today would have played out without you and your crew. Thank you." Ella and her team were escorted into the building.

Maverick shook each of his teammates' hands. "We did one hell of a job today. How's everyone doing?"

Each affirmed they were okay.

"Come to me with any concerns. Understood?"

"Thanks for listening this morning," Penelope said.

He tossed her a nod. "Always."

Gunner's lips curved. "Today is the last time I fix your dislocated shoulder. I'm a sniper, not a medic."

"But you do both so well," Penelope said with a smile.

"You do it next time," Gunner said to her.

"I hope there is no 'next time'," Maverick replied. "Drop the vehicles before heading home." They caravanned back to the office, left the SUVs, and rolled out.

Maverick slogged home in heavy rush hour traffic. As he pulled into his parking spot at the marina, Carly got out of her car. A jolt of energy shot through him. She was the perfect ending to a very stressful day.

Carrying two grocery bags, she had the sweetest smile on her beautiful face. One glance at those tight jeans and peasant top and he grinned like he'd won the fucking lottery. *She's the total package.*

"I knew you'd be hurting, so I brought you a steak. Two, actually. I'm hungry."

He took the bags, threw his good arm around her shoulder, and kissed the top of her head. "You are a perfect person. Perfect. I'm starving, cranky as hell, and my leg—"

"Yeah, I figured. You're a stubborn pigheaded man, you know that?"

He chuffed out a laugh and they ambled down the pier to his yacht.

Once onboard, she said, "Why don't you take a long, hot shower and I'll make us dinner?"

He wanted to throw his arms around her and kiss her gorgeous face, then invite her to join him, but even he knew when to throttle back. Instead, he said, "Thank you, ma'am," and headed downstairs.

Feeling refreshed after his shower, he threw on a T-shirt and shorts, and entered the galley. Carly nurtured his tormented soul simply by being there.

She extracted three giant baked potatoes from the microwave and shoved them in the oven to crisp before checking on the steaks, also in the oven. She'd tossed a salad and had poured them each a glass of sparkling water, but he popped open a bottle of beer and guzzled half down.

When they sat down to eat, she didn't ask him how his day went because she knew he didn't want to relive it. She understood his need for silence. He'd run on energy, then shifted to adrenaline. Now, he was depleted and needed to recharge.

Beyond his complimenting her on the delicious dinner and on how pretty she looked, he stayed silent. They shared a laugh when they reached for the same potato. He stroked her finger and she smiled in return.

If this wasn't love, he had no idea—*absolutely no idea*—what was. But that was the last thing he would bring up. After freezing him out for the past few days, she was there now. And he was so damn happy to see her.

When they finished eating, he collected her hands in his. "Thank you." The longer he stared into her eyes, the more alive he felt. A faint blush covered her cheeks. He wanted to kiss her, pull her into his arms, into his bed, and make love to her for hours, but reality smacked down the delicious fantasy when she tugged her hands away.

"I'm going to leave you to clean up." She pulled a gallon of mint chip ice cream from the freezer. "I bought you a treat."

"You're a saint. A beautiful, sexy, brilliant saint. Stay and have some with me."

Sadness blanketed her eyes "I can't." She curled her hands around his triceps and gave him a little squeeze. "Your mom would be proud of you. I'm sure your dad is busting."

He pulled her into his arms and held her close. "I don't want you to leave, and I'm not talking about sex. Please, stay and have a bowl of ice cream with me. If you don't, I'm going to eat the entire gallon."

Her light-hearted laughter made him smile. "I would love nothing more than that." She brushed soft fingers over his whiskered face. "But I have to go. Congratulations on today. You and your team did a kick-ass job." And with that, she dropped a soft kiss on his lips and left him, yet again.

In bare feet, he hurried down the pier to make sure she got safely into her car. "Text me when you get home."

With a quick nod, she hopped in, started the engine, and drove way.

"Time to lock that woman down and make her mine."

CARLY'S DISCOVERY

The media heralded Monday's gig, "Another Heroic Effort by ThunderStrike". Maverick preferred flying below the radar, but in light of the recent fallout from the senate hearing, he welcomed the accolades. They'd put an end to the calls from concerned clients doubting ThunderStrike's viability.

Wednesday, zero nine hundred. Maverick and Penelope finished reviewing current assignments. Two teams were out on local protection jobs. Five were overseas. Maverick hadn't heard from one of them and was about to make a call when his phone rang.

"Hmm, a blocked number." He flicked his gaze back to Penelope. "Call the team lead and confirm their whereabouts."

"I'm on it." Penelope left.

Maverick answered. "Hott here."

"Good morning, Maverick. George Internado, here. How are things going?"

"What can I do for you, George?" Maverick kept his tone curt.

"Several months ago, I introduced you to a number of key players. They've let me know they're concerned about your cockiness and rogue behavior. Quite frankly, so am I. They don't want to do business with a maverick, Maverick." Internado chuckled. "I've been reviewing the investigative report. To be honest, things look bleak, so I'm extending you an olive branch."

Acid churned in his gut. "Go on."

"Are you familiar with the Watergate steps?" Internado continued.

Those are on my Ironman training route. "The ones on Ohio Drive that butt up against the Potomac?"

"Yes." Internado cleared his throat. "Meet me there tonight... say...eleven thirty."

Maverick fisted his hand. "Why?"

"Poor decisions have consequences. Save yourself, boy."

"I'm not your *boy*. And I'm not some pawn you can manipulate for your own gain."

Neither of them spoke for several tense seconds.

"You're making a grave mistake," Internado said. "I'm going to bury you alive at Friday's hearing." The line went dead.

"Not unless I bury you first," Maverick said, anger coursing through his veins. He high-tailed it down the hallway. First stop, Penelope's office. She was on the phone.

"Hold on," she said before addressing Maverick. "The team ran into a snag, but we're working through it."

"Good job." Next stop, Gunner's office. His second-in-command looked up from his computer and waved him in.

"The doctor is in. What's out of joint today?"

"I need to leave for a few. Can you handle things here?"

"Of course." Gunner paused. "What's going on?"

"Internado's putting the squeeze on me."

"That can't be good."

"No, it's not."

"Do what you gotta do," Gunner said.

Once in his Porsche, Maverick tapped impatiently on the steering wheel while the security gate slowly clanked and squeaked open. *I have got to get a new gate.*

On the way to Stone Investigations, he made a quick stop at a nearby shop. With a surprise in hand, he strode into Carly's office. Desiree peered up at him with the saddest eyes. "Hey." She couldn't even muster a smile.

"What's wrong?"

She leaned over the reception counter. "We have to move out."

Maverick's mouth dropped open. "When did this happen?"

"Carly found out Saturday when she had dinner with her parents. She's been working nonstop with a realtor." His sister's shoulders sagged. "Friday is my last day."

Maverick's brain stuttered. *Why the hell didn't Carly tell me?* "How can I help?"

Desiree's expression perked up. "You are such a sweetheart. I told Hudson I'd help him manage the restaurant. He didn't argue because he's struggling."

Heat infused him and he loosened his tie. "Why am I just now hearing about all of this?"

The front door opened and Carly's older sister bounded in like she owned the place. Maverick's chest tightened. For as much as he adored Carly, he detested Cassie. The two sisters couldn't be more different, both in appearance and in behavior. At five feet eight, Carly was all curves, a natural beauty, and a competitive athlete. Cassie was rail thin, her platinum blonde hair plastered in hairspray. She dressed in high-end designer suits and always wore too much makeup. Despite being just three years older than Carly, thirty-six-year-old Cassie looked like she'd had a facelift. Her skin was stretched so tightly across her cheeks and forehead it pained him to look at her.

As much as Carly was emotionally guarded, Cassie was on a never-ending romantic rollercoaster having just divorced her third husband. These two women were polar opposites in every conceivable way. But none of that would matter if Cassie weren't such a bitch toward her sister.

Trailing after her was a slight man pecking madly on a tablet.

Cassie hitched her eyebrow and shot Maverick a sly smile. "I haven't seen you in a while, Ashton. You're looking hot, with one 't.'" She sauntered close. "Still keeping up your reputation as a D.C. playboy?"

Not anymore. He doubted Cassie's visit was a social one. "Hey, Cassie, what brings you by?"

"Business. And my name is Cassandra." She turned to the man with her. "Let's start in the kitchenette. It's nasty and outdated." She squared her shoulders before parading forward.

Maverick turned to his sister. "What was that all about?"

"It's bad," Desiree said, tracking Cassie as she disappeared into the break room.

The front door opened and Carly breezed inside. She'd thrown her hair into a messy updo and wore a simple brown dress with a black belt. Her beauty stole his breath and, for a split second, he forgot why he was there.

"There she is," he said.

"Hi." Her smile made his day. Always did.

"I need to talk—"

When Cassie flew into reception, surprise flashed in Carly's eyes. "What are you doing here?"

Cassie raised her chin and peered down her nose at Carly. "Mom is the new landlord."

"I know." Carly dropped her handbag on the reception counter. "I've got to be out of here by the end of next week. There's a new tenant moving in who's paying Mom a small fortune. I can't afford rent that steep."

"You could, if you were doing as well as me." Cassie's conceited tone turned Maverick's stomach. "Which is why I'm here. *I'm the new tenant. Cassandra Stone, Family Law. Sounds great, right?"

What the fucking fuck?

Carly's eyes grew cold. "I see." She eyed the man cowering behind Cassie.

"This is my architect. I'm redesigning." Her upper lip curled as she eyed the space. "There's no way I can work in this shithole. It's bad for my aura." She batted her lashes at Maverick. "Mine is bright yellow. Sunshine yellow, to be exact, and I've got to do everything possible to ensure it stays dazzling bright."

This chick is loco.

Still, no response from Carly.

"I know Mom gave you until the end of next week, but could you be out by Friday?" Cassie continued. "Two days is plenty. I mean, according to Mom, you're not busy, plus, she said something about you meeting clients in the park." She snickered. "What a joke."

"Cassie, I—" She cleared her throat. "Consider it done."

What a sweetheart. Her family doesn't deserve her.

Her sister stomped the floor. "Stop calling me Cassie! I'm not a child. My name is *Cassandra*." Her phone buzzed and she yanked it from her gigantic handbag. "Hello. Let me call you right back." She hung up. "I'm a busy, busy gal. Clients galore. Gotta run."

Cassie sashayed up to Maverick. "My number is on my website. Cassandra Stone, Family Law. We should hook up sometime." She flounced out, her architect scurrying behind her.

When the door banged shut, Maverick fully expected Carly to blow. He would have if one of his siblings had pulled that crap on him.

Instead, Carly smiled at Desiree. "Any calls?"

A total pro.

"Are you okay?" Desiree asked.

Carly shouldered her handbag. "It is what it is, right?"

"Your messages are on your desk."

"Thanks." She slid her gaze to Maverick. "I'll leave you two to catch up."

"I came here to talk to you."

As she headed toward her office, she waved him over. "Come on back." They entered her small office and she closed her door.

"This eviction has hijacked my world." She eased down onto the rickety wooden desk chair. "How are you doing?"

He took a seat in one of the guest chairs across from her. "I wish you'd said something to me."

"Ash, I told you plenty. Plus, you've got your own stuff going on."

"Have you found anything?"

"Nothing I can afford. I'm going to work from home and meet clients at a shared office space in Arlington."

"I'm sorry your mom is kicking you out. I know this place is special to you."

"I was worried about Desiree, but Hudson jumped at her offer."

"My sister's pretty resourceful."

"I was told I had until the end of the month, but, you heard the latest. It's probably better anyway. The less I see of my family, the happier I am."

Even as a kid, Maverick had never liked Carly's family. "I know that, babe. What can I do to help?"

"Thanks for offering. I'm okay."

"What are you doing with the furniture?"

"This desk is all I care about keeping. It was Grandpa Pierce's, plus, it's an antique and so beautiful." She ran her fingers over the weathered cherry grain.

"I'll grab Hudson and we'll move it out tomorrow."

When she smiled, her eyes crinkled in that way he loved. "Thank you…so much." She relaxed back and he forced himself *not* to check out how nicely the dress clung to her. "So, what brings you over?"

"I need you."

She hitched a brow.

"Your help. I need your help."

"Another background check?"

"Not this time. I could use your counsel. Internado wants me to meet him at the Watergate steps, tonight at eleven thirty."

"Good grief. What on earth for?"

"He didn't say. I'm guessing he didn't like my refusal to spy on his opponent in the governor's race. What I do know is that if I don't help him, I don't stand a chance at Friday's hearing. I'm concerned about my company. I've got payroll obligations to meet. I've got staff with families to feed."

"Hmm." While thinking, she fiddled with her stack rings. She planted her palms on the desk and stared into his eyes. "You're making the right choice. If you go there tonight, he owns you going forward."

"That's the confirmation I needed to hear."

Pushing out of her chair, she rounded the desk and sat beside him. Their knees brushed until she crossed her legs. His chest warmed. She was close enough to take her hand or cup the back of her neck and pull her close for a kiss.

"Okay, Ash. Why don't you tell me why you're *really* here? Unless something changed, you have an executive team you can talk to."

"I'm not dragging them into this. The fewer people who know the details about this, the better. I trust you."

She patted his thigh. "Thank you. And?"

"And what?"

"You could've called me."

He pulled the ring box from his suit pocket. "I bought you a little something."

Her eyes grew large. "It's not my birthday."

"I know."

"What's this for?"

"I miss you...*a lot*. I think what happened between us was a good thing. But you've been distant ever since."

She opened her mouth and he held up his hand. "You made me dinner Monday, but wouldn't stay for ice cream. That's our thing.

We *always* share a bowl. Look, if you don't want to be with me, that's okay. Actually, it's not." He opened the box. "It's the stackable diamond band you've been admiring for months. As corny as this sounds, it's a friendship ring. I want us to move forward, but backwards is better than losing you."

Her eyes grew moist. "Oh, wow. It's beautiful. Thank you, Ash."

He slid the gift onto her middle finger with all her other rings, then pushed out of his chair. "Think about what I said."

She jumped up, threw her arms around him, and kissed him full on. He held her like she belonged there. Because she did, dammit. Why the hell couldn't she see that?

"My heart is pounding so fast right now," she murmured.

With a smirk, he asked, "Can I feel it?"

She laughed as Desiree tapped on the door, then popped her head inside. Her gaze flitted from one to the other, then she grinned. "Your appointment is here."

Carly nodded. "I'll be right out."

Desiree shut the door.

He dropped a swoon-worthy kiss on her lips. "See you tomorrow, Carly girl."

Before Carly greeted her client, she caressed her lower lip, savoring the feeling of Ashton's mouth on hers. His delicious scent lingered in the air while her heart thumped out of her chest.

Just because she didn't talk about her feelings didn't mean she didn't have any. When it came to Ashton, she had plenty. She adored him. Craved him. Needed him. Loved the hell out of him. Not just as a friend, but as a man. But, she had *everything* to lose and nothing to gain if things didn't work out between them.

I love you so much, Ashton, and I'm flat-out terrified.

. . .

AT THE END of the workday, she leaned against the reception counter, her stomach tied in knots. She never imagined this day would come. "Hey."

Desiree was powering her computer down. "Ash said he and Hudson are moving you out tomorrow."

She nodded. "Since I'll be working from home starting tomorrow, today's your last day, but I'll pay you for Thursday and Friday, plus all the vacation you've accrued."

"This sucks."

"Yeah, it does. I've loved working with you."

"I'll miss seeing you everyday, but I won't miss the mice."

"Me either."

"I never told you this, but I almost declined your job offer," Desiree said.

"Why?"

"I worried that working together might hurt our friendship if things didn't work out. I mean, we're practically sisters."

That made Carly smile. "We are. So, how'd you get past it?"

"Ash reminded me that you're levelheaded, super smart, and that I'd learn a lot from you." She twirled a strand of bright pink hair around her finger. "Per usual, he was right. Now, I can pay that forward at Hudson's."

"I'm grateful he encouraged you to work here. Working with you has been one of the best parts of my job."

"Me, too. I'm soooo glad I trusted him." With a sly smile, Desiree rounded her desk. "You should, too." In a whoosh of pink-streaked blonde hair, Desiree hugged her, then hurried out, leaving Carly alone with her thoughts.

THE FOLLOWING DAY, Maverick threw open the door to Stone Investigations cradling two large moving blankets under his arm. He dropped them and opened his arms. "Gimme a Hott hug, baby."

Laughing, she complied. His arms blanketed her and she melted into his strong body. "You're in a good mood."

"It's a great day to be alive."

Hudson bounded in holding a half-eaten cookie from the bakery next door. "Behold, the cookie." He took a bite. "Yum."

Carly led them into her office.

"That looks really old," Hudson said. "You should buy a new one."

"It was my grandfather's."

"So?" Hudson bit off a chocolate chunk.

"It has sentimental value."

He shrugged.

"It's an *antique*, Hudson," Maverick explained. "Vintage."

"Okie dokie." Hudson circled the desk. "No way will that fit through the door."

Kneeling, Maverick examined the underside. "If we remove the top, we can carry out the pedestals and the top in sections." He slapped Hudson's back. "Nice job, my man."

Hudson grinned. "The power of the cookie. My God, I love sugar."

Laughing, Carly got busy unscrewing the top of the desk. Once separated, the guys leaned it against the wall.

"Hey, lookie here, a secret compartment," Hudson said peering inside. "There's something in there."

With the top removed, the right side of the antique desk revealed a hollow corner that, when pulled out, was large enough to store file folders.

"Did you know about that?" Maverick asked.

"No," Carly said as she slipped her hand inside.

Hudson grabbed her arm. "Spiders!"

Squealing, Carly yanked her hand out. Hudson started laughing and she punched him in the shoulder.

"Still afraid of spiders," Hudson said when he'd stopped laughing.

"I'm gonna get you back when you least expect it." After giving him a playful glare, she slid her hand into the hollow space and extracted a large white envelope with a string closure tied into a neat figure eight. There was no writing on either side.

"Oooh, cool," Hudson said. "Maybe your grandpa stashed a wad of cash in there and I'll get a finder's fee."

"I had no idea this was here."

"Open it." Hudson popped the last morsel into his mouth.

Carly unwound the string and peered inside before showing him. "Sorry to disappoint, Hudson. No money."

He scrunched up his face. "Just a bunch of papers. Bummer."

Carly stashed the folder in her computer bag while the guys wrapped both pedestals and carried out the desk in sections. After loading Hudson's truck, they followed her home.

Hands on hips, Maverick surveyed her living room. "Where are we setting it up?"

Carly glanced around. "I didn't realize how large the desk is and how small my house is."

"What about the lower level? It would make a great addition next to the pool table, or even in that far corner," Maverick said with a wink.

As they gazed into each other's eyes, Carly imagined them on the cherry desktop, him beneath her, while they connected in the most intimate of ways. The longer they stared the harder her heart pounded.

"Hellooooooo," Hudson said.

Carly blinked. "I'm sorry, what?"

Hudson chuckled. "You two are pathetic. The desk?"

"I'll make room here." She slid the Ficus tree out of the way.

The guys moved the pedestals into place and Maverick set the desktop over both. As he secured the pieces together, Hudson opened the secret compartment.

"Now that you know about this, you can stash all sorts of goodies in here. But you better shine a flashlight before you go sticking your fingers inside." He waggled his brows. "Spiders, Carly, *spi-ders.*" His playful expression made her laugh. "This has got to be the coolest thing I've ever seen." He slid the desk door closed. "Sorry to bolt, but I've gotta get to work."

"Thanks for helping me." She walked them outside. "Dinner's on me."

"Come to the restaurant and dinner is *my* treat." Hudson jumped into the truck, started the engine, and rolled down the window. "I hope those secret papers lead to a buried treasure."

Maverick stepped close and peered into her eyes. "I'll take you up on that dinner."

She stroked his arm, her fingers trailing down his bulging triceps. "Deal."

"My hearing is at nine thirty tomorrow. Will you be there?"

"Of course I will," she said, offering a reassuring smile.

Hudson laid on his horn. "Either get a room or get in the truck."

Maverick hopped in and shot her a smile that made her heart skip a beat.

Returning inside, Carly pulled the white envelope from her computer bag and laid the contents on the kitchen table. In all the years she'd worked with her grandfather, he never kept professional secrets. After sifting through the loose papers, she found his familiar-looking case summary sheet. At the top, he'd written:

JOE CLARK

Pierce Stone always posed as life insurance investigator Joe Clark when he didn't want people to know he was a private eye. Per usual, Grandpa Pierce's notes were sparse.

Client Alice Murphy, 67. Raised child as daughter. Erin Murphy, 39.
Aunt, not mother (murdered, CC). Has Alz. Wants Erin to know.
KILLER?

From what Carly could deduce, Erin Murphy's biological mother had been murdered and Erin's aunt, Alice Murphy, had raised her, but never told Erin the truth. Alice Murphy, who suffered from Alzheimer's, wanted her daughter to know the truth and this cold case solved. Alice Murphy had hired her grandfather to find her sister's killer.

She opened her laptop and searched his online files. This case had never been logged.

The front door opened. Her roommate bounded into the kitchen and screamed, then clutched her chest. "I about had a heart attack. What are you doing here?"

"You didn't see my car out front?"

"I didn't notice. I have a short story due tomorrow that I haven't even started. I was lost in thought. Hey, are you working from home?"

"Sure am."

"Yay, I'd love the company." Tabitha dropped her satchel on the table. "My imagination has shriveled up like a raisin." She snort-laughed. "Hey, that's good." Yanking a notebook from her backpack, she scribbled it down, then peered at the papers strewn on the table. "Client Alice Murphy, raised child as daughter. Aunt, not mother...Killer." Her eyes grew large. "Killer? Whoa, this is some serious stuff."

Carly crammed the papers back into the envelope.

"That would make one hell of a story!"

Oh, God, no. "You can't use this."

"No worries. I write fiction." Tabitha snatched an apple from the fridge. "I'll be working in my bedroom."

Never having run into this type of challenge before, Carly nibbled the inside of her lip. *I don't have an office and I can't work from here. I could ask her to move out. Then, I wouldn't have anyone snooping over my shoulder, but I'd lose her rent money. And I really need that extra cash.*

Her phone rang and she fished it from her handbag. "Hey, Cassie."

"Would it kill you to call me Cassandra?"

Carly rolled her eyes. "What's up?"

"Just confirming you'll be out of the office tomorrow."

"I moved out today. The space is yours."

Her sister popped her gum. "When were you planning on telling me?"

"I moved out ahead of schedule, so you're welcome."

"I'm not thanking you for doing something you were expected to do. I need the key."

"I'm working from home. Swing by and pick it up."

"I can't even remember where you live."

"Fine, whatever. I'll drop it by." She was anxious to put the move behind her, plus, she could tell her sister about all the office issues she'd been dealing with. After sliding the envelope into her handbag, she left.

The main lot of Cassie's condo complex was full, so she pulled around back and parked. Her sister emerged from the building and their mom's boyfriend, Ross, jogged over, pulled Cassie into his arms, and planted one on her.

Carly's mouth dropped. "Oh, my God. No way." *Mom is getting screwed in more ways than one.*

Arm in arm, the lovebirds hurried inside. Carly hung back a few. When she tapped on Cassie's door, her sister didn't answer, so she knocked harder.

A long moment passed before Cassie cracked the door open revealing flushed cheeks and disheveled hair. She thrust out her hand. "Give it."

"I drove all the way over here. Aren't you going to invite me in?"

Her sister grimaced, then jumped and yelped as if someone had pinched her ass. Carly didn't see Ross, but she heard him breathing behind the door. "I'm in the middle of something."

As soon as Carly dropped the key into her palm, Cassie slammed the door in her face. *She's busy, all right, but not with clients.* As she slipped on her shades and exited the building, Carly laughed out loud.

Had her sister invited her inside, she would have told her about the rodents, the updated surveillance system, *and* the problem with the back door sticking...to name a few. Per usual, she'd just gotten the royal bitch treatment, so Cassie could complain to her new landlord. *And while you're at it, you can compare notes about your sleazy, two-timing boyfriend.*

As Carly drove away, she glanced at her sparkly new stack ring.

Ashton is the best man I have ever known. I've gotta put my heart out there and take a chance. If I don't, I'll spend the rest of my life regretting it.

15

THE HEARING, ROUND TWO

F riday morning, round two of the senate hearing. Maverick held his head high, but his guts were in knots. *Execution day.* The crowd of spectators and media hovered like vultures outside the Dirksen Building. *How the hell am I supposed to get in?* Maverick's cell phone rang. Sinclair. "This is a madhouse."

"What did you expect?" Sinclair replied, the grogginess in his voice a sure sign he'd gotten little sleep. "You're innocent and about to be crucified. I'll get you into the building. I'm around the corner."

Maverick slid inside the town car. The chauffeur dropped them at the rear of the building. Free of the media, the two men sailed inside.

"Hang tight." After Sinclair spoke with a security guard, he returned with two badges and they were waved through.

Maverick couldn't help but smile. "You have the magic touch."

Sinclair shot him a wicked smile. "Black magic."

As they made their way down the corridor, Maverick asked, "How is it that you don't need an escort?"

"These aren't the droids you're looking for works every damn time."

In spite of the anxiety in the pit of his stomach, Maverick chuffed out a laugh.

They turned a corner and Sinclair slowed. "Let's take the Capitol Subway."

Once seated on the electric monorail that connected the Capitol Building to the senate offices, Maverick said, "Internado will be ruthless."

"Agreed, but once the gavel comes down, the *real* fun starts. He's messing with the wrong family," Sinclair said as the train rolled forward.

Someone tapped on the acrylic window and both men turned around. Two women sitting in the boxcar behind them were grinning. "I recognize you," one of them said to Maverick. "You're the guy who saved all those hostages."

Maverick shot them a smile. "How're you ladies doin' this morning?"

"We're good," said the second.

"Who's your friend?" asked the first.

"This is my brother."

"Oh, God, two from the same family." She homed in on Sinclair. "Are you on social media?"

"Not if I can help it," replied Sinclair, though his lips twitched in amusement.

"Have a good one," Maverick said before facing forward.

"What's wrong?" Sinclair asked. "You're usually full of bravado."

"I thought you'd want a turn."

"I'm not the showman. You are."

"Carly's got me by the balls."

"*More* sex?"

"No. She's freezing me out."

"She needs a helpful nudge in the right direction." The monorail slowed and Sinclair stood. "Leave that to me."

Maverick rose. "Carly won't fall for your Jedi mind games."

Sinclair flashed a devilish smile. "We'll see about that."

"Bye, boys," said one of the women.

"Be good, ladies," Maverick said as he and Sinclair exited the subway.

"I need to speak with someone, so follow this hallway to the end," Sinclair said. "Turn left and take the third door on the right. No badge needed. I'll see you in there."

Maverick found himself in the back of the hearing room and made his way to the table.

The same intern zipped over. "Good to see you, Mr. Hott." After pouring Maverick a glass of water, he flipped on the mic.

The committee members filed in. Now that Maverick had seen the *real* Internado, he knew that every other government official staring down at him was an irrelevant player. With his jaw set in a hard line, Maverick eyed the group.

Internado struck his gavel. "I call this hearing to order. This Senate Select Committee hearing is a continuation of our investigation into a recent mission undertaken by ThunderStrike, code named 'The Twelve.'" Internado glared at Maverick. "Good morning, Mr. Hott."

"Good morning," Maverick replied, stone faced.

"Mr. Hott, the committee would like to acknowledge the good press you've received of late, especially with respect to your stopping the bomber who targeted Qualitation. Once again, the media labeled you an American hero." The senator gazed around the room. "Unfortunately for you, government contracts are not awarded based on popularity contests."

A light wave of laughter washed over the room. "It is the committee's finding that you acted recklessly and in a way that was contrary to the government's interest and agenda during the mission known as 'The Twelve.'" As if punctuating his point with a pregnant pause, the senator sipped his water.

Bracing for the inevitable, Maverick steeled his spine.

"We've instructed all federal contracting officers to issue stop-work orders for all of your government contracts and to disqualify you for future awards." With a smug expression, he added, "I suspect this action will also have a negative impact on your commercial business. Going forward, it's the committee's hope that you will follow the letter of the law and not behave like the maverick you believe yourself to be."

Murmuring voices filled the packed room. Internado was throwing his authority around unchecked and Maverick was powerless to stop him.

The senator's chilling smile soured his stomach. "Do you have anything to say for yourself? Please, the floor is yours."

He glared at Internado. "The truth will come out."

"This hearing is adjourned." With the smack of a gavel, George Internado had all but shut down ThunderStrike.

Decades of tamped down anger billowed to the surface and Maverick gritted his teeth to keep from exploding in a blind rage. The senator's words, "I'm going to bury you alive," echoed in his head.

I am so screwed. He couldn't save his mother, so he'd dedicated his life to rescuing others. No way would he roll over and play dead to a bunch of out-of-touch politicians who ruled from an ivory tower.

As he inched his way toward the door, he spotted Sinclair in the back row. His brother's lips curved into a sinister grin. Sinclair fought dirty. His brother lived for revenge and would relish tearing George Internado down. He, on the other hand, did not.

In the corridor, a wall of reporters pounced. Maverick forced a smile and offered a few prepared statements. But inside, he was seething.

Carly waited off to the side, her lips set in a thin line, her eyes narrowed. Sinclair approached, thanked the press for their support, then took Maverick by the arm and led him away. Reporters shouted questions as Carly fell in line. To elude the press, they ducked down a hallway and escaped out a side entrance. Their sunglasses filtered out the hazy autumn sunshine.

"Was that a load of bullshit?" Maverick growled.

"Internado is a spectacle," she replied, her voice tight.

Sinclair patted his brother on the back. "Ready to have some fun?" He ushered them into his waiting sedan. "I've been biding my time for a reason to take him down. That day has come."

Sin's chauffeur dropped them at Maverick's vehicle.

"Meet me at my office," Sinclair said. "Use my code and park in the small gated lot behind the building."

Dazed, Maverick drove toward Georgetown, consumed by contempt.

At a red light, Carly caressed his arm. "We'll get through this. We've gotten through much, much worse, Ash. This is a blip."

While he appreciated her encouraging smile, he couldn't return one of his own. The light turned green and anger fueled him forward. His phone rang. Gunner.

"He crucified us," Maverick bit out.

"Penelope is with me," Gunner said. "We figured it was bad. Clients are bailing, big time."

"Are you coming back to the office?" Penelope asked.

"I'm meeting with Sinclair first."

"Oh, God." Penelope groaned. "We're playing dirty."

"We'll see what he comes up with. I'll be there ASAP." He hung up. "Penelope's right. I'm not sure I want to go there."

"Flinging mud used to be one of your favorite things to do," Carly said. "It'll be just like old times."

"That's because I was playing with *you*."

"You still are." Even her sweet smile couldn't quiet his fury.

Maverick parked in Sinclair's private lot. In silence, they walked into the office building that bore his name.

DEVELIN

Sinclair's crisis management firm occupied the entire top floor.

"Hold all calls," Sinclair said to his assistant before shutting the door to his corner office overlooking M Street in Georgetown. A conspiratorial smile filled his face as he eased into his executive chair. "Here we go."

Carly perched on the edge of a guest chair while Maverick gripped the back of the other. "Tell us what you know," he said.

"Internado's cheating on his wife—the one he made a public fuss over reconciling with—only, this time, he's gotten smarter about not getting caught. Instead of screwing his office staff or propositioning any attractive woman who gets within three feet of him, he's gone underground. There's chatter he's playing in a very exclusive, very discreet group. Everyone is hard-core. Masks and aliases are required. The onboarding process is lengthy."

Maverick scraped his fingers over his whiskered cheeks.

"Infiltrate the group and capture video of him," Sin continued. "Now *you* have the power. He's days from announcing his run for Governor *and* he's favored to win. Threaten to throw a monkey wrench into his campaign by going public with the video and he'll fly right."

"I stoop to his level and, what—blackmail him into reversing the committee's findings?"

"That hearing was theater. Internado pulled some nasty shit to throw you under the bus. If an X-rated video of him at a kink club went viral, he would be forced to drop out of the race. Possibly even resign his current position. His career means *everything* to him, Ash."

"I see." Shaking his head, Maverick pushed off the chair.

Sinclair's gaze hovered on Carly before shifting back to his brother. "Why aren't you fired up?"

"There's gotta be another way."

"There isn't. He's been running amok for decades. No one gets a free pass for this long."

Maverick respected the rules. He believed honesty was the *only* way.

"If you don't get the upper hand, your career is finished," Carly said.

He stared into her eyes, alight with energy. "You know I don't fight dirty."

She hitched her brow. "Maybe it's time you did."

"Carly's right," Sinclair said. "He's leaving you no choice. You do nothing, he destroys your company. You'll have to let your employees go. Families will suffer. Your clients will, too. What about future hostages ThunderStrike can't rescue? What happens to them?"

His clenched his hands. "Dammit."

Tense silence hung in the air.

"Or you fight back," Sinclair said. "And you show him who's *really* running the show."

If I do nothing, he wins and everyone else suffers. The truth has got to come out. Steeling his spine, Maverick slid his gaze from Sinclair to Carly. "I'll do it."

Sinclair made a call. "Greta, Sin. How are you, beautiful? I have a couple,"—Carly shot to attention—"who are close friends of mine. They're very discreet, very private, and they're ready to take their kink to the next level."

Carly stared at Maverick, intensity pouring from her.

"She was a Top. Now she's a Switch." As Sinclair listened, his eyebrow arched ever so slightly as his attention shifted from Maverick to Carly. "Exhibitionism."

She whipped her head toward Sinclair. "Oh, God."

"They're searching for something unique," Sinclair explained. "If they become members, it'll be my gift to them." He shot them a devilish smile. "They're newlyweds. Mr. and Mrs. Black."

16

MR. AND MRS. BLACK

Carly's stomach flipped while her pulse took off. She couldn't wait to play with Ashton again, but there was no way—*no way*—she could pretend to be his wife. She couldn't fake it with the only man she'd ever loved. When the ruse ended, her heart would shatter.

Propping her hands on her hips, she glared at Sinclair. "What the hell was that?"

"How's he supposed to get this done without you?"

"How much do I owe you?" Ash quipped.

Carly flicked her gaze to him. "Didn't you hear what he just did?"

"I did."

"You don't owe me anything," Sinclair replied. "Greta will bill me the hundred grand if she invites you into her inner sanctum and you accept. If you get what you need before that, I keep my dinero."

Carly whistled. "Welcome to the big leagues of kink."

"Ash needs you," Sinclair said. "You're the player *and* the private eye. How's he supposed to sleuth around on his own? He's got to participate or they'll become suspicious. This club isn't for voyeurs. It's for *players*."

Hugging herself, Carly shook her head. "I can't do the marriage thing."

"Too late now," Sinclair said. "You have an easy excuse as to why you're exclusive. You're crazy in love and only play with each other."

"You can't fake being hitched to me?" Ashton asked. "I'm kinda insulted."

"Okay, you two, you have a lot of work to do before tonight," Sinclair said.

"*Tonight?*" Carly and Ashton replied in unison.

"Greta does Meet-and-Greets every other Friday. You can't sit on this for two weeks." Sinclair texted them the address. "It's in the ritzy neighborhood of Lincoln Park, on East Capitol Street. Greta will invite you to have a drink with her, so create an airtight story. Make it simple. If she likes you, she'll ask you back or she might invite you upstairs to play. Be prepared. Keep in mind, hers is a tight-knit group. Word has it, the senator is one of them."

"Thanks for your help," Ashton said. "This had better work."

"I believe in you." Sinclair walked around his desk and gripped his shoulder. "*Together,* you two are unstoppable."

"Down the rabbit hole we go," Carly said. "Do you own a mask, Ash?"

"No."

"Take anything you need from my store at the club." Sinclair handed Carly a key to Uninhibited. "This is my spare, so I'll get it back from you whenever."

They walked the two blocks to Uninhibited and went into the boutique. As she browsed the masks, Ashton moseyed around. Sinclair stocked everything from masks, play costumes, and hand-held sex toys to specialty items like sex chairs and a sex machine.

She found him eyeing the sex machine. "This looks barbaric," he said.

"There's something for everyone in the world of kink."

"As long as you're *mine*, you won't need a contraption like this."

Her heart fluttered as they stared into each other's eyes. *I'm sure I won't.* They had a lot to do and little time, so she shoved down the butterflies and selected two black masquerade masks. One was a simple eye mask; the second would conceal three quarters of his face.

"How am I going to kiss you in that thing?"

"What's kissing got to do with this?"

"If we're having sex, there's kissing."

"Sex is our cover for sleuthing, Ash. Internado *cannot* recognize you."

"Right."

Sex with Ash. Eyeing his scruffy face and wild head of hair, her insides tightened in anticipation. "You'll need to wear a wig."

His boisterous laugh made her smile. "Are you kidding me?"

"No."

They left with the masks. While he weaved his way out of Georgetown, she ran through a mental checklist.

"You're quiet," he said, crashing in on her thoughts.

"We've got to get our story straight. I have to put a tracker on Internado's car. If he does play at Greta's, we'll need to bring the right kind of surveillance devices. I've got a camera watch, but my camera glasses won't work with the masks."

He placed his hand on her thigh. "Whoa, baby, slow down."

Heat ripped through her like wildfire. Going forward, they were a committed, married couple…in love. She stared out the window as he drove over Key Bridge into Virginia. *How am I going to manage through this?*

"We won't be able to strategize at my house if my roommate's home. She'll be salivating for details if she hears about our fake marriage at a hardcore kink club."

"What's going on with her?"

"Writer's block," she said as he parked on the slab beside her Acura. "That's her car on the street."

"I've got to swing by the office. Pack some clothing and I'll meet you at my place."

"What for?"

"Married couples live together."

She barked out a laugh. "Don't you think you're taking this pretend marriage a little too far?"

"No. I have no idea if this Greta woman will quiz us on which side of the bed we sleep on or who makes dinner on Tuesdays."

"It's a sex club, Ash, not a game show."

"You just said you can't work here. You've got the yacht to yourself on weekdays. Plus, I have a top-secret clearance. Your secrets are safe with me." He held up three fingers. "Scouts honor."

She fiddled her stack rings. "I don't know about this."

"Carly, I've got payroll obligations to meet and ThunderStrike isn't flush with cash. I have one pay period, maybe two, before I have to start letting people go. I'm offering you a paid gig. Don't let me down."

She stared into his eyes while the air grew thick with sensual tension. How could she desert him when he needed her...again? With so much at stake, she wouldn't refuse him. "I'll help you, but I won't take your money."

His relieved smile melted her. "Thank you. But I am paying you and you are *not* going to argue with me. If you get to the marina first, make yourself at home. You know where I hide my spare key."

"I do." She opened the car door and turned back to him. "I won't let you down."

"You never do."

Convincing everyone she was in love with him would be easy. Convincing herself it was just an act would be impossible.

Maverick stood before his staff, determined to bolster their spirits. "Today we suffered a tough blow, but we aren't giving up. I know you're anxious and worried about job security. Trust me to do my job of reversing the committee's decision. We'll overcome this challenge like we've overcome past ones. In the meantime, it's business as usual."

In truth, his world was imploding.

He answered questions as best he could without divulging his plan. Then, he gave his team the rest of the afternoon off.

On the way to his car, he called his dad. "Are you at home?"

"I will be in ten."

"Got a few minutes for me?"

"Always. C'mon by."

Fifteen minutes later, Maverick entered his childhood home, a two-story colonial in Fairfax. He found his dad pouring two iced teas in the kitchen.

"Did you work today?" Maverick sunk down on a cushioned stool at the center island.

His father, retired from his career as D.C.'s chief prosecutor, ran his own legal practice. "I had some details to iron out for Mom's annual charity tournament." He furrowed his brow, studied his son's face. "Things didn't go well at the hearing, did they?"

Maverick shook his head before chugging down the cold beverage. "No, but I'm going to fight to keep my business alive."

"I have every confidence you'll succeed. I'm here if you need my help." His dad took a long drink. "Is that what brings you by?"

"Carly agreed to work on a case with me. It requires we pose as a married couple."

Warren seated himself on a counter stool. "Is that a problem for you?"

"We have to get really close in order to pull this off."

"I can't think of anyone better suited to help you."

Maverick stayed silent.

"Ashton, does this fake marriage include real feelings?"

He paused for a few seconds. "Yeah."

"And that makes you feel vulnerable?"

"When the gig ends, we'll go back to being buddies."

"Why does it have to end?"

"Just thinking about giving my heart away, even to her, terrifies me. Keeping her in the friend zone is a safer choice. This way, I'll never lose her."

"I see." His dad's gaze hit the floor and the room grew quiet. Then, he regarded his son. "When I wake in the middle of the night, I reach for your mom. A few blissful seconds pass before I remember she's gone. The emptiness never goes away. But I wouldn't give up the years we had to avoid the heartache. If fear of losing your mom had kept me from marrying her, I would never have experienced deep, meaningful love. I wouldn't have you guys." He leaned back, a fatherly smile crinkled his lined face. "Don't let the love of your life get away because you're afraid you'll lose her. One day, you will. Hopefully, you'll both have lived a long and happy life together." He drank down more of the tea. "Ever since high school, women have chosen you. You'll be *much* happier if *you* choose your life partner. And if you're being honest with yourself, you'll admit you chose her a long time ago."

Silence while Maverick absorbed the weight of his dad's words. "You tell it like it is."

"I have to with you, Ash." His father stood. "Back in a second."

He's right. I've loved her for years.

A moment later, his dad placed two silver wedding bands on the center island. "You'll need these." His dad smiled. "Props, of course."

"But they're yours and Mom's."

"Mom adored Carly. I'm confident she'd agree with me on this one. Take the rings, son."

Maverick slid them into his pocket. "Thank you, Dad."

Warren walked his son to his car and gave him a hug. "Now, go and pretend propose to your real true love."

Maverick drove home inspired. He would do whatever it took to get his life back on track. And that included a fake marriage that appeared so genuine, even Carly would see how right they were together.

He found her cutting vegetables while chicken sautéed on the stovetop. Wearing shorts and a T-shirt, her hair in a ponytail, she looked like she belonged there.

"There's my wife." He popped a sliced cucumber into his mouth.

A tight knot occupied the small space between her eyebrows. "Hey." She rinsed the cherry tomatoes before dropping them into the salad.

"What's going on?"

"Nothing." She refused to look at him.

"That chicken smells fantastic. I'm *starving*."

That elicited a brief smile. "You're *always* starving. It'll be ready soon." As she tossed the salad, she said, "Let's work out our story."

"We keep it simple, like Sin said. We've been close friends for years. We're crazy in love, been married for a few months. No kids. No pets. If she presses us on where we live, we'll tell her Maryland. You're an exhibitionist. I'm vanilla and I love to satisfy your needs. We're Mr. and Mrs. Black. Boom. Done."

"If she asks about careers, we tell her retail."

"Got it," he said. "What about condoms? We *are* married."

"It's standard protocol to use them at kink parties." Pausing, she spun her rings. "And if they invite us to play tonight?"

"We play."

"I'm nervous."

Maverick collected her hands in his. "Why the jitters?"

"Your career is riding on this. Combining work and kink and you…it's a lot to process."

"You can *absolutely* pull this off. I believe in you and, like Sinclair said, 'together we're unstoppable.'"

She squeezed his hands. "Right. Of course we can do this." She broke away to flip the chicken in the skillet.

"I've got something for you." Clasping her hand, he led her to the sofa. She eased down and gazed up at him.

Despite the fact that theirs was a faux marriage, his heart pounded double time. He was giving her something that had once symbolized the union of his beloved parents.

He fished the rings from his pocket and sat beside her. "I stopped by to see my dad." He opened his fist and revealed the silver bands.

Her eyes grew large. "You told him what we're doing?"

"I told him we're working a case posing as husband and wife. He offered these. Let's see if my mom's ring fits." As he slid the ring on her finger, a sense of completeness washed over him. Then, he gazed into her eyes. "Carly, will you be my pretend wife?"

Sadness flashed in her eyes. "It's lovely."

"It fits, too." He held out his dad's ring. "Make it official, woman."

She stared at that ring like it had grown a set of razor-sharp teeth. Then, with trembling fingers, she slid the band onto his finger. She had to shove it over his thick second knuckle, but once she'd cleared it, the ring looked like it belonged there. "Ash, we are bound together until the end of this gig."

"Gotta seal it with a kiss."

Her eyes widened. "Ash—"

"This has *got* to look and feel real. If Greta or someone on her staff thinks we're up to something, we'll get booted out. Kiss me, and make it good."

She pressed her lips to his. He loved how her eyes fluttered closed, how she didn't pull away when he kissed her, again and again. Soft, doting kisses that had him wanting more.

"Was that convincing enough for you?" she murmured.

He'd started to harden. "Oh, yeah."

During dinner, she kept sneaking peeks at their wedding bands.

Maybe there's hope for her yet.

When it came to her fetish, he needed more info. Rather than bumble through anything at Greta's, he asked, "When you're playing, what do you like?"

"To be watched, to be in control." She sliced off a piece of chicken. "But you're a total alpha, so I'd be a Switch, which means I would alternate between top and bottom depending on the situation and our sexual needs."

"Got it. And just so that we're clear, my fetish is pleasuring you."

She held his gaze while a pink hue flooded her cheeks. No denying she liked that answer.

After they'd eaten, Carly grabbed two shopping bags. "Your burner." She pulled out two phones, handed him one. "I programmed my burner number into your address book. Your password is my birthday and vice versa."

"Now, when's your birthday again?"

"May—"

"Fifteenth." He winked. "I know your birthday, Carly."

Smirking, she swatted his arm, then pulled three wigs from the second bag.

"What the hell are those?"

"Your new 'do."

"This is insane."

He tried on the first wig and Carly could not stop laughing. "You look like a surfer dude. So not you." Glancing in the mirror, he cringed.

The second wig was a marked improvement. Light brown hair styled in a tidy business cut.

"Hmm, that might work. Let's see the back." She ran her

fingertips across his neck, her soft touch sending sparks flying through him. "Your hair is popping out back here."

He tried on the third. The chocolate brown wig fully covered his dark blond hair. She crossed her arms and cocked her head. "I like." Then, she checked the back. "It's the most realistic."

He examined himself in the mirror. "It'll work."

"You look great." She caressed his scruffy cheek. "I'm going to get ready. Don't shave and no underwear. Bring two condoms, in case we're there a while."

He grinned. "I like the sound of that. What should I wear?"

"White shirt, dark pants. Shirt stays on, but I'll unbutton it. You'll drop the pants, but keep those on, too."

Just thinking about sex with Carly turned him hard. They headed toward the master cabin, but she veered into the smaller stateroom.

Dammit. "Hey, what happened to being married?"

"I'm good in here." Before he could object, she shut the door.

He got ready and waited for her on the stern. He felt ridiculous in the rock-star wig, but if he could get some dirt to shove down Internado's throat, it would be worth it. Carly sashayed out, both masks in hand. His heart took off.

Holy hell, she's breathtaking.

She was wearing a black dress with a reverse halter top, lace sleeves covering her arms. She'd styled the long dark wig into an elegant updo. Besides the wedding band, she wore no jewelry.

He rose. "You look phenomenal."

She spun around. "Do you approve?"

He nodded. "My God, you're a total knockout. You'll be the hit of the evening."

She held up her left hand. "I'm a happily married woman who *only* plays with her husband."

He loved hearing her call him that and stepped close. "Your husband's a *very* lucky man."

Her eyes softened and the knot between them disappeared.

The longer they stared, the more he wanted to wrap his arms around her, pull her close, and kiss her.

After blinking several times, she cleared her throat. "Okay, so, I need to show you how this dress works." She pulled apart the slotted material over her breasts, revealing bare skin and pink nipples.

"My God, woman, I won't last five minutes."

"Makes it simple, huh?" She anchored her hands on his shoulders and rose on her stilettos. Leaning close, she whispered, "I've got on a thong with an elastic center. Easier to move out of the way."

He placed her hand over his crotch so she could feel his excitement. "I'm going to forget all about Internado."

She patted his junk before removing her hand. "While I'm very impressed with your *massive* erection, we should make sure our surveillance equipment works." She handed him her watch and showed him how to activate the camera. "It's video only."

He strapped it on.

She held up her mask and pointed to the middle of three sequins affixed over her left eye. "This is a tiny transceiver that captures video *and* audio."

"Impressive." He clasped her hand. "Ready to roll?"

"Ash, I don't think you should say much. You've got a very distinct and booming voice." She shrugged. "It's the showman in you."

"Should I say nothing?"

"Less is more and quiet is better than loud. I love that I can find you wherever we are, but at Greta's, you're someone else."

"I'm Mr. Black." He had lowered his voice and spoke quietly.

She smiled. "Perfect."

On the way to Greta's, Carly told him she never drank while working.

"Neither do I." He glanced over at her. "You doin' okay?"

"A few jitters, but I'll settle down once we get there. You?"

"In some ways, this is like a mission. While waiting for you, I checked for my weapon, but this isn't that kind of assignment."

Their eyes met in the darkened car. "I hope it doesn't devolve into that."

"Me, too, babe."

They parked a block from Greta's end-unit townhouse, tied on their masks, and headed out. In a very affectionate move, she slipped her hand into his. Warmth flooded his chest as they walked up the brick stairs to the front door.

Presuming there were surveillance cameras located on the home's exterior, he placed his mouth to her ear. "Show time, wife." She turned. The air sizzled with wild excitement, the attraction undeniable.

He dropped a kiss on her mouth. "For luck." Then, he tapped the doorbell.

A ghost of a smile curved her lips. "You're a very doting husband."

"You're easy to dote over, Mrs. Black." He kissed her again as Greta swung open the door.

"Ah, how romantic." A petite, middle-aged woman in a modest black dress offered a gracious smile. Her jet-black hair was pulled into a tight French twist. "Can I help you?"

"Mr. and Mrs. Black, for Greta," said Carly.

"Friends of Sinclair," she said, eyeing them up and down. "I'm Greta." She extended a bony hand with several black and silver bracelets lining her thin wrist.

They shook her hand.

"Please, come in." She closed the front door and snapped the dead bolt into place before moving toward the cozy bar tucked in the corner of the room.

Sinclair had gotten them in. Now it was up to Carly to take them the rest of the way. *Everything is riding on this. It had damn well better work.*

17

GRETA'S DEN OF INIQUITY

As Carly followed Greta toward the bar, blood whooshed through her veins. She loved working, but this was different. She'd never combined kink with her career, nor had she imagined she'd be doing either with Ashton.

The entire first floor served as a mingling room. There were four beautiful sofas covered in an elegant fabric of muted reds, browns, and blacks. Each of the mahogany end tables boasted clawed wooden feet. Beautiful artwork of pastoral landscapes hung on the walls. Jazz streamed from invisible speakers while sweet vanilla wafted in the air. Soft light from three table lamps added to the sensual ambiance.

Several couples and a group of five spoke in hushed tones. Most wore clothing similar to what she and Ash wore; a few showed more skin. Only Greta and her bartender were unmasked. After the barkeep poured Greta a glass of red wine, he asked what they'd like.

"Two sparkling waters," Carly replied.

"No wine?" Greta asked, before sipping from the goblet. "I have whiskey, vodka, whatever you'd like." She eyed Ashton. "You look like a Martini man."

"Just water tonight," he replied.

Carly loved how he'd morphed into Mr. Black. His voice wasn't just quieter it was deeper, too.

With glasses in hand, the three sat around a cozy round table. Relaxed and pleasant, Greta came across as someone who'd been in the business for a long time. Perhaps she'd been a madam. In what sounded like a canned speech, she touted the uniqueness and discretion of her club.

"I guard my members' identities like a lioness protects her cubs." Greta played with her bracelets. "Everyone here is family and, when they play here, they're in a safe, clean environment. My wish is that my guests have an immensely erotic experience. I won't lie, I talk with a lot of people eager to join, but I only accept a small percentage."

Carly acknowledged her with a nod. "We're looking for something different. I played in a club briefly, but prefer the ambience of a home environment. It's more intimate."

"And you?" Greta asked Ashton.

"When my beautiful wife's erotic needs are met, so are mine." The huskiness in his voice set her insides on fire while his words melted her. She so wished they were true.

As Greta continued talking, Carly flicked her gaze to him. The showman who had one volume—*loud*—had a stealth-like appearance. He moved nothing, except his eyes. And he had taken the chair which gave him the clear advantage...the one that put his back against the wall so he could watch everyone come and go. His quiet strength aroused her in ways she never imagined.

"Tell me about your sexual needs," Greta said. "I want to make sure you'll fit in."

"I love the rush of being watched in a safe, secure environment," Carly said.

"Ah, yes, Sinclair did tell me you're an exhibitionist."

"I am."

"Very nice." This smile touched Greta's eyes. "I was, too, in my younger years. Nothing like the rush from an erotic experience in a roomful of spectators." Greta's gaze lingered on Carly. "What about rough play? Do you like role playing or dressing up?"

"No rough play. The other two are fun."

"Didn't Sinclair tell me you're newlyweds?"

"We are," she said as Ashton clasped her hand. Even though they were pretending, her heart fluttered.

"Most of my couples find mixing things up enhances their marriage," Greta continued. "Are you open to playing with others?"

"No." The intensity in his voice surprised Carly.

"I see." Leaning back, Greta crossed her ankles. "Overly possessive, perhaps?"

"If playing with others is something you'd expect—" Carly began.

"I expect nothing," Greta interrupted. "I offer the environment. My staff entertains with a show. Members are free to do what gratifies them. You're both young, attractive. Sexual delights with others oftentimes enhance a marriage."

Ash started to get up. "This probably isn't the right environment for us."

Greta pursed her lips.

Hell, no! Carly squeezed his hand. "Baby, before we rule this out, maybe Greta can show us around."

"An excellent idea." Greta rose. "Join me on a tour."

Ashton winked at Carly and she bit the insides of her cheeks to keep from smiling. He was playing the bad cop, the hard ass. Greta introduced them to a few members before heading toward the staircase.

"What's in there?" Carly asked as they passed a closed door with a keypad.

"My basement."

"Is that your private residence?" Carly asked.

"I don't live here." As Greta climbed the stairs, Carly eyed Ashton. He squeezed her hand in response.

On the way up, he slipped his hand up her dress and massaged her bare ass. His slow, unexpected caress jolted her, eliciting a soft moan.

Greta brought them into the upper level main room where two women and a man were playing in front of a small group of about twenty. Sofas and futons filled the large space; a St. Andrew's cross was attached to the wall.

"Those three are on my staff." She kept her voice low, so Carly leaned close to hear her. "After the show, my team will mingle. Some engage in sex with members; others don't. I leave it up to the individual to decide. Guests play until two in the morning, when the festivities end."

Though aroused by the tantalizing performance, Carly's focus shifted from one person to the next. Internado wasn't there. Though disappointed, she couldn't stop the rush of endorphins as she returned her attention to the live sex show.

One of the women was lying on plush blankets near a gas fireplace. She wore a crotchless corset, her breasts exposed. A garter belt tugged at her fishnet stockings.

The second woman, wearing a baby doll nightie, had her face between the first woman's legs, her ass in the air while the man knelt behind her, thrusting. Initially, Carly couldn't tell if the sex was real or simulated, but when the man withdrew, her breath hitched. This was the ultimate in naughty, and she loved every filthy second of it. She turned to Ashton. He was waiting, his gaze fixed on hers, lust pouring from his eyes.

He nuzzled close. "You like, Mrs. Black?"

She moistened her lips. More than the show, she liked that he was by her side to watch it.

Greta didn't let them stick around long enough to watch the climactic finale. Curling her thin fingers around Carly's arm, she ushered them into a room marked "Salon". Besides the futon covered with a bright, white sheet, a fluffy down comforter and two pillows, there was an oversized chair large enough for two. In the corner, a door opened to a bathroom.

"This is one of two aftercare salons," Greta explained before continuing on.

They passed an open door marked "Powder Room" and stopped in front of a small bedroom. "I have two privacy rooms." She flashed a red manicured fingernail across the hall to a similar room. "Some members don't like an audience. Here they can play alone or invite a third person or a couple to join them."

"Very nice," Carly replied.

Greta faced them. "You won't find anything more upscale or discreet than my club. You're welcome to stay and watch, but I don't permit prospective members to play on their first visit. I'll be in the lounge on the first floor. See me before you leave."

With a tight smile, she disappeared down the stairs.

Carly leaned up and whispered in Ash's ear. "Let's make one more pass through." He threaded his fingers through hers and a burst of warmth traveled up her arm. Together, they checked out the entire top floor. Both aftercare salons and the private rooms weren't in use, so they returned to the playroom.

The show had ended, but the smell of sex hung heavy in the air. Guests mingled, but most had gotten busy getting to know each other. One couple had parked themselves in the corner. The man's pants pooled around his ankles while a woman knelt before him. She feasted on him with such slow, deliberate strokes that Carly's breath hitched. More times than she could count, she'd imagined taking Ash into her mouth and sucking him to the edge of ecstasy. Then, when she was ready to give him what he desperately needed, she would send him hurtling over the edge. Sex here could be fun. Sex *anywhere* with Ashton would be crazy hot.

As much as she wanted to get caught up in the hedonistic fun, she was there to do a job. Find Internado. But it appeared the senator wasn't there.

As Ash stroked her bottom, her insides throbbed for a release. "I need you." The edginess in his voice made her go wet.

Framed by the dark mask, his feral eyes glowed wildly. The animal in him had been unleashed. How could she resist the one man she desperately wanted?

I can't.

He wrapped his arms around her and she nestled close. His long, hard shaft pressed against her tummy and her insides hummed with a need she couldn't refuse. As if freed from the mayhem that had become their lives, they got lost in each other's eyes.

His mouth found hers and their smoldering desire ignited into a blaze. He kissed her with a roughness that rocked her to her toes. His throaty groan vibrated through her, landing in the sweet spot between her legs. She ground against him, relishing in his hardness, in the power of his kiss, and the strength of his touch.

Gasping for breath, she broke away. The sensual haze was like a drug. He kissed her again, this time with tenderness. "You are delicious in *every* conceivable way," he whispered.

So are you, Ash.

For a split second, she'd forgotten she was working. Was his kiss an act? *This feels so real.*

She kissed him, relishing how their lips melded together, how natural it felt being with him in this kinky environment.

They returned to the main floor and waited while Greta finished talking with an employee. Carly looked everywhere but at him. Her defenses were crumpling and she would break if she didn't keep her emotions in check. He held her hand, stroking her skin with his thumb. His performance so convincing, she believed they were a married couple, deeply in love.

"Hey." His husky voice vibrated through her. His gaze drilled into her. He squeezed her hand while the ends of his mouth curved in the most delicious way. Even masked and wearing the ridiculous wig, his beauty shone through, like a beacon in a stormy sea. Resisting him was futile.

He nuzzled her neck and dropped a soft kiss on her shoulder. "I love the way you smell." Lifting their entwined hands, he kissed hers.

Her heart leapt, her pulse picked up, and her body yearned for his. Ash's ability to turn her inside out required little effort on his part.

"Watching you two gives me hope that true love still exists," Greta said, interrupting their fiery connection. Her hand was on her heart, a sincere smile touching her eyes. "My line of work is exciting and provocative, but it's also hardened me. Members are eager to play with someone new. My gut tells me your love will last." Her eyes flitted between them. "But enough of romance. Did you like my club?"

"At first pass, we did," Carly said.

"Delightful." Greta plucked a business card from the tray, jotted something on it, and handed it to her. "My website. Enter the password I wrote down to access the members-only section. Your two-week trial starts when you set up your account."

"When are your parties and what type of events do you offer?" Carly asked.

"I host parties on Fridays and Saturdays that begin with a sex show. Every other Friday includes a theme. And Thursday events are by invitation only."

Hmm, invitation only. She shifted her attention to Ashton who, in true form, gave nothing away. They told her they'd be back and Greta appeared delighted to hear that.

In silence, they walked to the car.

Before Maverick opened the passenger door for Carly, he peered down at her. She was scorching hot in that number and he had to have her. He tipped her chin, dipped down, and kissed her. Her soft moan sent streaks of desire racing through him.

On the way home, they removed their masks.

"I was disappointed Internado wasn't there," Carly said.

"Me, too, babe."

"My money is on that locked basement or the invitation-only events." The conviction in her voice filled him with hope.

As soon as they stepped into the cabin, the air shifted, her heavenly scent surrounding him. He captured her in his arms and kissed her, their collective moans roaring in his ears. Her husky sounds and impassioned kisses drove him wild.

Breathing hard, she broke away and stared into his eyes with half-hooded lids. She tugged off his wig and raked her hands through his hair, then pulled off her own wig and freed her wild mane from the pins.

Every bone, every muscle craved her. He kissed her again, their tongues colliding in an explosive embrace. The raging fire that burned inside him was out of control. He had to have her. Had to feel her skin on his, her mouth on his, her body on his.

"I need you, Ash. Take me on the sofa." Her words tumbled out, her warm breath heating his face. She fished a condom from his pocket. "Take off your pants."

Lifting her, he set her gently on the sofa. Even separated from her for a few seconds was too much. He dropped his pants and his erection jutted out. "Tell me what you want."

She patted the cushion. "Sit."

The second he did, she straddled him. "I *need* this. I need *you*." She rolled on the condom, then dipped down and kissed him.

Her lips were soft; her kiss was not. Raw and untamed, she stroked his tongue while her sexy, throaty coos filled his ear. He squeezed her shoulders, stroked her back. She slowed then, gasping for breath, she stared into his eyes.

She shuddered in a breath. "Yes?"

"Always, yes." He couldn't stop touching her, his hands roving hungrily over her sexy body.

Still in her dress, she rose up and gripped him like a gearshift, like he was already hers to do with as she damn well pleased whenever she damn well wanted.

Fucking nirvana.

Sinking down on him, she cried out. Her kiss was greedy and filled with an edginess that had him biting her, fisting her hair and tugging. Her heat surrounded him in the ultimate pleasure. In the moment, he had everything he needed.

Their raw passion exploded in a torrent of rough kisses. She arched forward, pushing her breasts into his face while driving him deeper inside her hot, silky flesh. He parted the material covering her luscious tits and took one nipple into his mouth. Her long, sexy-as-hell groan had him sucking harder. Her breathing became erratic.

She dug her fingers into his hair and murmured, "You feel so fucking good." He bit her other engorged nipple. "Yes, that's so perfect. I like it like that. Harder."

He fondled her breasts, reveling in their perfection. When he kissed her and drove his tongue inside her mouth, she ground harder.

Then, she slowed the kiss and stopped gliding. Even in the darkness, he could see her clearly. Her face so beautiful, his heart swelled. This connection, while wild and intense, was filled with undeniable love. Her eyes were jet black, her mouth pressed gently to his. Carly was all woman and he reveled in her silky skin, the curve of her hips, and her delectable ass. Her lips curved. His did, too.

"Ash." She whispered his name like a prayer. "I can't get enough of you."

Three dangerous little words were perched on the end of his tongue. He was ready to tell her, to share his most intimate thought with her. To let her into the deepest part of his heart, the one he'd cut off from the world a long time ago. More than anything, he needed to bare his soul to her and only her.

He studied her face. Would she be able to handle his raw honesty? *Not yet.* Instead, he uttered three very different words.

"Don't deny me." The warning in his voice elicited a muffled cry from her.

She thrust her tongue into his mouth, her intense passion stealing his breath. This time, she began slowly moving on him while she pressed her breasts against his chest. The pleasure so perfect, he released a long, husky moan.

Her speed increased, as did her sultry coos. "Take me. I need you to make me come." She arched her back, raised her arms over her head and closed her eyes.

He anchored his hands on her hips and took control. His slow, deep thrusts were met with whimpers and moans. Her voice had grown throaty, desire spilling from her like the rush of river water spewing over an open dam.

"Kiss me." His words were an order.

She framed his face in her hands, stared into his eyes and murmured, "I'm coming…so good." Her insides squeezed him, her shudders sending earthquake-like spasms through him. Staring into her eyes, he surrendered to her.

Seconds of perfect ecstasy turned into minutes of kissing and touching. He floated back to earth wrapped in a Carly cocoon. "Holy fucking hell."

Another long, voluptuous kiss was her only reply.

Sex for Maverick filled a physical need. Sex with Carly filled *all* his needs. His only question: Did he fill all of hers?

18

MEETING MRS. MURPHY

M averick woke early, tugged on cotton lounge pants, and headed to the main cabin. While he wasn't angry with Carly, per se, he wasn't thrilled with her, either. After their mind-blowing sex, they'd stayed locked in an embrace. Then, she'd slain him with three little words. "This changes nothing."

He'd wanted to laugh. In truth, *everything* had changed.

What really pissed him off was her refusal to sleep in his bed with him. He was the one who never stuck around long enough to cuddle, but Carly really slammed him back to reality when she flat-out wouldn't get in his bed. *Stubborn, headstrong woman.*

As he cooked breakfast, he decided to give her a dose of her own medicine. If she wouldn't give him what he really wanted, he would deny her sex. Though that thought scrambled his brain, he would not continue to fuck her if she wouldn't admit how she felt. He could feel it in her kiss, see it in her smile and in the way she looked at him. And she still hadn't stopped sneaking glances at their borrowed wedding bands.

Carly trudged in. "Caffeine."

One look at her and his grumpiness dissipated like fog lifting in the morning light. Life was too short for him to be frustrated with her simply because she was too scared to admit her true feelings. She was on *her* clock, not his. He had every confidence she'd open up to him. It was only a matter of time before their fake marriage felt so real even she would acknowledge the truth. If Greta could see it, she would, too.

"Hey, sleepy head." He handed her a piping hot mug of coffee and poured a second cup for himself. He gave her the creamer he'd bought for her. She thanked him with an adorable sleepy smile.

"What time is it?"

"Seven thirty." He checked her out. "You're covered in pussies."

Her groggy chuckle was sexy as hell. "Kitty-cat pajamas."

"I always imagined you slept in the nude."

Her brow hitched ever so slightly. "Sometimes I do. These were a Christmas present from Desiree. Aren't they cute?"

"The alternative would have been better." With a sly smile, he sipped his java. "Can you play racquetball with me today?"

"I don't think your leg is ready for that kind of a workout yet. But even if it were, I'm working."

Though he frowned, he loved how he couldn't get one past her. He could hide his pain from the world, but he couldn't conceal his true self from her any more than she could from him.

She poured their orange juice and buttered the toast. "I have to put tracking devices on Internado's vehicles today." She slid onto the kitchen bench and opened her laptop.

"But, it's Saturday." He set down two plates of grub. "Scoot over."

She looked up at him. "Why don't you sit across from me?"

Time to get cozy. "I want to watch you work."

She slid over. He loved having her by his side, their shoulders brushing against each other, her beautiful peach scent wafting in his direction.

After logging in to a people-search database used by private eyes and law enforcement, Carly entered 'George Internado' in the search field.

"Your breakfast is getting cold." He offered her some scrambled egg. She opened her mouth and he slid the fork inside. While she chewed, he eyed her mussed hair, sleepy eyes, and puffy cheeks.

Seeing her in jammies took him back to his childhood. Sometimes, when they'd have family sleepovers, Carly would be included. Following a huge pasta dinner, they'd play a board game, then pile on the family room sofa for movie night. Midway through, his mom would slice apples or watermelon while his dad made popcorn. When the movie was over, the kids would crawl into their sleeping bags and his parents would snooze on the sofa. He loved when his parents included her. Having her there was the best part.

Maverick had been to Carly's house enough times to know that if her mom wasn't criticizing her, she was bickering with her dad. Even as kids, Carly was closer to Desiree than to her own sister.

Carly drank down the orange juice. "I can see the gears turning. What are you thinking about?"

"Do you remember the time you stayed over and we watched Snow White?"

"That's probably my favorite memory. Hudson laughed so hard every time he saw Dopey." Her heartwarming smile tugged at him. "Those movie nights were the absolute best. I loved when your parents included me."

"I loved having you there."

They peered into each other's eyes, the magnetic pull impossible to ignore. "What's happening here?" he murmured.

"We're reliving a special childhood memory."

"I think we're doing a hell of a lot more than that."

Carly's computer pinged and she dragged her gaze away. "We've got a hit."

"Woman, you're killing me." He held up his hand, displayed his wedding band. "What happened to the perks of marriage?"

"There would be a ton of them…if we were *actually* married." A flash of sorrow flickered across her face before she clicked on a tab. "Look what I found."

The database displayed Internado's home address and the vehicles registered to him and his wife, Kathy. While they ate, she shared her plan. His phone buzzed on the table, a text illuminating the screen. They glanced over. No name, just a phone number.

"Hey, Maverick, I haven't seen you in months. Stop by. I'll make it worth your while." There were several kiss emojis.

Carly nudged him. "I should get dressed." He didn't budge. "Can you let me out?"

"Not until I reply." His large thumbs flew across the screen. "No can do," he texted back. "I got hitched."

"*Ashton.*"

He kissed her full on. "Why don't you chew on *that* for a while, *Mrs. Black?*" He pushed out of the cozy booth, dropped his plate into the sink, and walked downstairs to his stateroom.

This is gonna be fun…except for the blue balls. That, not so much.

After dressing in cargo shorts and a T-shirt, he brushed his teeth and returned to the stern to bask in the morning sunshine. A few moments later, she joined him. She'd changed into jeans and a nondescript black shirt. No jewelry, save for the wedding band. She wore a chestnut wig and a baseball cap.

"Where's your disguise?" she asked.

"Come help me."

She followed him into his suite. Having her in his stateroom exacerbated his need. He sat on the bed, pulled on the short dark wig. With a tender touch, she tucked in his hair around the edges while he watched her with keen interest.

"Wear your sunglasses and don't take them off, no matter

what." She handed him a transceiver. "You'll keep watch while I hide the tracker."

"Now I can talk dirty into your pretty little ear."

"And I can talk dirty right back, mister." While she peered into his eyes, a flush covered her cheeks. "We have to pick up a van I use for these type of stakeouts."

"I've got a half a dozen Suburbans in my parking lot. Can we use one of those?"

"Not if they can be traced back to you."

"You're good at your job."

"I better be." She slipped on her shades. "A lot is riding on this."

After renting a white van and smacking magnetic construction logos on each side, she drove to Internado's upscale McLean neighborhood and parked half a block away from his home. They waited. And waited. And waited. Over an hour later, a car backed out of the driveway and headed toward them. Kathy Internado was alone in her sedan.

"I was hoping she'd leave in the other direction." Carly lowered her face as the car sped past.

Hanging a U-turn and following at a respectable distance, Carly trailed her to a nearby shopping center. With a package in hand, Kathy headed toward the post office. The senator's wife appeared to be in her mid-sixties with shoulder-length dark-blonde hair. She dressed in jeans and draped a shawl over her shirt.

"This isn't ideal," he said. "There's surveillance everywhere."

"I can do this." Carly exited the van, kept her head lowered, and wove her way through the sea of parked cars.

Maverick couldn't help but admire her boldness, not to mention her fantastic ass, accentuated by the swing of her hips. She knelt beside Kathy Internado's sedan and vanished from view.

Maverick trained his attention on the post office, watching the shoppers come and go. Kathy exited the store and walked with purpose toward her vehicle.

"Subject is hurrying back," Maverick said. "Ten seconds out."

"Crap. I dropped the tracker."

"Five seconds."

"Got it."

"Show time, babe."

"Sorry to startle you," Carly said while still on the ground. "I was playing with my wedding band and it fell off."

From his location, Maverick couldn't see if Kathy was helping her look for the ring or getting into her vehicle.

"No, but thanks for the offer," Carly said while still on the ground. "I'll find it. It's gotta be right around here."

Kathy Internado opened her trunk and extracted several reusable grocery bags.

"I found it!" Carly rose. "Have a good day," she said, before taking off toward the stores and ducking into the nail salon.

"She's heading for the grocery store." Maverick waited until Kathy had rolled a cart inside. "All clear, babe."

Though wearing sunglasses, they locked gazes as Carly made her way back to the van. Never having worked with her before, he admired how she'd gotten the job done, even with the snafu.

She slid behind the wheel. "Thanks for having my back."

"Always. Nice job under pressure."

"Thank you." She flipped open her laptop. "The tracker is active. One down, one to go."

They returned to Internado's neighborhood, but the senator didn't emerge. After several hours, Maverick's stomach growled so loudly that Carly called it a day.

"We don't even know if he's there," Maverick said, after wolfing down a sandwich at a sub shop.

She leaned across the table. "Until I can track his vehicle, I have no way of knowing where he is."

That evening, Maverick endured another night alone because his make-believe wife slept in the damn stateroom next door.

Monday, five in the morning, Carly hurried into the main cabin, her leather workbag clutched in her hand. After spending Sunday staking out Internado's house, she'd made no progress whatsoever. Internado hadn't ventured out, but his wife had driven to Richmond. Carly had endured another night of restless sleep. She was desperate to accept Ashton's invitation and sleep in his bed. But she refused to allow her feelings to direct her actions. Sex the first time to help him out; the second time was for her. Going forward, she'd cool her jets, except for whatever was required during their sleuthing at Greta's. Just because she adored the man didn't mean she had to act on it going forward.

She couldn't allow their relationship to devolve into a "friends with benefits". She didn't just love Ash, she adored his family, too. If things didn't work out, she would lose her best friend *and* his beloved family. *Nothing is ever simple when Ash is involved.*

She found him finishing a bowl of cereal and dressed for work in a pink button down and suit pants. Her heart stuttered as she soaked up all that masculine beauty. No matter what he wore—or didn't wear—he was a striking man.

"Hey, babe."

She wanted to touch him so badly her fingers ached. "Good morning."

He took his time checking her out. "Headed back to Internado's?"

She'd worn the chestnut wig, a baseball cap, and workman's clothing.

"I want to catch him when he leaves for work."

"Call me if you need anything."

"Same." Unable to stop herself, she leaned down and brushed her lips against his. Their sizzling connection sent tingles skittering through her.

"Stop fighting this," he murmured.

"I'm keeping things in perspective." She bolted out and slipped on her sunglasses.

My "perspective" is skewed when it comes to that man. I'm really just trying to keep myself together.

She drove the rental van to Internado's neighborhood and parked down the street. At ten minutes past six, a black sedan backed out of the driveway. Though she wanted to reach for her binoculars, she didn't. As it drove by, she confirmed the sole occupant was the senator himself.

After unearthing a small device from her leather bag, she set it to "jam" and drove forward. As she rolled past Internado's home, she pressed the activation button, but the light stayed red. *Dammit.* She drove around the block to try again.

As she neared Internado's home, a neighbor walking a Rottweiler flagged her down. She pulled over, cracked open the window.

"I noticed you've been driving around the block," he said. "Are you lost?"

Her stomach dropped. Being spotted was never a good thing. "I'm cool. Thanks."

"Maybe I can help. What's the address or who are you looking for?"

"I'm waiting for my partner. We've got a job on Holly Lane. This is Holly, right?"

"That's around the corner." The dog jumped on the door of the van and barked, startling her. The man stepped closer. "He's real friendly. Come on out and pet him."

Hair on the back of Carly's neck prickled. Using her elbow, she locked the van door. "I've gotta get to work." She pressed the gas pedal and rolled away.

Carly waited several minutes before returning to Internado's street. This time, as she drove past his house, she aimed the jammer at his garage and held the button down. The light turned green. *Much better.*

With step one completed, she returned the rental van and drove to the marina. Once onboard, she removed her disguise and sat at the kitchen table to review the contents of the white envelope. Her curiosity had been piqued. Why would her grandfather hide a case from her when they'd collaborated on everything?

She read the copy of a clipped newspaper article on the death of a twenty-three-year-old woman named Rose Aurora. The article wasn't dated nor was there anything identifying where this story had been printed.

He'd jotted notes at the bottom of the newspaper article.

R. police — no leads
Evidence file — no fingerprints
Hair strands found in motel — no match
Skin cells under fingernails — no match
Cold case
Photo

Her gaze lingered on the word "photo", which Pierce had underlined. *C'mon Grandpa, you've gotta help me out here.* Though she doubted she'd find anything, she accessed Stone Investigation's client files and checked the database again. No matter how many different keywords she used, this case had not been logged. It didn't exist, except on the written page.

This could have been resolved decades ago. She reread Grandpa Pierce's notes.

Client Alice Murphy, 67. Raised child as daughter. Erin Murphy, 39. Aunt, not mother (murdered, CC). Has Alz. Wants Erin to know. KILLER?

For her grandpa's sake, she decided to give the search one more try. Pulling up the people-search database, she plugged in the name, "Alice Murphy".

There were thousands of Alice Murphy's scattered across America. *This'll take me twenty years*. She added "Erin Murphy" to the same search and the possible matches dropped to seventy-eight. Determined to lower that number, she added Virginia, Maryland, and D.C. to the geographic field. The number of matches dropped to twelve. *This, I can work with.*

If these didn't pan out, she'd widen her search to the East Coast. She spent the afternoon pouring over data, narrowing her findings to three possible Alice-Erin pairs. There was a phone number for an Alice Murphy in Silver Spring.

"Hello," said a woman.

"I'm looking for Alice Murphy."

"Wrong number."

"Do you know an Erin Murphy?"

"What's this about?"

"I'm following up for a coworker who was in communication with Alice."

"I got this cell phone number about six months ago and can't help ya."

Carly called the second Alice Murphy, but after twenty rings, she hung up. There was a corresponding number for Erin Murphy, so Carly called her.

"Hello," said a woman.

"I'm looking for Erin Murphy."

"You got her."

"Ms. Murphy, your mom, Alice, was in communication with a coworker of mine and I'd like to follow up with her."

"'Bout what?"

"I'm not at liberty to discuss."

Silence.

"Who is this and what do you want?" Her abrupt tone didn't surprise Carly, but she couldn't discuss the nature of her call.

"It's confidential. Is there any way I can get Alice's phone number?"

"Look, lady, I can't help you. My mom moved to Texas and I ain't talked to her in years." The woman hung up.

Carly dialed the number for the third Alice Murphy.

"It's a happy day at Presley Valley Nursing Home. How may I direct your call?"

"I'm hoping you can help me. One of your residents, Mrs. Alice Murphy, was a friend of my grandfather. Unfortunately, he passed away and I'd like to provide her with information she requested of him. Can you confirm she still lives there before I stop by?" Carly held her breath. *Please be the right one.*

She Googled the name of the nursing home. It was located in Springfield.

"I'm not at liberty to disclose the name of our residents. I'm sorry."

"I understand. I'll just follow up with her daughter, Erin. Thanks for your help."

"Oh, you know Erin?"

Not yet. "If at all possible, I'd love to stop by and see Mrs. Murphy this afternoon. You're in Springfield, right?"

"That's right. Who should I tell Mrs. Murphy is coming?"

"My name is Carly Stone."

Forty minutes later, Carly checked in at the nursing home. The woman she'd spoken with had left for the day, so the current attendant called for a nurse.

A rotund woman bustled out, a warm smile on her face. "I understand you'd like to see Mrs. Murphy."

"Yes."

"Are you a friend?"

"My grandfather, Pierce Stone, was. I'm following up with her about a conversation they had."

The nurse ushered her out of the way of a resident rolling by in his wheelchair. "Mrs. Murphy is struggling today. Some days are better than others."

"I'm sorry to hear that. Because of the Alzheimer's?"

The nurse nodded. "But she might like having a visitor." Carly was escorted to Mrs. Murphy's room.

Alice Murphy rested in a chair near the window, a knit shawl covering her tiny frame.

"Mrs. Murphy, you have company."

Mrs. Murphy turned. "Hello."

"I'm Carly. Can I sit with you for a little while?"

Mrs. Murphy looked to the nurse.

"This young lady said her grandfather was a friend of yours." The nurse told them she'd be back after checking on a patient.

Carly pulled over a chair. "It's a pretty day. You have a lovely view of the changing leaves."

"What's your name?"

"Carly Stone. You spoke with my grandfather, Pierce Stone, about your daughter."

Mrs. Murphy smiled. "Where's my punkin? Is she here?"

"Erin isn't here right now. Do you remember talking to Pierce Stone?"

The woman shook her head. "I don't know who that is."

Carly tried several different approaches to spark Mrs. Murphy's memory, but nothing worked. When the nurse returned, she escorted Carly to the lobby.

"Mrs. Murphy would be interested in what my grandfather found out for her." Carly handed the nurse a business card.

"When she's feeling better, I'll let her know."

When Carly returned to the yacht, she found Ashton setting the table for dinner. "Hello, wife. How was your day?"

Hearing him call her that made her smile. "Good day, hubs. You?"

He stepped close enough for her to delight in his earthy scent.

But when he didn't kiss her, a pang shot through her chest. She stroked his arm, finding joy in running her fingers over his solid muscles.

"I met with a prospective client who's considering us for some local security gigs."

"That's good news." She lifted a lid to find pasta boiling in a pot of water. "Yummy, tortellini."

"Nothing but the best for my pretend woman."

With a snicker, she washed her hands and made a simple dinner salad. "You are spoiling me."

"That's the plan."

Next, she heated a jar of tomato sauce. "Where's the protein? You can't live on pasta."

He pulled four chicken breasts from the toaster oven. "Voila."

She kissed his cheek. "Best husband ever."

"Best husband ever deserves way more than a peck on his cheek."

He's right.

During dinner, she told him about jamming Internado's garage door opener so he'd have to leave his car outside. "I'm going back there tonight to hide the tracker." Then, she told him about the guy with the dog.

"Whoa. You can't go back there alone."

"I'll be careful."

"I hired you, so, technically you work for me. I'm going with you."

At midnight, she changed into black clothes and braided her hair, then confirmed Kathy Internado was still in Richmond. On the way out, she handed Ash a black ski mask.

He drove Carly's Acura into Internado's neighborhood, pulled over, and killed the lights, including the interior ones. After sliding on their ski masks, Carly covered the license plates with diffusional shields. They continued to the senator's street, parking two houses away.

"Good luck, babe."

She acknowledged him with a tight nod before exiting the vehicle and quietly closing the door. Using trees and parked cars as cover, she made her way to Internado's house. To her relief, he'd parked in the driveway, but his front porch light illuminated his yard.

As she crawled up the dark side of the driveway, lights on the garage flicked on, bathing her in bright light. She froze. When Internado didn't emerge, she shoved the tracker in the rear wheel well. Then, she pressed the button on the device to unjam his garage door. As she turned to leave, the front door opened.

"Who's there?" shouted Internado.

SNUGGLING

Internado's voice bellowed through the quiet night. Maverick's instinctual urge to rescue Carly sent adrenaline surging through him. Several agonizing seconds passed before he spotted her hiding behind a tree. Like a cat, she slinked from one to another. Thirty-eight long seconds later, she slipped inside the car.

She inhaled a deep breath. "That was some rush, huh?"

"You're cool under fire."

"That's the goal. Freaking out only makes things worse."

Without turning on the headlights, Maverick drove out. Once they reached Chain Bridge Road, they yanked off their ski masks. He pulled onto the shoulder and she removed the license plate covers. Then, he flipped on the lights and hit the gas.

On the way home, she kept watch for a trailing vehicle. After ten minutes on the G.W. Parkway, she gave the "all clear".

While Maverick lived for rescue missions, working alongside Carly brought a special element of excitement. "Mission accomplished. Nice job, boss."

"Back atcha." She pulled out her laptop and verified the tracker's signal. "Good thing we love the thrill of adventure."

Not as much as I love you.

Once back home, he reminded her he was leaving before dawn.

Sidling close, she peered into his eyes. "Is your mom's charity golf tournament in Ocean City again this year?"

The air crackled with irresistible desire. "Yeah. I'm spending a couple of days at my training facility since it's on the way."

"You want me to head back to my place?"

Desperate to touch her, he ran his hands down her arms. He wanted their clothing gone so he could press skin to skin. "Absolutely not. And that's an order."

"So bossy," she said, cracking a smile. He loved how her eyes crinkled at the corners. "I'll stay. When are you coming back?"

"Late Thursday, after the tournament." He broke away to fish out a key from his kitchen drawer. "Since you'll be here alone, make sure you lock up at night." Though hungry to kiss her, he didn't. "G'night." It about killed him to walk away from her, but he was sticking with his damn plan.

"Ash."

Hopeful, he turned.

"We should talk when you get back."

You think? "Be good Carly girl." He retreated into his stateroom and shut the door, frustration coursing through him.

The following morning, Maverick drove out before sunrise. He spent the next two days at ThunderStrike's Eastern Shore Training Facility. His fourteen newest employees were completing their eight-week boot camp. Several asked about the rumors, so he spoke candidly about ThunderStrike's current challenges, but emphasized he believed justice would be served. At the end of his meeting, two quit. Maverick took each resignation personally, the weight of the situation bearing down on him.

First thing Thursday, he headed to Ocean City. No matter what was going on, he never missed a year to celebrate his mom's life. His dad relied on him to help run the annual event, and act as Master of Ceremonies during the dinner and awards ceremony. Maverick was always humbled and grateful for the two hundred golfers who participated and donated generously to honor Sarah Hott. All proceeds benefitted Medicine Without Borders.

The event was a rousing success. It raised over one hundred thousand dollars for the organization whose physicians were willing to place themselves in danger to save lives.

That evening, several of the guys stopped at a local bar before heading home. Maverick helped his dad settle up before joining them. The place was packed, but he made his way over to the bar and ordered a beer.

"What's going on tonight?" he asked the bartender.

"A women's business convention is in town." The bartender set Maverick's beer on a napkin. "From the crowd, I'd guess half of 'em are here. Good for business."

Maverick found his golf buddies. Most of the men were talking with women. One of the golfers raised his beer bottle to Maverick. "When the cat's away, the mice will play. And I see a lot of very cute mice scurrying around here tonight."

"You're married, man." Maverick tossed back a mouthful of ale.

"So? I wear a condom. Plus, it's not like I'm getting much at home anyway."

Maverick's stomach soured. The dude's personal life wasn't his business, but he lost respect. In his rulebook, cheating was unacceptable.

Another golfer flagged him over and introduced him to the two women he was chatting with.

Maverick shot them a smile. "How's everyone doin' tonight?"

After a few minutes of small talk, he was ready to roll.

"You want to get out of here?" asked one of the ladies. "We could go somewhere where I don't have to shout."

Maverick displayed his wedding band. "I'm going home to my

THE HOTT TOUCH | 211

woman. I miss her." He thanked the guys for playing in the tournament and took off.

On the drive home, he thought about what he'd say to Carly. When it came to matters of the heart, he was unskilled. Maverick was a man of action, not words. His plan? Show her how much he loved her. *Time to make some serious life changes.*

His thoughts were interrupted when Douglas Hill called. "Hey, Douglas. How are you, my friend?"

Douglas was president of Lakewood Technologies, a thriving Northern Virginia tech company. For the past two years, they'd been ThunderStrike's biggest commercial client and had booked seven jobs over the next ten months, both domestic and abroad.

"Maverick, welcome back." Normally upbeat, Douglas's voice was sullen.

"What's going on?"

"I was summoned to the Hill this afternoon."

The hair on the back of Maverick's neck prickled. "What for?"

"Internado wanted a heart-to-heart, though I'm convinced he doesn't have one."

Maverick's stomach dropped. "This doesn't sound good."

"It's not. A few years back, I needed support to get legislation passed on certain codes for our products, along with a big push for the green initiative that put us on the map. I asked Internado for help. He did way more than expected and never asked for anything in return. No contribution to a PAC, not even my vote. It sickens me that he called in that favor today."

Maverick wished this nightmare would end.

"He *suggested*—and I use that word loosely—I sever my relationship with you. If I don't, he's going to make things very difficult for my company."

Despite his soaring pulse, Maverick stayed in control, refusing to let his emotions get away from him. "These political games are annoying as hell."

Douglas's jittery laugh morphed into a coughing attack. "Unfortunately, I've got to put our upcoming missions on hold."

The twelve point five mil ThunderStrike would have earned from those gigs vanished in a puff of smoke. The call ended with Douglas apologizing profusely.

Once again, Maverick's frustration morphed into a seething rage. That was the final nail in his coffin. ThunderStrike wouldn't make it past Halloween.

I've hit rock bottom.

That evening, Carly hurried toward the front door of Presley Valley Nursing Home. Mrs. Murphy was interested in speaking with her. After signing in at the front desk, Carly was directed to the library.

When she entered the cozy book room, an alert Mrs. Murphy smiled from her wheelchair. "I'm Carly Stone, Stone Investigations." She shook her hand before easing onto the chair beside her.

"Thank you for coming by," Mrs. Murphy said. "The nurse explained you were delivering a message from your grandfather. Why didn't he come by himself?"

"He passed away in February."

"I'm sorry for your loss, dear. He was such a nice man." Mrs. Murphy had the kindest eyes. "How did you know I'd contacted him?"

Carly pulled the envelope from her bag. "I found this in his desk. It's your case, which he never discussed with me. Since his notes aren't dated, I didn't know if everything had been resolved."

"I asked him to be discreet. I'm guessing that's why he never said anything to you."

A woman in her mid-thirties hurried into the room. "Hi,

Mom. I got here as soon as I could." The woman turned her attention toward Carly and the warmth drained from her eyes.

"This is my daughter, Erin Murphy," said Mrs. Murphy.

This wasn't the first time Carly had encountered a potentially hostile situation, so she offered a friendly smile and one of her business cards. "I'm Carly Stone with Stone Investigations."

Erin snatched the card. "What are you trying to sell my mother?"

"It's okay, dear," said Mrs. Murphy. "I hired Ms. Stone's grandfather to help me."

Erin's lips were slashed in a thin line. "Help you do what?"

"Fear has kept me quiet for decades, but I'm ready to talk," said Mrs. Murphy. "Ms. Stone, can you give me a few minutes with my daughter, please? Help yourself to coffee or tea in the cafeteria. It's right across the hall."

"Can I bring you both something?"

"A black coffee would be lovely," said Mrs. Murphy. "Use the plastic lids. The coffee is very hot."

Carly entered the quiet cafeteria, poured two coffees and waited. Ten minutes later, Erin entered the break room and sat beside Carly. "I'm sorry. I had no idea."

"Totally okay."

"A lot of people have tried to take advantage of her. I've become overly protective." Tears filled Erin's eyes. "I feel like I've been hit by a bus."

Carly offered her a napkin. "It's a lot to take in. I would offer to come back—"

Erin squared her shoulders. "My mom is lucid and she would like some answers. Let's talk this out."

The two women returned to the library.

"Mrs. Murphy, you were my grandfather's client," Carly began. "How would you like to handle this going forward?"

"I'll hire you," Erin said. "We need to get to the bottom of this."

Mrs. Murphy nodded in agreement.

Carly showed both women her grandfather's notes, along with the newspaper clipping about the death of Rose Aurora.

"I gave him that." Mrs. Murphy read over Pierce's notes. "He got the main points. In February, he told me he was getting close, but I never heard from him again."

"I'm sorry to ask you to repeat what you told him, but this is all I have." Carly pulled out her small notebook.

"My sister, Rose, was twenty-three when she died," Mrs. Murphy began. "She'd been strangled in a motel room, but her infant daughter, Erin, had been spared, thank the good Lord. No one heard or saw anything. There were no suspects. The police never even brought anyone in for questioning. I was seven years older than Rose, already married with two young sons. My husband and I raised Erin as our own."

Carly jotted notes. "I see."

"Several months after my sister died, we moved to Northern Virginia. My husband and I never told anyone the truth about Erin for fear the killer would come after her or our boys."

"Where was Rose murdered?" Carly asked.

"Richmond."

"What can you tell me about the men in Rose's life?" Carly asked. "Anyone special?"

A smile flitted across her face. "My sister was very pretty and always got a lot of attention." Her smile fell away. "But she was attracted to the wrong kind of men."

"Meaning?" Erin asked.

"The married ones," Mrs. Murphy replied. "I did tell your grandfather about that, but it wasn't in his notes. When she got pregnant, I asked her if her fella had a name. Her answer stayed with me forever."

"What did she tell you?" Erin asked.

"She said, 'Let's just call him Mr. Virginia,'" Mrs. Murphy continued. "When I pressed her, she told me he was leaving his wife for her and that *her* man might end up in the big house one day."

Erin grimaced. "Prison?"

"No," said Mrs. Murphy. "She was talking about the White House."

"So, he was a politician?" Carly jotted everything down.

"Might have been. I don't know." Mrs. Murphy shook her head. "I've kept this secret for almost forty years. Someone has gotten away with murder. I hope you find the son of a bitch who killed my sister."

"That's the plan," Carly said. "Erin, can I get a DNA sample from you? I use a lab in Arlington that's known for their discretion. Your profile won't be entered into any databases, but it *will* be checked for any matches to those currently in them."

"Sure," Erin said. "Whatever you need. How long will that take?"

"About a week."

Erin held up her water bottle. "Will this work?"

"Sure will." Carly pulled out latex gloves from her satchel, along with a plastic baggie. Erin drained the bottle and dropped it in. "Mrs. Murphy, do you have a photo of Rose?"

"I gave Pierce her picture."

"I didn't see it. That's not like him to lose things."

Mrs. Murphy asked her daughter to retrieve her wallet. "It's in my—"

Rising, Erin smiled. "I know where your purse is, Mom."

"I'm so sorry to hear of your grandfather's passing," Mrs. Murphy said. "Was he ill?"

"He took a bad fall down a flight of stairs."

Hurrying back in, Erin handed her mom the wallet. Mrs. Murphy extracted a small photo. "I've been carrying this with me for years." She showed Erin.

"Hard to believe she's my mom."

Mrs. Murphy passed the photo to Carly. "I'm afraid that's my only photo, so I can't give it to you."

"Do you mind if I take a picture of it?"

"You young people are so smart with technology."

Rose Aurora was petite with bright blonde hair and a big smile. Carly snapped a shot. "Your sister was very pretty."

"She was bursting with energy and full of life. I hope you find something."

"Thank you for calling me," Carly said to Mrs. Murphy. "Erin will be my point of contact going forward."

"I understand." Mrs. Murphy extended her wrinkled hand. "If I think of anything else, I'll tell Erin."

Erin escorted Carly to the lobby. "I'm going to need weeks to process what I've learned today."

"I admire how well you're handling the news."

"I'll lose it later, when I'm alone with my wife."

"Please say as little as possible."

"But I trust her."

Carly stepped close. "I'm not referring to your spouse. I wouldn't tell anyone else and I would advise her to do the same. Whoever murdered Rose might have moved far away or could still be living in Richmond, if they're even alive. The press would love to get their hands on a forty-year-old cold case. You'd be hounded, your mom, too."

"I understand."

"If your mom mentions *anything* to you about Rose, please call or text me right away."

"Where will you start?"

"By finding Rose's lover."

CARLY WOKE TO garbled shouting coming from somewhere in the boat.

"Hey, heyyyy. *No!*"

She shot out of bed, grabbed her weapon from the night table drawer, and hurried out.

"No! Don't!" Ash's shouts sent fear pounding through her.

She bolted into his stateroom to find him thrashing and muttering on the bed. She shoved her gun into his night table drawer.

"Hey, Ash." She kept her voice soft.

He stopped flailing. "I can do it," he said, his tone adamant.

No response. She sat beside him. "Ashton." She touched his leg. He jerked awake, his eyes unseeing. "It's me, Carly." She caressed his arm. He was shaking, his breathing jagged.

She held his hand. "You were having a nightmare. It seemed pretty intense."

He leaned up on his elbows, perspiration covering his face. "I'm sorry you heard that."

She brought him a glass of water. When he sat up, his chest was drenched in sweat, the sheets soaked.

After he guzzled the drink, she retrieved her weapon. "Come on. You can't sleep here." Together, they went into her stateroom where she dried him with her towel. The dips and striations of his muscles were sublime, his physical form perfection to touch. But now, all she cared about was comforting him.

He climbed into bed. Grateful he didn't argue, she slid in beside him. He laid his head on her chest while she caressed his hair and stroked his back. His breathing calmed down. A few moments later, he stopped shaking.

"I'm sorry," he said again.

"Why didn't you tell me you suffer from PTSD?"

He moved onto his pillow, stared into her eyes. "I've been having this nightmare for years."

"What's it about?" she asked, propping onto her elbow.

"I don't want to talk about it." He rolled onto his back, stared at the ceiling. Not wanting to push the subject, she rested her head on his chest and stayed quiet.

He wrapped his arms around her. "It's always the same dream," he said, after a moment of silence. "I'm trying to save my mom."

Her heart broke. He strummed his fingers up and down her back, warming her through her T-shirt. "I see."

"She's being held captive, but I find her. Sometimes I can get her out, but most times they kill her and I can't stop them."

A lump formed in her throat. "Have you told anyone?"

"No. I wish you hadn't heard me."

Like always, Ashton bore the hardship alone. She pushed off him, peered into his eyes. "I'm grateful I did. You shouldn't go through this alone." She offered a soft smile. "Your mom was…she was awesome and an amazing person. I see so much of her in you."

"The emptiness never goes away. It haunts me. On every mission, I look for her in the faces of the hostages."

Her heart was heavy, the tears welling in her eyes. This man was there for everyone, yet he refused to lean on anyone…*ever*. She had no idea he'd been struggling like this for so many years.

"She would be proud of the work you do, of the man you've become. You might feel like you're alone, but I'm here. I've always been here."

Pulling her close, he folded her into his arms. "You always know what to say or do to make me feel better. You are the only person who knows the good and the bad." He dropped a tender kiss on her head. "We've got something pretty damn special, you know that?"

She wiped away the tears. "Yeah, I do." She breathed easier knowing his secret. They were together and that was all that mattered.

"Thank you for…for being you. For being my rock. For being my beautiful Carly girl."

"We've always been each other's besties."

"I missed you so much these past few days."

She melted. "Me, too, Ash."

They grew quiet. Moments later, his breathing changed, his sleep peaceful. She lay awake a long time, appreciating their tender embrace. She loved sharing a bed with him, loved the feel of his skin on hers. Loved how he let her comfort him. She loved so much about this man that she couldn't imagine living her life without him.

THINGS GET HOTT

"What's that beeping?" Maverick asked.

Carly bolted upright. "One of the trackers." She rushed out and clicked on the software, silencing the alert. "Internado's driving home."

Maverick followed. "From where?"

"Greta's."

"At four forty in the morning?"

"Must've been one hell of a private party. I hope he goes back there tonight."

"If you aren't here, how do I stop the beeping?"

"My password is Carly the PI, all one word. Then, click the stop tab in the tracking program."

Maverick's boner bobbed, snagging Carly's attention. She arched her brow before reaching into the cupboard for a can of coffee, causing her T-shirt to ride up, exposing her sexy ass. Now his boner was really bobbing. He bit back a smile. She was playing this way too cool.

"Kathy Internado is still in Richmond because their youngest daughter had her third child," she said. "I'm guessing she drove down there to help out."

"Do *you* want children?"

She whipped around. "*What?* Where did that come from?"

"I do." He smiled. "Plus a dog, too."

She sauntered close, peered up at him. "Were you asking because you're ready to make one...*now?*"

He chuffed out a laugh. "What does Mrs. Black want?"

"The Mrs. would love a family one day, but today, she wants to catch Internado doing something morally reprehensible so Mr. Black can continue saving the world from bad guys."

"I like your priorities. I'm going to take a shower and get to work." Maverick draped his arms over her shoulders and stared into her sleepy eyes. "Thank you for being there for me last night."

"Always."

He wanted to kiss her, take her to his bed, and love her. He wanted to whisper all the words he'd been ready to say for years. But, he was not deviating from his plan, so he shot her a wink and walked away. As he stepped into the shower, an idea began to formulate as to how he could win her over...forever.

Carly sucked down a breath. Resisting Ashton was hard. The more time she spent with him, the more her walls crumpled. Telling him how she felt would be a big, bold move. She'd have to put it all out there and risk what they had for the complete unknown. She was good with following the evidence and piecing together a puzzle, but leading with her heart? That scared the hell out of her.

After getting ready, she headed out, relieved Ash had already bolted for work. That evening, Greta was hosting a leather and latex party, so she drove to her house to grab a few things, including her latex cat suit.

She parked out front, hurried inside, and stopped short. The living room was trashed with empty beer bottles and plastic cups, most of them piled on the antique desk. The secret drawer was wide open.

"What the hell?" Carly's stomach dropped as she climbed the stairs and headed toward her bedroom. The door was open and the lights were on. Several pieces of clothing had been tossed on her mussed bed. Tabitha emerged from the small walk-in closet, locked eyes with Carly, and shrieked.

Carly's cheeks flared. "What's going on?"

Tabitha clutched the latex cat suit, dangling from a hanger. "I… er…um. Oh, hey. I wasn't expecting you."

"Clearly."

Two women floated into the bedroom, one with a lit cigarette in her mouth.

"My head is pounding," said the non-smoker. "I need aspirin. What time is it?"

"No smoking in my house," Carly said, before shifting her gaze to Tabitha. "You know my house rules."

"Put it out," Tabitha said to her friend.

"Geez," said the smoker. "Fine, whatever." The woman sauntered out, followed by a trail of smoke, the stench of tobacco making Carly's eyes water.

"I had a party and those two were too drunk to drive home." Tabitha hung the outfit in the closet. "They slept in my bed, and I slept here."

Hating confrontation, Carly pushed down the anxiety as she gestured to the clothing strewn on her bed. "And this?"

"You have great clothes. Can I borrow your cat suit?"

"Got coffee?" asked the second woman. Carly shot her the death stare and she trudged out.

Leaning against her bureau, Carly crossed her arms.

Tabitha's cheeks flushed. "I…um…I'm not sure what you want me to say. *Sorry?*"

That sounded heartfelt. Not.

"So, er, I think one of my friends broke the secret drawer on that beat-up old desk." Tabitha's gaze stayed glued to the floor. "He found an old calendar in it." She snorted. "You know...the *paper* kind."

Narrowing her gaze, Carly forced herself to continue, despite her soaring pulse. "I gave you a place to live while you looked for something permanent. One month turned into three and you're taking advantage of the living arrangements...and of me."

Tabitha's shoulders slumped. "You weren't supposed to see any of this."

"But I did. Look, it's time for you to find somewhere else to live."

"Sure, okay." Sighing, Tabitha left the room.

As Carly put away the clothing her roommate left out, she shook off the anxiety. Whenever possible, she avoided conflict. That left her vulnerable to her mom and sister, who took advantage of her all the time. Today, however, she found the gumption to speak up for herself. With a touch of pride, she made her bed and packed her cat suit, plus a few other things. With bags in hand, she found Tabitha cleaning up the living room.

"I tried fixing the secret compartment, but it's busted," Tabitha said.

Carly spied her grandfather's pocket calendar sitting in a bowl of chips and tucked it into her handbag.

"I'm sorry," Tabitha said. "You've been super nice to me and I was taking advantage of your not being here. It's just that things have turned around for me since I wrote that short story about the case you were working on." She clamped her hand over her mouth. "Ah, shit."

Muscles running along Carly's shoulders tightened. "I thought so."

"I can check with my friends and be out in a day or two. Thanks for letting me stay as long as you did."

Carly nodded. "Leave the key on the kitchen table and lock the door behind you on your way out."

Driving back to the yacht, Carly smiled. *Ashton's boldness is finally rubbing off on me. Now, if only I can be that brave with him...*

She settled in on the back deck and read through her grandfather's day planner, hunting for a clue that would help her with Rose Aurora's case. Her grandfather kept his appointment entries to a minimum. Years ago, she asked about his cryptic notes.

"A *good* PI gets to the truth," Grandpa Pierce had explained. "A *great* PI gets to the truth *and* is invisible. The best of the best can sit in the middle of a busy hotel lobby for hours and go undetected. By the end of the day, you're part of the scenery. If someone finds my planner or my notes, the information is meaningless. When clients put their faith in us, we have to protect them and their identities."

Carly flipped to the day before he died. Friday, February 22. He had a meeting that evening at eleven thirty. *He never worked that late.* He woke every day at five thirty and was in bed by nine thirty without fail.

11:30 PM: WS w/I — bring RA photo

She stared at his familiar handwriting. "What does that even mean?"

Over the next forty minutes, she plugged the initials WS into Stone Investigations' database. Her search yielded no results. She flipped back to January and examined each page for a clue.

Pierce's shorthand made no sense, so she crosschecked it with her own schedule. An evening event on February 13 snagged her attention. In all caps he'd written,

JC, DONOR EVENT
MEET GI, DC HOTEL
BRING RA PHOTO!

JC might stand for Joe Clark, Pierce's alias. Carly checked her own schedule. She'd spent the afternoon tailing a wife whose husband wanted to learn if she was cheating with her grad school professor. After work, she'd met Ashton at the shooting range.

The morning bled into the afternoon. At some point, she went inside for a glass of water, then paced—back and forth—before stopping and staring out at the water. Normally, she wouldn't have thought twice about this calendar entry, but Pierce had used his Joe Clark alias only a handful of times. And each time, he was hunting for a killer. That made her shiver.

"There's my gorgeous wife," Ashton boomed.

Carly whirled around. "Oooieeee."

His massive body filled the doorway, but it was his smile that jolted her heart. His button-down shirt and dress pants clung to his body while hers heated in response. Tonight's assignment at Greta's was all about bringing him pleasure under the guise of blending in at a kink party. *I won't have to fake a thing.*

He dropped his computer bag, then continued toward her. She couldn't look away. She couldn't step out of his way, either. When he wrapped her in his arms, she could only delight in his touch.

"What's got *you* so jumpy?" With the tenderness of a lamb, he kissed her forehead.

"It's nothing."

He stepped back, crossed his arms. She wanted to tug him back, sink her fingers into his hair, marry their lips, and give her faux spouse the kind of hello he'd remember for hours.

"Talk to me," he said, snapping her out of her fantasy.

"I stopped by my house to grab a few things and told my roommate to move out."

As if pulled by a magnet, she'd inched so close she had to tip her head back to stare into his eyes. His smile, a mix of playfulness and a whole lotta sexiness had her checking out his mouth.

He didn't back up, but didn't wrap her in his arms again,

either. What he did do was stroke her cheek with the back of his finger. "Don't even *think* about moving out."

"I'm not leaving."

"Good." He furrowed his brow. "Now, what's got you so tense? I saw you pacing, then stop and do that thing you do."

"What thing?"

"Rub the back of your neck when you're trying to work something out."

Ash had this way of breaking down her guard without putting forth any effort. "I didn't realize I did that." She arched an eyebrow. "What are my other tells?"

"For one, your dilated pupils. You're dying to kiss me hello…or better yet, you want *me* to kiss *you*."

Busted. She bit back a smile. "You're a cocky one, you know that?"

"Cocky, bold, brave, and your favorite: loud. Now, if you don't spill, I'm going to spank you." He winked. "Would you like that?" He started unbuttoning his shirt.

I might. She huffed out a breath, then retrieved the day planner. "This was in the secret drawer in my grandfather's desk."

"I haven't seen one of these in a while." With his shirt open, he leafed through the book. "Find anything worthwhile?" he asked before handing it back to her.

She slid her gaze from his bare chest. "His shorthand is hard to figure out. He had some late night meeting the night before he died."

Ashton dragged his shirt over his shoulders and tossed it onto the sofa. As he knelt to untie his shoes, she couldn't tear herself away from his flexing muscles. He peered up at her, the intensity in his gaze halting her breath. She knew his tells, too, and he wanted her. He toed off his shoes, then yanked off his socks. "Was his late night meeting atypical?"

"Uh-huh," she said, struggling to concentrate.

He rose. "Who was it with?" His minty breath warmed her cheeks.

"That's what I'm trying to figure out." She blinked several times. "But it can wait."

"Are you sure? If you need my help…"

Her gaze roamed greedily across his chest, down his guns, and over his abs. She couldn't wait to trail her fingers over his skin, kiss him breathless, and grind against him. "Let's talk about tonight instead."

"Right, so about that." He curled his finger around a chunk of her hair. "Do you want me to take care of you on the cross? On the sofa? Against the wall? With penetration?"

Her lips parted and heat pooled low in her belly. *I want all of that…and all of you.* "Whatever it takes."

He gave her hair a gentle tug before letting go. "I'll take that as a 'Yes.'"

Clearing her throat, she pushed past him and pulled out two chilled beers from the refrigerator. "We'll know what to do when we get there."

The ice-cold liquid tamped down on her white-hot heat. Trying to compose herself, she checked the tracking devices. "Kathy Internado is still in Richmond. With any luck, Georgy-boy might get an early jump on the evening."

After a quick dinner, they got ready. When she sauntered into the main cabin, she spied Ash standing on the back deck, staring into the night, the harbor lights illuminating him in a soft glow.

Her insides heated while her heart took off in her chest. Ashton Hott was power personified. His black dress shirt and black slacks accentuated his hard body. Even the wig couldn't detract from his charisma and intoxicating persona.

He turned. The intensity in his gaze ratcheted up the heat, and his moan confirmed his approval. She had dressed for him…and *only* him.

Maverick's brain screeched to a halt at the same time his libido kicked into overdrive. "Whoa, baby." Glossy black liquid covered Carly's body, leaving nothing to his imagination. She'd blown way past sexy. She'd left sublime behind, too. Plain and simple, she rocked his world. The image of her in that outfit would be tattooed on his brain forever.

My God, she's stunning.

One slow, deliberate step at a time, she slinked closer. He burned to touch her, to taste her, and listen to her whisper her sweet needs in his ear. A breath away, she stopped. Her eyes shone like lasers on the darkest of nights. He'd had so little to drink, but he was already intoxicated from everything Carly. For the next few hours, he would live out that fantasy as if it were reality. She would be his wife, his soul mate, his kink partner, his spy.

"You like?" The spark in her eyes turned him on, the subtle upturn of her sultry lips turned him hard. She stroked his shoulder, trailing her fingernails down his biceps.

His temperature skyrocketed. For all the crispness in the evening air, it might as well have been midsummer in the Mojave.

"*Do I like?*" Eager to touch her second skin, he ran his hands down the hourglass curve of her body. "'Like' isn't a word I would use to describe you. Amazing, breathtaking, gorgeous. I'm not sure I'll ever recover from seeing you in this."

Her eyes bled black with desire. She stroked his cheek, tugged on his beard. "You, Mr. Black, take sexy to a whole new level."

"No, Mrs. Black, it's all you." He kissed her, cherishing how her lips melded to his.

Her sweet moan rumbled through him. He caressed her back and squeezed her ass. "You're right. We *will* know what to do when we get there." When he pulled her close, her breasts pressed against his chest. "You. Are. Mine."

Her lips parted and she exhaled a soft sigh. "Do you want me to show you how the outfit works?"

The first zipper stopped at her navel. A second zipper covered her crotch.

"I got this."

Breaking with his plan, he brushed his lips to hers, had to feel her silky mouth on his again. "The tracker went off while you were getting ready. He's on the move."

He clasped her hand and they walked inside to check Internado's whereabouts. Just past twenty-one hundred and the senator's car was parked around the block from Greta's. Maverick slipped his hand into his pocket and pulled out a small drone that resembled a housefly. "Crockett's Spy Fly."

"What's your plan?"

"Leave it near the bar."

"I'll divert the bartender's attention while you maneuver it into place."

Maverick chuffed out a laugh. "One look at you and he won't notice me at all."

"And if the bartender is a woman?" she asked, nuzzling close.

"Regardless of who's tending bar, you're gonna steal the show, baby doll. *Steal. The. Show.*" He clasped her hand. "Ready to roll?"

On the short ride to Greta's, he took every opportunity to check her out. She caught his gazes with seductive looks of her own. By the time he parked, their pent-up energy had turned the air electric. Before exiting the car, they tied on their masks.

"I'm not letting you out of my sight for a millisecond."

"I wouldn't want you to," she said and caressed his leg.

They stayed connected for several beats. Her soft hand stroking his thigh, their eyes locked in a passionate gaze.

"You ready to do this?" he asked.

"More than ready."

Hand in hand, they sauntered toward Greta's brick-front townhome. This felt more like a date than a stakeout. More like an erotic night out with his sizzling hot wife. More like what his heart had always needed but he'd been too walled off to realize. Neither had removed the wedding bands since they'd first put them on. His pretend marriage to Carly was the easiest thing he'd ever done.

He rang the doorbell. The gentle breeze cooled him, but when their eyes met, the flame reignited.

Greta swung open the door. "Welcome back."

While Greta raved over Carly's outfit, he swept the room for Internado as the hypnotic sounds of Delerium played in the background. *Come on. Show your slimy face.*

A tall woman rounded the corner and strolled over. Her black leather body harness hid her nipples and a lacy thong covered her snatch. She touted a black choker collar and cat mask. Otherwise, she was all skin. She sidled beside him, waiting for a break in the conversation. "Greta, introduce me to your friends."

"This is Mr. and Mrs. Black."

She smiled at Carly. "Love the body suit. So hot." She winked, then slipped her hand into Maverick's. "What's your poison, big boy?"

"My wife," he replied, untangling his hand from hers.

"She can play, too."

"They're exclusive," Greta chimed in.

"If you change your mind, we're in the first bedroom upstairs. My Master loves meeting new people." She strolled over to the bar.

"I saw you set up an online account," Greta said. "Your two-week trial begins tonight. As I mentioned, kink happens upstairs only. You'll find condoms on all the tables up there. Use one if you play. I'll be around if you need me." With a tight smile, she ambled away.

Maverick wrapped his arms around Carly and pulled her close. After dropping a kiss on her mouth, he nuzzled her neck.

"You're up. The bartender has been fixated on your backside. Wait until he sees the rest of you."

"Should I give him something to look at?"

"Go ahead. Unzip yourself."

"You do it." Her husky, commanding voice ripped through him.

Taking his time, Maverick tugged down the zipper, admiring her breasts as they spilled from the tight suit. He stopped just below her cleavage.

She glanced down. "Nice."

"Yes, they are." He kissed one breast, then the other. "I love the girls." With his hand clamped on her ass, he ushered her to the bar.

As the bartender rattled off a short list of cocktail specials, Maverick scoped out a spot to land his drone. Carly walked to the far end of the bar, leaned over, and pointed to a bottle. "What's that?"

Using his phone app, Maverick piloted the tiny insect to the top shelf, then sidled over to Carly and pulled her close. "We'll save the alcohol for later. Two sparkling waters."

"Yes, sir." The bartender eyed his phone. "Ms. Greta has a no phone policy."

"Good to know." Maverick slid his phone into his pocket and dropped a kiss on Carly's temple.

The bartender set two goblets on the bar. "Your first beverage is on the house."

Maverick dropped a ten in the tip jar, collected the drinks, and they moved away from the bar.

"To us," Carly said, her voice full of promise.

"Always." Maverick tapped her glass and drank down the cold beverage.

She had a few more sips before abandoning the drink to curl her arms around his neck. He was buzzing with tension. The press of her lips against his sent a current through him. Her breath hitched, her tongue toying with his.

Here, she was free and open with her affections and he loved how she never held back. He slid his hands down to her curvy hips and around to her sensational ass. The air crackled with chaotic energy, desire springing from her eyes. He wanted to see that degree of heat every moment of every day. Not just while sleuthing at a kink party.

As they headed upstairs, they instinctively reached for each other and entwined their fingers together. First stop: The playroom, where Maverick did a sweep. The majority of the couples were playing while a handful of folks watched from the sidelines. No sign of Internado.

Dammit to hell. Where the hell is he?

Taking their time, they moseyed around. One of the aftercare salons was in use, as was a private room. "Maybe he's in there," he murmured.

"Let's hope so."

They returned to the playroom, but stood against a wall where they could see who exited those rooms.

The upside to this evening was the erotic activity. Three couples, partially clothed, were exploring various degrees of intimacy. A man's face was pressed against his partner's pussy while she moaned and writhed on the leather couch. Another pair was screwing against the window, and the third had tucked themselves away in a darker corner of the room for a blowjob.

A small group had gathered around the St. Andrew's cross. A woman in a two-piece latex outfit was strapped to the apparatus while a tattooed man dressed only in leather pants flogged her.

When Maverick shifted his attention to Carly, she pushed off her stilettos. Again, she kissed him, her body undulating with the deep, slow strokes of her tongue. Ending the kiss, she whispered, "I didn't come here to watch." Her throaty whisper sent sexual energy humming through him.

"Good," Maverick growled, "because I came here to satisfy my wife." He backed her into a corner, cradled her face in his hands, and kissed her. Internado *should* have been his priority, but the need to be with her had been burning a hard line to his raging hard-on all the damn day. He'd come here for one reason, but her unrelenting sex appeal had hijacked his every thought and every action.

Opening her mouth, she welcomed him inside and he deepened the kiss. She raked her fingernails down his back and moaned into him. When the kiss ended, he murmured, "I've waited days for this. *For you.* No more waiting. Have I made myself clear?"

Her lips parted, her eyes dark with desire. "Message received."

He pressed his mouth to hers and gave her another long, lustful kiss.

She flicked open one shirt button at a time, then teased her fingernails down his chest while her half-hooded eyes drilled into his. "We should canvas the entire level." She licked his nipple, kissed his chest. Another burst of energy shot straight to the cramped space between his legs. Then, she ran her tongue over his other nipple and bit it.

Pleasure ricocheted through him. "We will, after I take care of you. Unzip your suit."

With her gaze cemented on his, she pulled down the zipper. The latex gave way, exposing her full breasts. "What should I do now?"

He dropped his mouth on her chest, ran his tongue over her heated skin. "Pinch your nipples."

She did, her breath coming in short gasps.

"Very nice. Do you think they're ready to be sucked?"

She nodded.

"Feel how hard I am for you."

She palmed and fondled his erection through the cotton pants. "Do you like?"

"So much."

"I want you to be seen, watched, admired." She swallowed, hard, her jet-black eyes fluttering closed. "Look at me."

She did.

"I'm going to fuck you against this wall and give you more pleasure than you thought possible. You won't deny me that, will you?"

Framed by the mask, her eyelids were heavy and she kneaded his triceps with her fingers. "No, I won't."

He pressed his mouth to hers, savoring her pouty lips. He deepened the kiss, dipping his tongue inside to tangle with hers. Every act, every breath was deliberate. He moved to her neck, trailing a line of kisses to her shoulder. She began writhing against him, but when he collected her engorged nib into his mouth and sucked, she gasped and arched toward him.

Her long, deep moans clouded his thoughts, turning his already stiff dick to stone, but his sole intention was showing her that she was all that mattered.

When finished, he stepped back, leaving her panting against the wall. "Show me your beautiful pussy."

She unzipped the shiny vinyl, revealing her glistening, bare skin. He slid a finger into her dripping wet folds, withdrew, and licked it. On a husky moan, he snaked his arm around her back. "You're so hot, so wet, Mrs. Black. I cannot wait to make you come." He snagged a condom from his pocket. "Take off my pants."

With nimble fingers, she started to unzip him, but her attention was snagged when the door to the aftercare salon opened. Three members exited, none of them Internado. Maverick shifted his focus back to Carly and she continued to strip him of his pants. They hit the floor and she curled warm fingers around his shaft and caressed him. Slowly up and slowly down before coating its head with his arousal.

"I need you inside me." Her voice gritty with lust. "So badly."

Maverick rolled on the condom, then slipped two fingers inside her delicious sex. "Is this good?"

"Yes," she hissed. She kissed him with so much force any other man would have staggered back. But Maverick was an immovable object. He played with her clit, circling her engorged button with so much gentleness she trembled. "I'm...you feel so good. Oh, God, yeah."

He withdrew his fingers and sucked, her fiery gaze tracking his every movement.

"You are the sexiest man I have ever known." Her voice came out in a breathy whisper, meant only for him.

"This is for your pleasure, Mrs. Black." Lifting her, and using the corner walls for support, he positioned her over him. She wrapped her arms and legs around him as he held her by her buttocks.

"Am I too heavy?" she whispered.

"No, sweet baby. You're as light as a feather and perfect in my arms."

Her relieved smile ratcheted up the heat. He lowered her down onto him, their mirrored groans drowning out any sounds around them. Her blazing eyes burned into his.

Her mouth crushed his, the clash of tongues and moans whirred together as he created the friction they both desperately needed. "You feel incredible. Sooooo good." She chugged in another breath when he captured her breast in his hand.

"It's gonna be fast and deep."

"*God, yes.*"

With her clinging to him, he gripped her hips and thrust again and again, the euphoria spreading over him like a wildfire. Panting, he gasped, "You are fucking *delicious.*"

They peered into each other's eyes, drunk from the primal passion.

She silenced her garbled cry when her mouth found his again.

"Too good. I'm gonna—" Her insides tightened around him as she convulsed and moaned in his arms.

He ground hard against her, pumping until his passion exploded and ecstasy overtook him. Their embrace was a maelstrom of tongues and teeth, of biting and growling. The intensity of their coupling had him soaring. When their orgasms subsided, she dropped her forehead on his, panting in his arms.

"You are so special to me, Mrs. Black." Even sleuthing at a kink club, he couldn't hold back his true feelings.

Her sexy, just-fucked smile slayed him.

They stared at each other, the truth as plain as the love in her eyes. Regardless of where they were and what they were doing, they were each other's missing piece. Only they'd never been missing. They'd been right in front of each other the entire time.

Seconds later, Carly's attention was diverted and he followed her gaze. The door to the private room opened and two couples entered the playroom, one of them being the woman who'd approached them downstairs.

They'd struck out again. "Where the hell is he?" Maverick murmured, frustration tingeing his tone.

"We'll find him."

For another precious moment, they stayed tucked away in the corner. Again, Carly peered over his shoulder, then back into his eyes. "He's here," she whispered.

That smacked him back to reality. "Hold on to me, babe. I'm putting you down."

As soon as he did, she nuzzled his neck. "Over your left shoulder," she whispered.

Maverick zipped up. "Did we catch his attention?"

"Oh, yeah. We'll pass him on the way to an aftercare salon." Carly closed her crotch, then zipped up the latex suit, but left enough to give Internado an eyeful. Maverick didn't want that pig leering at *his* woman. Shielding her, he zipped her up.

"Don't you want to give him something to look at?"

He tipped her chin, brushed his lips to hers. "No."

As she adjusted her mask, she pressed the center sequin. With clasped hands, they made their way toward one of the salons as Maverick zeroed in on his target.

George Internado.

His impressive disguise consisted of a salt and pepper toupee along with a matching beard and moustache. Like Maverick, he wore a black mask, black pants, and a black dress shirt. Had he been just another guy at this kink party, Maverick would have joked about their identical clothes. But there was nothing funny about this situation. Nothing funny at all.

Internado had zeroed in on Carly. His sleazy gaze had Maverick holding her closer. It took all his restraint to walk past the asshole and not deck him.

"Excuse me," Internado said to Carly as Maverick activated his video watch.

"Hey, how are ya this evenin'?" Carly spoke an octave higher.

"You're new to Greta's, aren't you?" Internado's attention lingered on her chest and his creepy smile made the hairs on the back of Maverick's neck prickle.

"Tryin' out the club. Lookin' to turn up the heat, ya know?"

He hadn't even glanced in Maverick's direction, which was to their advantage. No need for the two men to have a stare down.

"How do you like it so far?"

"S'okay." Then, she leaned closer. "Not as dark as I was hopin'." She squeezed Maverick's hand. "Good chattin' with ya." And with that, they moved on.

Once behind the closed door of the aftercare salon, she pulled him close. "Could be cameras in here."

He kissed her, stayed close enough to share breath. "You were fantastic with him," he murmured. "He took the bait, though I'm not happy it was you."

"I can handle myself."

"I know that, babe." He walked into the bathroom to clean up and she followed close on his heels.

"I really have to pee." She sat on the toilet.

For some reason, this was a defining moment. If she could pee with him standing a foot away, she was truly comfortable around him.

When she finished, he captured her in his arms. "Ready to execute the plan?"

Nodding, she caressed his shoulder. "Do you need aftercare?"

"Absolutely." She moved toward the bed, but he drew her hand to his mouth and kissed her soft skin. "Mrs. Black, one of the perks of being hitched is that I get to enjoy aftercare at home in *our* bed with my stunning wife."

Her sultry smile was her only reply.

FLYING HIGH

After paying for their drinks, Maverick eyed his drone on the top shelf behind the bar. Several more couples had arrived, so Mr. Black escorted the stunning Mrs. Black to a spot where they could see Internado if he went on the prowl.

While they waited, the basement door opened and a masked woman wearing leather lingerie made her way to the bar. Her back had been marred by several fresh whip marks. Inwardly, Maverick winced. *That looks painful.*

He kissed Carly's ear, then whispered, "Woman at the bar is from the basement."

After eyeing the club member, Carly leaned up, kissed him, letting her lips linger on his. "Nice catch, Mr. Black."

"You are such an attentive wife. God, I love that about you."

Greta had been making the rounds, greeting people and checking in with them.

"Here she comes," he murmured. "Ready to do this?"

"Absolutely."

Greta finished chatting with a couple nearby, then sauntered over. "Downstairs so quickly?"

"We had a little fun," Carly said.

"Just a little?"

"You have a beautiful place, Greta. The club is lovely, but I'm not sure it's what I'm looking for. I'll let Sinclair know we won't be returning."

Greta frowned. "I'm surprised to hear you've made your decision already. What's missing or what didn't you like?"

Carly leaned close. "It's definitely classy and you take all the appropriate precautions. I appreciate that you allow penetration."

"Are you looking for more equipment?" Greta asked. "More entertainment from my staff?"

"I'm looking for something darker, maybe even a little dangerous."

"What about you, Mr. Black? How was your evening?"

The basement door opened and a masked man wearing a latex kilt and mesh shirt passed by on his way out. "Maybe your basement crowd would better suit my wife's needs."

Crossing her arms, Greta arched an eyebrow. "The dungeon is a closed group."

Carly set the glass on a tray. "I'm sorry it's not going to work out."

Out of the corner of his eye, Maverick spied Internado leering at Carly. In a protective move, he draped his arm around her before escorting her out.

Once in the car, he activated the Spy Fly. They watched real-time on his phone as a couple discussed their drink order like it was the most critical decision of their lives. While their conversation droned on, Maverick checked the video on his watch. "The lighting is so low, I think Internado would deny this was even him." He showed Carly.

"Maybe, but he wouldn't want us showing that to the press." Using her phone app, she played back her video clip. "That's definitely his voice, but we need to catch him doing something beyond chatting me up. I'm more concerned our bluff with Greta will backfire. We don't have confirmation he plays in the basement."

"But now we know it's a viable option."

The couple finally decided on two beers. Internado stepped up to the bar and ordered a drink as Greta sidled over. Maverick zoomed in on them.

"Packed house tonight," Internado said. "Good for business."

"How's your evening going?"

"Fun, as always. Who's the new couple?"

"I have several floating around. Which one?"

"Latex jumpsuit. Dark hair. She wore it up."

"Hmm, was she alone?"

"No. She was with a silent, muscular guy. Six two or six three."

"Ah, yes, Mr. and Mrs. Black."

"Who are they?"

"No idea." Greta sipped her red wine. "They're shopping around. Said they're exclusive. I don't ask a lot of questions. You know that. A hundred grand is a hundred grand."

"I'd love to play with her," Internado said. "She looks like she'd be one hell of a good time."

"Don't think they're returning. She's got her own private group and said this isn't much different from that. She's looking for something darker."

The senator's eerie smile sent a shiver down Maverick's spine.

"Invite her into the dungeon," Internado quipped.

Carly and Maverick exchanged glances.

"She won't play with you," Greta continued.

"She might if she likes my talents."

Greta shook her head. "I have rules regarding the dungeon."

"Break them."

"If they become members, I'll consider it."

"How 'bout I sweeten the pot? Invite her and her dolt downstairs. If they agree, I'll give you ten grand."

"You know I'm all about consent. I'll boot you out if you try anything."

Even in the dimly lit room, Maverick couldn't miss Internado's sneer.

"I'm a lot of things, but I have no intention of forcing myself on anyone," Internado said. "I, too, am into consent, dear friend, so you have nothing to worry about. I'll charm her, then wow her with my talents."

Maverick's stomach dropped.

"Ew," Carly blurted.

"Are you talking about tomorrow?" Greta asked.

Internado sighed. "No, I have to go out of town tomorrow for a fucking family obligation. I'm playing the role of excited grandfather. Let's plan on next Thursday."

"I'll let you know."

"You'd be a fool to turn down that much cash for such little effort."

"Oh, boy," Maverick said.

Internado collected his glass and walked out of the frame. A couple headed toward the front door. As soon as it opened, Maverick piloted the drone out, down the street, and into the car.

"I hope Greta accepts his offer," Carly said.

"No fear of going into the lion's den?"

"Not when I have the biggest, fiercest, most loyal lion of all on *my* side," she replied.

On the short ride home, Carly made a decision. Matters of the heart terrified her, but she was done freezing Ashton out, done sleeping alone.

Before stepping onboard, she removed her stilettos. Once on the yacht, she took his hand. "Ash."

"Yeah, babe."

"Help me out of this cat suit."

His eyes locked on hers. When he stepped close, he lifted her hand to his mouth and brushed his lips over her knuckle. "I won't want to stop there." That deep, sexy-as-hell voice of his rumbled through her chest.

"Neither will I."

His intense gaze made her go damp. And then, his mouth found hers. The kiss turned incendiary, their breathing erratic. She couldn't slow herself down, the desire to mate with him overpowering her rational thought. He clung to her like she was the only woman in the entire world. Without question, her heart, her soul, and her body were his.

The wild kiss slowed, morphing into tender pecks. A smile dancing on his mouth had her opening her eyes.

"I'm not going to make love to you."

His words slashed her heart. "It's okay."

"Unless you spend the night in my bed, in my arms," he said, caressing her back and palming her ass.

Her pulse fluttered. "I will."

"Hmm, that sounded too easy. Not putting up a fight?"

"No."

"Finally, some damn progress." He dropped kisses on her forehead, both cheeks, and another on the tip of her nose. Then, he dragged the zipper down, his eyes blackening with desire as he revealed her naked form.

"You are stunning in *and* out of this," he said, kissing the nape of her neck and the dip between her collarbone before helping her out of the costume.

"Thank you. Let's get you out of this wig." She tugged it off and combed soft fingers through his wavy hair.

His growly sounds made her insides thrum. "By God, woman, I love your touch."

"I love touching you, Ash."

244 | STONI ALEXANDER

He captured her face in his hands. "You mean everything to me." His kiss was soft and filled with so much tenderness.

Her heart soared while her body tensed. Mr. and Mrs. Black's gig would end and where would they go from here? He kissed her, plucking her from her angsty thoughts.

After pulling off her wig, she brushed her fingers through her hair. "You aren't the only one who doesn't like wearing wigs."

"Let me do that for you." He gently stroked her scalp, then inhaled. "You smell incredible. Like summer peaches."

That made her smile. In high school, he'd call her "Peaches", but only when they were alone.

Though eager to strip him naked, she plucked one button at a time, pausing to bite and nip at his warm skin. By the time she dropped his pants, her insides were on fire.

As he led her downstairs toward the sleeping quarters, his phone rang. "Dammit."

"You have to see who that is."

While he checked, she slipped into his stateroom. The cool sheets felt delicious against her hot, bare skin.

He handled the call and entered his bedroom. She was peeking out from beneath the linens. "Are you the captain of this vessel?"

He paused for a split second before a smile danced in his eyes. "I am. Who the hell are you and what are you doing in my bed?"

She bit back a smile. "I need to get out of the country."

"Sorry, darlin', I don't harbor stowaways. I'll have to turn you over to the authorities."

Her eyes grew large and she pushed back the cover to reveal her breasts. "Captain, please no. You can't. You just can't."

He glanced at her chest. "I'm not that easily swayed, ma'am. Can you offer me money?"

"No."

"Can you cook for my crew?"

"Nope."

"Well, then, what *can* you do?"

She tossed off the blanket. "I can fuck."

His guttural growl landed between her legs while he perused every naked inch of her. "I'll be the judge of that."

With her gaze locked on his, she licked her finger, then rubbed her erect nipple until it glistened. "Can you wet my other nipple, Captain?"

He slid into bed and laved her delicate pink flesh with his tongue. "Like that?"

"Mmm, that was perfect." She ran her fingers down his shoulder, chest and abs, appreciating the striations in his defined muscles. When she curled her hand around his shaft, he bit out a throaty moan. "I'll fuck you so good, you'll never want to throw me off your ship."

As he peered into her eyes, his breathing shifted. "Never?"

She leaned in and kissed him, letting her tongue tangle with his. "No. Never." Her breathy whisper elicited another long deep moan from him.

Within seconds, he had sheathed himself. She rolled away and bent one leg, giving him easy access to her pussy. He positioned himself behind her, caressing her breasts and stomach before sliding two fingers inside her heat.

"Damn, woman, you are so wet for me."

"Mmm, you've got great hands. So big and strong."

He thrust and withdrew his fingers before teasing her clit. Then, he positioned himself at her opening. "Last chance to cook for my crew."

"I'm a much better screw than I am a cook," she said with a hint of a smile.

He tunneled inside. "Baby, you feel phenomenal."

So. Much. Pleasure. *Everywhere.*

And then, he started moving. Her moans were drowned out by his groans and grunts. He caressed her tits, rubbed her nipples, stroked her tummy.

"We shouldn't kiss," Carly rasped out.

"No, that would be wrong, very wrong."

As soon as she craned her neck, his mouth found hers. The kiss turned savage. She bit his lip and he stroked her tongue, hard. He fondled her clit and waves of ecstasy exploded through her. Crying out, she came.

"Carly, babe, you're making me come." He poured himself into her, moaning through the euphoria.

Once she caught her breath, she murmured, "How did you know my name?"

He laughed. "No matter how many different ways we make love, you'll always be my Carly." He wrapped his arm around her and hugged her. Moments passed before he withdrew. As soon as he did, she rolled toward him. Cupping her chin in his hand, he kissed her.

Boneless, she lay on his chest and threw her leg over his. "Too heavy?"

"Carlyle, look at me."

Lifting her face, she peered into his eyes. "You are not heavy. Do not ever ask me that again. You are perfect and perfect for me. You have a rockin' hot body and I'm going to worship you all night long. Understood?"

"Yes, sir." She shot him a playful smile. "I…I…I like you."

He chuckled. "How many years did it take to figure that one out?"

"I liked you the first day I met you, but I wanted to let a couple of decades slide by…you know…just to make sure."

He nudged her onto her back and planked over her. Peering into each other's eyes, they shared a smile. "I like you, too." He dropped a long, luxurious kiss on her lips. "With everything I am."

THE MORNING SUN streamed through the window. Carly was alone, so she padded into her stateroom and threw on a sweatshirt and yoga pants, stopped in the bathroom to brush her teeth, and ventured out to find her man.

Ashton sipped coffee on the ship's bow. Shirtless and in long shorts, he looked too sexy and adorably sleepy. "Good morning, my beautiful angel. Sleep okay?"

She bent over and kissed him. "What little sleep we got was perfect. You're the best cuddler."

"I don't cuddle." He pushed off the bow and ran the back of his finger down her cheek. "*You* bring that out in me."

As they stared into each other's eyes, romantic words played on the tip of her tongue. She wanted to tell him, but she couldn't. Not yet.

The boat owners in the next slip started chatting with him, so after she said hello, she retreated inside and filled a mug with hot, steaming java.

Not long after, he eased down beside her on the kitchen bench and she topped off his coffee. "Internado's headed to Richmond, like he told Greta."

"How long have you been awake?" She rubbed her eyes, trying to push out the grogginess.

"An hour. I've got a surprised planned for today."

"What about work?"

"It's Saturday and everyone, *even you*, is entitled to a day off." They sipped their coffee as a flock of geese flew south.

"Boat ride?" she asked.

"No. Dress in layers. We'll be outside for part of the day." He shot her a smile. "And that's all I'm going to say."

Excitement skittered through her. "When are we leaving?"

"After breakfast."

The crisp fall morning was cloudless and Carly settled into the passenger seat of the Porsche. As they weaved their way out of D.C., Ashton punched up a playlist of jazz tunes. Not long after, they were headed west on Route 66 in Virginia.

"Does this have something to do with your birthday?"

"My birthday isn't for another week and a half, and when have I ever celebrated that?"

She studied his profile. "Not even a hint?"

He glanced over. "No way."

They sped west, leaving the bustle of Northern Virginia behind them. An hour later, Carly commented on the beautiful color of the changing leaves. "We're going to a winery."

He claimed her thigh with his large hand and gave her a little squeeze. "You'll see."

Her chest warmed as she studied his wide knuckles. She loved his touch, the gentle way his fingers wrapped her leg. Just as she was about to thread her fingers through them, his cell phone rang and he took the call.

"Hott here."

"Maverick, it's Darren. Can you hear me?"

"I can and you're on speaker. I'm not alone."

"Yes, sir. We had to go quiet the past twenty-four hours, but we've got confirmation on our target."

"Good. How's your team doing?"

"High spirits, decent sleep. No one's drunk the water."

Ashton chuckled. "Are you on schedule?"

"Affirmative."

"If you run into any issues, call me right away. Thanks for checking in. Good luck, Darren."

"Thank you, sir." Darren disconnected.

The wrinkle between his brows had returned from the pressure he imposed on himself. Despite his silence, she knew he worried when a team was on assignment in hostile territory.

Exiting Route 66, he downshifted, continuing west on a pretty country road.

"You've got so much going on at work," she said. "We don't have to do this, you know?"

"Yes, we do. We need a break from the mayhem." He turned onto a farm road. In the distance, the rolling hills of the Virginia countryside created a picturesque landscape. A farmhouse and two smaller buildings were the only structures in the area. Carly was stumped until they rounded the corner and saw three hot air balloons in various states of inflation.

"Oh, wow. No way." Beaming, she grasped his arm. As soon as he parked, she hopped out. "Are we taking a ride?"

"Damn straight."

"This is the *best* surprise."

"I thought you'd like it."

"I cried so hard when my mom wouldn't let me go with you guys." She curled her hand around his biceps as they made their way across the field. "Well, she can't stop me now."

"Can I go?" Carly had asked her mom. "I really, really want to."

"Absolutely not," said her mom. "What a stupid way to spend the day. Those Hotts are such a pretentious family. A balloon ride... how ridiculous. You'll thank me if their balloon crashes to the ground and they all die."

Two short months later, Ashton's mom was dead.

Carly shivered away the bitter memory as a burly man shot them a friendly wave and ambled over.

"Howdy, folks. You Maverick?"

"Sure am." The two men shook hands. "Kevin, right?"

"Last I checked. I'll be your pilot today. Hang out for a bit while I help my guys get this balloon airborne."

Once the craft lifted into the air and sailed away, Kevin pointed to a giant nylon balloon lying fifty feet away. "You guys ready to soar like a bird?"

Over the next thirty minutes, they learned about balloon safety while assisting Kevin and his team prep for their flight. Once the lemon-yellow and peacock-blue nylon balloon was fully

250 | STONI ALEXANDER

inflated, they climbed into the gondola and Kevin's team disconnected the cables.

"Here we go," the pilot said as the basket lifted into the air.

Carly grinned up at Ashton.

"It's a great day for a balloon flight," Kevin said.

Carly's heart soared as they sailed above the treetops. "Beautiful."

Ash dipped down and stole a kiss. Her heart swelled and she threaded her fingers through his. Save for the roar of the burner, the flight was silent. The majestic Blue Ridge Mountains lay before them, a breathtaking sight from the air.

"This is amazing. Thank you, Ash."

"You're welcome, babe. Glad you like."

"Are you guys celebrating an anniversary?" Kevin asked.

"This has been on my wish-list since childhood," Carly replied.

"Been married long?" Kevin asked.

"Oh, we're—"

"First year." Ashton grinned.

Her heart flipped. *If only...*

"The wife and I were high school sweethearts," Kevin added. "Three kids later and we're still going strong. Got kids?"

"Not yet," Ash replied.

Thinking about little Hott babies made her smile.

The wind shifted and the balloon sailed westward. From every direction, the views were spectacular. Rolling farmland and pastures framed by a jutting mountain range. The sun beamed down in a cloudless sky and the mild breeze carried them for miles. More than the scenic vistas and the stunning beauty of the Virginia countryside, the man beside her had captured her heart, fully and completely.

Even with all the stress and pressure he'd been under, he'd arranged something special just for her. As she shifted her gaze to him, she felt so incredibly loved. He anchored his arm around her and she leaned into him. *If this isn't love, I have no idea what is.*

"This is perfect." She stood tall, and kissed him. His tender kiss was his only reply.

An hour later, Kevin landed in an open field. The chase vehicle waited on the dirt road and the crew ran over to secure the lines. After Carly got out, she threw her arms around Ash, then kissed him again. "You are the best. Thank you. This was *so much fun.*"

"I wanted to do something special for you, something I knew you'd enjoy."

"I loved this and I…" The rest of that sentence stuck in her throat.

He raised a brow before they piled into the van. The crew whisked them back to the old farmhouse.

"We had a great time," Ash said as he palmed Kevin's hand with a tip.

"My pleasure." Kevin stashed the cash in his pocket. "So, you're all set up on the far side of the building overlooking the mountains. I'm here for the afternoon helping my crew get their balloons airborne if you need anything." The two men shook hands. "Enjoy yourselves."

As they headed toward the farmhouse, she caressed his back and he flashed her that panty-melting grin. "Time to talk, Carly girl."

Energized by the awesome balloon ride, Maverick was done playing things safe. Time to break past his barriers, put it all out there, and tell Carly how he felt.

They walked around the brick red farmhouse.

She stopped short. "Oh, wow."

Before them was a breathtaking vista of farmland and rolling hills, a stunning portrait of autumnal glory provided by Mother Nature. In the foreground, a red-checkered cloth adorned a table with place settings for two. Linen slipcovers wrapped the folding chairs. Awaiting them was a platter of cheeses and an assortment of crackers, sliced pears and apples framed in a heart of plump blueberries. A bottle of champagne chilled in an ice bucket.

The quaint setting was the perfect romantic backdrop for him to profess his love. She strolled past the table and admired the countryside. As he caressed her back, she tucked her hair behind her ears and turned toward him.

"It's so peaceful here," she said. "We've been so busy with work and with everything going on—"

Touching his lips to hers, he released the last remaining tension. He inhaled her beautiful scent, reveled in her soft pecks and quiet murmurs. "I've been holding back, withholding the truth." His voice was hushed, his tone serious. "I love you so damn much, Carly."

To his utter surprise, she broke away, fixed her gaze on the vista. "I can't lose you."

What the hell? "Why would you say that?"

Kevin jogged around the farmhouse. "Hey, guys. Just checking in. Everything good?"

"We're doing great," Maverick replied.

"Need help uncorking the bottle?"

"No, thanks. Just admiring the view."

"Doesn't get any better than that." With a wave, Kevin left.

When Maverick turned back, Carly had removed the foil on the champagne bottle and was untwisting the wire. She popped the cork, sending it skyward, and, with a shaky hand, poured two flutes. Though she offered him one, she didn't look at him.

They sat, staring into the valley. Unnerved but undeterred by her reaction, he forged forward. "Why did you say that?"

"I have everything to lose if we don't work out."

"We both do, babe."

"It's not the same," she said, shifting toward him. "If we broke up, I would lose my best friend *and* his family. I would lose *all* of the people I love the most." The sadness in her eyes wrecked him.

Holy hell.

He set down the bubbly, held out his hands. A long moment passed. When she placed her hands in his, she was trembling.

"My family adores you. Nothing will ever change that."

"Losing you could."

Tell her.

"Carly, my job is all about taking risks, but when it comes to love, I've taken none. When my mom died, everything changed. Over time, I learned to hide my sadness, but you saw past all that. You always see the *real* me."

With gentle fingers, she caressed his bearded cheek.

"I have loved you most of my life. Somewhere along the way, I realized I'd fallen in love with you, but I refused to act on it. For me, love meant the pain of loss. I vowed I would never allow myself to experience that grief again, so I've been playing things safe with you."

Her gaze stilled on his while the air between them hummed.

"I'm done playing it safe. This pretend marriage is the best thing we've ever done. I love starting and ending each day with you. I love making you happy. Being around you has always been one of my absolute favorite things. Being in love with you, and admitting that, is the best decision I've ever made."

Her smile urged him onward and filled him with hope.

"I need you in my life in *every* conceivable way. I'm terrified of loving you and losing you, but I'm not letting fear stop me. You are it, Carly girl. You've always been it and I'm going to do everything in my power to ensure you stay safe. If something happened to you..." He shuddered in a breath. "I couldn't go on."

Tears blurred her vision. "Oh, Ash."

When he patted his thigh, she moved to his lap. A kaleidoscope of emotions beamed from her eyes.

"When I was in the hospital, all I could think about was coming home to you." He kissed her cheek. "Seeing you with those two men lit a fire in me. Then, when we *finally* got together,

I knew I had to make you mine. Because I knew I was already yours. I asked you to be my girlfriend in middle school and I'm *still* waiting for your answer."

As she stared at her hands, folded in her lap, a single tear rolled down her cheek. A moment passed before she lifted her face, their eyes locking gazes. "What is love to you?"

He drank in her beauty and uttered the truth. "I'm looking right at it."

Her expression softened, the smile shining in her eyes. Threading her arms around his neck, she kissed him. "If you can push past your fear, then so can I." She married her lips to his and kissed him again. "I've been in love with you for years. You stole my heart a long time ago and now it's yours to keep." Her smile overflowed with happiness. "I love you so much, Ash."

After twenty-five years, Ashton Hott had finally won over the girl of his dreams.

2 2

CONNECTING THE DOTS

Carly floated on a cloud, rejoicing in Ash's love. Their picnic had been more about kissing than eating. They admired the beauty in each other over nature's colorful vista. When finished, he lifted her to her feet and drew her into his arms. "Let's go home."

Home. That simple word elicited another smile.

His kiss melted her, his embrace made her feel safe and deeply loved. *I am his. And he's mine.* Hand in hand, they thanked Kevin and left.

On the drive back, Sinclair called. Ashton hit the speaker. "Hey, brother. What's happening?"

"Greta said you and the Mrs. might not be returning. No luck finding Internado?"

"Hey, it's the Mrs.," Carly said. "Internado plays in the dungeon. We don't have access."

"Need my help?" Sinclair asked.

"Internado got one look at Carly and was chomping at the bit," Ashton said. "I'll let you know if we run into an obstacle."

"Are you guys going there tonight?"

"No, his daughter had a baby," Carly said. "He's in Richmond."

"That's not the real reason he's there," Sin said. "He's announcing his run for governor this weekend."

"Because Richmond's the capital?" Ashton asked.

"No, because he's *from* Richmond and always returns home for significant political announcements," Sinclair replied. "They treat him like royalty. Stroke his ego and God knows what else."

"Hmm," Carly said. *Rose Aurora was from Richmond.*

"Good luck," Sin said and hung up.

"I can hear your brain churning," Ashton said.

Smiling, she leaned over and pressed her lips to his cheekbone. "I'm working a cold case that may involve a politician. When Sinclair said Internado is from Richmond...nah, never mind. I have an overactive imagination."

He waggled his eyebrows. "I cannot wait for you to use that imagination on me."

"Drive faster." She massaged his corded thigh with anxious fingers.

"Do you want to stop at Hudson's for dinner?" he asked.

"Only if you do. Are you hungry? Of course, you're hungry. You're always hungry."

He stopped at a light. His eyes darkened with impatient desire. "I *am* starving. For you."

When the light turned green, he hit the gas. With an edgy delight, she felt herself go damp. No masks, no kink club, and no role-playing. She couldn't wait to make love to him.

By the time they got back, the sun had set. Once inside the yacht, she slammed into him, their bodies afire, their mouths greedy. Ravenous, they stripped each other bare and tumbled into bed. She fastened her lips to his, his sexy sounds sending currents jolting through her. His mouth was hot, his hands hotter. His intensity sent flares straight to her center. Their rough kissing yielded to softer pecks and murmurs of love.

As they lay facing each other, his thumb tenderly teased her nipple, while she stroked him beneath the sheet.

"I need a condom." His husky voice vibrated through her.

"No condom. I use an IUD, plus, my partners gloved up."

"I'm king of the condoms." His smile crinkled his eyes in the corners. "I'm clean."

She guided him to her opening and, in one glorious slide they were connected.

"You're all mine," he murmured, "and I want to show you exactly what that means." He took her slowly, his eyes never leaving hers. With every thrust, her body bowed to his. The rise was slow, decadent. The touch of his hands on her breasts, the feel of his mouth on her skin, exploring and tasting.

His moans rippled through her. She couldn't stop writhing beneath him, couldn't stop stroking him, reveling in his hard muscles and strong body. His ravenous kisses stole her thoughts and sent her flying high.

She got close to cresting, but he slowed them down, then built her back up. When he finally propelled her to a crescendo, the orgasm shattered her, shaking her to her soul. He, too, let go, the euphoria enveloping them in layered sensations of ecstasy. They became each other's world. They were all that mattered.

Without question, she had found her soul mate. They stayed wrapped around each other while they drifted down to earth.

"You're my angel." He drew her closer still, dropped a kiss on her heated skin. "I'm going to spend every day making sure you know how much I love you."

"From the moment you sat next to me at school, I adored you," she said with a smile.

"And you always will." He kissed the corner of her mouth, where her lips curved into a smile.

"So cocky."

"Yes, ma'am. I also know I'm the luckiest guy on earth. So, what's your answer, Carlyle Stone? Will you be my girl?"

"You have me, Ash."

He held up his pinky. "That goes double for me."

258 | STONI ALEXANDER

She hooked her small finger around his. "Pinky promise."

"Forever," he said and pressed his lips to hers.

Maverick woke, his heart pounding out of his chest, the nightmare too fresh in his mind to ignore. He stood alone in a cemetery, staring at a casket that had yet to be buried. While he'd assumed his mother's body lay in that wooden box, the sinking feeling in the pit of his stomach gave him every reason to believe he was burying Carly.

In the pre-dawn hour, her rhythmic breathing calmed his palpitating heart. He was spooning her, his arm and leg protecting her like a shield.

She's okay. Better than okay. She was with him and she was safe. He had no reason to believe anything to the contrary, but the chilling dream had left him unsettled and overly protective.

As his heart rate slowed back down, he replayed their lovemaking. Passionate and intense one minute. Tender and slow the next. Stirring, she rolled toward him.

"Nightmare?" Her voice was soft and soothing, but knowing, too.

"Yeah, but I'm okay."

"Let me make you feel better." A sly smile graced her mouth and lit up her beautiful eyes.

Heat suffused his chest as she traced her fingertips over his skin. Her slow, provocative kiss had him moaning, but when she slithered beneath the sheet and took his hardened cock into her mouth, every muscle in his body turned to steel.

Carly drew primal sounds out of him with her licking and sucking. Her hums and moans turned him harder still. He tossed back the sheet and moved her hair out of the way to admire her sensual talents. She cradled his balls and he murmured her name.

Her pace was deliciously slow, the build sending a constant stream of pleasure surging through him.

"Oh, Christ, Carly, you're sending me to the fucking moon."

Her throaty hum vibrated through him. When she increased her pace, he closed his eyes and surrendered to the ecstasy until he had no more left to give. As he drifted back to earth, she attended to his knotted thigh with gentle kneading, then crawled on top of him.

When she finished with another tantalizing kiss, he offered a drunken smile. "You've rocked my world." He rolled them over, peered down at her cradled in his arms. "This is it, you know that, right?"

As the cresting sun reflected in her eyes, they shone with love. "I do."

"I love you so damn much. I want you to relax and let *me* love *you* now."

She caressed his cheek. "I'd love for you to put your hot mouth on me, but that was an early birthday present."

"Dear God, that was the best birthday present...*ever*."

"Better than the go-kart?"

"No contest. That go-kart was way better." On a laugh, he kissed her. "You are the best present I get to unwrap every single day. I am *so* damn lucky you're mine."

"You sure are." With a playful gleam, she pushed out of bed. "Come take a shower with me. I need help washing those hard-to-reach places."

He threw back the linens. "Yes, ma'am. I can do that and a whole helluva lot more."

An hour later, they'd finished breakfast when Maverick got a call from Gunner. One of the teams overseas had run into a problem and Maverick needed to strategize with his executive team. He threw his arms around her and nuzzled her neck. "I'm sorry to leave you, especially on a Sunday."

"Make sure they're safe. I've got work to do." One luxurious kiss before she ordered him out. "Go."

"So bossy." With a wink, he jumped onto the pier.

———

As Ashton walked down the pier, Carly was relieved he had way more swagger than limp. She retrieved her satchel and settled on the back sofa beneath the overhang. The day was clear, the sky bright, and her heart was bursting with love. *Settle down, missy. Time to work.*

After laying out the contents of Rose's file along with Pierce's day planner, she read through everything again.

Pierce's calendar.

11:30 PM: WS w/I — bring RA photo

Pierce's notes.

Client Alice Murphy, 67. Raised child as daughter. Erin Murphy, 39. Aunt, not mother (murdered, CC). Has Alz. Wants Erin to know. KILLER?

R. police — no leads
Evidence file — no fingerprints
Hair strands found in motel — no match
Skin cells under fingernails — no match
Cold case
Photo

A gust of wind blew the papers off the table. On the flip side of one, Pierce had written "Archived Newspaper Photos" and underlined it three times. She stared at his familiar handwriting. *How'd I miss this?*

Spurred by that new clue, she logged into a website giving her access to vintage newspapers, but that search yielded nothing.

Then, she thought about the story Mrs. Murphy had shared about Rose getting involved with married men and how "Mr. Virginia" had his sights set on the White House. Had Rose worked for a political candidate? Carly searched the Internet for Virginia campaigns from four decades ago.

There were several local political races that year, but the one that stole her attention was the race for U.S. Senator.

"Oh, God."

George Internado, then a prosecutor for the Richmond D.A.'s office, was one of a slew of candidates running for the U.S. Senate. After digging deeper, she found that the primaries had spit out three candidates—a democrat, a republican, and an independent. Internado was the frontrunner.

She found a focus piece on Internado and stared at the accompanying photo. A young, slim man with a full head of hair smiled at the crowd. The thirty-year-old candidate lived in Richmond with his wife and young family. Since graduating from law school, he'd put in long hours as a hard-nosed prosecutor in the D.A.'s office.

> "My job," he was quoted as saying, "is to make Virginia the strongest, safest, most law-abiding state in the union. I'm a candidate of the people. Their concerns, fears, and dreams are mine. My platform is built on strong family values because family comes first. As our popular slogan states, 'Virginia is for Lovers.'"

"Hmm. Was Rose Aurora your lover, Georgy-boy?"

Based on the story, George Internado appeared to be a saint, but Carly wasn't buying the load of crap he was selling. Still, her search yielded another big fat zero.

Frustrated by her lack of progress, she redirected her attention to Internado's foremost opponent. Helen McDay was a strong-minded woman fighting for a seat in a male-dominated U.S. Senate. Though more experienced, she didn't appear to possess Internado's charisma.

Carly eyed a photo of Helen McDay surrounded by staff at her campaign headquarters. A young, pretty woman with bright blonde hair and a baby bump stood beside her. Carly skimmed the names until she found the one that matched.

Rose Aurora.

Acid churned in her stomach.

Was Rose Aurora feeding Internado information on his opponent like he'd asked of Ashton? Had he played with that young woman's heart simply to gain a competitive advantage?

Fueled by her find, Carly located the vintage newspaper article from the day following the senate election. Internado's face was splashed on the front page.

Internado Takes Virginia by Storm
Landslide Win for Former Prosecutor

"Hey, babe." Ashton's booming voice startled her. He set down grocery bags, sat beside her, and kissed her hello. "You smell like home."

Her heart bloomed as she threaded her arms around him and kissed him back.

"Have you been at it this entire time?"

"Yeah." She eyed his watch. Nearly four hours had passed. "Everything go okay?"

"All good." He glanced at the computer screen. "What are you working on?"

"One of my cases."

"Getting anywhere?"

"It's slow going."

As he put away the food, she turned back to her computer in

search of Rose Aurora's date of death. She logged in to an online database containing vital stats.

Rose Aurora had died on December thirty-first. Carly returned to the archived newspaper website and narrowed the dates to coincide with Rose's death. Up popped the January second article Mrs. Murphy had clipped about her sister's murder.

Above it, and emblazoned across the front page, was a photo of George Internado on the steps of the Virginia state capitol building. The headline read:

Virginia's Senator-Elect George Internado to Take Oath of Office in Washington, D.C.
Promises to be a "Senator of the People"

The photo captured Internado waving at the crowd. Standing beside him was his wife, Kathy. Something wasn't right about Internado's face and Carly zoomed in. Internado was sporting what appeared to be the remnants of a black eye. She skimmed the article. When asked about his shiner, Internado was quoted as saying, "My youngest daughter is energetic. My face just got in the way of her fun."

The hairs on the back of Carly's neck prickled while a chill streaked down her spine. Rose Aurora had died three days before Internado's inauguration. Coincidence? In her line of work, Carly followed the evidence. *Is Erin Murphy his child?*

She reread her grandfather's notes, this time focusing on his handwritten appointment the night before he died.

11:30 PM: WS w/I — bring RA photo

"Babe." Ashton crashed in on her thoughts. "I'm going for an easy run. Take a break and join me. I'd love your company."

She stood and stretched. "I've been sitting for so long, my butt hurts."

"I promise a Hott rub later."

"No argument from me. You have *the* best hands."

As she ambled past, he caught her in his arms and touched the spot between her brows. "Relax, babe."

But the gnawing in her gut wouldn't go away. After changing into running clothes, they drove toward a familiar destination. Riverwalk Trail offered a twenty-mile pathway bordering both sides of the Anacostia River. The lovely October afternoon attracted everyone from athletes to parents pushing their baby carriages and owners with their dogs.

They eased into their workout with a brisk walk. Ten minutes into it, he suggested a slow jog. "This feels great."

Halfway through, he increased his speed and Carly pushed harder to keep pace.

"It's pretty busy this afternoon," he said. "I wonder if we'd have had less foot traffic on my Ironman route."

"That's a great route, except for the Watergate Steps. I'm always worried I'll lose my footing and tumble to the bottom."

"I didn't know those were an issue for you. Going forward, I'll reroute us."

She flashed him a smile. "You are so good to me."

"Right back atcha. I'm glad I listened to you and didn't meet Internado there. What a cluster fuck that would have been."

Pierce's mysterious calendar entry popped into her head.

11:30 PM: WS w/I — bring RA photo

Oh, my God. She stopped short. "WS" stood for Watergate Steps. The "I" was Internado. "RA" was Rose Aurora. The night before her grandfather died, he'd showed Internado a photo of Rose Aurora at the Watergate Steps.

Nausea clouded her thoughts. Bending over, she gripped her

thighs and tried to suck air into her lungs. But she couldn't breathe at all.

In an instant, Ashton was by her side. "What's wrong?"

She couldn't speak.

Kneeling in front of her, he gripped her arms and stared into her eyes. "Talk to me, Carly. Are you hyperventilating? Cramping?"

His touch relaxed her and she gasped for air while he rubbed her back. When she straightened up, she wrapped her fingers around him for support.

"Drink some water."

She did. After a moment, she regained her composure. "I'm okay. I can run."

"We'll walk this down."

After swigging more water, they forged forward.

"You okay?"

She nodded.

"You want to tell me what's going on?"

"I need your help with one of my cases."

"I'm listening."

"Not here," she replied.

On the drive home, Maverick kept checking on her. Her pasty white complexion had improved to rosy cheeks, but he couldn't shake his worry. In all the years they'd run together, he'd never seen her *that* pale.

She caught one of his glances. "I see you watching me."

"I'm not trying to be subtle. I'm concerned about you."

Once onboard, he filled their water bottles and sat beside her in the boat's stern, the afternoon sun warming their skin. He couldn't take his eyes off her, not just because he was worried, but because she was so beautiful. Her skin glistened with a sheen of perspiration and her ponytail was askew. She was makeup free, totally natural, and completely captivating. He adored her with his entire being. "Feel better?"

She nodded. "I've been working the cold case from the envelope Hudson found. A woman with a newborn was murdered almost forty years ago and her sister raised the child, posing as her mother."

"Okay."

"The woman hired my grandfather to find out who killed her sister."

"Got it."

"But he died before solving the case. I've been trying to piece together his clues, but Grandpa wrote in his own style of shorthand, so it's been slow going. During our jog, you said something that made total sense, but now I'm not so sure."

"Show me his notes."

She opened his calendar to Friday, February 22 and pointed to the last entry on the page.

11:30 PM: WS w/I — bring RA photo

"I think grandpa had a late-night meeting with George Internado at the Watergate Steps."

His eyes grew wide. "What the hell?"

"It might sound like my over-active imagination has gone off the rails, but I've pieced together clues that put Internado in Richmond at the time of the young woman's death. During the time she worked on his opponent's campaign, she became pregnant, gave birth, and was later found strangled in a motel room on New Year's Eve. Three days later, Internado was sworn in as a freshman U.S. Senator." She showed Maverick the picture on her laptop.

Leaning close, he studied the photo. "Is that a black eye?"

"He claimed his daughter hit him by accident. I'm not buying it. My grandfather also saw him at some donor event the week prior." She showed him the calendar entry.

JC, DONOR EVENT
MEET GI, DC HOTEL
BRING RA PHOTO!

"You knew my grandfather. He *never* went to political fundraisers. I know this was work-related because he attended using an alias." Carly sipped more water. "I think he had come to the same conclusion I have regarding this young woman, so he met with Internado at the fundraiser, then again on the Watergate Steps, where Internado pushed him to his death."

Maverick stared at her for several seconds. "Holy fuck."

"I know this sounds crazy. I need to get the specifics on how and when Pierce died."

"I thought you knew."

"My dad said he passed away as a result of a fall. I assumed it was on his regular morning power walk and never suspected anything."

"If you're right, then Internado killed this woman *and* your grandfather. Going forward, you're under my protection twenty-four seven."

She laughed. "You're not serious, are you?"

"Very serious."

"Ash, honey, Internado has no idea I'm investigating this cold case or that I'm Pierce's granddaughter. I think you're overreacting."

He hitched a brow. This was not up for negotiation.

A sly smile lifted the corners of her mouth. "A prisoner under your protection day and night. Could be a lot of fun."

Maverick loved her wild mind, but this wasn't something to joke about, not even when it included a seduction. "This is serious, Carly."

Her gaze flitted over his face. "I can't change your mind, can I?"

"Not this time."

She kissed his cheek. "Thank you for protecting me."

"If anything happened to you…"

"Ashton, *nothing* will happen to me. I've got this." She rose. "I'm going to shower. You should join me, that way you can keep close tabs on me." She vanished inside.

As her self-assigned protector, what choice did he have but to follow?

23

CARLY TAKES THE LEAD

C arly and Ashton stood outside the first district police station in southwest, D.C. While waiting for his dad, Carly forwarded Erin Murphy her DNA results. No paternal match had been found, but Carly wasn't surprised or deterred. She'd find Rose Aurora's killer one way or another.

Her phone rang. "Hey, Mom."

"I got your text. Grandpa Pierce fell down some stairs."

"Where?"

"No clue. Look, I need your help. Can you spy on Ross, as a personal favor to me? I think he's seeing someone else."

You got that right. "Have you asked him?"

"He's a liar."

"And you picked *him* over Dad?"

"I got caught up in all his machismo. Do it for me, 'kay?"

"Ask your other daughter to help you. I'm *confident* she can find him. Gotta run."

"Don't you dare hang up on—"

"Goodbye."

Carly had texted her dad, but he never replied.

"No help?" Ashton asked.

"Of course not. That's why I called your dad." She gave him the once-over. "You look handsome. Why the suit?"

He moved the jacket to display the Glock tucked into his pants.

She raised a brow. "What's *that* for?"

"I want you safe, babe. Do you have your weapon?"

"Not at the moment."

"Seriously, you should carry it," he said. "So, what's with the getup?"

Faux prescription glasses framed her eyes and she wore a brown wig with bangs. "After we meet with your dad, I have another stop."

"*We*. We have another stop. We're back to the buddy system. You like the buddy system."

She smiled up at him. "I love the buddy system."

Warren Hott joined them, coffee cup in hand. "Good morning, you two."

"Hey, Dad."

"Thanks for meeting us, Warren," Carly said.

"Why the disguise?" Warren asked.

"I'm working on a case."

"It's dangerous, Dad."

Warren slid his gaze from one to the other. "That didn't just leave me unsettled. No, not at all. Maybe one day I'll stop worrying about you kids, but today is not that day."

They walked into the building, stopping at the front window. Warren introduced himself and asked to speak with the commander. After a brief moment, the officer buzzed them in.

"I have a weapon," Ashton said. "I'm registered to carry."

"You'll have to check that," said the officer.

The three entered the duty area, which was brimming with activity. After Ashton checked his Glock, an officer led them to the commander's office.

Commander Morgan Rush shook Warren's hand. "Always a

pleasure to see our former chief prosecutor. How've you been, Warren?"

After a moment of small talk, Warren said, "This is my son, Ashton, and his friend, Carly Stone."

He shook their hands. "What can I do for you?"

"I need a copy of a police report," Warren said.

Morgan chuckled. "And here I thought you were gonna ask me for the key to the city. I love when it's this easy. I'll get one of my officers to help you. Everything else good?"

"We missed you at Sarah's golf tournament."

"I'm sorry I couldn't make it. I was asked to speak at Howard University's Family weekend. As an alum, I like to offer support whenever I can. Next year for sure." After a hardy handshake, the commander escorted them to the records officer. "Grimes, can you give my friends a hand, please?"

"Yes, sir," said the officer. "What can I help with?"

Carly stepped up to the desk. "I need the police report for the death of Pierce Stone. His body was found either February 22 or February 23 of this year."

"It'll be a few minutes while I pull this up."

Ten minutes later, they exited the police station. Carly had the police report and the coroner's report in hand.

"Thank you so much, Warren."

"You could have gotten those reports without me."

"Not that quickly," Carly replied. "I don't have a week to wait."

"I'm glad I could help, then." Pausing, he regarded them. "How's the pretend marriage working out for you two?"

After exchanging lingering gazes, Carly and Ashton smiled. "Best thing we ever did," he declared.

"I'm *very* pleased to hear that. Let me know if you need anything else. Be safe," Warren said and took off down the sidewalk.

Ashton fixed his gaze on Carly. "Where next, boss?"

"The Dirksen Building."

"You want to tell me what you're up to?"

She stepped close and inhaled his fresh scent. "The congressional motor pool provides government vehicles to members of congress and high-ranking government officials."

"And?"

"I want to see if Internado checked out a vehicle on February 22."

"Because he's an idiot?"

"The senate was in session that day. I know it's unlikely, but when working a case, I ask myself 'what if'. Plus, I never overlook anything. Those vehicles are equipped with tracking devices."

"How do you know?"

"I called and asked."

"Smart, beautiful, super fine. That's my woman." He clasped her hand. "I couldn't hold you in my arms tightly enough the past two nights. I want you safe, honey."

Years ago, he'd captured her heart. Now, he owned it.

They drove to the senate building and Ashton parked around the corner. "I don't like leaving you alone."

"No worries. Back in ten." She dropped a kiss on his mouth. "Mmm, you are delicious."

She hurried inside and showed her badge to a security guard. Sinclair had gotten her a government ID showing a different name and a photo of her in disguise. After getting directions, she took the elevator to the lower level, entered the motor pool office and waited in line.

When it was her turn, the clerk waved her over to the counter. "Here to check out a vehicle?"

"I'm hoping you can help me."

"I'll give it a try."

"I need to know which cars were checked out on February 22."

"You gotta fill out a form online. Takes a couple weeks to get the report."

"Is there any chance we can rush the order? I needed it like, you know, yesterday."

"I hear ya. Demanding boss?"

"Something like that."

"I can fill it out here." He swung the computer screen around. "Might speed things up."

"Anything you can do is appreciated. Actually, is there a way to check on a particular senator?"

"Yup. Which one?"

"George Internado," she murmured.

"Busy man. He uses the service every week. Let's get this done for you. What's your name?"

"Pierce Stone."

"Address."

"Can we skip that?"

"Nope."

She provided her former work address, where her sister had set up shop.

"What dates do you want us to check?"

"February 21, 22 and 25."

"I need an email address to send the report."

She provided her work email.

"Reason you need this info?"

"Does the report include GPS locations?"

"I can check that field. I need a reason for your request."

"My boss."

"Name."

The clerk looked up and grinned. "Hey, Senator. We was just—"

Carly's heart jumped into her throat. Rather than waiting in line like everyone else, Internado waddled over to the counter. "How's the day treating you, Byron?"

"Just fine, just fine. How's things goin' for you?"

Carly nudged the screen back toward the clerk.

"Hello there, young lady." The senator's friendly smile turned her stomach.

"Hello."

"How are you today?"

"Fine, thanks." Carly pushed away from the counter. "Thanks for your help," she said to the clerk.

"What brings you into our fabulous motor pool office?" Internado asked.

She blanked for a brief second. "You're Senator Internado, right?"

He puffed out like a peacock. "Why yes, yes I am."

"Good luck with your campaign," she said and hurried out.

George Internado wasn't just trying to tear down Ashton's company, he could be Rose Aurora's killer. *And Grandpa's, too.*

Her blood ran cold as she slid into the car. "Internado walked in while I was there and chatted me up."

Ashton's eyebrows jutted over his sunglasses. "Any chance he recognized you from Greta's?"

"I didn't stick around long enough to find out."

"When do you get the report?" he asked, merging into traffic.

"A couple of weeks."

"I'm running out of time, babe."

"I know, Ash. I'm pushing hard to get answers. And we still have Greta's."

He drew her hand to his mouth and kissed her palm. "I know you are."

Ten minutes later, they waited while ThunderStrike's chain-link gate slowly squeaked open. "I've gotta get this thing fixed. It's too damn slow."

As soon as they entered the building, Ashton's demeanor changed. She'd noticed it when she worked there yesterday. He exuded the same high level of confidence and charisma, but the loud showman had been replaced with a quiet strength that kept her locked on his every word.

He checked in with Anne at reception.

"Penelope and Gunner are waiting for you in the mission room," Anne said. "I brewed a fresh pot of coffee and spoke with Douglas Hill."

Ashton raised an eyebrow. "Let me get Carly situated and I'll circle back."

"Carly might like working in the empty office at the far end of the building rather than the safe room."

"She stays in the safe room."

Carly loved that he was vigilant about her safety. They walked down the hallway, but Ashton pulled her to a stop outside a closed door marked, MISSION CENTRAL.

"Your security clearance doesn't permit you to join me in here."

"That's okay. I need to get started—"

"I want you to see the hub of ThunderStrike, so Gunner made a few modifications."

He peered into her eyes. The energy between them shifted. His power and magnetism tugged her closer. She tilted her face and gazed up at him. "I would love that."

"Are you tempting me?"

She couldn't look away. "Always."

He leaned down, brushed his lips to hers. "You are irresistible."

The door opened and Gunner chuckled. "When did this become the romance zone?"

Her cheeks warmed while Ashton huffed out a laugh. "Busted," he replied.

"Hey, Carly. Come on in, you two lovebirds."

Eight screens hung on the wall. Four were dark. The other four monitored different teams on assignment. A large console filled the center of the room.

"How's Henson doing?" Ashton asked.

"So far, so good," Penelope replied. "Hey, Carly, how's the sleuthing going?"

"Slower than we'd like."

Penelope tossed her a nod. "You'll get there."

Gunner zoomed in on screen number two as three ThunderStrike team members escorted a man wearing a suit and dark sunglasses through an outside market. The room grew quiet as the men took him into a building and up a flight of stairs. One knocked once on a closed door. All three had their guns at the ready.

The door opened and they entered. After sweeping the room, they lowered their guns.

"We're in," said Henson through the comm. "All clear."

"Nice job," Gunner replied.

Gunner zoomed back out, then turned to Ashton. "What's the latest?"

"I'm going to excuse myself." Carly headed toward the door. "I'm dying to get this wig off, plus, I'd like to review the police reports."

"Let me run Carly to the safe room."

"Ash, I'm good, really. I know where I'm going." She opened the door. "This room is awesome. Thanks for showing me."

She hurried into the safe room. After removing her wig, she read the police report. At the time of her grandfather's death, he carried no ID and the officer referenced him a John Doe. Her heart dipped. *Poor Grandpa Pierce.*

A jogger stopped just after seven Saturday morning to assist a man on the ground. Police notes said he tried to revive him, but that the "older gentleman was stone cold and gray".

Tears pricked her eyes.

She skimmed the paperwork and found where her grandfather had passed.

LOCATION OF INCIDENT: Sidewalk on Ohio Drive, S.W., at the base of the Watergate Steps

She broke out in a cold sweat, the hairs on her arms standing straight up. Jumping out of her seat, she poured herself a glass of water and guzzled it down.

Despite not having any hard facts or evidence, Carly was convinced that George Internado had invited her grandfather to that location on the evening of February 22. Somehow, he ended up at the bottom of the steps, dead.

Did Internado push him?

She flipped to the coroner's report.

TIME OF DEATH: Between 2200 on Friday, February 22, and 0100 on Saturday, February 23
CAUSE OF DEATH: Head trauma, resulting from a fall

Oh, my God.

The report also stated that Edward Stone, the son of the deceased, had identified the body at the morgue. Sadness blanketed her. Her dad had shouldered that burden alone.

Even with the unusual time of death, both the police and coroner reported no signs of foul play. Pierce's death had been ruled an accidental fall and the case had been closed.

Accident, my ass.

There was a knock on the door.

"Come on in."

When their eyes met, Ashton's brows lifted. "Well?"

"I'm going to clear your name and nail that son of a bitch for the murder of my client's biological mother *and* the death of my grandfather." Carly steeled her spine. "No way is Internado getting away with this."

24

BREATH PLAY

Zero eight hundred Thursday morning and Maverick was starting the day with a major fucking chip on his shoulder. According to the tracker, Internado had driven his vehicle to an auto dealership.

Carly slid beside him on the kitchen bench and stroked his leg. "Babe, are we going in to work today?"

"That feels good." He blinked. "What did you ask me?"

"Work?"

He nodded, then turned his attention back to the screen. "Internado's at a dealership. He's either there for service or he's buying a new car." Acid churned in his stomach. "Either way, we're flying blind. That really pisses me off."

"Would you feel better if I carried today?"

He loved her morning face. Sleepy eyes, puffy cheeks. He kissed her. "Yes, even though I'm not letting you out of my sight. I'll have my weapon, too."

"I'm surprised it wasn't in the bed between us last night."

That elicited a smile. "Nothing comes between us." He tugged gently on her hair. "It was on the night table and I was up half the night."

Carly's burner phone rang. "It's Greta." She answered, put the call on speaker. "Hello?"

"Hello, Mrs. Black. It's Greta. I hope I'm not calling too early."

Carly flicked her gaze to Maverick. "Not at all."

"I wanted to extend you and Mr. Black an invitation to my *private* party tonight. I'm sorry for the last-minute notice. I hope you'll reconsider joining my club and attend."

"Sounds intriguing. We'll have to check it out. What time?"

"Excellent. See you tonight, ten o'clock." Greta hung up.

Carly snapped the flip phone shut. Her confident smile sent adrenaline pumping through him. "We're getting that video *and* a DNA sample."

"How do you plan on doing that?"

"Wear a suit jacket. If Internado has a drink, we'll hide his glass under it."

"That's risky."

"But worth it. If it doesn't work, we'll go for Plan B."

"Which is?"

Carly brushed her lips to his. "I'll let you know when I figure that out."

The kiss continued. He slipped his hand under her hair and around the back of her neck, inhaled her beautiful, just-washed scent, and deepened the kiss. Her breath hitched. She slipped her arms around him and slid closer on the bench. He wanted to carry her back to his bed—*their* bed—and make love to her all morning long.

But she ended the heated embrace and slid out of the booth, taking his salacious thoughts with her. "Two minutes and I'll be ready to go." She glanced back at her laptop. "Maybe Internado will wait if he's getting his vehicle serviced."

"Let's hope so. No matter what, I've got your back, babe. No one is going to hurt my woman. If he tries, he gets a bullet to the head."

She spun around. "*Oh, God, no!* You *can't* kill him."

Pushing out of the booth, he shouldered his satchel. "I wasn't trained to hit him in the foot."

"If he did murder two people, he has to pay for his crimes. If he dies, the truth dies with him."

Though he didn't like her strategy, he stayed silent.

THAT EVENING, Mr. Black admired Mrs. Black as she modeled her black, lace-up latex romper with black, leather thigh-high boots.

"You like?"

"You're so damn hot. I am pleased to see the girls aren't on full display this evening."

"Internado doesn't get to see my tits."

"You read my mind."

She ran her fingers down his back and cupped his tight ass. "You're damn hot yourself."

Dressed in all black, Maverick collected their masks.

"A kiss for luck." Carly pressed her mouth to his and warmth flooded his chest.

"I love you, Carly, and I won't let *anything* happen to you."

"I love you, too, Ash, and I won't let anything happen to you, either."

At a traffic light a block from Greta's, they tied on their masks.

Moments later, Greta welcomed them into her townhome. "Tonight, the fun happens downstairs in my dungeon. The same rules apply. No is no. Alcohol is permitted, but if my bartender thinks you've had too much, he'll cut you off and I'll call a car service to drive you home."

"Understood," Carly replied.

"Penetration is optional. Condoms are not. It's wilder downstairs. I hope you find this group more to your liking." She escorted them to the basement door, punched in the code, and they descended.

Once in the dungeon, he took in the large space. Faux candles bathed the room in flickering light, the smell of vanilla filled his nostrils. Total nudity was more prevalent here and most of the members were participating, rather than watching.

There was a foursome on the futon in the corner, their naked bodies grinding and pumping in an erotic rhythm. Across the room, a naked woman lay on a bondage bed while a man in leather pants secured her with rope. His skillful performance had garnered a small audience. Off to the side, a man wearing a black kilt pleasured a blindfolded woman, her naked body strapped to a St. Andrews cross.

Maverick wasn't aroused, nor did he care about the kink. Tonight, he'd come prepared to complete a job. As his focus roamed from one masked person to the next, his chest tightened. Internado wasn't amongst them. When he spied a closed door off to the side, he squeezed Carly's hand. She followed his gaze. "Patience," she whispered and kissed him.

He stroked her ass. Her soft moans and deepening kiss had him clutching her tighter.

She slowed the kiss and whispered, "He's exiting that private room." With her eyes fixed on Maverick's, she unfastened a button on his shirt. And then another. She pressed her mouth to his heated chest and kissed his pecs.

"Three seconds out," he whispered.

As he strutted over, Internado's naked paunch protruded over his black leather pants. Once again, he wore the fake beard, stache, and toupee, his eyes framed by a black mask. "Hello, Mrs. Black." He didn't even throw a glance Maverick's way.

She stopped kissing Maverick and peered at him. "Oh, hey. Hiya." She shot him a cool smile. "I remember you from last time."

A stone-faced Maverick fought the urge to land a right hook on Internado's jaw. His protective instinct had him threading his hand around Carly's waist and pulling her close.

Two women sauntered out of the same room and joined them.

Their leather bondage attire left nothing to the imagination. As far as Maverick was concerned, they'd be more comfortable if they ditched the harnesses and walked around buck naked. He acknowledged the women with a nod.

The taller of the two curled her hand around his biceps. "Can we steal you from your partner?"

"We'd *love* to get to know you better," said the second.

"No thanks." Maverick lowered his voice.

Internado stroked the ass of the shorter woman, but directed his attention on Carly. "Come play with us. We're having some wild fun."

The tall woman clutching Maverick's biceps said, "The danger really spices things up."

"It's like *nothing* I've ever experienced before," said the shorter one. "It'll blow your mind, it's so intense."

The first woman tugged Maverick forward, but he wouldn't budge, so she let him go and sauntered back toward the room.

"Sure, we'll check it out." Carly held Maverick's gaze an extra beat before they forged forward.

He hated that Carly was the bait.

Once inside, Internado shut the door and Maverick activated his video watch. Aside from a four-poster bed and a night table with a bowl of condoms, the room was bare. The only light came from the battery-powered candles, their plastic wicks swaying back and forth. No kink equipment and no other members.

Internado extended his hand, but Carly shook her head. "Show me." She fiddled with her mask, her finger pausing over the middle sequin.

The taller woman lay sideways on the bed while the other one bound her wrists to the posts. Internado dropped his pants, revealing his erection.

Our video equipment had better be working.

As soon as the senator positioned himself between the woman's legs, she drew her knees up. The second woman tossed a large dildo on the bed, then kissed the woman lying down. As their kiss began heating up, Internado thrust inside her, not bothering with a condom. Maverick gritted his teeth. *He's above the rules, here, too.*

Cheaters sickened Maverick. When he turned to Carly, her beautiful face calmed him. Normally, arousal would emanate from her eyes, but tonight confidence and determination shone from them.

The woman's moans hijacked their attention and they turned back to the erotic show.

Internado stopped thrusting and leered at Carly like she was his next victim. "I'm an expert on breath play." And then, he placed his hand on the woman's throat and applied pressure. The second woman lubricated the dildo and worked it into Internado's ass.

Maverick fought the grimace.

Internado paired loud, deep moaning with hard, fast thrusting, all while eyeing Carly. Maverick held her closer, gripped her tighter, and stood there unmoving while this graphic scene played out.

"Fuck me harder," he instructed the woman behind him. And then he placed his second hand around the woman's throat.

Maverick swallowed down the bile. He never imagined erotic asphyxiation would be Internado's kink. As he groaned and bucked through his orgasm, he tightened his grip around the woman's neck until she stilled.

When he stopped thrusting, he removed his hands and the woman behind him withdrew the dildo.

The woman on the bed appeared lifeless. Maverick fought the urge to rush over and begin CPR. That scumbag, still high from his own orgasm, did nothing to address his limp play-partner lying on the bed.

The other woman sat beside her and gently patted her face. "Hey, honcy. Come on, wake up."

She patted her face again. "Hello, wake up."

The woman's eyes fluttered open and she inhaled a deep breath. "That was uh-maaazing."

"Take care of her needs," Internado barked as he pulled up his pants.

The women began kissing. Maverick stared down Internado, repressing the urge to unleash his own pent-up anger. *He's savage and selfish and reckless as hell.*

Carly had been gripping his hand so tightly his fingers tingled.

Internado walked into the bathroom and shut the door. Maverick wanted to yank that fucking door open and rip off his damn wig, exposing him as the pervert he is.

Even Maverick knew that communication and consent were *everything*, in life and in the BDSM world. He also understood that erotic asphyxiation was all about ensuring the person getting choked achieved orgasm, not the other fucking way around.

Carly must have sensed his fury because she'd been stroking his back, her soft touch doing little to stifle his anger.

A moment later, the bathroom door opened and Internado rolled out. He paid no attention to the women frolicking on the bed.

"Did you enjoy our little show?" Internado asked Carly.

"It was somethin' all right. Do ya do that a lot?"

"As often as I can." Internado ogled her breasts. "Have you ever experienced breath play?"

"Nope."

"Let me teach you. I'd have total control over you, down to what might be your last breath." The excitement in his eyes was nothing short of evil. "But I'm an expert, been doing it for years, and know when enough is enough."

Maverick was trying to save people's lives and this monster was toying with them.

"I'll give that some thought over a drink," Carly said. "Can I bring ya something?"

"Whiskey, neat."

"Hang tight." Back on the main level, they waited in a short line at the bar.

Greta had been speaking to a couple, but hurried over. "I thought you'd be downstairs for hours."

"Intermission," Carly said before ordering three whiskeys.

"On the house," Greta said to her barkeep. "Did you like my dungeon?"

"Very nice," Carly said. "One of your members invited me to do breath play with him."

"Sounds fun," Greta said.

You wouldn't think so if you saw the crap he just pulled.

With drinks in hand, they returned to the dungeon. Internado couldn't get to Carly fast enough.

"To kink," Carly said, and they tossed back the alcohol. "I ain't familiar with breath play, but ain't it about the person bein' choked."

Inwardly, Maverick smiled. He and Carly were in total sync.

"Yes, you're correct, but when I play with those two, we mix things up. I like to come when I'm suffocating them and they get off on pleasuring me. It's a win-win." His creepy smile had Maverick gritting his teeth. "If you put yourself in my care, I can promise you an extremely gratifying experience."

"Is choke sex your thing?" she asked.

Maverick admired how Carly stayed in character and maintained her composure. He wanted to deck him, then shove that dildo down his throat.

"I'm also an expert with rope play. Either way, my focus is on control. Sometimes I like to inflict pain, so I engage in rough body play." Those words rolled off Internado's tongue like he was reciting a memo to his assistant.

"A true sadist," Carly replied.

Internado nodded. "What's your poison?"

"My husband."

Fortunately, Internado didn't even glance in Maverick's direction.

"What's your kink?" Internado asked her.

"Exhibitionism."

His breath hitched. "Very nice. How do you like Greta's?"

"It's a good time." She plucked the empty glass from his hand. "Thanks for a fun show."

"Wait, is that a no?" Internado glanced at her chest again.

"Afraid so," Carly replied.

As they walked up the stairs, Carly reached back and handed Maverick Internado's tumbler. At the top of the stairs, he was about to duck into the restroom when Greta intercepted him.

"I can take those for you." Maverick watched as Internado's DNA got whisked away and placed on a tray filled with dirty tumblers.

Dammit to hell.

His eyes met Carly's. They'd come so close.

"Why don't you stay and play?" Greta asked.

"We aren't feeling it tonight," Carly replied. "Thanks for inviting us. We'll be in touch."

Silence filled the car as he drove home. For most of the ride, Maverick had no words. No words at all. Then, he found them.

At a light, he removed his mask and placed his hand around her thigh. "Carly, I love you...so much, you know that, right?"

She smiled. "I do."

"I've gotta be honest...the kink scene isn't my thing."

After taking off her mask, she threaded her fingers through his. "I know that."

"I don't want you giving up what you need. I want you happy and sexually fulfilled."

She leaned close, dropped a lingering kiss on his cheek. "I choose you, Ashton Hott. When the need for kink arises, I'll let you know."

"Fair enough." The light changed and he hit the gas.

"We got quite an eyeful tonight," she said. "I'm still having trouble processing his reckless behavior."

"He's a monster."

"Erotic choking is dangerous. Some kink communities don't allow it. So much can go wrong."

"You mean, like *death*?"

Their gazes locked. "Yeah, like death."

As soon as they returned home, Maverick yanked off the wig and removed his shoes and socks. Carly slipped out of her stilettos while he checked the playback from the video watch. They'd captured him screwing and choking a play partner. Though he should have been relieved they finally had what they needed, he wasn't. Internado was more reckless than he'd expected.

But the second he dropped a lingering kiss on her bare shoulder and breathed her familiar, peachy scent, his anger evaporated. "Let's take a midnight cruise down the river."

Her sultry smile was the best medicine for his suffering soul. "Let me get out of this wig first."

"Do *not* change," he called as she retreated down the stairs.

She pivoted, a fiery look blazing in her eyes. "Yes, sir."

After readying the vessel, he found her waiting in the main cabin and draped a light blanket around her bare shoulders.

"It's a beautiful night. Should we head upstairs to the flybridge?"

"I'd love that."

He motioned for her to climb the stairs while he admired her backside. However, this time, he didn't touch her. He took his seat in the captain's chair and she sat on the built-in sofa bench across the aisle.

The night was still, the air crisp. Boating was one of the few things that quieted the rage living inside him. Once out of the channel, he increased speed.

"Sit on my lap."

After doing so, she slipped her arm around him and snuggled close. He kept one hand on the wheel, threaded the other around her waist. She felt so right in his arms, especially now, after witnessing Internado's disturbing behavior.

Several minutes into their trip, he slowed to a stop. To their right was a park, to their left, office buildings. Save for a few errant offices bathed in light, they were surrounded by darkness. He dropped anchor, cut the engines.

When he peered into her moonlit eyes, her beauty halted his breath. Her undeniable attraction pulled him closer until their lips touched. The longer they stared, the more he needed her. But tonight wasn't about him or his needs. Tonight, he would show her that a life with him would be just as sensual, just as kinky as the party he'd barged in on at her place, or any event at Greta's.

He kissed her again, this time anchoring his hand on the back of her neck and tilting her head back. He gobbled up her moans with his mouth while his tongue explored and teased.

Her breathing increased, her fingers kneading his thigh. He ended the kiss. "Stand up."

When she stood, she tossed the blanket on the sofa bench. He swiveled toward her in the captain's chair.

"Face me. Untie the laces on your romper."

She moistened her lips, then tugged on the latex drawstring. One by one, she unlaced the romper.

"Show me your breasts."

She shrugged out, leaving the garment to pool at her waist. He pushed out of the chair and stared into her eyes.

He brushed a thumb across her hardened nipple. Her throaty moan landed between his legs. He drew circles around her other nipple with the tip of his finger. Her breathing intensified.

He dipped his head, kissed the swells of her breasts, moving closer and closer to her swollen nibs.

"Yes," she murmured. "Suck them."

"Not yet. Take off your clothes."

"Mmm, yes." She shimmied out of the romper and stood naked before him.

His gaze lingered on her face. Her lids were heavy, her eyes dark with desire. Parting her lips, she sucked in a harsh breath. Her nipples were pert, her back arched, tempting him to caress those magnificent breasts.

But he did not touch her. Instead he dropped his gaze to her tight abs, curvy hips, and muscular legs. He paused an extra beat to admire her hairless pussy.

"Your body was made for sex, but tonight, I want your mind."

"Oh, God, Ash." Her breath was jagged, her eyes fluttered closed for a brief second.

"Take off my shirt."

She ripped it open, sending buttons flying in every direction. Then, she pressed her mouth to his chest and kissed him before burrowing her hands inside his shirt and dragging it over his shoulders. It fell to the floor.

"Lay on your back and spread your legs."

After easing onto the sofa's soft fabric, she shuddered in a shaky breath.

Still wearing his pants, he stalked up her body and stared into her eyes. "I have wanted to taste you for a long, long time."

She responded with an aching whimper. His kiss was deep and intense. Instead of touching him, she rested her arms over her head and laid them on the throw pillows. Now, she was completely open and totally vulnerable.

He nibbled her ear, nipped at her neck, and dotted her collarbone with a trail of kisses. He bit her shoulder, fondled her breast, but he denied her any nipple foreplay.

"You're killing me. Suck my tit."

"No." His exploration continued. He licked the skin between her cleavage and whispered, "Delicious."

"I need you inside me."

"Patience, my love."

Another deep groan shot out of her, the huskiness reverberating in his chest. He kissed her tummy and hovered over her pussy. She pushed a throw pillow beneath her head to watch.

"This is one of my favorite fantasies," she whispered.

"Mine, too." He ran his tongue up the inside of her thigh. She spread her legs wider.

"Please, Ash. Please."

"Not yet, baby." Planking over her, he kissed her. Then, he placed his mouth around her nipple and sucked it gently as she mewled and writhed beneath him. When he'd had his fill of her breasts, he dotted her tummy with a line of kisses until he reached the apex between her legs. "I can't wait to taste your sweet juices."

She shuddered in a jagged breath and murmured, "Yes."

He slipped his hands beneath her ass, lifted her off the cushion, and ran his tongue over her glistening skin. And he breathed deep, savoring her sweet, sweet scent.

She arched up, pressing into him. He tasted her, drank in her juices, listened to the grittiness of her groans while she dug her fingernails into his shoulders. She writhed while he thrust his tongue inside her soft folds. Again and again and again. He was drunk out of his mind on pleasuring her. When he took her to the brink and slowed back down, her throaty growl made him smile. Again, he brought her to the crest of ecstasy, only to deny her one more time.

On the third time, her body shook. Her moans were husky and raw and sexy as hell. "So good, Ash. Fuck, you're taking me."

As soon as he slid two fingers inside her and flicked her clit with his tongue, she fisted his hair, tugging hard. He massaged her breast, teasing her hardened nipples with his thumb.

A smaller boat motored by, its headlight casting diffused light on them. "They can see you, baby."

Moaning through her release, she surrendered. When the tremors subsided, she relaxed and he slowly withdrew his fingers.

He kissed her pink flesh, then held her in his arms and kissed her breathless.

"Because you need me inside you, I'm going to fuck you." He pushed off the sofa and dropped his pants.

Her lips parted, her breathing erratic. She spread her legs and arched toward him. "I need you so badly."

He speared her in one fluid slide. Sheer pleasure radiated through his every muscle, every nerve. She wrapped her legs around his back, her arms around his neck, securing him to her.

"I love how good you love me." Unleashing a torrent of energy, she bucked her hips against him and pulled his ass toward her, ensuring he thrust to her end. Passion hummed in her throat while her kisses grew rough. The build was wild and brutal, the intensity drenching him in streams of euphoria. When he bit her earlobe, then her neck, he triggered her second orgasm.

This time, she cried out his name. Before he found her mouth, he whispered, "I love you, Carly." And he poured himself into her, waves of ecstasy washing over him.

Not wanting to put his weight on her, he repositioned himself and she lay boneless on him while he stroked her back. As the water lapped against the side of the boat, they floated in each other's arms.

"You are a total alpha. God, I love that about you."

"You are a total hottie, Carlyle Elizabeth Stone. And I'm so in love with you."

She lifted her head and they shared a smile. "I'm just as in love with you, Ashton Miles Hott." She laid her head back down on his chest and snuggled close.

"If we admitted this years ago, would we be married with a litter of little Hotts wreaking havoc and ruling our lives?" He kissed the top of her head.

He could feel her smile as she caressed his chest with delicate fingers. After a bit, she lifted her face and stared into his eyes. "I'm happy you...um, how should I put this...experienced your playboy lifestyle. And I needed to explore my own sexuality, independently of you. We've come full circle. What we wanted as kids is what we've necded all along. We just weren't ready then."

"But we're ready now," he said, wrapping her in his arms. "I can't imagine my life without you."

"I can't, either," she said before her lips found his once again.

25

CARLY'S LAST BREATH

"I must be crazy," Maverick said after breakfast.

"We need his DNA," Carly replied. "This seems like the surest way to get it."

"I'm checking in with Sinclair first." Maverick dialed while Carly cleared the table.

Sinclair answered. "Hey."

"Hey, bro. We got what we needed from Greta's, so we won't be returning."

"I'll tell her. You got enough to bury the SOB?"

"Let's hope so. How are you doing?"

"I've got some shit going down. Dakota's calling me. Gotta go." The line went dead.

"Hmm," Maverick said.

"What?" Carly asked.

He slid his gaze to her. "He and Dakota are up to something."

"That's nothing new."

"True," he said. "Wish me luck. I'm calling Internado."

Leaning down, Carly kissed him. "You've got this."

"That's cuz I've got you, babe." He flashed her a smile before dialing the senator's private number.

"Hello?" Internado answered.

"It's Maverick."

"What can I do for you?" The senator's brusque tone came as no surprise.

"We should talk. How's Rudy's, say, noon today?"

"Why?"

"I'm ready to help you with your campaign." Bile rose in Maverick's throat.

"Good. I'll meet you there at four." The line went dead.

Carly checked the tracker. Kathy Internado had returned home. George Internado's car was still at the dealership. "Let's hope he doesn't ask you to drive him to pick up his car."

"I'm getting his damn DNA one way or another."

Maverick drove them to his office, determined to have the day go off without a hitch. *I need some damn normal.*

Later that afternoon, as Carly fitted Maverick with a wire, Gunner entered his office. "What trouble are you two getting into?"

"I'm meeting with Internado," Maverick said.

Crossing his arms, Gunner leaned against the wall. "This can't be good."

"No alternative." Maverick slipped on his shirt.

Gunner slapped his back. "That's one of the reason's why I love you, man. You don't give up."

"No, I don't." Maverick tucked his shirt into his pants. "Let's test the sound." After confirming they could hear him, he peered into Carly's eyes. "Wish me luck."

Her smile was brimming with love. "You'll do great. I have complete faith in you."

"Nothing better than a woman's love," Gunner said. "Now, go get 'em."

Maverick arrived early, got situated at Rudy's private table in the kitchen.

"Good seeing you, Maverick." Rudy set two water glasses on the table. "Meeting with the senator?"

"Sure am. How've you been?"

"Can't complain. Business keeps me hoppin'. You two eating?"

"Absolutely."

"You want me to wait until the senator arrives?"

"I'm here." Internado brushed past Rudy. "Bring me a cold one, will ya, Rudy?"

"Yes, sir. Two?" Rudy asked Maverick.

"Sure." As Maverick slid his grin from Rudy to Internado, his blood chilled. Since first meeting there, so much had happened. Maverick's good opinion of the senator had plummeted to rock bottom. But he'd put on a good show to get what he needed. He extended his hand. "Thanks for meeting me."

The senator shook it and his skin crawled. "How have things been going for you, Maverick?" Letting out a sigh, he eased onto the rickety wooden chair.

"Not good. I have to let my training recruits go. I burned through a quarter mil just to bring them on board. Kills me to have to fire them."

Internado shrugged. "You brought this on yourself."

"I did, and I regret my decision."

That snagged his full attention. "Tell me more."

"I'd like to offer you my services. Take you up on that generous offer you made me, right here, last month."

Internado smiled while Maverick gritted his teeth. Rudy set down their ice-cold brews. "Ready to order?"

"Dinner is on me, Senator," Maverick said.

"I don't have much time," Internado said.

"Bring us a couple of appetizers." Maverick scanned the menu for anything that would warrant using a fork. "Steak tips. Got any scallops?"

"You want those wrapped in bacon?" Rudy asked.

"I'm not into finger foods. Let's eat 'em with a fork."

"Senator?" Rudy asked. "Those sound good to you, sir?"

"Whatever." Internado checked his watch.

"And two whiskeys," Maverick added.

"I'll get right on that." Rudy high-tailed it toward the bar.

Maverick waved the white napkin. "You win, George. I concede."

Internado's smug expression repulsed him. "You've seen the light. Very good." The senator downed half the beer and Maverick eyed the glass like it was the Holy Grail.

"I have."

"If you help me, there's a chance I might be able to throw you that much-needed lifeline. Some new evidence could emerge that drops the charges against ThunderStrike, but you have to prove yourself first, boy."

Maverick nodded. "You and I both know ThunderStrike did nothing wrong."

"But the members of the committee don't know that because I —how shall I say this—*adjusted* the subcommittee report."

Gotcha. "You mean you falsified it?"

"That's a weighty word. 'Adjusted' sounds better."

Maverick's blood boiled as Rudy set down their whiskeys. "Food'll be out in a minute."

"To you, George." he said, raising his glass. "I'll do everything possible to ensure you get what you deserve and nothing less."

"Now, that's what I'm talking about." Internado swigged the whiskey.

"Let's get back to how I can help you, Senator. What do you want me to do?"

"I'm hosting a donor dinner Wednesday night. Two hundred loyal supporters give me the perfect alibi. While I'm there, I want you to break into the campaign headquarters of my opponent."

"And do what, exactly?"

"Are you a fucking idiot?"

"Do you want me to bug his office? Tap into the phone lines?

Do you want me to take anything? I have no idea what the hell you want me to do."

"I want you to bug the office and the phone lines. Hell, if you could shove a bug up his ass, that would work, too." He laughed. "I'm going to need his donor records and a list of his strongest supporters. I'm going after them, hard."

"Understood."

Rudy delivered their appetizers.

Internado raised his beer glass. "Here's to a new and *improved* relationship." He ate a few beef tips and a scallop, but kept checking his watch.

As if on a mission, Maverick inventoried everything Internado touched. Whiskey glass. Beer glass. Napkin. Fork. "Don't let me keep you."

"My wife is headed out of town this weekend. I'd like to see her off."

I'm sure you would. "I know how devoted you are to your family." Maverick's skin prickled. "Thank you again for giving me the chance to show you my *full* capabilities." That made him smile.

The senator drained the beer, wiped his mouth with his napkin, and stood. "I'll be in touch. Going forward, I'll be calling from a burner." And with that, he bustled out the employee entrance.

Without wasting a second, Maverick pulled latex gloves from his pocket and tugged them on. Then, he dug out the plastic baggies and placed each glass in a bag. As he dropped the senator's fork into another bag, Rudy popped around the corner.

Fuck.

"Oh, boy." Rudy stared at the bagged items.

"I'm sorry you had to see this, Rudy."

"I'm sure you have your reasons."

Maverick handed him a Ben Franklin.

Rudy waved away the money. "Too much, Maverick."

"I insist."

"Thank you." Rudy pointed at Internado's crumpled napkin. "Better take that, too."

Maverick shoved the napkin into a baggie and took off. On the way out, he called Carly. "I'm headed to the lab."

"You got it!"

"I sure as hell did, baby doll."

"They're closing in ten minutes."

"What's their number?"

After she rattled it off, he hung up and called the lab.

"Falls Church DNA Center, Steve-O here."

"Hey, Steve-O, you're closing in ten minutes, aren't you?"

"Sure am. Whatcha need?"

"I work with Carly Stone and—"

"Oh, yeah, Carly uses us all the time."

"I need a rapid test completed."

"I can help ya Monday, first thing."

"I'm thirty minutes away, but I need you to stay open."

"Sorry, I've got a life. Look, Mister—"

"The name's Maverick and I need you to complete a rapid DNA test *tonight*. How long does that take?"

"Two hours, but…"

"I'm going to make this worth your while. How's five hundred?"

"Seriously, I—"

"I'll run to an ATM machine while we wait. Cash is yours. Name your price."

"I'd do it for a thousand."

"Done."

"Wait, what? No way! Really?"

"I'm serious. Carly will be calling you with details on who to check the DNA against."

"Boy, you must really need this information."

"You have no idea." Slogging through Friday rush hour traffic, he called Carly again. "Hey, babe, I need you to call the lab for me."

"They close at five."

"I'm paying Steve-O a grand to stay open and run the test while I wait."

"Whoa, Ash."

"Instruct him on who to run Internado's profile against."

"I will."

"Did you hear Internado admit he falsified the report?"

"I did. That's the evidence we need."

"Is anyone at the office with you? I won't get back 'til after eight."

"Penelope is here, but she shouldn't have to babysit me. I'm fine, Ash. This place is like Fort Knox."

"All right, babe. I'll see you in a few."

"Ashton?"

"Yeah?"

"I love you, and I love that you *never* take no for an answer."

His heart swelled. "I love you, too, Carly girl. So damn much."

Carly called Steve-O and gave him the DNA cross-reference, then continued working, though she was having trouble concentrating. *George Internado could be Erin Murphy's biological father...and a cold-blooded killer.*

Thirty-five minutes later, Penelope tapped on the open door. "Where's Maverick?"

"Running an errand. He'll be back around eight thirty."

"I'm happy for you two," Penelope said. "He's been waiting a long time for you, you know?"

Happiness filled Carly's soul. "Same here. Timing is everything, right?"

"Tell me about it. I met my husband the last week of flight school. If I hadn't been running late to an exam, I wouldn't have met him at all."

"Some things are just meant to be."

Penelope nodded. "I love that about life. You want me to stick around and wait with you?"

It was a little past six. "Go and enjoy your weekend."

Penelope left and Carly turned her attention back to her laptop. At quarter past eight, her phone buzzed with an incoming text.

"It's Cassandra. I locked myself out of the office. Bring the spare key. I'm at a bar down the street and borrowed a friend's phone. Text when you're on the way."

She fished out her key ring, eyeing the spare. If she left now, she could be back before Ash returned. Although angry with her sister for being such a bitch, she wouldn't leave her stranded.

She jotted a quick note.

Ash, Cassie is locked out of her office.
Bringing her the spare key. See you shortly.
I love you, honey.

The cool evening breeze chilled her and she tugged her suit jacket around her as she jumped into her car. The cloudy night sky blanketed the evening in a murky darkness. She texted back, "On my way."

Maverick was flying high when he rolled back into ThunderStrike, but a quick scan of the parking lot had him running full tilt into the office.

"Carly!"

No answer.

"Carlyle, where are you?"

Her beeping laptop sent him bolting into her office. He typed in her password. Kathy Internado was beyond Fredericksburg, heading south on I-95. George Internado was traveling down Pennsylvania Avenue in the vicinity of Carly's old office.

He read her note and his blood ran cold. Carly was walking straight into a trap.

After parking around the corner, Carly hurried down the street. Evenings in this part of town were quiet, especially on Friday nights. She inserted her spare in the lock and opened the door. As she entered, someone shoved her inside and shut the door.

Shrieking, she fell to the floor.

"Shut the fuck up or I'll slice your throat."

Adrenaline streaked through her, while her heart climbed to a frenetic pace. The familiar voice turned fear into sheer terror.

Before she could get up, he threw a burlap bag over her head, plunging her into darkness. Within seconds, he tied her hands behind her back and yanked her up, then hurried down the hall and pushed her into a hard chair. *The break room.* He hog-tied her wrists to her ankles.

Afraid she'd pass out, she tried calming breaths.

"You and I are going to have a little chat, missy. If you scream, you die. Do you understand?"

"Yes."

He removed the scratchy burlap and she gasped.

Wearing the toupee and fake facial hair, George Internado dragged over a metal chair, spun it around, and sat.

"What do you want?" she asked. His eerie smile made her want to vomit, but she swallowed down the hysteria and glared into his evil, wicked eyes.

He leaned forward. "Your last breath."

Oh, God. Her mind raced, her heart thumped in her ears. In an attempt to stall, she asked, "Is this a robbery? There's nothing of value here and I don't even—"

He smacked her face and tiny yellow stars swarmed in front of her. "You're a stupid, stupid girl to think you could outsmart *me*."

This time, she said nothing, her stinging cheek a painful reminder of who was in control. Behind the chair, she fiddled with the rope, but every tug yanked at her ankles. She was trapped. Perspiration dotted her brow.

"I met your grandfather several months ago," Internado began. "He was a spry old man. Well, he was until he took a terrible tumble down some very hard stairs." Internado's rough laugh was sandpaper on her soul. She continued tugging at the rope, desperate to get to Internado and claw his eyes out for what he'd done to her beloved grandfather.

"No point in trying to escape. I'm a rope expert." He stroked her cheek with the back of his finger and she gagged from his touch. "If we'd met at a different time, in a different place, we could have had some real wild fun together, you and me." He sighed. "But I digress."

"Do you know my sister?" She braced for another slap, but none came.

"I met her a few days ago after a dutiful clerk at my office told me a young lady had been snooping around about me. He gave me this address, which led me to Cassandra. What a blabbermouth. She even told me you had her spare office key."

"You're going to kill me, aren't you?"

"That sounds harsh, even to my ears. Let's say I'm going to *silence* you. You know too much about Rose Aurora." He leaned close. "Are you familiar with breath play, Carly?"

Maverick had been on hundreds of missions, but none mattered more than this one. Every second counted.

He grabbed his go-bag and ran into the parking lot. Once behind the wheel of the Suburban, he punched the gas and plowed through the gate, sending metal clanging in every direction. One of the pieces clung to the front grill as he peeled onto the street.

Slowing for a red light, he threw the thermal and night vision goggles around his neck, then looked both ways and blew through the intersection. His heart beat hard and fast in his chest, his mind raced. Did Carly have her Glock? Would she go in or wait outside? *Please don't go into that building.* Despite wanting to remain hopeful, he feared the worst. That primal fear spurred him forward. He would do whatever necessary to stop Internado from hurting her.

He screeched to a halt a half-block from the office and grabbed his gun before charging down the street. He'd honed his skills, worked his ass off for years to ensure safe and successful hostage rescue missions. Tonight, those skills would be put to the ultimate test. And he would not fail the love of his life. *Failure is not an option.*

As soon as he entered the alley behind the building, he activated the thermal goggles. Hugging the wall, he stopped shy of the back door. Heat sensors showed the images of two people in the break room, both seated.

Maverick switched to his night vision goggles and shot open the lock. He burst through the back door and stormed into the room where he'd seen the figures.

For a split second, his mind froze, the sight too heinous to be real. Internado had his gloved hands around Carly's throat. Her head was back, her eyes closed. She made no sound, didn't fight back.

"NOOOOO!" Maverick charged toward the senator.

Pure evil shone from his eyes, but he wouldn't release his hold around Carly's throat. Maverick threw him aside and he crashed against the small kitchen table before slamming to the floor.

Carly didn't move and panic turned to dread, but Maverick shoved down the emotion and went to work. He found a kitchen knife and cut the ropes, freeing her. She slumped forward into his arms and he laid her on the floor.

Behind him, the tiniest sound roared in his ears and he turned as Internado rained down on him with a metal chair. He grabbed the chair before it hit him and shoved Internado back with such force he hit the wall and bounced off.

As Maverick stood, Internado came at him again. Maverick grabbed his Glock and aimed for his chest, but Carly's words crashed into his thoughts. *If he dies, the truth dies with him.*

In that split second, Maverick lowered his aim and shot him in the thigh. As Internado screamed, Maverick hammered his head with the butt of his weapon and dropped him cold. After storing his Glock and yanking off the goggles, he turned his attention back to Carly.

She was still as death. Forcing down the panic, he knelt by her side and felt her carotid artery.

Nothing. No pulse.

God, no. No, no, no.

Adrenaline coursed through him as he placed the heel of his hand on her chest, laid one hand over the other, and performed thirty compressions.

No change.

"C'mon, Carly. Breathe."

He tilted her head back, lifted her chin, and breathed life into her.

She remained lifeless.

"Breathe, Carly." Dread surged through him.

He repeated the maneuver.

No change. "No, no, no. You can't leave me."

Determined to bring her back, he moved into position and resumed thirty more compressions. Still, she offered him no sign of life.

"Carly, come back to me." Dread was morphing into panic, but he flat-out refused to give up on her.

Again, he tilted her head back, lifted her chin, and breathed into her. Twice.

She lay there lifeless, but he forged forward. *No way in hell are you leaving me.*

"Fight, Carly. Fight your way back to me. I *can't* live without you." He performed another set of compressions. On the seventeenth, she gasped air into her lungs.

Hope coursed through him. "That's it. Breathe."

She inhaled another raspy breath and coughed. "Nice and easy. Slow, easy breaths." He covered her with his suit jacket, checked her pulse. It was faint. He called 9-1-1.

"Nine-one-one, what's your emergency?"

"My girlfriend was strangled. She had no pulse and I performed CPR. I need police and an ambulance." He kept his voice steady, though his heart was exploding out of his chest.

"Is she breathing now, sir?"

He placed two fingers over her carotid artery. "Yes, but her pulse is weak. She'd been bound with rope. I had to shoot Internado. Send two ambulances."

"Sir, did you say you shot someone?"

"Yes."

"Is he breathing?"

"Yes. I shot him in the leg to stop him from attacking me."

"What is your name, sir?"

"Ashton Hott." He gave her the address. "Tell the first responders to enter through the alley behind the building."

"All right, Mr. Hott, they'll be there in a few minutes. Stay on the phone with me."

"Ahhh, my head," moaned Internado. "My leg."

Maverick tapped the speaker button before he hog-tied Internado, then checked him for weapons.

He felt Carly's pulse again. *It's too damn weak.* "I'm right here, honey. Carly, you're doing great. Ambulance is on the way." He slipped his hands beneath the jacket and clasped her cold fingers. "I love you, Carly. You gotta stay with me."

Her eyes fluttered open, then closed again.

"I've got you." When she started trembling, his greatest fear consumed him. "Operator, where are they? She's going into shock."

"The police have entered the alley."

"Police," called an officer.

"We're in the kitchen," Maverick replied.

The officers entered the room and flipped on the lights. Seeing Carly in the stark fluorescence was a punch in the gut. Her bruised neck had turned purple and her face was ashen. She hadn't stopped shaking. The rage that Maverick forced down on a daily basis burst to the surface. He wished he'd killed the son of a bitch.

"Her name is Carly. She's my girlfriend." He turned back to her. "Carly, honey, the ambulance is here. You're going to be okay."

Internado groaned. "Help me. I've been shot."

Paramedics hurried in.

"The paramedics are here." Maverick gave her hands a gentle squeeze. "We're gonna get you to the hospital." Rising, he moved out of their way so first responders could treat her.

"I'm Officer DeLuca. What's your name, sir?"

"Ashton Hott."

"Mr. Hott, I understand you shot this man. I'll need your weapon as evidence. Do you have a permit to carry?"

"Yes, for my job." Maverick relinquished his Glock. "Carly has been working a cold case that could link this man to a murder. He found out and tried to kill her."

Paramedics untied Internado and he tried standing, but couldn't. "That's total bullshit. I'm in a lot of pain. He shot me!" he said, grabbing his thigh.

THE HOTT TOUCH | 307

"Please hold still, sir." The EMT dressed Internado's wound, then placed him on a gurney.

"What's your name, sir?" asked the second police officer.

"Internado. *Senator* George Internado."

The paramedics fitted Carly with a neck brace and lifted her onto a gurney. Maverick gently stroked her hair before turning back to the officer. "Internado's hairpiece and facial hair are a disguise," Maverick said. "He lured her here to kill her. When I got here, he had his gloved hands around her neck. She had no pulse and I had to perform multiple cycles of CPR."

"I need to phone my lawyer." Internado tugged off his glove and began sliding his hand inside his pants pocket.

"Keep your hands where I can see them," said Officer DeLuca. "You can make that call after you've been treated at the hospital."

"We're taking them to Washington Hospital," said a paramedic.

"Senator, you have the right to remain silent," the second officer began. "Anything you say can and will be used against—"

"How dare you! I'm a United States Senator." Internado's face turned beet-red, his bulbous nose a bright pink. "You'll regret this. It's my word against his. You should be arresting him. He tried to kill me! *I'm* the victim here."

As the paramedics wheeled Carly by, Maverick leaned down and kissed her cheek. "Babe, I'll be right behind you." But Carly remained unresponsive. Another jolt of panic surged through him as she disappeared through the doorway.

"I'm heading to the hospital." Maverick handed DeLuca his business card. "My contact info."

"Mr. Hott, you look familiar," said DeLuca. "Aren't you that guy who rescued all those American hostages?"

"Yes, sir. I'm one of them."

Internado sneered at Maverick. "I should have known you'd be behind this."

"I told you you'd get what you deserve," Maverick replied. "And I'm a man of my word."

26

KICK-ASS CARLY

D ecades of training had brought Maverick to this moment, with this woman. As Carly slept, her chest rising and falling with each breath, he kept telling himself she was safe.

She's alive. She's going to be okay. She is okay.

He leaned down, kissed her forehead. "I love you. You're doing great." He held her hand, stroked her soft skin with his thumb.

But the intensity of the evening still curled his fingers into fists, the anger festering just below the surface. He'd wanted to kill Internado. One bullet would have accomplished that. Maverick hadn't been trained to shoot someone in the leg. The image of Internado strangling Carly haunted him. He squeezed his eyes shut, but the picture remained.

The emergency room staff had examined her. While waiting for the test results, Maverick had paced. Then he'd parked himself in the chair beside her bed and talked to her, watched her breathe and calmed down. Then he'd paced again. He couldn't settle down.

Carly needed rest. She'd been through a horrific ordeal. Physically, she'd suffered tremendous trauma. Who knew what the emotional toll would be? She'd been lifeless, but he would not let her go. Not on his watch and not in this lifetime.

The ER physician returned, but Carly didn't stir.

"The results are looking good. No obvious brain damage, no heart damage." The doc paused. "Since we don't know how long she was deprived of oxygen, she's not out of the woods yet."

"What do I watch for?"

"Wide swings in her blood pressure. Memory or perception issues. For the next week or so, she'll tire easily. She'll have to ease back into her routine, and that includes work. No physical exertion for a week while her body heals."

"Understood."

"Performing CPR saved her. *You* saved her." The doctor patted his back. "The staff is right outside if you need us or if she has questions when she wakes up." He left and pulled the curtain closed.

Unable to stop the myriad of emotions careening over him, he dropped his head into his hands. Ever since his mom's death, he'd fought the demons every day. Now, as the woman he loved slumbered, he couldn't stop them.

Maverick prided himself on maintaining control. His team looked to him for leadership and he didn't let them down. His family relied on him and he wouldn't fail them. His friends trusted him and he'd been their rock when they'd needed him.

He couldn't get through this one alone. Not this time.

"Hey." Carly's hoarse whisper cut through the silence.

Some of the tension pinching his shoulder blades eased when he peered into her eyes. "Welcome back, my love."

For Maverick, displaying emotion was a sign of weakness, but as he folded his hands over hers, he couldn't hold back the tears of joy at touching her warm skin, so full of life. He could have lost her, but he hadn't. And that's what he'd cling to while he got them through this.

She wiped his tears with her thumb. "It was bad, huh?" Her raspy voice a harsh reminder of what she'd endured.

"Nothing I couldn't handle." No need to scare or upset her. There would be time, later, for the blatant, terrifying truth.

"Did we get him?"

"He was arrested and charged with kidnapping and attempted murder. That said, I'm sure he has a team of top-notch attorneys working to get him out on bond."

She started to sit up, but he placed gentle hands on her shoulders. "Easy, babe."

"I don't want Internado to get away—"

"He won't be able to slither out of this. The DNA results showed a match with your client. The police stopped by while you were sleeping. They'll be back."

"What time is it?"

Maverick checked his phone. "Five o'clock, Saturday morning."

She sank back onto the pillow and stared at the ceiling. "I'm sorry."

He leaned close, kissed her. Her warm lips calmed his tormented soul. The emotion burbled up again, tears welling in his eyes. "I love you, so damn much."

The pinch between her brows faded, a tiny smile lifted her lips. "I love *you* so much, Ashton."

He pressed his lips to her forehead and breathed. "I can't—*I won't*—live without you."

She placed her hand over her heart. "So romantic." Then, her smile fell away. "I should never have fallen for his text."

"Do *not* blame yourself. He's been manipulating people for decades."

A nurse entered the room. "Looks like someone woke up. That's good to see. How are you feeling?"

"Like I've been hit by a train," she rasped out.

"It's going to take several days for you to feel back to normal. Your sweetie pie hasn't left your side."

Carly cracked a little smile.

After checking her vitals and recording them on the tablet, the nurse filled Carly's water bottle.

"How are her numbers?" Maverick asked.

"Blood pressure is still low. The good news is that she's awake and alert. Her heartbeat is strong. Whatever you've been whispering in her ear the past several hours, keep doing it." The nurse addressed Carly. "Before I remove the IV, I'd like you to start sipping the water. It's going to hurt, so drink a little at a time. I'll be back to check on you."

Over the next couple of hours, Carly drifted in and out of sleep while Maverick remained her vigilant guard and protector. At seven, he slipped out of the room.

"Hey," he said to his dad. "Sorry to call so early."

"Everything okay?"

"Carly is in Washington Hospital ER."

"Oh, God, what happened?"

"Tell you when you get here."

"I'll be out the door in fifteen." His dad hung up.

He called Sinclair.

"Yeah." He'd woken his brother.

"Internado tried to kill Carly."

"Fuck, no. Where is she?"

"Washington Hospital ER."

"Is she okay?"

"She will be."

"On my way."

Maverick returned to her bedside and watched her sleep. Thirty minutes later, Warren arrived. So as not to wake her, they spoke in whispers outside her room.

When Maverick finished giving his dad the short version, Warren couldn't speak for several seconds. "I'm so thankful you got to her in time and that you know CPR."

"I've kind of been a wreck and you know I'm a rock."

"Son." His dad gripped his shoulder. "You adore her. She's the one."

He nodded in agreement. "She is."

"I'll represent you both."

"We don't need lawyers."

"Like hell you don't. You shot a United States senator. Let me tell you one thing...George Internado is going to get a heaping dose of justice when I'm finished with him."

"Thanks, Dad."

"Can Carly have visitors?"

"I'm sure she'd love to see you, but she's been sleeping pretty much this entire time."

"Have you gone to the bathroom? Gotten something to eat?"

He shook his head. "I don't want to leave her."

"Did you call Sinclair?"

"He's on his way."

"Desiree and Hudson?"

"I'll call them in a few."

"Why don't you intercept Sinclair and take ten? You're wound pretty tightly. I'll stay with Carly."

Maverick hesitated.

Warren nodded. "Clear your head, Ashton. She'll be okay. I'll call you if anything changes."

"I won't be long." He rubbed the back of his neck, hoping for some relief.

Carly was still asleep, so he kissed her forehead, watched her breathe, then left. He found Sinclair in the ER lobby. The woman manning the check-in desk was smiling way too big for someone who worked in an emergency room.

"Hey," Maverick said.

"How is she?" Sinclair asked.

"Groggy, in pain. Been sleeping, mostly."

"Thanks for your help," Sinclair said to the woman.

"Where do men like you hang out?" she whispered. "I *never* meet guys who look like you. Wow, you two are something else."

"Thank you, darlin'," Maverick said. "Point us in the direction of coffee."

As soon as she did, they took off.

"Tell me everything," Sinclair said.

On the way to the cafeteria, Maverick gave him the long version, including Internado's interest in choke sex.

"I'm not surprised. Greta has a reputation for walking the line between consent and downright dangerous. Where's Internado now?"

"In jail, I hope. I have no idea. I met him at Rudy's yesterday and got him to admit he altered the subcommittee report."

"Were you wired?"

"Damn straight."

"Get that over to me. I'll make sure it ends up in the right hands."

Even at this early hour, the cafeteria was busy. "You want something?" Maverick asked.

"Coffee."

Maverick bought three.

"You aren't eating?" Sinclair asked. "You never turn down food."

"My stomach's in knots."

"So, now what?" Sinclair asked on the way back to Carly's room.

"Dad's representing us, though I doubt we'll need legal counsel."

"I'm at your disposal. Whatever you need."

"I need Carly to make a full recovery."

"She will."

"She has to," Maverick replied. "Because I can't live without her."

Sinclair's lips split into a smile. "Finally. The damn truth."

Carly opened her eyes and gasped. Then, she wrapped her fingers around her sore neck. The vivid memory of her ordeal crashed into her reality and her heart raced in her chest.

"You're okay and you're safe."

She expected to see Ashton, but his dad sat at her bedside. Since childhood, Warren Hott had been a positive role model in her life. She'd turned to him for advice when it was time to apply for college and, later, for career advice.

Over the years, he'd been a great sounding board when a case stumped her. She admired his quiet strength, strong moral compass, and deep love for his children. Ashton was so much like his dad...only brimming with that intoxicating bravado she loved so much.

He held out the Styrofoam cup and she sipped through the straw. Cool water trailed down her burning throat. After she'd drunk some more, she breathed deeply, grateful she could breathe at all.

"Ash will be right back."

"Thanks for coming." Weak and raspy, she didn't recognize her own voice.

His smile was fraught with concern. To her surprise, tears filled his eyes and he cleared his throat. "I'm relieved you're okay. You know, Carly, I consider you one of my own."

That made her smile. "In many ways, *you* are my dad."

This time, his smile touched his eyes. "Internado won't get away with his crimes. I'll make sure of that."

She hoped that was true. "Was he arrested?"

"Yes."

Ashton and Sinclair entered her room and she mustered a little smile. Ashton dropped a light kiss on her lips. "You look more alert, honey."

"You are one tough chick," Sinclair said. "I love that about you. 'Kick-ass Carly.'"

"Funny," she rasped out. "Thanks for coming."

"Whoa, sister, I would rest that voice." Sinclair kissed her forehead. "You sound like something out of a sci-fi flick."

Even in the worst of times, Sinclair always made her smile. "My phone was in my pants pocket," she whispered to Ashton. "Where's my clothing?"

He unearthed her cell phone from the plastic hospital bag filled with her belongings. "Do you want me to call someone for you?"

"Check the office surveillance app," she said.

"There's a recording from last night," Ashton replied.

"Oh, wow," Warren said.

Sinclair's lips split into a sardonic grin. "Nice."

After easing down beside her, Ashton tapped the video.

The four of them watched in horror as the nightmare played out on the screen. When Internado's hands folded around her neck, she looked away. "I don't need to see any more."

He paused the video. An eerie silence fell over them. Filled with dread, Carly started shivering, so Ashton covered her with an extra blanket before warming her hands in his.

"Did I have a pulse when you found me?" Her hoarse voice cut through the silence.

Unable to utter the words, he shook his head.

"If you hadn't come, I would be dead."

His confident smile calmed her. "This is the *beginning* of our love story, Carly. Not the end."

Though weak, she squeezed his hand.

As Warren shook his head, he narrowed his eyes. "He's *not* getting away with this. You have my word."

"He's messing with the wrong family if he thinks he can beat us." Sinclair's words spilled out like a growl.

"Internado deserves to rot in hell," Ashton bit out.

The anger these men displayed reminded Carly just how loved she was. "Thank you for having my back," she said, tears pricking her eyes.

The nurse pulled open the privacy curtain and frowned at the men. "Sounds like a party in here. I'm delighted our patient is feeling better, but she needs her rest."

"I'll walk these guys out and be right back, babe," Ashton said to Carly.

"Warren, can you show the video to the police and FBI?" Carly rasped out.

"I'll handle everything," Warren said. "Don't you worry about a thing."

"Kick-ass Carly, you're going to be just fine." Sinclair shot her a smile and left.

Maverick returned to Carly's room, pulled the chair over, and kissed her hand. "Can you close your eyes for a little while? I'll be right here when you wake up."

She pushed up, winced, and lay back down.

"What are you doing?"

"I wanted to kiss you."

He pressed his lips to hers. "Go easy, please."

"You saved my life."

He tightened his grip on her hands. "In truth, you saved mine...a long time ago. I owed you one. We can call it even."

They shared a smile. "I'm so tired."

"You rest while I call your mom."

"Don't bother. She doesn't care about me."

His chest tightened. He couldn't imagine what that felt like. "I'll be right outside and back in two minutes," he said as her eyes fluttered closed.

Maverick called Lisa Stone.

"Hello."

"Lisa, it's Ashton."

"Who?"

"Ashton Hott, Carly's friend."

"Oh, yeah. What's up?"

"There was an attempt on Carly's life and she's in the hospital."

"Is she okay?"

He was floored at how unconcerned Lisa sounded. "She will be. Someone tried to kill her at her old office."

"You mean Cassandra's law firm?"

"Right. I had to shoot out the back lock to get to her."

"That sounds...uh...action-packed."

Wow, she's cold. "The locksmith will fix it this afternoon."

"When did this happen?"

"Last night."

"So, the office has been unlocked this *entire* time?"

Maverick wanted to shout a string of obscenities at this stupid, selfish woman. "What the hell is your problem, Lisa? Your daughter almost died."

"I have my own problems. I'll let Cassandra know. She's a very important lawyer." And with that, Lisa hung up.

Carly's better off without her.

He called Ed Stone next.

"Ed, this is Ashton Hott, Carly's—"

"Hey, Ashton. How've you been?"

"Carly is in the hospital and—"

"What happened?"

"Someone tried to kill her."

"Oh, dear. Was it because I suggested she meet clients in the park?"

What the hell is wrong with this family? "I shot out the back lock of your office building to get to her. I let Lisa know—"

"That bitch doesn't care."

"Since you own the building, I thought you'd want to know I arranged for a locksmith."

"Thank you. Can I talk to Carly?"

"She's sleeping."

"When she's better, you guys should visit. Florida is a nice change for me. Give her my love."

Maverick hung up. He couldn't fathom his family being so hard hearted. As her words floated back to him, he grasped the full weight of her fear. *If we broke up, I would lose my best friend and his family. I would lose the people I love the most.*

He returned to Carly's bedside. "You're not going to lose me," he whispered. "Not ever. I will love you and keep you safe *forever.* You are my life, Carly."

Her eyes fluttered open. "You are mine, too," she whispered.

TOGETHER

Ashton had fallen asleep in the hospital chair, his head resting on Carly's lap while she stroked his hair and back. Being able to touch him made her deeply happy. Despite her exhaustion and pain, she was grateful to be alive.

The doctor entered and he sat up.

"How are you feeling?" the physician asked.

"About the same," she rasped out.

"Were you able to eat something?"

She wrinkled her nose. "A few bites."

He shone his light into one eye, then the other. "Open your mouth." He shone the light, then switched it off. "Your blood tests look good. While you did go into cardiac arrest, your heart is otherwise very healthy." He examined her neck. "Those bruises will heal." He checked her wrists and ankles. "I'd get some aloe for those rope burns."

She nodded.

"The EEG came back and it's normal."

"Great news," Ashton said.

"You may experience PTSD symptoms. Have you heard of post-traumatic stress?"

"Yes," she whispered.

"Take it easy for a week, longer if you need it. You've been through a lot, so listen to your body. Talk to your healthcare professional if you experience any night terrors or trouble sleeping. Any kind of anxiety that you would consider unusual or excessive. Unfortunately, PTSD affects people in many different ways."

She nodded.

"And that goes for you, too," he said to Ashton. "Talk about what you're feeling. Help each other through this."

"Absolutely," he replied.

"You're young, healthy and I expect you'll make a full recovery. Unless you feel the need to be admitted, I'm going to discharge you."

"Sounds good," she whispered.

"No driving for at least a week. Your chest and ribcage endured intense pressure from your husband's CPR. Be patient with recovery. Rest your voice. Ease back into your exercise routine. Are we good with that?"

"Yes."

"What questions do you have for me?"

"None."

"Sir, any questions?" the doctor asked.

"No. Thanks for everything," Ashton replied, shaking his hand. "I'll make sure Carly takes things slowly."

"Take your time getting dressed. Everything I mentioned will be on your discharge papers. Good luck to you both." With a smile, the physician left.

"He thinks we're married," Carly whispered.

"I wonder who gave him that idea," Ash said with a smile.

An hour later, the nurse came by with discharge papers. After Ashton helped Carly dress, they walked slowly out of the hospital.

"Babe, would you feel more comfortable heading to your house or mine?" he asked once he'd tucked her into his car.

"I don't care as long as I'm in your arms."

Tired and sore, she said nothing on the way to the marina. The simple act of holding his hand brought her tremendous joy. That evening, Carly had a restless night's sleep. Her nightmares woke her and her throat hurt, but she felt safe and loved in Ashton's strong embrace. She awoke alone and feeling anxious. It was after ten in the morning.

Moving with care, she dressed and padded out. She found Ashton with Warren and Sinclair on the ship's back deck.

"There she is," Ashton said.

Carly sat beside him. "Hi, guys." Her voice was gravelly, her throat parched. She sipped his orange juice and winced.

"We brought your car back," Warren said.

"Thank you." She picked up her keys and stood.

"Whoa, where are you going?" Ashton asked.

"To get my Glock out of the trunk."

"I'll go with her," Sinclair said.

Pushing past the pain, Carly hotfooted it down the pier.

"Hey, slow down there, mama. What's the rush?"

She opened her trunk and shouldered the holster, then tucked her weapon inside. That soothed her down. "I feel restless. I can't explain it, but I need this."

"Do what makes sense. Just don't shoot *me*."

"Don't piss me off and I won't."

He laughed. "You're coming back with quite an attitude."

"No one's ever tried to kill me before."

"Welcome to the club."

She lifted her gaze to his. "Hmm, that's new information."

"The past is the past for a reason."

Side by side, they returned to the boat to find Warren on the phone. "She's still recovering. I'll call you back." Warren shifted his gaze to her. "The police and FBI need to speak with you."

"I want to talk to my client first. I'll call her now."

"Carly, are you pushing?" Ashton asked.

"No." She shot him a little smile. "Yes."

Worry lines creased his forehead. "Don't."

"It's one phone call and two conversations with law enforcement. The defense is building its case. We need to make sure Internado doesn't get off." She dug out her phone. "Warren, I believe Internado pushed my grandfather to his death. Will you help me prove it?"

"Give me what you have and I'll get to work."

As Carly called Erin Murphy, Ashton set a glass of water on the table in front of her. "Thank you." She shot him a smile, drank down a few sips. "Erin, it's Carly Stone." Her throat hurt, but she had to have this conversation.

"You don't sound so good. Are you sick?"

"Not exactly. I have information regarding your case."

"Great."

"I found a paternal match that's ninety-nine point nine percent accurate. And he may have murdered Rose Aurora."

"Oh, God. Okay, lay it on me."

"Senator George Internado is your biological father. He's been arrested for attempted murder."

"Only 'attempted'? But Rose is dead."

"He tried to kill *me*."

"Oh, no! Are you okay?"

"I will be. The police and FBI need evidence in order to build a case against him. I'm going to email you the DNA results, but I'll have to provide them to law enforcement, as well."

"Totally fine."

"One more thing. I have reason to believe the senator also murdered my grandfather."

"Am I in danger?"

"Hold on a sec." Carly hit the mute button. "Warren, where's Internado?"

"In jail."

"Not released on bond?"

"Kidnapping and attempted murder don't get you a free pass to roam around the city."

Carly unmuted the call. "Erin, Internado is being held without bond, but if you fear for your safety, you should take precautionary measures. I'm sure the police will be in touch." She hung up. "Okay, Warren, I'm ready to give my statement."

"The video speaks for itself, but I'll be here when you talk to them," Warren said.

"I'm heading out," Sinclair said. "Ash, I'll check in with you later."

"Thanks for everything," he replied.

"Kick-ass Carly is loaded for bear," Sinclair said. "Of the two of you, who's the better shot?"

"I am," Carly said at the same time Ashton said, "Carly is."

"Loaded for bear *and* packing heat." Sinclair squeezed his brother's shoulder. "Relax. She's gonna be just fine."

Maverick was concerned Carly was pushing herself too hard. A police detective stopped by and she recounted everything, beginning with the cold case and ending with the attempt on her life. As he was leaving, an FBI agent showed up, so she had to repeat her story all over again.

An hour later, FBI Agent Mark Rodriguez closed his tablet. "Having the video is huge. Disturbing as hell, though. I'm sorry for what you've been through."

She slipped her hand into Maverick's. "I'm lucky to be here."

"It's been a rough weekend for you guys." He stood. "Get some rest. I'll be in touch."

As soon as Rodriguez left, Carly thanked Warren before Maverick walked his dad down the pier. When he returned, Carly had conked out on the sofa, her holstered weapon on the table. He sat beside her and she crawled into his lap.

"I'll be right here when you wake up." He rested his head on the back cushion. The adrenaline rush had worn off and he was beat. He was drifting to sleep when a woman's shrieking voice jolted him awake. Carly jumped off the couch, her eyes wild with fear. She grabbed her Glock.

"Where the hell is she?" the woman screamed.

Maverick went outside. Cassie Stone glared at him from the pier. "Where the fuck is my sister?"

Carly sidled up beside him. "What do you want?"

Carly's hoarse voice, black and blue neck, and Glock in her hand *should* have been a clear sign something was severely wrong. Rather than showing any concern for her sister, Cassie hitched her hands on her hips.

"Mom said the lock on the back door of my office was busted and that *you*"—she launched her finger toward Maverick—"did it. I demand an explanation."

Carly's mom's boyfriend, Ross, rolled up beside Cassie wearing a snug suit, his clingy shirt unbuttoned to his navel. *What the hell? I thought he was with the mother.*

Ross slid his sunglasses down his nose and eyed the yacht. "I'll bet she's a sweet ride." He eyed Maverick. "This baby yours?"

"What do you want, Cassie?" Maverick asked.

Rolling her eyes, she harrumphed. "You broke into my office. Explain yourself."

Maverick threw a protective arm around Carly. "A man in his sixties visited you last week, interested in Carly."

"Yeah, so?"

"You told him Carly had your spare key and he used that information to impersonate you and lure her to your office. When she dropped everything to help you, he forced her inside and strangled her."

Cassie flicked her gaze to Carly and barked out a laugh. "Ha! Good one. I don't believe you." She pointed at Maverick. "You need to pay for damages or I'll...I'll sue you!"

Ross shifted back and forth. "Hey, baby, maybe we should go easy. Your sister's got a piece." Pausing, Ross eyed the vessel. "I wouldn't mind going out for a...a...what do you call it? A sail? This ain't no sailboat. A spin? A roll down the Potomac?"

"Oh, shut up, Ross," Cassie said. "You sound like a blathering idiot."

A deep growl shot out of Maverick. "If you'd shown any concern for your sister, I would have paid for the damn locksmith."

"Just because you saved a few hostages doesn't mean a goddamn thing to me," Cassie said, glaring at him. "It only adds to your arrogance and pretentiousness."

Stepping forward, Carly glared at her. "Shut your mouth. Do *not* talk to him like that."

"What's your problem?" Cassie asked, furrowing her brow. "Speak up. I can barely hear you."

Moving with care, Carly climbed onto the pier. "You've been a total witch to me my entire life and I've let you walk all over me. Not anymore," she said, hitching her hands to her hips. "You don't get to talk to Ash like that and you don't get to talk to me like that anymore, either. I don't want *anything* to do with you. We're done."

"Go to hell. You're lucky I'm being so nice about this. I'm a lawyer, and a damn good one!"

Maverick stepped onto the pier, dwarfing everyone. He placed a protective arm around Carly and drew her close to him. "For the past twenty-five years you've been nothing but a bitch to your sister. I've never opened my mouth, never interfered, but that all ends today. Here's what I have to say to you, Cassie: Go. Fuck. Yourself."

"What...er...how dare you talk at me like that!"

Ross removed his sunglasses. "If your sister and the dude have known each other for twenty-five years, are they, like, fifty?"

Cassie rolled her eyes. "No, you idiot, they met when they were kids."

"Now, get the hell off my pier and don't ever set foot on my property again."

Cassie flipped Maverick off and marched away, with Ross trotting after her.

Maverick jumped into his yacht and pulled Carly into his arms, then he kissed the top of her head. She hugged him tightly, then stared into his eyes. "My family is an example of everything that doesn't work. Now, do you see why I'm so scared of losing you?"

He smiled at her. "Do you know now that my family *is* your family?"

Her rueful smile was filled with love. She nodded. "I do."

"C'mon, honey, time to sleep." He guided her back inside.

"Will you stay with me?"

"Only for the rest of your life."

Rising on her tiptoes, she laid a tender kiss on his lips. They returned to the sofa and cuddled while he caressed her back and reminded her how much he loved her.

But reminding her and showing her were two completely different things...

28

A BIRTHDAY TO REMEMBER

Carly woke excited to give Ashton an early morning birthday present, but the other half of the bed lay empty. Five days had passed since her horrific ordeal. While her body continued to heal, she was struggling mentally. In addition to wearing her weapon everywhere but in bed, she felt restless and unsettled.

She also worried that the stress was starting to take its toll on Ash. He'd figured out a short-term strategy to keep his recruits on ThunderStrike's payroll, but confided he was running in the red.

She padded out to find him in the galley, on the phone. He mumbled a quick goodbye and hung up.

"Happy birthday, babe," she said as she slipped her arms around him.

He poured her a cup of coffee and handed her a teaspoon for the creamer.

"It's your birthday," she said. "I should be waiting on you."

"Nah, you know my birthday is no big deal."

"I want to get you something special. What would you like? A weekend away? Something special for the boat? Sex everyday for a year?"

He laughed. "I'll take *you*...and sex everyday for a year."

"Let's start now," she said and stroked his butt cheek.

"I'm glad you're feeling better." His smile fell away. "Let's sit down. I want to talk to you about something."

Her stomach clenched. *It's Internado. He's getting out.* They sat on the sofa and he scooped her hands in his.

"Carly, you know I've never been big on celebrating my birthday."

She swallowed. "Uh-huh." *Oh, God, what is going on?*

"I've given this a lot of thought and there *is* something I want for my birthday."

She didn't realize she'd been holding her breath and inhaled deeply. "Whew, you scared me. You look so serious."

He stroked her hand. "I am serious. I want to turn my birthday into something I'll look forward to celebrating every year."

She was drawing a total blank. "Okay."

He knelt and, with the most sincere expression, said, "Carlyle Elizabeth Stone, I love you with all my heart. Our pretend marriage feels so real and so right, I want to make it official." He pressed his lips to hers. "Marry me. Today."

"Ha-ha. Very funny."

"I'm not joking. I want us to get married. You asked me what I want for my birthday. I want you to become my *real* wife. *Today.* Please don't disappoint the birthday boy."

Everything Ashton ever did was full throttle. Why would she expect this would be any different?

As her gaze floated over his face, her heart rejoiced. Without question, she knew what her answer would be. What her heart had always wanted. To be this man's wife for all eternity. She cradled his face in her hands. "Ashton, I would be *honored* to marry you, today."

He swept her into his arms. His kisses were tender and passionate, sweet and panty melting. "Best birthday ever."

"Hellooooooo," Desiree called. "Where's the birthday boy?"

His sister bounded onboard carrying garment bags. Ashton took them and hoofed it down the stairs to the staterooms.

"You look much better today," Desiree said, examining Carly.

"Well?" Desiree asked when Ashton returned.

He grinned. "She said, 'Yes'!"

Desiree hugged Carly. "Congratulations! Finally...real sisters." Then, she hugged her brother. "Happy birthday, old man. Thirty-four. Yikes, you two better start popping out the babies."

Carly laughed. "Slow down there, sister. I can barely process that we just got engaged. How does this work? Do we just show up at the courthouse?"

"We have an appointment at noon with a judge."

"You planned this?"

"Hell, yeah."

"Not concerned I'd say no?" Carly asked him.

He laughed. "Hell, no."

"So cocky." Her smile faltered. "I don't have anything to wear."

"What do you think is in those garment bags?" Desiree asked. "Let's go try on some dresses."

Carly kissed her fiancé. "This is the best surprise, *ever*."

The two women retreated into the guest stateroom. One at a time, Desiree held up each of the cocktail dresses. Varying in color, they were as simple as they were elegant.

"They're all fabulous," Carly said. "Thank you so much for doing this for us." She tried on a blush pink one and both of the white dresses. Despite the yellowish bruises on her neck, she loved the fit and feel of the white, off–the-shoulder mermaid dress with a delicate lace overlay. "This is absolutely beautiful. But the other white dress has a high neck, which hides my bruises. What do you think?"

With hands fastened on her hips, Desiree studied Carly. "Wear the dress of your heart."

Carly examined herself in the mirror. "This is definitely the one."

Desiree beamed. "I thought so, too. It's like that dress was made for you." She flipped open her makeup box. "I might be able to hide some of the bruising with make up."

"That would be awesome."

"How 'bout an updo?"

"Do I need a tie?" Ashton called through the closed door.

"Of course," Desiree replied. "It's your wedding day."

Forty minutes later, Carly was ready to go. She stared at her reflection in disbelief. "I look like a bride."

"You're stunning."

"Thank you. You are the best sister." Carly's eyes misted.

"Oh, please no," Desiree said. "You'll smudge your eyes."

Carly fanned her face. "Will you be my maid of honor?"

"I'd love to." Desiree changed into a pale blue chiffon cocktail dress. Before leaving, Carly tucked her Glock into her handbag.

Desiree's eyes grew large. "Whoa, what's that for?"

She wished Desiree hadn't seen her do that. "Just a precaution."

"I thought the senator was behind bars." Desiree put a comforting hand on Carly's shoulder. "Are you okay?"

"Yes and no. I have a permit to carry and I'll let security at the courthouse know. I feel better when I have it with me."

"Well, let's hope you never have to use it," she said and cracked open the door. "Ash, are you there?"

"You two ready?" he asked.

"I'll drive Carly. It's bad luck to see your bride before the ceremony. You go ahead."

"Oh, wait." Carly pulled off Sarah Hott's wedding band and Desiree passed it out the door.

"You two are funny," Desiree said. "You're going to put these back on in an hour."

"Yeah, but this time it's for real," Ashton replied.

Maverick spied his family waiting in front of Judge Reynolds's chambers. "Hey, guys." He could not stop smiling. "Thanks for being here."

His dad hugged him. "Congratulations! I'm very happy for you, son. You two are perfect for each other."

Hudson pulled him in for a handclasp. "You look good. What happened to Grizzly Adams?"

Laughing, Maverick ran his hands over his clean-shaved jawline. "Gotta look sharp for my bride."

"This wedding is a long time coming," Sinclair said.

Warren looked around. "Where are the ladies?"

"Desiree is driving Carly. Something about bad luck."

"Our sister is a hopeless romantic," Hudson said.

"Dad, I need to borrow your wedding bands a little longer." He handed the rings to Sinclair.

"This does *not* make me your best man."

"Why the hell not?"

"I'm too much of a sinner to be a 'best' *anything*."

"A sinner with a pretty face is a dangerous combo."

Sinclair chuckled. "I know, right? Nobody suspects a thing."

"Just the opposite." Maverick threw an arm around his brother. "Everyone sees you coming a mile away."

The door opened and the judge smiled at Warren. "Good to see you, Warren."

"You, too, Emily."

She glanced around. "Where's the bride?"

"En route," Maverick replied.

Judge Reynolds ushered them into her chambers and Warren introduced his sons. Her office was stately, yet functional. Built-ins filled with law books lined one wall. The room's focal point was the judge's oversized desk that faced into the room.

A few moments later, there was a knock on the door.

"Here we go," Sinclair said.

The judge opened the door. Desiree spoke with her for a brief second before entering the room alone and whispering to Warren. Maverick's stomach dropped. Had Carly backed out?

"Are you ready?" Desiree asked him.

"I can't do this without my bride."

Desiree placed a small Bluetooth speaker on the table, pulled up Pachelbel's Canon on her phone and nodded. Warren opened the door. Carly crossed the threshold and Maverick's heart jumped into his throat.

"Wow," he murmured.

Her fitted white dress hung off her shoulders. She'd worn her hair up, tendrils falling softly against her silky skin. But it was the happiness in her eyes that stole his heart.

She slipped her hand into the crook of Warren's arm.

"Ready?" Warren asked her.

Maverick couldn't take his eyes off his bride as his dad escorted her over to him. His dad kissed her cheek, patted him on the back, and stood beside Desiree.

As Carly and Maverick faced each other, he collected her hands in his. "You are beyond gorgeous."

Her smile was filled with love. "Thank you. I love that you shaved." She stroked his cheek with soft fingertips. "So handsome."

When they faced the judge, the anguish and heartache that plagued him lifted a little as peace settled into his soul.

"Welcome, Ashton and Carly," Judge Reynolds said. "Your wedding is a special day for you and your family. It signifies the beginning of a new adventure that you're choosing to take together. From this day forward, you are a team. Every decision you make will affect the other. Every day you share is a gift. Cherish it and each other. Are there wedding rings?"

"Yes." Sinclair displayed both bands.

"Would you like to say something to each other?" the judge asked.

"I would," Maverick said. "But you're welcome to go first."

"You go," Carly replied.

"Carlyle Elizabeth Stone, I promise to love you always, treat you with respect and kindness, protect you, and make you laugh. I will make the most of every moment we have together. I will listen when you speak and only yell if something is on fire...or if one of our children throws up."

Laughter filled the room.

"You were always the cutest girl in school and you're the most beautiful woman now," he continued. "You're smart and kind, patient and funny. You work hard and never give up. You and I made great work partners and, now, we're going to make great life partners. Thank you for turning my birthday into a celebration I will look forward to every year. I love you so much."

Sinclair passed him the ring and Maverick slid it onto Carly's ring finger. "My wife, my friend, my lover, my life partner, my spy...for the rest of our lives."

With an adoring smile, Carly clasped his hands in hers. "Ashton Miles Hott, there's never been anyone for me, but you. You are the bravest man I have ever met and I love that about you. You go out of your way for others, but you shoulder so much alone." Love danced in her eyes. "From this day forward, we're in this *together*. Our friendship and your family have been such an important part of my life, I can't imagine going through it without you, without all of you." She paused to look at each of them before turning back to her groom. "You will always be my best friend and I will always be so proud to call you my husband. I love you completely."

She slid the wedding band onto his finger, pausing to shove it over his thick knuckle. "I will be your life partner, your friend, and your lover for the rest of my life. We are bound together for all eternity."

Gazing into her eyes, a sense of completeness washed over him. Before turning back to the judge, he whispered, "Love you, wife."

Carly threaded her fingers through his. "Love you, husband."

The judge cleared her throat. "That was lovely. I have every confidence you'll have a beautiful life together. I'd like to add my two cents, if that's okay."

"Please," Carly said.

"Life is short. We don't realize it until we have more days behind us than ahead of us. Cherish each one of them. Keep your individuality and grow as a couple. You'll find if you put your spouse first, the love you show them will be returned tenfold." She smiled. "By the power vested in me by the District of Columbia, I now pronounce you husband and wife. Congratulations to you both. Ashton, you may kiss your bride."

Maverick pulled Carly into his arms and his lips melded with hers to loud applause. When the kiss ended, he grinned. "We did the deed, woman. It's you and me, baby, for the next seventy years."

Beaming, she said, "That sounds perfect."

The judge snapped a few pictures of the happy group. After hugs and congratulations, they decided to celebrate at Hudson's.

On the way to the restaurant, Maverick's phone rang. "Caller ID is blocked."

"You should answer," Carly said. "Could be work."

He picked it up on speaker. "Hott here."

"Mr. Hott, this is Senator Wynona Applegate from the Senate Select Committee."

"What can I do for you, ma'am?"

"As the newly appointed committee head, I'm reopening the case made against ThunderStrike by Senator Internado. New evidence has been brought to my attention. Can you come in Friday morning, ten thirty?"

"I'll be there. Same location?"

"Yes. If you have questions, call my office." She rattled off her phone number and hung up.

"Sinclair made sure the audio file from my conversation with

Internado at Rudy's got into the *right* hands." Maverick clasped Carly's hand and kissed it. "This day couldn't get any better, wife of mine."

She shot him a coy smile. "Oh, yes, it can, hubs. And it will. I haven't given you your *other* birthday present yet."

29

THE FORMAL APOLOGY

Maverick soldiered through the throng of onlookers and media with his head held high. Flanked by his wife, his brother, and his father, he entered the Dirksen Senate Building.

Like the previous hearings, the room was packed. Word traveled fast in the nation's capital.

After Maverick was escorted to the table, he turned to his family, seated in the row behind him. "Thanks for being here with me."

"I have a good feeling about this." Carly kissed his cheek, then sat back down between Warren and Sinclair.

"I'm right here if you need your attorney," his dad replied.

Maverick tossed him a nod.

"Thank you for this," Maverick said to Sinclair.

"Anytime, brother. It's what I do."

The same young intern hurried over. "I hope three's a charm, sir." The staffer poured him a glass of water and flipped on the mic as the senators filed in and took their seats.

After calling the hearing to order, Senator Applegate addressed Maverick. "Good morning, Mr. Hott."

"Morning, Senators."

"Thank you for meeting with us on such short notice. The past week has been a difficult one for you and your family. We'd like to extend our sincerest sympathies to you, to your wife, and to anyone else affected by the events involving Senator Internado."

"Thank you."

"For the record, are you the Chief Executive Officer of ThunderStrike?"

"Yes, ma'am."

"The purpose of this hearing is to report on startling new information regarding ThunderStrike's top-secret mission known as 'The Twelve'. Glaring discrepancies between the original report and the one Senator Internado provided us were brought to my attention by an anonymous source. The subcommittee concurs that the senator falsified the report."

Maverick nodded. *Sounds about right.*

"On behalf of us all, I offer you and your employees a sincere apology. For the record, ThunderStrike did nothing wrong or illegal during the mission in question. While you did choose to rescue the twelve American hostages in the most extreme and dangerous conditions, you operated within international laws and did not, as the Senator suggested, 'go rogue.'"

After weeks of constant anxiety, the gnawing in Maverick's guts finally stopped.

"Furthermore, Mr. Hott, we are lifting the freeze placed on your government-related missions and future contracts, effective immediately. The committee will see to it that all contracting officers are personally contacted and provided a formal correction. You and your team are true American heroes who risk your lives every day to ensure the safety and successful return of Americans everywhere." She smiled. "I understand you served in the Navy."

"I did, ma'am."

"Thank you for your service, Mr. Hott. Congratulations on a successful mission. We wish you and your team the best in the future. Do you have any questions for us?"

"I want to thank you and your committee for uncovering the truth and clearing ThunderStrike of any wrongdoing. Our motto at ThunderStrike is 'Above and Beyond'. We appreciate that your committee did the same."

"Thank you, Mr. Hott. This hearing is adjourned." She rapped her gavel.

The grin Maverick had waiting in the wings flashed across his face. Elated by their decision, he rocketed out of his chair, kissed his wife, bear-hugged his dad and brother. "I couldn't have done this without you."

Together, they exited the room and faced the media. Phones and mics were shoved in Maverick's direction. Soaking up the moment, he basked in the spotlight.

"Maverick, how do you feel now that you've been vindicated?" asked a reporter.

"I'm indebted to private investigator Carly Stone of Stone Investigations, who worked tirelessly to clear my name. I also owe a debt of gratitude to my ThunderStrike team for their brave efforts every day."

"Rumor has it that your brother, Sinclair Develin, had a hand in this," said a journalist. "What can you tell us about his role in how this went down?"

Maverick regarded his brother. "Let's just say Sinclair has his finger on the pulse of this great city and we'll leave it at that. I'm grateful justice was served. It's time to get back to what we love doing…our jobs."

"What's next for ThunderStrike?" asked another journalist.

"That information is classified, darlin'," Maverick said with a wink. He thanked the press and, flanked by those he loved, left the building.

Once outside, he slid on his sunglasses, captured Carly in his arms and spun her around. Her melodious laughter was music to his soul.

"Congratulations, Ashton," said his dad. "I'm thrilled you've been exonerated."

"Thanks for everything, Dad."

"I've got to get to a meeting." Warren aimed his finger at each of them. "You three…stay out of trouble."

"Where's the fun in that?" Sinclair flashed his devil-may-care smile and sauntered toward his car, his driver waiting at the curb.

Shaking his head, Warren headed down the street.

"We owe Sinclair big time for our fake marriage," Carly said.

Maverick dropped his arm over her shoulder and kissed her temple. "We sure as hell do."

On the way to ThunderStrike, Carly checked her email. "The report from the congressional motor pool came in. Internado checked out a car on February 22. At 11:08 PM that evening, he drove to the Lincoln Memorial. The GPS tracker clocked him there for forty-two minutes. It's a five-minute walk from the memorial to the Watergate Steps."

"Great news, babe."

"I'm forwarding this to your dad and Mark Rodriguez."

A minute later, FBI Agent Rodriguez called her.

Carly answered. "Hi, Mark, you're on speaker. Ash is with me."

"Hey, guys. How's everyone doing?"

"I guess you saw my email about the motor pool," she said.

"Not yet, but thanks for sending it over. I have some info for you. We tested the skin cells collected from under Rose Aurora's fingernails. Unfortunately, the DNA wasn't a match with Internado. Neither was the hair found at the crime scene."

Hairs on the back of her neck prickled. *God, no.* "Does that mean Internado will get released on bond?"

"No way," Mark said. "We've got a solid case based on the kidnapping and attempted murder charges. Our challenge is the missing link in the Rose Aurora case. He had motivation to kill Rose, but the evidence says otherwise. If anything develops, I'll let you guys know."

"Thanks for the call." Surprised and disappointed by the news, Carly hung up. "If Internado didn't kill Rose, then who did?"

"He could have hired someone." Ashton pulled up to ThunderStrike. The newly installed gate glided open and he drove inside.

Maverick was talking, but Carly was obsessing over Rose Aurora's killer. "I was certain Internado killed Rose," she said.

"Carly."

"I just can't believe it."

"*Carlyle.*"

She stared at him. "I'm sorry, babe. What did you say?"

"I'd like to bring Stone Investigations under the ThunderStrike umbrella. You'd operate as a separate entity, but your office would be here. It's secure and you'd never be alone."

She loved that he was vigilant about keeping her safe. "Wouldn't you have to reconfigure the offices to accommodate my clients?"

"We'd share an entrance and reception, but separate the companies by a locked door. You'd have access to ThunderStrike, but your clients wouldn't."

She leaned over and kissed him. "I love it."

The front door to ThunderStrike opened and the employees rushed outside.

Gunner was grinning. "We heard the news!"

"And the phone hasn't stopped ringing," Penelope added. "You gotta help us manage these bookings. It's fantastic!"

Before following them inside, Carly called Erin Murphy. If Internado didn't kill her biological mother, Erin needed to be warned. A shiver skirted through her and she glanced through the chain-link fence, dread returning like an ominous storm cloud.

The killer's still out there.

THE H.O.T.T. FOUNDATION

C arly and Maverick reviewed the email invitation.

Subject: WE GOT MARRIED!!!

Please join us in celebrating our recent nuptials at the home of Warren Hott on Saturday, October 26. The party starts at 1:00 PM and ends when the last guest leaves. Dress is casual.

In lieu of gifts, a donation to our charity—The H.O.T.T. Foundation —would be greatly appreciated.

The H.O.T.T. FOUNDATION—Helping Others To Thrive—has been created in honor of Ashton's SEAL teammate, Enrique Rijado. All monies donated will go toward helping veterans with PTSD receive the care they need in order to live long and healthy lives.

We can't wait to see you!

Ashton and Carly Hott

Carly beamed at him. "I'm Carly Hott."

"And hot you are, wife of mine. Gimme some more of those smokin' hot kisses."

The last forty-eight hours had been a blur of lovemaking, some food, and not nearly enough sleep. Despite being deliriously happy, Carly kept her Glock close by. Though concerned, Maverick would support her through the healing process, no matter how long it took.

When the smooching ended, he asked, "How many are we inviting?"

"Around ninety. That includes your family and the Rijados, all our friends, and everyone at ThunderStrike." She hit the send key.

"Will you be—what did Sinclair say—loaded for bear and packing heat at our party?"

"Yes, and you should be, too."

"Internado is in jail and the FBI is doing its job. We're safe."

"I feel more secure when armed. Speaking of which, I'm headed to target practice. Come with me."

"I definitely want to come with you." He stroked her breast, hidden beneath her shift. "But shooting a gun wasn't what I had in mind."

"C'mon, horndog," she said and kissed him. "We'll fool around when we get back."

WARREN'S BACKYARD was bustling with activity the day of the big event. Hudson's catered, with Desiree in charge. The tables and chairs had been set up. Both open bars were fully stocked. At one o'clock, guests began arriving.

Internado's high-profile case had garnered both Carly and Maverick a lot of attention. In the last week, several new clients had contracted with Stone Investigations, along with one Craig Pluckett. According to Carly, he'd apologized for his rude and unprofessional behavior, then hired her to complete so many background checks, she was able to afford a solid advertising campaign.

Still, Maverick worried about her. She toted her weapon

wherever she went, even into their bedroom. Today, her holstered gun was hidden beneath her shawl.

When Crockett and Alexandra Wilde arrived, Maverick bear-hugged his friend. "Thanks for coming."

"Congratulations!" Crockett replied. "It's about damn time you two admitted what everyone else already knew."

Maverick laughed.

"You two were always meant to be together." Alexandra introduced the couple they'd brought with them. "This is my friend and cameraman, Gavin Aviato, and his husband, Bruce."

"We're so happy you're all here today," Carly said.

Crockett slung an arm around Maverick. "No way would we miss this."

"Thanks for letting us do a story on your foundation," Alexandra said.

"For you, baby girl, anything," Maverick said. "We appreciate you getting the word out."

"I'm going to set up for the interviews," Gavin said.

"There's a ton of appetizers," Maverick said. "Grab a bite first."

Colton Mitus and Brigit Farnay walked around back.

"There's my golden man!" Maverick hugged his friend.

"You married up," Colton said and everyone laughed.

"Way, way up," Maverick replied as he locked eyes with his wife.

"Congratulations," Brigit said as she hugged Carly. "Colton and I brought you a surprise." She pointed to the back deck.

Jagger Loving and Taylor Hathaway waved. "Surprise!" Hand-in-hand, they hurried down the stairs.

Grinning, Maverick said, "I thought you couldn't make it."

"I lied," Jagger said with a smile. "Congratulations!" The two close friends hugged. "I miss you, man."

"Miss you, too, bro."

Jagger pulled an envelope from his sport coat. "From Taylor and me." He handed the envelope to Carly.

Sinclair joined the group and Carly waited until everyone greeted him before reading the card out loud. "Please honeymoon at our Malibu resort and stay as our guests." She grinned. "This is *awesome*. Thank you both so much."

"I'm definitely in." Maverick put his arm around Carly. "We could use some R&R."

"And my jet is available to take you there." Sinclair said.

"Thank you, brother. Carly and I want to thank you for the fake marriage set-up. You're brilliant."

A cool smile lifted Sinclair's lips. "You had a problem and I fixed it. It's what I do."

"I should have known you were involved," Crockett said with a smile.

Colton gripped Sinclair's shoulder. "This one here is the real wizard behind the curtain."

"As long as he's not the Wicked Witch of the West," Maverick said. "I'm—"

"We know, honey," Carly interrupted. "She scares the living hell out of you." While everyone laughed, she dropped a light kiss on his lips. "No worries, my love. I've got your back."

"I know you do and I love that about you."

A waiter appeared with a tray of flutes filled with champagne. After they'd each taken one, Maverick raised his glass.

"To the six," he said.

"The Harvard six," the guys replied in unison.

Gratitude washed over him as they toasted their friendship, and love filled his heart when he clinked glasses with his wife. Today, he was celebrating a relationship that began decades ago with a girl he'd cherished for most of his life.

Two hours later, the guests had eaten and Carly and Maverick rose from the head table.

"Can I have everyone's attention?" Maverick shouted.

Gavin Aviato grabbed his camera and started filming. The

chatter continued so Desiree, seated beside Carly, blew an air horn. Carly clutched Maverick's arm.

"It's okay," he whispered. "Just Desiree."

Conversations ceased and Desiree handed her brother a mic.

"You don't need that," a guest yelled.

"Can everyone hear me?" Maverick boomed. "How 'bout in the back?"

"You have one level," Gunner said on his way back from the bar. "Loud."

The crowd cracked up.

"That's the man who saved my life," Maverick said. "Everyone, say hello to my man, Marshall Young." After the applause died down, Maverick began. "Thank you all for joining us today. My wife—I love saying that—my beautiful wife, Carly, and I aren't just celebrating our recent wedding, we're starting a new venture together."

Maverick and Carly exchanged smiles.

"Our foundation, 'Helping Others to Thrive', is in honor of my friend and SEAL teammate, Chief Enrique Rijado. Sadly, Enrique is no longer with us, but his wonderful family is here today. Please give a warm welcome to the Rijado family." He paused for applause. When the backyard quieted, he continued.

"PTSD—post traumatic stress disorder—affects thousands every year. Carly and I want to provide former or retired military personnel with support as they heal. We want to make a positive difference in the lives of those who've served. Thank you to everyone who dropped an envelope into the basket."

As the guests applauded, Sinclair picked up the mic and stood. A female guest whistled and a second shouted, "Woo-hoo!"

Maverick draped his arm over Sinclair. "This is my brother, Sin."

"I'll get sinful with him," shouted the first woman.

Chuckling, Sinclair raised his glass. "Help me toast the bride and groom." He turned his attention to the newlyweds. "Ash,

Carly, you two were always meant to be together. Mark my words. Five loud children and three stinky mutts." He flashed a smile. "Congratulations. I love you both."

Everyone toasted.

"Ashton isn't just my brother, he's one of five men I trust with my life," Sinclair continued. "Colton Mitus, Crockett Wilde, and Jagger Loving, please stand up." He paused while the men stood. "Unfortunately, Dakota Luck couldn't make it today. The five of us want you and Carly to make a *real* difference, so we're *each* donating a million dollars to your foundation."

Silence.

Maverick lowered his head, the emotion gripping his throat.

"Wow." With tears in her eyes, Carly hugged him. "Thank you guys, so, so much. Let's show these amazingly generous men some love." After the hoots and hollers ended, she continued. "Your donation will be life-changing for so many veterans in need."

"Love you, my brothers." Maverick put his hand over his heart. "In addition, Carly and I want to acknowledge my sister and brother, Desiree and Hudson, for their hard work in putting this event together. And a big thanks to our dad for letting us take over his house for the past three days."

Rising, Desiree sounded the air horn. Carly startled again and Maverick placed a calming hand on the small of her back.

"Hi, everyone. I'm Desiree Hott. Hudson, and I have a surprise for the newlyweds. I hope everyone saved room for dessert!"

Over the next hour, Carly and Ashton chatted with their guests. At one point, Carly left him to catch up with Crockett and Alexandra, but he made his way over to her and clasped her hand. She loved how he wanted to be by her side and how he referred to her as "my beautiful wife".

She was thrilled her investigative firm was flourishing and that

ThunderStrike's calendar was booked solid for months. Despite the FBI reopening Rose Aurora's case, she was still so unsettled. Was the killer out there, long dead, or lurking nearby? Tormented by that, she lay awake for hours each night. Since the unsolved crime had become a top news story, she feared she and Ash were sitting ducks.

Even at her own wedding reception, she struggled to relax. Her back muscles were in knots, but she forced herself to put on her party face and mingle.

At some point, Desiree and Hudson rolled a beautiful wedding cake into the yard. "Do you like?" her sister-in-law asked.

Carly admired the three-tiered cake with the miniature bride and groom fixed to the top layer. "It's beautiful. Thank you for doing all of this for us."

"My pleasure." Desiree pulled aside the white tablecloth covering the cart and peered inside. "Oops, I forgot a knife," she said and sprinted toward the deck.

Hudson sounded the air horn. This time, Carly reached for her weapon, tucked under her arm. *I have got to calm down.*

"We'll be cutting the cake as soon as my sister returns with the knife," Hudson announced. "This is fun." He blew the horn again and, again, Carly startled.

Ashton pulled her close and whispered, "Deep breath. I'm right here and I've got you."

After taking what should have been a calming breath, she nodded.

"It's okay, babe."

BANG!

The echo of a firecracker reverberated through the air.

Everyone flinched, including Carly. Several guests ran screaming behind trees, while a smattering hit the ground. The remainder stood frozen in place.

When Carly followed the sound, her heart leapt into her throat. A woman stood on the deck with Desiree in a chokehold, a gun pointed at her sister-in-law's head. *Oh, God no.* Carly's pulse soared as she slipped sideways behind Ashton, shielding herself. "Kathy Internado," she whispered.

"I'll try to talk her down," he murmured.

"Do you have your weapon?"

"No."

"I have mine."

"Hello, Kathy." Ashton's strong, calm voice cut through the chilling silence. "What's going on up there?"

Carly's heart banged against her ribcage, but she inhaled slow, controlled breaths. Moving at a snail's pace, she extracted her gun from its holster. She clutched the weapon to her chest and clicked off the safety.

"You and that stupid bitch have ruined my life," Kathy screamed from the deck.

"Why don't you put the gun down and we can work things out." Ashton kept his voice low and steady.

"Work things out?" Kathy's shrill laugh iced Carly's blood. "You two think you're so smart. You bask in the spotlight and play the heroes while my husband, *Senator* George Internado, rots in jail. He's the real hero. That man dedicated forty years of his life to public service and what does he have to show for it? *What?*"

Carly peeked out from behind Ashton. Kathy's face was bright red and her wide eyes were bulging out of their sockets. She'd released her chokehold, but still had the gun pointed at Desiree.

"I've stood by him my entire life, coaching him, encouraging him. And cleaning up his stinking messes, including that stupid, doe-eyed slut he knocked up. Did she actually think I would step aside so she could become a senator's wife? That little whore never saw me coming."

"Kathy, put down the gun, my sister—"

"Shut the hell up! You don't get to bark orders. This isn't a mission you can win, Maverick."

"Why are you throwing your own life away?" he asked. "What about your children and grandchildren?"

"You didn't just ruin his life, you ruined mine, too. I stuck with him and endured all his philandering. Who the hell do you think found him a place where he could get his jollies in secret? I had the governor's mansion in my sights. I paid my dues and was ready to claim my reward as First Lady of Virginia. Then, that meddling old man came along, poking around about the past. Just another obstacle we cleared out of our way."

Carly's blood boiled, anger replacing anxiety. "Get me a clean shot."

"I'm working on it," he whispered. "Kathy, you don't want to hurt my sister. She's got nothing to do with this." Ashton raised his arms. "I don't have a weapon. Shoot me. Then, we'll be even."

Oh, dear Jesus. Carly shuddered in a shaky breath. She was flying blind. She couldn't jump out from behind him and fire her weapon. *If I miss, I kill Desiree.*

Warren stepped forward. "Do *not* kill my children."

"Stay out of this," Kathy yelled before another shot rang out.

"Carly, now," Ashton said, then shouted, "Desiree, drop!"

Carly jumped out from behind him, aimed, and fired.

BAM-BAM-BAM-BAM!

Kathy Internado staggered backward, then crumpled to the deck.

"Anyone hit?" Ashton shouted over the chaos.

No one answered.

"Gunner, Penelope!" Ashton hollered.

"Go!" Penelope yelled. "We've got this!"

Carly raced up the stairs behind Ashton, Warren and Sinclair close on their heels. On the deck, Warren lifted Desiree and hurried her into the house. Carly froze at the sight of Kathy Internado, blood oozing from her wounds. Both men jumped into action. Ashton yanked off his shirt and used it to apply pressure while Sinclair felt for a pulse.

Gunner flew up the stairs. "First responders are on the way. No one was hit. We're looking for the bullet. Need my help?"

"Keep everyone calm and get me confirmation on that bullet," Ashton replied before Gunner hurried back down.

"No pulse," Sinclair said.

"God, no." Carly couldn't stop shaking. Everything was happening so fast, yet it felt like time had stopped. She hugged herself, but she couldn't tear her gaze from Kathy Internado's lifeless body.

Ash flicked his attention to her. "Sin, take over for me."

As soon as Sinclair did, he pulled Carly into his arms. Her heart beat out of her chest and she was shaking violently.

"I've got you." Leaning back, he stared into her eyes. "Talk to me."

Clinging to him, she tried deep breaths to steady her erratic breathing. Unable to speak, she shook her head.

"Let's get you some water." He ushered her inside.

As soon as Desiree spotted her, she rushed over.

"I was so scared," Desiree blurted, throwing her arms around Carly and bursting into tears. "I thought I was going to die." Carly hugged her while her own tears flowed.

As she stood there comforting Desiree, Ashton stroked her back. Carly's anxiety was replaced with an overwhelming sadness. She'd been forced to fire her weapon to save others, but that didn't make Kathy Internado's death any easier to bear.

Darkness had fallen when the mayhem finally settled down. The police and paramedics had come and gone. Most of the guests had left. Family and close friends had moved inside. Maverick walked the Rijados to their car and returned to the house. The somber mood was to be expected, but he was concerned his friends had been traumatized by what they'd witnessed. One by one, he checked in with them before turning his full attention on his wife.

After pulling Carly into the foyer, he peered into her eyes. "How are you doing, honey?"

"I'm struggling with what happened. I've replayed it over and over in my mind, but I don't see any other outcome. When she fired into the crowd, I had to...I had to shoot her." She shuddered.

"I'm sorry I doubted you. I'll never do that again."

"I almost left my Glock at home. If I had, she would have unloaded on Desiree and your dad." She choked back a muffled sob. "She could have killed you, too."

"But she didn't because you were prepared."

Struggling with the intensity of what might have happened, she swiped away a fresh tear. "Kathy must have given Internado that black eye when she found out about Rose Aurora."

"And here I'd pegged her for the innocent wife who'd been wronged."

"She *had* been wronged, but she was every bit as guilty."

Sinclair sauntered over and kissed the top of Carly's head before gripping his brother's shoulder. "You two make one hell of a team."

Carly's smile was laced with sadness. "Thanks."

"You guys okay?"

"We will be," Maverick replied.

"I've got to head out of town for a while," Sinclair said.

"*Now?*" Carly asked.

"Where are you going?" Maverick asked.

"I've got to take care of something with Dakota."

Silence.

"That can't be good," Carly murmured. "What are you two up to?"

As if amused, Sin's lips curved. "The past is the past, until its rears it's ugly head. I'll be flying under the radar, so I'm leaving my phone at home."

"Oh, boy," Maverick said. "Is that all we get?"

"That's all you need to know." He clasped Maverick's hand and pulled him in for a hug. "My GM will be running Uninhibited. Do me a favor. Can you two drop by and check on things for me?"

"Of course," Carly replied.

"Be safe, brother," Maverick said as Sinclair opened the front door and slipped into the night.

"I worry about him," she said.

"If anyone can take care of himself, it's Sin." Maverick drew Carly into his arms and dropped a tender kiss on her forehead. "Thank you for saving Desiree's life."

"No one hurts my family," she said with conviction. "No one."

EPILOGUE

D*ecember, two months later*

Maverick and Carly stood in the spacious lobby of the Loving Malibu Resort with Jagger and Taylor. Rested and relaxed from their honeymoon, they'd spent the week enjoying the beautiful California coastline, their close friends, and each other. Maverick considered himself the luckiest man on earth to have Carly as his life partner. Each day, he discovered something new to love about his wife.

"Thank you for an amazing time," Carly said to Jagger and Taylor. "Your hotel is gorgeous, the food was amazing, the entertainment was—"

"*Exotic*," Maverick said, finishing her sentence.

Carly laughed.

"We like to mix up the fun, along with the heat levels," Taylor said.

"Thanks for inviting us to stay with you guys next week," Jagger added.

"Wouldn't have it any other way," Maverick replied.

"We look forward to a tour of the new house you're having built," Taylor said.

"Right now, it's support beams on a slab of cement," Maverick said. "But we'll squeeze it in somewhere between Colton and Brigit's rehearsal dinner, their wedding, and our day cruise down the Potomac with my boys and their better halves."

The limo pulled into the hotel drive-through. After hugs goodbye, Carly and Maverick headed out.

"That was a fantastic vacation," Carly said as the driver whisked them to the airport.

"I had no idea you had *that* much energy," Maverick said. "Please note, I am *not* complaining. I'm a very lucky man."

"What can I say?" She grinned. "I *adore* my husband."

Maverick tucked her hair behind her ear and dropped several worshipful kisses on her lips. "Love you, wife."

Two hours later, their flight took off. Within minutes, Carly fell asleep, her head resting on his shoulder.

As the plane flew east, he stared out the window at the twinkling city lights below. The past two months had been a whirlwind of activity, but neither of them had lost sight of what mattered most.

Each other.

Three weeks ago, FBI Agent Mark Rodriguez had informed them that Kathy Internado's DNA had been a match to the skin found under Rose Aurora's fingernails, and Carly stopped toting her Glock everywhere. But she never missed a week at the shooting range and Maverick was always there, honing his skills right alongside her.

After a minor building renovation at ThunderStrike, Stone Investigations had relocated to its new home. Maverick loved the days when they could drive in to work together.

They'd also moved out of the yacht and into Carly's house in

Arlington while waiting the spring completion of their new digs, not far from Crockett and Alexandra.

Carly stirred and Maverick kissed the top of her head. She shot him a contented smile before nuzzling closer. Maverick closed his eyes, but sleep wouldn't come, so he scrolled through emails.

His dad had sent one with an update on the case they were building against Internado for the murder of Pierce Stone, but he rolled past that one. While Maverick had every confidence justice would be served, he was still on his honeymoon. Just thinking about Internado had him clasping Carly's hand and listening to her steady breathing, grateful she was by his side.

The former senator had pleaded guilty to the kidnapping, assault, and attempted murder of Carly, in exchange for a reduced sentence of twenty years. He got another two years for admitting to being an accessory after the fact in the death of Rose Aurora.

Maverick put down his phone, closed his eyes, and let his wife's comforting touch lull him to sleep. The following morning, the jet touched down at Reagan National.

"Home sweet home," Carly said as they waited to deplane.

He smiled. Returning home always felt so damn good.

As Maverick drove out of the airport, he told her he needed to make a quick stop at the office. Because it was Saturday, the parking lot was deserted, save for his company-owned SUVs. He bolted inside, retrieved the gift from his safe, and returned to the vehicle.

"What are you up to?" she asked.

"Nothing but trouble." With a wink, he drove home.

"Did you tell anyone about our special delivery?" Maverick asked as he set their bags in the living room.

"No, but I was dying to tell Desiree." She hung her coat in the hall closet. "You?" She took his parka and hung it up for him.

"Not a word to anyone."

Thirty minutes later, the doorbell rang and they hurried outside.

"It's been over a week since our last visit," Carly said to the woman. "I'll bet he's grown a lot."

"He's done nothing *but* grow." The woman laughed as she opened the back of her SUV.

The seven-month-old German shepherd barked once, his tail whipping back and forth in the travel crate.

Maverick grinned. "There's my boy. Hey, Whiskey, welcome to your new home."

Before the trainer opened the crate, she said, "Whiskey, platz."

The fluffy pup with the gigantic paws dropped down.

"Good boy." After opening the crate, she said, "Whiskey, aus."

Whiskey scrambled out and Carly knelt to give him some love. The dog's tail swished back and forth.

"Platz means lie down," the trainer said as she leashed Whiskey. "Aus means out."

They entered the house and the trainer instructed Whiskey to sit so she could unleash him. Like proud parents, Maverick and Carly marveled at how well behaved he was.

The trainer discussed the dog's progress since the last time they'd seen him, provided a full packet of information, and reminded them that she was available for any questions or concerns they might have.

"The word 'free' is a command that lets Whiskey know he can do as he pleases," the trainer explained. "As a working dog, he'll learn the difference between assignments and lounging around at home."

"We're looking forward to continuing his training and making him a part of our family," Maverick said.

The trainer knelt and said goodbye to the puppy. "He's a great dog. I wish you guys the best."

After she left, Whiskey looked up at them with innocent, brown eyes.

358 | STONI ALEXANDER

"It's like having a baby." Carly sat on the floor, but the dog didn't move from his sit position. "Whiskey, free." The dog bounded over. "Good boy. Good boy, Whiskey," she said while loving on him.

Maverick grabbed the shopping bag off the sofa and eased down beside them. "Whiskey, we bought you a bunch of presents, little buddy." He offered the dog a pull toy.

The frisky pup latched on to it and the two got busy playing tug of war. The adorable dog growled and pulled with all his might.

"He's got some power behind him," Maverick said.

"He's too cute." Carly laughed. "We'll need to work with him daily. Especially since he's going to become an active member of ThunderStrike."

Maverick let the dog win and he dropped to gnaw on his prize. "Good boy, Whiskey." He rubbed the pup's head before heading to the coat closet. There, he extracted the gift tucked in the pocket of his parka.

She waggled her eyebrows. "What's that, Mr. Hott?"

He eased onto the floor beside her, excitement coursing through him. "For the past three weeks, I've been waiting for the right time to give this to you. I decided that the beach in California would be the perfect setting, but I forgot to bring it. On the flight home, I realized that if I wait for that perfect moment, I'm missing the point." He dropped a soft kiss on her lips. "Our life is filled with so many wonderful moments because we're together."

"You are so romantic," she said with a smile.

Maverick held up his inked ring finger. "I love my wedding band and want you to have something just as special. I designed this myself, based on what you told me."

He opened the ring box to display a dazzling, diamond eternity band.

Gasping, her eyes grew wide. "Wow. It's breathtaking."

The center row of round diamonds was flanked by a row of smaller diamonds on either side.

"Carly, I love you with everything I am." He waited while she removed his mom's wedding band, then he slid the eternity band onto her finger. "You are mine and I am yours. *Forever.*"

After thanking him with several doting kisses, she admired the sparkly wedding ring. "It's stunning. I will treasure it and the life we're building together." Her loving smile filled him with happiness. "I love you so much, Ashton."

Maverick kissed his wife, relishing the tender way she held his face and the love that shone from her eyes. The girl who'd captured his heart twenty-five years ago had always been the girl of his dreams.

And *always* would be.

Another Happily Ever After by

Stoni ALEXANDER

Sign up for Stoni's newsletter at
StoniAlexander.com
and she'll gift you Metro Man, a steamy short story available only
to her Inner Circle.

A NOTE FROM STONI

Thank you so much for reading THE HOTT TOUCH!

THIS BOOK! This book was quite an adventure for me to write. From the moment Maverick burst into THE WILDE TOUCH, he captured my heart. He was larger than life and loaded with testosterone. He reappeared in THE LOVING TOUCH and, once again, showed me his brash, bold, cocky self. Only, this time, he let me see what a huge heart he has for those he loves. I received *a lot* of positive feedback about this secondary character. Excited readers were eager for him to have his own story.

I wanted that, too...but the emerging storylines weren't the right fit, so, I moved on and wrote BEAUTIFUL STEPBROTHER.

At some point, I concluded that Maverick's story wasn't mine to tell, but my amazing, supportive, and very loving husband, Johnny, would *not* let me abandon ship. When the right storyline finally did emerge, so began my exciting journey into THE HOTT

TOUCH. The challenges I encountered ended up being blessings and lessons learned. I'm so grateful for all of them!

Writing this love story was a wonderful experience, especially because I introduced readers to Sinclair Develin. And Sin was as much of a handful as his brother. They were both fighting for the page, but this was Maverick and Carly's story, no doubt about that.

Are you ready to read Sin's story? Here's Book Five...

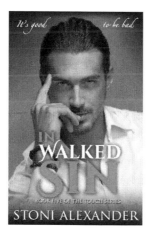

IT'S GOOD TO BE BAD...

I have no soul.

And that suits me.

How else could I wield absolute power in the nation's capital?

I own this town and everyone in it. The public thinks the politicos run Washington. Who do you think is pulling their strings?

I am.

Some hate me for it…until they find themselves in the center of a scandal. That's when I become their savior.

When I step out of a limo, men stare in envy while women gawk and blush. There's always a pretty young thing draped on my arm, sometimes two. Window dressing to fill a void or keep me warm on a chilly night.

They're all gunning for the same thing—to be *The One*. But these women don't hold my attention and they can't snag my heart.

Then, *she* crashes into my sinful world and I'm pulled by an invisible force even I can't resist. She becomes my obsession, my reason to breathe.

Everything changes the moment her gaze meets mine.

Everything.

Grab IN WALKED SIN or Read FREE on Kindle Unlimited!

READ THE ENTIRE TOUCH SERIES
EXCLUSIVELY ON AMAZON
& FREE ON KINDLE UNLIMITED!

WANT EVEN MORE ROMANTIC SUSPENSE?
YOU'LL LOVE MY EXCITING NEW SERIES

DAMAGED
The Vigilantes, Book One

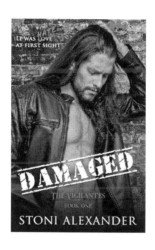

I'm *not* one of the good guys...not even close. I'm a heartless savage hunting down the thug who murdered my mother. Watching her die in my arms has turned me into a killing machine. Revenge runs bone-deep for me. It's burned into my soul, baby.

When I become the one with a damn target on my back, my life turns into a raging dumpster fire. But not because my company gets breached or because some SOBs are trying to off me.

There's this woman...the *one* woman I can't freakin' stand. An impulsive cop who arrested me for a crime I didn't commit. She gets too close to me, she's gonna learn about all the ones I *did* pull off.

The problem is, I'm crazy attracted to her. Insane, over the top, can't-get-her-outta-my-head kind of attraction. She pushes all my buttons and makes me madder than hell. If anyone can bring me to my knees, it's her.

Turns out, I took a vow of celibacy. And I don't break so easily.

Except the hot cop is now a detective...and I gotta help her with a serial-killer case 'cause I got wicked-good hacking skills. But that's all I'm gonna help her with...

Grab DAMAGED or read FREE on Kindle Unlimited!

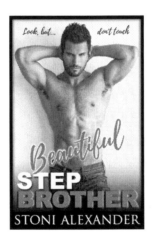

ACKNOWLEDGMENTS

Each of my novels has a hero and a heroine. The following people are my real life ones who inspired and supported me as I penned this novel.

To my husband, Johnny. Thank you for believing in me. Thank you for making me laugh 'til I cry, and for the abundance of patience God has blessed you with. This journey is magical because we're in it together.

To my beloved son. Thank you for your fierce love. I am beyond grateful to be your mom. You *are* Maverick in so many ways.

A big shout-out to my fabulous editor Nicole for her talents and hard work. I am thrilled you loved this book so much so that you stayed up until 4:30 in the morning to finish it! That means the world to me.

My continued gratitude extends to Carole, my eagle-eyed proofreader, who catches things each and every time. Thank you for your awesome efforts and for all the texts that put a smile on my face or make me laugh out loud.

Thank you to my beautiful ARC team for loving my stories and for being uber-excited to read this one in particular!

My heartfelt gratitude to Kira for her vast knowledge of BDSM and for supporting my extensive research. Kira, the line, "Don't you dare die on me," is yours. You thought of it, you got excited over it, and you gave it to me. What a special gift!

A mountain of thanks goes to Colonel Jonathan Brazee, USMC (Ret) for answering my never-ending stream of military questions. I appreciate your willingness and generosity in helping me navigate through those Naval waterways.

An appreciative shout-out to Anna Davies for her *Redbook* piece that catapulted Carly Stone's character. I've been a fan of your writing ever since and I'm grateful for the conversations that have ensued since our first correspondence.

Meeting Lisa Cron was an absolute pleasure! Lisa, I am a huge fan of your work. You have a magical ability to break down the art of writing a story that speaks to my soul. I have to give you all the props for driving your point home about misbelief. Understanding the value of that was essential in creating Maverick's deep-seated pain. My heartfelt gratitude for your brilliance and warmth. What a great lady!

Thank you, thank you, thank you to my readers! I am deeply appreciative that you take the time to read my love stories. You guys *ROCK IT OUT*!

And finally, thank you to my muse who has been with me for a lot longer than I was willing to admit. I envision you to be like Marjorie McAllister from MITUS—smoking, gravely voice, pacing. Shoving that unlit cigarette behind your ear while you bark your smart-ass remarks at me. And then screaming at me because I ration our potato chips. Lady, this is some fun adventure we're on, isn't it?

ABOUT THE AUTHOR

Stoni Alexander writes sexy romantic suspense and contemporary romance about tortured alpha males and independent, strong-willed females. Her passion is creating love stories where the hero and heroine help each other through a crisis so that, in the end, they're equal partners in more ways than love alone. The heat level is high, the romance is forever, and the suspense keeps readers guessing until the very end.

Visit Stoni's website:
StoniAlexander.com

Sign up for Stoni's newsletter on her website and she'll gift you a free steamy short story, only available to her Inner Circle.

Here's where you can follow Stoni online. She looks forward to connecting with you!

a amazon.com/author/stonialexander
BB bookbub.com/authors/stoni-alexander
f facebook.com/StoniBooks
g goodreads.com/stonialexander
o instagram.com/stonialexander

Made in the USA
Monee, IL
27 September 2021